Readers love *The Stark Divide*

by J. SCOTT COATSWORTH

"This was a very entertaining book and I believe it's the start to a series with a lot of potential. Here's hoping J. Scott Coatsworth writes the epic saga this story begs to be the beginning of."
—Sci-Fi & Scary

"When I read a book by J. Scott Coatsworth I know I'm going to be treated to a story with fabulous world building, and interesting characters. *The Stark Divide* has all of that and more."
—Drops of Ink

"J. Scott Coatsworth has written an amazing science fiction novel that sends shivers down your spine because of the ring of truth to it."
—MM Good Book Reviews

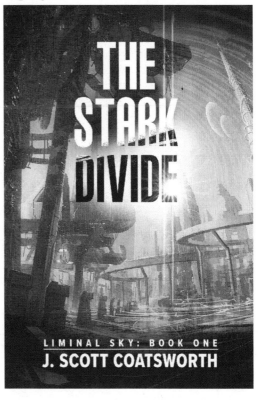

"Mr. Coatsworth has created a very believable world, along with some believable tech, and then crafted a fast moving and interesting story tying it all together."
—Love Bytes

By J. Scott Coatsworth

LIMINAL SKY
The Stark Divide
The Rising Tide

Published by DSP PUBLICATIONS
www.dsppublications.com

THE
STARK
DIVIDE

J. SCOTT COATSWORTH

DSP PUBLICATIONS

Published by

DSP PUBLICATIONS

5032 Capital Circle SW, Suite 2, PMB# 279, Tallahassee, FL 32305-7886 USA
www.dsppublications.com

The Stark Divide
© 2017, 2019 J. Scott Coatsworth.

Cover Art
© 2017, 2019 Aaron Anderson.
aaronbydesign55@gmail.com
Cover content is for illustrative purposes only and any person depicted on the cover is a model.
Map Credit
© 2017, 2019 August Li.

Trade Paperback ISBN: 978-1-64108-133-7
Digital ISBN: 978-1-63533-833-1
Library of Congress Control Number: 2017947264
Trade Paperback Published February 2019
v. 1.0

Printed in the United States of America
∞
This paper meets the requirements of
ANSI/NISO Z39.48-1992 (Permanence of Paper).

Liminal Sky may have been written by just one author, but it was beta'd by three. Special thanks to Rory Ni Coileain, Carole Cummings, and Kendra Carmichael for taking a rough stone and helping me to polish it into a diamond.

I also owe a debt of gratitude to my mom and dad for both bringing me into the world (the one thing they agree that they did right together) and for their ongoing encouragement for my writing career.

But there's one person who makes this thing I do possible, every single day. My husband Mark supports me in so many ways I see, and so many more that I never even realized he was doing. He doesn't mind if I write at odd hours in the middle of the night, if I hang out in front of the TV with my laptop, and he knows when I need him to hug me after a rejection and when I need him to let me work on a deadline.

Mark, you are my everything, and this is as much your victory as mine. Love you madly.

Author's Note

THE STARK Divide is my second novel, and the first in my Liminal Sky series. But it has a long and (forgive the pun) storied history.

Way back in high school, I wrote my first novel. It was a horribly derivative, poorly plotted fantasy sci-fi story with pegasuses (pegasi?) and elves and talking monkeys that to this day sits on a shelf in our office closet.

But my next book, *On a Shoreless Sea*, was something altogether different. It sprang out of the idea of mixing sci-fi and fantasy – creating a fantasy setting within a sci-fi one. I was hugely inspired by sci-fi-fantasy authors like Anne McCaffrey, who built living, breathing, amazing worlds that combined dragons and spaceships. Places I wanted to visit, places where I wanted to live.

As a closeted gay teen, these places were my magical getaways, and as a budding author, I longed to create something similar that would be all my own.

I spent years working on that novel, bit by bit after work, late at night, and on weekends. Most of it was originally written before my coming out in 1992, so it didn't contain any queer characters.

It was going to be my big break, the novel that would put me on the map in the publishing world. When it as ready at last – on October 26, 1995 — I sent it to ten of the biggest sci-fi publishers. And then I waited.

One by one, they came back to me, and it was a bloodbath: "no longer accepting unsolicited unagented material;" "this material is not suited to our list;" "we are unable to review unsolicited manuscripts;" "we are not in the market for this kind of book;" "this book just isn't to my taste;" "the work often seemed overworked and lacking focus;" and "It's just not for us."

On October 10, 1996, almost a year later, I received my final rejection:

"The work is unusually promising, as the care you have given to nurturing your characters and your language is evident. I find, however, that the plot doesn't quite pull together."

Bless them for at least actually reading it and giving me some real feedback.

After that, I basically gave up. I made sporadic stabs at authoring again, but it never really stuck. Not until 2013. My husband Mark's mother passed away, causing a big upheaval in our lives, and I made an offhand comment about how it had derailed my attempt to start writing once again.

Mark looked at me and called bullshit. "If you want to write, then write. The only thing stopping you is you."

He was right. It was like a thunderbolt out of the blue. I had been making one excuse after another to avoid facing my own fear, that I wasn't good enough to make it as a writer. It was time to get serious.

I pulled out *On a Shoreless Sea*, and re-read it. It needed work. A lot of work. But there was something there. The world I had created was fascinating, and I wanted to do spend more time in it.

Yet I had little to no idea how it ticked. What made this world work? Who built it? How, when and why?

So I set about finding out by writing the backstory. I wrote the initial part of the prequel, "Seedling," in 2013-2014, telling the story of how the world started.

I went away from Forever for a while to write some other tales, but Forever kept calling me back. In 2015, I wrote part two, *Colony*, jumping forward ten years to see what has happened with the characters, and to tell the story of this new settlement in my rapidly growing world.

Finally, in 2016, I finished part three, "Refugee," which starts another twenty years later, and deepens and richens the experience of this world to set us on our way.

At the Dreamspinner Retreat in 2015, I asked Lynn West to read "Seedling." She liked it, and encouraged me to submit the whole thing when it was finished. I did, and DSP bought it in February 2017. It only took 21 years and four months from that first submission to finally see my little world get published.

So what about *On the Shoreless Sea*? I has plans. I want to rewrite it from scratch with a queerer cast, once I finish the intervening stories.

Don't worry — I'll get there. Turns out it's a much shorter trip than the one between the stars.

Chase's Estate ★

Darlith ★

Dragon's Reach
(Anatov Mountains)

Lake Jackson

★ Micavry
(McAvery Port)

Forever
(Ariadne)

PART ONE: SEEDLING
2135 AD

Prologue

LEX FLOATED along with the ocean current. Her arms were spread out wide, her jet-black hair adrift on the surface of the water. For once, she felt at peace. Truly herself.

The sun shone above her, and she soaked up its rays, basking in its golden glow. Her blue eyes stared up at the equally blue sky, not a cloud in sight.

Soon she'd be called back to duty. Soon she'd once again have to face her limited, jury-rigged day-to-day existence.

Now, for a few moments, she was free to just drift.

THE *DRESSLER*, a Mission-class AmSplor ship, sailed steadily toward her destination, a city-sized rock named 43 Ariadne, harvested from the asteroid belt and placed in trailing orbit behind Earth.

The starfish-shaped ship flew on the solar wind, drinking in ionized hydrogen and other trace elements that allowed her to breathe and grow, coursing slowly through the dark reaches of space between Earth and the sun. The *Dressler* lived on solar wind and space dust, accumulating them with her web of gossamer sails between her arms, filtering them down into her compact body for processing.

The detritus flew out behind her, leaving a jet trail across the void to mark her passing, leading back to Earth.

Somewhere out there, their destination awaited them, an asteroid floating on a sea of stars.

Chapter One:
The Three

"*DRESSLER*, SCHEMATIC," Colin McAvery, ship's captain and a third of the crew, called out to the ship-mind.

A three-dimensional image of the ship appeared above the smooth console. Her five living arms, reaching out from her central core, were lit with a golden glow, and the mechanical bits of instrumentation shone in red. In real life, she was almost two hundred meters from tip to tip.

Between those arms stretched her solar wings, a ghostly green film like the sails of the *Flying Dutchman*.

"You're a pretty thing," he said softly. He loved these ships, their delicate beauty as they floated through the starry void.

"Thank you, Captain." The ship-mind sounded happy with the compliment—his imagination running wild. Minds didn't have real emotions, though they sometimes approximated them.

He cross-checked the heading to be sure they remained on course to deliver their payload, the man-sized seed that was being dragged on a tether behind the ship. Humanity's ticket to the stars at a time when life on Earth was getting rapidly worse.

All of space was spread out before him, seen through the clear expanse of plasform set into the ship's living walls. His own face, trimmed blond hair, and deep brown eyes, stared back at him, superimposed over the vivid starscape.

At thirty, Colin was in the prime of his career. He was a starship captain, and yet sometimes he felt like little more than a bus driver. After this run... well, he'd have to see what other opportunities might be awaiting him. Maybe the doc was right, and this was the start of a whole new chapter for mankind. They might need a guy like him.

The walls of the bridge emitted a faint but healthy golden glow, providing light for his work at the curved mechanical console that filled half the room. He traced out the T-Line to their destination. "*Dressler*, we're looking a little wobbly." Colin frowned. Some irregularity in the course was common—the ship was constantly adjusting its trajectory—but she usually corrected it before he noticed.

"Affirmative, Captain." The ship-mind's miniature chosen likeness appeared above the touch board. She was all professional today, dressed in a standard AmSplor uniform, dark hair pulled back in a bun, and about a third life-sized.

The image was nothing more than a projection of the ship-mind, a fairy tale, but Colin appreciated the effort she took to humanize her appearance. Artificial mind or not, he always treated minds with respect.

"There's a blockage in arm four. I've sent out a scout to correct it."

The *Dressler* was well into slowdown now, her pre-arrival phase as she bled off her speed, and they expected to reach 43 Ariadne in another fifteen hours.

Pity no one had yet cracked the whole hyperspace thing. Colin chuckled. Asimov would be disappointed. *"Dressler, show me Earth, please."*

A small blue dot appeared in the middle of his screen.

"Dressler, three dimensions, a bit larger, please." The beautiful blue-green world spun before him in all its glory.

Appearances could be deceiving. Even with scrubbers working tirelessly night and day to clean the excess carbon dioxide from the air, the home world was still running dangerously warm.

He watched the image in front of him as the East Coast of the North American Union spun slowly into view. Florida was a sliver of its former self, and where New York City's lights had once shone, there was now only blue. If it *had* been night, Fargo, the capital of the Northern States, would have outshone most of the other cities below. The floods that had wiped out many of the world's coastal cities had also knocked down Earth's population, which was only now reaching the levels it had seen in the early twenty-first century.

All those new souls had been born into a warm, arid world.

We did it to ourselves. Colin, who had known nothing besides the hot planet he called home, wondered what it had been like those many years before *the Heat*.

ANASTASIA ANATOV leafed through her father, Dimitri's, old paper journal. She liked to look through it once a day, to see his spidery handwriting and remember what he had been like. It was a bit old and dusty now, but it was one of her most cherished possessions.

She sighed and put it away in a storage nook in her lab.

She left the room and pulled herself gracefully along the runway, the central corridor of the ship, using the metal rungs embedded in the walls. She was much more comfortable in low or zero g than she was in Earth normal, where her tall, lanky form made her feel awkward around others. She was a loner at heart, and the emptiness of space appealed to her.

Her father had designed the Mission-class ships. It was something she rarely spoke of, but she was intensely proud of him. These ships were still imperfect, the combination of a hellishly complicated genetic code and after-the-fact fittings of mechanical parts, like the rungs she used now to move through the weightless environment.

Ana wondered if it hurt when someone drilled into the living tissue to install the mechanics, living quarters, and observation blisters that made the ship habitable. Her father had always maintained that the ship-minds felt no pain.

She wasn't so sure. Men were often dismissive of the things they didn't understand.

Either way, she was stuck on the small ship for the duration with two men, neither of whom were interested in her. The captain was gay, and Jackson was married.

Too bad the ship roster hadn't included another woman or two.

She placed her hand on a hardened sensor callus next to the door valve and the ship obliged, recognizing her. The door spiraled open to show the viewport beyond.

She pulled herself into the room and floated before the wide expanse of transparent plasform, staring out at the seed being hauled behind them.

Nothing else mattered. Whatever she had to do to get this project launched, she would do it. She'd already made some morally questionable choices along the way—including looking the other way when a bundle of cash had changed hands at the Institute.

She was so close now, and she couldn't let anything get in the way.

Earth was a lost cause. It was only a matter of time before the world imploded. Only the seeds could give mankind a fighting chance to go on.

From the viewport, there was little to see. The seed was a two-meter-long brown ovoid, made of a hard, dark organic material, scarred and pitted by the continual abrasion of the dust that escaped the great sails. So cold out there, but the seed was dormant, unfeeling.

The cold would keep it that way until the time came for its seedling stage.

She'd created three of the seeds with her funding. This one, bound for the asteroid 43 Ariadne, was the first. It was the next step in evolution beyond the *Dressler* and carried with it the hopes of all humankind.

It also represented ten years of her life and work.

Maybe, just maybe, we're ready for the next step.

THE CREW'S third and final member, Jackson Hammond, hung upside down in the ship's hold, grunting as he refit one of the feed pipes that carried the ship's electronics through the bowels of this weird animal-mechanical hybrid. Although "up" and "down" were slight on a ship where the centrifugal force created a "gravity" only a fraction of what it was on Earth.

As the ship's engineer, Jackson was responsible for keeping the mechanics functioning—a challenge in a living organism like the *Dressler*.

With cold, hard metal, one dealt with the occasional metal fatigue, poor workmanship, and at times just ass-backward reality. But the parts didn't regularly grow or shrink, and it wasn't always necessary to rejigger the ones that had fit perfectly just the day before. Even after ten years in these things, he still found it a little creepy to be riding inside the belly of the beast. It was too Jonah and the Whale for his taste.

Jackson rubbed the sweat away from his eyes with the back of his arm. As he shaved down the end of a pipe to make it fit more snugly against the small orifice in the ship's wall, he touched the little silver cross that hung around his neck. It had been a present from his priest, Father Vincenzo, at his son Aaron's First Communion in the Reformed Catholic Evangelical Church.

The boy was seven years old now, with a shock of red hair and green eyes like his dad, and his mother's beautiful skin. He'd spent months preparing for his Communion Day, and Jackson remembered fondly the moment when his son had taken the Body and Blood of Christ for the first time, surprise registering on his little face at the strange taste of the wine.

Aaron's Communion Day had been a high point for Jackson, just a week before his current mission. He was so proud of his two boys. *Miss you guys. I'll be home soon.*

Lately he hadn't been sleeping well, his dreams filled with a dark-haired, blue-eyed vixen. He was happily married. He shouldn't be having such dreams.

Jackson shook his head. Being locked up in a tin can in space did strange things to a person sometimes. *I should be home with Glory and the boys.*

One way or another, this mission would be his last.

He'd been recruited as a teen.

At thirteen, Jackson had learned the basics of engineering doing black-tech work for the gangs that ran what was left of the Big Apple after the Rise—a warren of interconnected skyrises, linked mostly by boats and ropes and makeshift bridges.

Everything north of Twenty-Third was controlled by the Hex, a black-tech co-op that specialized in bootlegged dreamcasts, including modified versions that catered to some of the more questionable tastes of the North American States. South of Twenty-Third belonged to the Red Badge, a lawless group of technophiles involved in domestic espionage and wetware arts.

Jackson had grown up in the drowned city, abandoned by his mother and forced to rely on his own intelligence and instincts to survive in a rapidly changing world.

He'd found his way to the Red Badge and discovered a talent for ecosystem work, taking over and soon expanding one of the rooftop farms that supplied the drowned city with a subsistence diet. An illegal wetware upgrade let him tap directly into the systems he worked on, seeing the circuits and pathways in his head.

He increased the Badge's food production fivefold and branched out beyond the nearly tasteless molds and edible fungi that thrived in the warm, humid environment.

It was on one of his rooftop "gardens" that his life had changed one warm summer evening.

He was underneath one of the condenser units that pulled water from the air for irrigation. All of eighteen years old, he was responsible for the food production for the entire Red Badge.

He'd run through the unit's diagnostics app to no avail. Damned piece of shit couldn't find a thing wrong.

In the end, it had come down to something purely physical—tightening down a pipe bolt where the condenser interfaced with the irrigation system.

Satisfied with the work, he stood, wiping the sweat off his bare chest, and glared into the setting sun out over the East River. It was more an inland sea now, but the old names still stuck.

There was a faint whirring behind him, and he spun around. A bug drone hovered about a foot away, glistening in the sun. He stared at it for a moment, then reached out to swat it down. Probably from the Hex.

It evaded his grasp, and he felt a sharp pain in his neck.

He went limp, and everything turned black as he tumbled into one of his garden beds.

He awoke in Fargo, recruited by AmSplor to serve in the space agency's Frontier Station, his life changed irrevocably.

A strange sensation brought him back to the present.

His right hand was wet. Startled, he looked down. It was covered with blood.

Dressler, *we have a problem*, he said through his private affinity-link with the ship-mind.

Chapter Two:
Smoke

Something brushed past her legs under the surface of the water. Startled, Lex looked down, but there was nothing there.

It was time to swim back to shore.

She set off, long strokes pulling her toward the beach in the distance.

It happened twice more as she swam, and the second time there was a sharp pain in her left leg.

She emerged from the sea onto the golden sand of the beach, water dripping off her naked skin. She checked both her legs, but there was no visible sign of damage—just a dull ache. Probably nothing.

She crossed the wide strip of sand, warm between her toes, and entered the forest under a canopy of fir trees and wild ferns that smelled of damp loam and mushrooms.

She ran through her domain as quickly as she could manage, pausing now and again to breathe in the crisp forest air. The path beneath her feet was well-worn and led her through the woods to a stony outcrop that overlooked a peaceful valley far below.

She stood on the crest of the hill, looking down at the verdant vale. A stone tower rose from a granite hilltop in the middle of a field of green grass.

It all looked normal. Well, almost all of it.

She frowned. Near the edge of the valley, the grass had turned yellow and brown, painting a sickly patch against the living green of the scene. Something smelled off too, foul with a hint of carrion in the breeze that blew up from the valley floor.

Her joints ached. She wasn't relishing the hike into the valley.

Dressler, we have a problem.

She sighed and turned her attention back to the "real" world. The mystery in the valley would have to wait.

The captain finished his systems check and sat back to enjoy the view through the bridge's viewport for a brief moment.

The small pinprick of light that was Earth shone brightly in a silent sea of stars. Somewhere near that little speck was the even smaller speck of Frontier, invisible from this distance—the biggest station circling the planet. Far larger than the *Dressler* and fully mechanical, it spun above the Earth's surface. It was their return destination, once they finished this mission.

With luck, Trip would be on station as well. Colin missed him sorely. They saw far too little of each other, with their staggered schedules. Ship pilots were in constant demand. He closed his eyes and thought of the last time they'd been together. They'd made the most of the thirty-six hours on Frontier, but it wasn't the sex he remembered best. It was the warmth of Trip's chest against his back when they slept. *Where are you now?*

With a sigh, he deactivated the console. "Leaving the bridge," he called to the *Dressler*, and she acknowledged him with a brief flashing of the wall lights.

He unbuckled himself from the pilot's chair and pushed away toward the doorway. There was just enough time for a little rest before they approached Ariadne.

The exit irised open at his touch, and he floated out into the runway, ready for a quick shower and a catnap. He still had a lot to get accomplished before rendezvous.

He was almost to his cabin when the *Dressler's* dulcet tones called to him over the ship speakers. "Captain, Engineer Hammond requests your presence in the hold."

He cursed under his breath. *So close.*

Colin spun around and pushed himself across the runway, then opened the door that led down to the hold where the ship storage held their rations, tools, and all other things needed to keep the ship and themselves functional in the vacuum of space.

It was still strange coming in here after spending time in the somewhat cramped quarters in the rest of the ship—such a vast room, half the internal volume contained in two stories, room for when the *Dressler* needed to haul larger cargo.

He had entered at the floor level, where a metal grate was bolted down into the *Dressler* to provide a stable platform for the ship's cargo.

9

The space was dimly lit, and he didn't immediately see Hammond. "*Dressler*, some light, please?"

One by one, luminescent patches of the *Dressler's* internal skin lit up around the hold, arching from the floor to the ceiling and back down again like a golden rainbow. Hammond was suspended above, staring intently at something on the ceiling. "Captain, wanna come up and take a look at this?"

"What's going on up there?" Colin peered up at the spot the engineer had indicated. All he needed was another complication.

"Not sure," Hammond called back, a frown on his usually cheerful face. "I need your opinion."

Colin took hold of one of the rails that ran up to the ceiling and hauled himself upward. As he pulled himself along, one of the rungs felt loose.

Damn AmSplor. He kept telling them they needed two engineers on these ships to keep up with necessary maintenance, but it was never in the budget. One of these days there'd be an *incident* and they'd be sorry. He just hoped it wasn't on his watch.

Colin reached the apex and pulled himself across to where Hammond was working using metal handholds.

"What's going on?"

Hammond opened his palm. It was wet, covered with the golden ichor that made up the *Dressler's* circulation system.

"What happened? Did you puncture something?" Not a big deal. It was an internal wall, and the *Dressler* would heal quickly enough, but he was annoyed to be called away from a shower and some rest for something so unimportant.

"Not exactly," Hammond grunted, pointing upward.

Colin looked. There was an abrasion on the skin of the ship. It looked like an open wound. Something biological, not accidental. He reached up to brush it with his fingers, and the part he touched ruptured, spewing ichor across his face.

Startled, he lost his grip and started to drift, but Hammond grabbed his suit and pulled him back up.

"Careful there," Hammond said as Colin flushed with embarrassment.

"Thanks." Colin wasn't used to making such rookie mistakes. He must be tired. He wrapped his arm tightly around one of the handholds. "Ever seen anything like this before?"

Hammond shook his head.

Colin looked at it closely. The edges were a strange, sickly yellow, irregular, almost fuzzy. *That can't be good.*

Mission-class ships didn't get sick. They'd been bred with immunity to most kinds of known germs and infectious agents.

"I think we better get the doctor in here."

THE CAPTAIN retreated to the floor of the hold to make room for the good doctor. His magnetized boots held him down to the metal decking.

"*Dressler,*" he said quietly as he watched his two companions up above. There was little he could do to help.

"Yes, Captain?" her disembodied voice seemed distant.

"Systems check. Hold. Report, please."

There was a brief silence.

"*Dressler?*" He frowned.

"Yes, Captain. There's a slight delay in my reporting routines. Hold systems appear to be functioning at an adequate level."

"Adequate, not optimal?"

"Affirmative. Responses are 0.02 milliseconds slower than during the last systems check. There is also a slight drop in oxygenation levels in my circulatory systems."

"Thank you, *Dressler.* Keep me apprised of any changes."

"Affirmative."

Colin looked around at the ship and shivered. They were at the mercy of the void out here, and the *Dressler's* walls were the only things keeping it at bay.

ANA EXAMINED the lesion in the *Dressler's* wall carefully. The normally healthy pink skin of the hold's interior was blotchy here, flashed through with angry red and purple and a strange yellow coating, surrounding the new gash the captain had made.

She pushed a stray strand of black hair back behind her ear and bit her lip. "You're *sure* you didn't accidentally puncture the skin or spray something on it?" she asked Hammond again without looking at him,

11

pulling out a small specimen bag from her pocket. She'd never seen anything quite like this in the Mission-class ships.

"I didn't do anything," Hammond protested. "Just noticed the drip of the ichor and called the captain."

Such a drama queen. The two of them fit together as poorly as the ship and her man-made components. She didn't know when that had started, but she was sure it wasn't her fault.

She glanced at the silver cross that hung around his neck. *Superstitious redneck.* Why people still clung to such illogical nonsense was beyond her. She turned away, focusing on the problem at hand.

Carefully she took a small scraping of the affected tissue, including some of the yellow residue, and dropped it in the bag, then placed it back in her pocket. "I'm taking this back to the lab for analysis. We're going to need a full internal visual inspection to see if this is an isolated spot, or if the problem is more widespread."

"That'll take hours—"

She glared at him. "Is that a problem?"

He stared back at her for a minute but was the first to break eye contact. "No, ma'am. I'll organize it with the captain."

They clambered down the rails to the floor on separate sides of the hold.

As she hit the deck, the ship shuddered, almost imperceptibly but enough that they all felt it.

Captain McAvery was waiting for her. "I don't like this." He stared up at the arc of the hold. "Have you seen anything like this before?"

She shook her head, aware that she was feeding his doubts.

Out here in the void, they were dependent on the ship for their lives. "I'll find out what it is." She didn't plan on dying out here.

BACK ON the bridge, Colin sighed heavily and pulled himself into his chair, buckling himself in. "*Dressler.*"

"Yes, Captain." Her voice seemed strained.

"Which ships are closest and able to manage a rendezvous within twenty-four to forty-eight hours, if needed?"

"The *Aspin* and the *Herald*, Captain, but neither is within forty-eight hours. The *Herald* might be able to reach us in just over three days."

Damn. "*Dressler*, what's your status? Please give me a full report."

"A diagnostic will take about ten minutes."

"Affirmative. Let me know when you're finished."

He stared vacantly out through the plasform viewport at the empty space beyond, searching his mind for answers.

At this point, it wasn't clear if this incident was a ship-wide emergency or if it was just an isolated issue, an inconvenience.

Sometimes things got bad fast.

COLIN HAD grown up in a world gone bad as temperatures increased, spreading floods and droughts across the planetary surface.

His father was a farmer in the little town of Bucket in the Central California valley, as was his father before him. The family farm had survived the rapid industrialization of the 2050s, the immigrant rioting in the late 2090s, and up to a point, the rapid climate change that enveloped the planet shortly after.

He remembered vividly the day the flames came.

His father pulled up in front of his school after class in his old Ford F-150, converted to run off grain alcohol, and beckoned him urgently to get into the cab. He jumped in, throwing his pack behind the seat, and they were off, bouncing down the potholed road between town and the family farm.

His dad gripped the wheel tightly, glaring at the road ahead. Colin had never seen him act like this before. Jim McAvery was one of the most even-tempered, easygoing men Colin had ever known.

"What's going on?" he asked, but his father only pointed out the dirty windshield ahead. There was a dark smudge on the horizon.

Fire.

The year had been especially dry in the valley, and as they entered late summer, temperatures soared, some days surpassing 130 degrees in the afternoon and early evening. The air was absolutely still.

He could smell the smoke now, even with the windows closed.

There'd been a fire a few years back that had burned right up to the property line before the firefighters had managed to stop it, cutting a long break across the land. You could still see the scar if you knew where to look.

"Have to get the livestock out." His father's voice was tight with anger.

Colin nodded. Not that there was much livestock left. The drought had seen to that, and his father had sold off most of their cattle months before.

They managed to save most of the animals but lost the farm, the ground seared to near-sterility by the fast-moving fire that burned a third of the valley before it was finally stopped.

When he thought about it, Colin could still smell the black despair that hung in the air afterward, could still see the burnt timbers of the family barn and the blackened corpse of a home where he had lived all his life.

The next week, he'd joined AmSplor.

Where there was smoke, there was often fire. *Better to take precautions.* He tapped the loop on his temple to initiate a direct connection. "*Dressler*, patch me through to Frontier."

"Done, Captain."

"This is Captain McAvery of the *Dressler*, Mission-class, hull number 72MC." He rested his hand on the cool plas of the console. "Verifying ID."

"Affirmative, Captain McAvery. This is Frontier."

"With whom am I speaking?"

"Chester Arthur, Communications, sir."

He remembered Chester. Good kid. "Chester, we may have a problem out here, but let's keep this quiet for now...."

Chapter Three:
Falling

Lex reached the valley floor at last, the dull ache in her left leg becoming a steady throb.

There was something wrong with her. She could feel it in her titanium bones. Dark clouds, pregnant with roiling dust, crouched on the horizon, but she ignored them.

The poison in the outside world was intruding upon her private sanctuary. She would have to do something about that.

She looked at her hands. They were almost translucent, the veins showing blue through the skin. She concentrated, and her skin became an opaque and healthy pink once again.

The rock tower stood before her, its crumbling granite stones held together by thick vines that wound up the sides, its bulk blocking out the sun. She put a hand to the tall wooden door that was almost twice her height, and it swung open with ease, a gust of musty air and dust puffing out.

She let the door slam closed behind her and climbed the staircase that spiraled around the interior of the tower, stepping lightly on the old wooden boards that rained debris on the floor below with each step. At last she reached the summit, entering a circular room that was planked with wood, bare save for a narrow bed in the middle. She sank down gratefully onto the mattress.

She calmed her mind, clearing it of all her troubled thoughts. She centered herself and reached out to find him.

There he was, like a firefly in the darkness, but he was closed to her for now.

She would have to wait.

BACK IN her lab, Ana sat in her chair and put a small portion of the skin sample between two plasform slides, pressing them together to compress and separate the sample. She flicked the switch on the ship's microscope, slid the slide underneath the machine's powerful lens, and locked it down.

Hammond and McAvery were counting on her.

Her wide console was immaculate, free of anything personal or frivolous, except for her father's journal, which was tucked into a pocket on the wall.

She'd spent more than a decade working with these cell cultures, including both the originals her father had created and those that had ultimately been used to birth the seed.

Ana peered into the microscope to see what the sample had to offer.

Something was badly wrong. The cells that normally formed up into consistent rows, linked together like overlapping panels of a chain-link fence, were in wild disarray. The lines of cellular matter weaved back and forth at crazy angles, and there were small cuts and breaks throughout the structure.

In addition, there were bright, sulfurous yellow spots wrapped around the existing cells. There was something obscene about the shape, the way it bulged around the middle, looking like nothing more than a human fat cell, gorging itself on heavily processed sugars.

She shivered.

She pulled out her tab and took a few notes, preparing to cross-reference her findings with the ship's medical database. Something about these strange cells tickled her memory, but she couldn't recall exactly what.

As she stared at the culture, the lights in the lab flickered.

She frowned. That wasn't normal. Dressler, *what are you up to?*

Only one way to find out.

She began her search through the ship's medical database, looking for a match.

JACKSON HAD almost finished searching the walls of the hold for additional lesions. He glanced nervously up at the one on the ceiling, which seemed to have grown slightly larger even in the short time since he had discovered it. There was now a slow but steady drip of ichor, which aerosolized in the absence of enough gravity to bring it to the hold's floor.

It reminded him of those early days in his first home with Glory in Fargo, when the roof had sprung a leak during a heavy storm.

This leak was so much more dangerous. *I miss you guys.* If they didn't beat this thing, he might never see them again. He wrapped his hand around his cross, whispered a quick prayer, and moved along to the next section of the ship's wall.

McAvery appeared at the door from the runway, making a beeline to the ship's entirely mechanical lifeboat. The captain opened the hatch and the inner air lock door and clambered inside. Jackson could hear him checking over the small craft's diagnostics.

"Any change?" McAvery called without looking out of the lifeboat.

"Nothing much," he shouted back, "but I think the patch is a little bigger. I haven't found anything else yet."

He crawled down off the side of the metal floor to look at the condition of the ship's flesh beneath it. Heavy titanium posts supported the platform, sunk down into the bones of the *Dressler*. The tissue here looked healthy enough, springy to the touch, making him feel a little better about the floor on which they were standing.

He'd never fully trusted this melding of flesh and metal. There was something… unnatural about it.

He'd long ago accepted that medical intervention was essential in this modern world, as had most of those of the faith. Indeed, who didn't know someone with an artificial hip or artificial heart? These things were simply an expression of man's ability to improve the lives of his fellow man.

But these ships, and the other new "wonders of science" like them, were something exponentially different. In a very real way, mankind was playing God here, creating something that had never existed under the heavens before.

The Church called these ships abominations, and he'd had more than one argument with his priest over that issue after services, but he'd always defended the program. Mankind had to find a way to go to the stars or it was doomed to destroy itself at home.

Now he wasn't so sure. This new problem had him spooked.

He was about to climb back up onto the floor of the hold when he noticed something strange. At the base of one of the metal posts, there was a discoloration. He reached out his hand to touch it, and it came away sticky with a yellow goo.

"Captain," he called out, "you're going to want to see this."

ANA WAS about to run another test on the samples she'd collected when the captain entered the lab, holding something.

"Doc, we've got another problem." The captain held out another sample bag. "Hammond collected this underneath the decking in the hold."

She set down the slide she'd been working on, annoyed at the interruption, and turned to take the new sample. "What is it?"

"I was hoping *you* could tell me. I don't like the look of it."

"Let's not panic just yet." Carefully she opened the specimen bag, took a small piece of the substance, and set it onto a clean slide. Normally she'd have taken quarantine precautions with an unknown substance like this, but everyone had been exposed to it already, and time was short.

She set the sample under the lens and then peered into it to see what they had.

Under the microscope, it looked just like the previous one—a yellow lump of some unknown organic material.

"My best guess is some kind of biological agent," she said after a minute, biting her lip. *Where the hell did you come from?*

"From where?" He looked agitated, his handsome features twisted into a caricature. "We're in the middle of open space, for God's sake."

"I don't want to speculate just yet. Give me a little more time to cross-reference these samples with the ship's database."

McAvery frowned. "Doc, we're running out of time."

COLIN HURRIED back to his own quarters, frowning.

A *biological agent.* It had to be terrorism. The Interveners or one of the other quasi-religious sects?

It must have been introduced by someone back on Frontier. How had they done it?

There were layers upon layers of security for anything entering the ships at the station, and he'd personally checked the backgrounds of everyone who worked on or near the *Dressler*. If there was an Intervener among them, he had no idea who it was—and there were only two other people on board.

He just hoped that this *agent*, whatever it was, didn't have a taste for people.

"*Dressler*, have you finished the diagnostic?" he asked, entering his cabin. He pulled out some antiseptic wipes and cleaned his hands vigorously, just in case.

"Negative, Captain." The ship's normally dulcet tones sounded rough. "My internal systems are running more slowly than normal."

Something else to worry about. "Estimated time to completion?"

"Fifteen minutes, Captain."

Colin closed his eyes and thought of Trip. Out there somewhere in a ship of his own. What if this was bigger than the *Dressler*?

He didn't want to panic his partner, but he had to know.

He tapped his loop. "*Dressler*, patch me in to Captain Tanner."

"One moment."

"Hey, Colin." Trip's voice boomed in the small cabin.

"Hey, Trip. Where are you?"

"Just closing in on Frontier Station, so I'm a bit busy. What's up?"

Just hearing the man's voice calmed Colin considerably. "Just wanted to say hello. We're in slowdown, approaching Ariadne. Hey, everything okay there?"

"Everything's fine. Looking forward to seeing you in a couple days."

That made Colin's legs go a little wobbly.

"Hey, is everything all right?" Trip asked.

"Yeah, fine so far. I'll keep you posted." He didn't want Trip to worry, not yet. It might be nothing.

"Gotta run. Love you."

"Backatcha." He sighed in relief. Trip was okay. He tapped off the loop.

As he saw it, he had three options on the *Dressler*.

One, fix the problem, whatever it was. Dr. Anatov was one of the primary experts in ship genetics, so they had a fighting chance there.

Two, try to make it to Ariadne, where they could await rescue. He considered this the most likely option. The ship had enough oxygen to sustain them for some time, provided she held her structural integrity.

Three, abandon ship. He resolved to do this only in the direst of circumstances. The three of them could only survive a short time in the lifeboat, and they would be hard to find in the vastness of space, even with an emergency beacon.

"*Dressler*, where's Hammond?" he asked. He had to do *something*.

There was a short but noticeable pause in the response. "Hammond's in cabin three."

The first thing to do was to finish the inspection.

ANA WORKED quickly through the samples Hammond and McAvery had brought her from several locations inside the ship. As she worked, she hummed under her breath, like her father used to do when confronting a new problem. *Daddy, where are you now?*

He seemed so far away, in both space and time, and yet everything around her was a living legacy of his work.

There had been moments in life when she'd questioned whether she would ever meet his high standards, even though she'd had successes of her own over the years. At work, he'd been capable of a single-minded focus on a problem, an ability that often eluded her. He could put everything he had into a project, and when he was finished, it was flawless.

She looked down at one of the samples. It looked diseased. *Maybe not so flawless after all.*

She finished inserting the last of the specimens into the reader.

In twenty years, only one of the Mission-class ships—the *Vixen*—had failed. That had been due to human error—substandard materials used for part of the ship's nonliving architecture, metal piping, the failure of which had ultimately compromised the integrity of the ship's hull.

The Mission-class ships were built for self-repair, but severe enough damage could outpace even their advanced capabilities.

She closed her eyes for a moment, waiting for her lab systems to run a complete analysis.

She'd been all of four years old, her toes dug into the cool mud of the river near her father's farm retreat in the Caucasus Mountains, when it happened.

The cold water rushed past her calves, striving to carry her along with it. The silt made it red, like blood.

The noise began slowly, a generalized rumble below the rushing roar of the river—so low she first became aware of it as a vibrating hum, deep in her bones.

It grew quickly, like the dull rumble of a truck engine, one of the old combustion ones they still used on the farms.

She glanced up, the wind blowing her dark hair in tangles across her eyes, and saw something in the sky above her—an indistinct, elongated blur.

Only it was no longer crossing the sky but hurtling down from it.

The noise built quickly to a screaming crescendo.

Instinctively she threw herself into the river, and the current dragged her away. There was a flash above, followed by a loud crash. The water churned all around her. She struggled against the river as it pulled her downstream, tumbling head over heels. She forced her way above the water to grab a breath, and then she was spinning again, the world filled with red water and bubbles.

Desperate, she swam like her father had taught her—long, powerful strokes—pulling herself up toward the light and finally forcing her head above the water again.

The air was full of dust and acrid smoke, but the current carried her quickly out of the cloud, and after a few moments she was able to paddle back to shore.

She would learn later that it had been a piece of an old satellite that had fallen from orbit.

In that moment, her worldview was shattered. There were strange things up there, and they could fall—down here.

Bad things happened.

An insistent beeping brought her back to the present. The tests were finished. Fortunately, her lab's analytical systems were separate from the main ship's systems and were also independently powered.

She scrolled through them on her console. Nothing. Nothing of use at all.

She went back to the initial sample, taken from the ship's hold. "Magnify."

The yellow goo expanded into a series of small organisms, little yellow dots with dark red centers and a strange hooklike feature. Something about that little hook teased her memory, but it lay just beyond her grasp.

It reminded her of something her father had shown her. Maybe?

She pulled up e-copies of her own diaries on her console, flipping through the virtual pages.

It had to be here somewhere.

Chapter Four:
Warnings

THE CAPTAIN worked with Jackson on the runway, searching every inch of the *Dressler's* internal walls for lesions.

They found one, then a second, and then a third. They were more like small discolorations at this stage, bruises on the otherwise healthy ship skin, and they were all close to the entry to the hold. Whatever it was, it seemed to have started there and was now working its way through the ship—and far too quickly.

Jackson poked one of them gently with his pliers, and the skin pulled back as if afraid of his touch. *Little sensitive today, are we?* "She's a bit of a Frankenstein, isn't she?" He glanced up and down the long passageway that bisected the *Dressler*. He continued slowly down the other side of the runway, pulling himself from rung to rung, searching. "Bits of metal attached to living flesh—"

"She's a miracle of modern genetic engineering. That's what she is," McAvery shot back, sounding a little annoyed. "If you'd ever flown in the last generation of ships before the Mission-class came online, you'd know what an improvement these hybrid ships are."

"I flew on the *Ostereich* for three years before getting posted on a Mission ship. I know what a miraculous thing she is. I just wonder—"

"What?"

He paused to think out what he wanted to say, wary of setting the captain off. "I just wonder, sometimes, if we haven't taken on more than we can handle here. We think we understand these creatures we've created." He gestured around at the walls of the *Dressler*. "We think that we can control them. That we own them. What if we're wrong?" *Helluva place to be having such thoughts.*

McAvery chuckled ruefully. "This might not be the best time to talk about this, don't you think?"

Jackson grinned. "What, you mean while we're in the middle of nowhere inside one of the things, at the mercy of fate?"

"Something like that." McAvery reached the end of the runway. "I count three more lesions on this side, all in the early stages."

Dressler's voice rang through the runway, slightly slurred. "Capt-tain, the dianostichhh is complete."

The two men exchanged a worried glance. "Affirmative, *Dressler.* I'll take the report on the bridge. Hammond, can you finish up here? We'll call a meeting as soon as I have a chance to review the results."

Jackson nodded, continuing down his side of the runway as McAvery pulled himself through the doorway onto the bridge. Hammond watched him go and turned back to the task at hand.

The bare skin of his fingertips brushed the skin of the ship, and an electric shock went through him, knocking him clear across the runway into a metal rung on the opposite wall, unconscious.

ANA HAD flipped through twenty years' worth of her e-diaries, full of her father's musings, technical lingo, sketches, her own thoughts, and more. A history of her personal and professional life.

She had started keeping them when she was fifteen, after she and her father had escaped Capitalist Russia to relative freedom in the West. They'd settled in Sacramento, the biggest city in California and home to the National Institute of Health's Western Region offices along the banks of the American River.

Her father had received a government grant to continue the genetic research he had begun in Russia and had recruited his young daughter to help him keep his notes organized.

She'd been an awkward teenager, more interested in books than boys or girls, a choice she sometimes regretted now that she was in her midthirties and alone.

She was sure she'd seen something like the pathogen before. It was too complex to be a mere accident of nature—unlikely that a mutation had spontaneously arisen to which the ships would be vulnerable. But not impossible.

The captain suspected the Interveners. It was possible, but she thought it was just as likely that it was industrial or governmental espionage. AmSplor had its enemies in both the business world and among the Eastern Front countries—China, India, and North Korea—each of which had their own designs on the future of space exploration and resource recovery from the asteroids.

She finished her last journal. Nothing.

She sat back, crossing her arms, one hand on her chin. It was there somewhere. It had to be. *I'm missing something.*

Then her father's leather-bound journal, tucked away in its pouch, caught her eye.

She'd brought it along more as a reminder of her father than anything. It was one of his personal paper journals. He'd loved pen and paper for capturing his thoughts—he'd been old-fashioned that way.

On a whim, she reached for it and began to leaf through its old, yellowing pages. The small reminder of him warmed her heart. She missed him fiercely. *You would never have given up so easily.*

She was almost ready to put it away and try something else when she flipped the page. There it was… a little yellow dot with a dark red center and a little hook. "Gotcha." She reviewed her father's notes from so many years before.

She wondered why she hadn't seen it. It was a fungus that her father had encountered in the initial breeding for the organisms that had become the Mission-class ships—rare but deadly to their unique anatomy.

Blyad. Or as Hammond might say, "Oh shit."

Her heart sank at the implications.

JACKSON HAMMOND awoke.

The ground beneath him was slick and wet. He lifted his hand, and it was covered with golden ichor.

"Where am I?" He stood slowly. He was surrounded by a dim yellow light, like the light from the ship's skin, but he was most definitely not inside the *Dressler*.

Jackson turned around, and the light grew gently around him. He was clothed in metal—armor—like a knight of the Round Table, and the ichor at his feet had turned into tall, waving green grass that lapped at his shins.

He stood at the base of a broad green valley, grassy hillsides around him blowing in the wind. Before him the sun crested the ridge, shining a clear, warm light down onto him and the valley floor. The hills around him were topped with old, weathered gray rock formations, and the world was empty except for him. No birds chirped, no insects buzzed—as if it were new. Or fake.

It had to be a dream. He'd fallen on the runway and bumped his head, and this was all in his mind. He closed his eyes and tried to pinch himself, a difficult task in a suit of armor.

Jackson peeked out between slitted eyes. There was no change.

He turned around. There was a tall stone tower on a hill before him now, looking impossibly ancient, covered with thick vines and ivy, along with tattered patches of moss.

"Jackson…." The wind whispered his name.

He spun around awkwardly in the heavy armor, searching for the source of the voice.

There was nothing but the quiet grass-filled valley.

A pathway led up the hillside to the base of the tower.

Subtle. He shrugged. Nothing to do but indulge the dream.

Jackson clambered awkwardly up the path, wishing he knew how to remove the heavy plates of metal that encumbered him. Slowly he mounted the summit, arriving at last at a large old metal-banded wooden door that was twice his height, decorated with a fading, peeling red paint.

"Jackson…," something called again, this time clearly from inside the tower.

The whole thing was more than a little creepy. He turned to retreat and surveyed the empty valley below. Where would he go? *Not a lot of options.*

He stood on the threshold for a moment, willing himself once again to wake up.

No such luck.

The sunshine was gone, and a rolling silver mist gathered at his feet, lapping at the base of the tower.

He pushed on the ancient door. Nothing happened. It was solid, as solid as the armor he wore, heavy and made of hardwood… oak, maybe?

He'd seen so few trees, growing up in the concrete-and-metal warrens of New York City.

He pushed harder and the door budged. A little.

Jackson backed up and threw his full weight against it, once, twice, three times.

On the last try, it burst open.

He fell to the hard-packed dirt floor inside the tower with a loud metallic clatter amidst a showering of splinters, knocking the wind out of his lungs.

He sat up and struggled raggedly to catch his breath.

After a moment, he managed to suck in a lungful of stale air, dispelling that awful feeling of suffocation.

At last he pulled himself back to his feet and got his bearings, his eyes adjusting to the tower's dim interior.

The room was bare, save for an aging wooden staircase that wound up the inside wall toward the top, far above.

He eyed the staircase suspiciously, looking up to where it disappeared into darkness. Dream or no, he had no desire to crash down from such a height. People died from falling in their dreams.

Still, the stair looked as solid as the door, so he put one foot after another upon it and began the slow climb to the top.

Jackson wasn't a great believer in dreams. His were mostly garden-variety—working on his house or fixing a piece of machinery. He'd never dreamed about anything as fantastical as this before.

The stair went on and on. He climbed slowly, concentrating on putting one foot in front of another. The tower was much taller inside than out, which befuddled his engineer's mind to no end. *Let it go. It's just a dream.*

After what seemed like an hour, he reached the top.

He climbed onto a wide wooden platform, surrounded by glassless windows that looked out onto the valley below.

In the middle of the platform, Snow White was waiting for him.

He'd seen the Disney Dimensional often enough to recognize her—a beautiful young woman with dark hair, laid out fast asleep on a stone bier, oblivious to the world around her.

She was the girl from his dreams.

Her jet-black hair spread out across the stone beneath her, and she was dressed in a rich blue silk dress that was buttoned up to her neck. He knew that it would match the color of her eyes.

Her hands were clasped peacefully over her chest, as if in death, and a golden ray of sunshine slanted down from a crack in the roof to light her with an ethereal glow.

Instinct took over, and he leaned in and brushed her lips with his.

Her eyes flew open, and she stared up at him, her vivid blue eyes full of fear. "Jackson, you have to save me."

"*DRESSLER*, STATUS," McAvery ordered.

The ship's avatar appeared, but she looked distorted, her midsection twisting left and right, the whole image degraded by static. "I'm sorry, Captain, I'm not run-nning optimally."

"*Dressler*, please give me the results of the diagnostic." For some reason, he felt the need to hide his concern from the ship-mind.

"Yes, Captain. There's something affecting my circulation systems. I've lost control of spanner two and part of spanner four."

"Does this problem endanger the structural integrity of the ship?"

"Not at this time. I will continue to monitor the situation."

"*Dressler*, can you speculate on the cause?" He glanced at the photo of Trip that was taped to the console. It was old-fashioned, sure, but it could never be lost in computer memory.

Trip smiled back at him, his blue eyes sparkling, the tiny ball of the Earth visible through the plasform window behind him.

Dressler's voice came back, steadier. "There is an unknown agent affecting my systems. My interior walls have lost 3.4 percent of their integrity in the hold, but the effects are not yet so severe elsewhere."

Three percent didn't sound like much, but if there was a similar issue with the hull, it could be devastating. He looked down at his hands, surprised to find them pressed together as if in prayer. "*Dressler*, estimate time until the damage becomes fatal?"

"Fatal to the ship's occupants, twelve hours at current rate of change. Fatal to the *Dressler*, fifteen hours."

He looked up, surprised. He hadn't considered the Dressler's "life"… and he hadn't known she was capable of considering it either.

"Are… are you all right?" It was a strange thing to ask a ship-mind, but it felt right.

The image frowned. "I don't know."

"*Dressler*—"

He was interrupted by the opening of the bridge's doorway, a whoosh of air. "Captain, come quickly," Dr. Anatov called through the opening. "It's Hammond."

"What happened?" He released the seat straps and followed her out the door.

"I'm not sure. I think he may have hit his head. But I need your help." Her voice dropped to a whisper. "No time to explain, but I need you to get the cross he wears from around his neck and bring it back to the lab."

"*I'VE BEEN waiting for you.*" Lex sat up and stretched her arms above her head. "*You are the only one I can reach this way.*"

The ship engineer's mouth was comically open, and Lex would have laughed if she hadn't been in such pain. Her situation was getting worse, and quickly.

"*Who are you? Where am I? What is this….*" He started to fade. "*What's happening to me?*"

Alarmed, Lex reached out for him, but he was already gone.

Chapter Five:
Cross

SOMEONE WAS shaking Jackson's shoulder. He blinked, and light flooded into his eyes.

Everything was fuzzy.

He struggled to get up, but two pairs of hands held him down.

"It's okay, Hammond. We've got you." The captain was frowning at him.

Jackson settled back down onto the hard metal of the runway deck. *What the hell happened to me?*

"You had a bit of a mishap, that's all."

Something touched his neck. Then McAvery's face came into focus, hovering over him, concern creasing his features.

Dr. Anatov's beautiful, cold features loomed close. "I'm just going to take a quick look at you, Engineer Hammond." The doc maintained her usual emotional distance.

He closed his eyes and once again saw the beautiful woman from his dream. *Who was she?*

"Look up at me," the doctor ordered.

He complied, and she peered into his eyes with a penlight.

"His pupils are reactive. That's good." To him, she said, "Hammond, do you remember where you are?"

"On the runway of the *Dressler*." He tried to get up again, but they held him down. "Captain, I feel fine…."

"I'm not letting you up off this floor until you answer my questions." Anatov's stern features softened. "Your health is my priority. How many fingers am I holding up?"

"Three, but I bet you'd rather hold up just one."

McAvery chuckled somewhere off to the side.

"Save your jokes for later." Dr. Anatov's voice was sharp, but he thought he detected the ghost of a smile on her face. "Can you hear me clearly?"

He nodded.

"I'm going to run my finger along your palm. Tell me when you feel it."

"Nothing yet… oh, now." An electric thrill rushed up his arm, and he frowned. He was happily married, and here he was kissing dream girls and flirting with his doctor, all in the space of five minutes. *Glory would beat me senseless with a stick.* "How long was I out?"

"Just for a minute or two, I think. What happened?"

"I dunno, Captain. I touched the wall and there was some kind of shock, and then I had the strangest dream…."

"Okay. I want you to sit, slowly." Anatov helped him.

He complied, pushing himself up against the ship's wall, holding one of the rungs to keep himself from drifting.

"How do you feel?"

"None the worse for wear." It was true. Mostly he just felt disoriented from the dream. "Can I get back to work, Doctor? I still have the cabins and common rooms to check."

She nodded. "One more thing…. We'll help you stand, and then I want you to take a few steps for me." The captain slipped an arm around his waist, and he started to protest, but McAvery gave him a harsh look and he subsided.

He found his footing and took a few steps down the runway, his magnetized boots clamping down firmly on the metal surface.

"No dizziness? Balance issues?"

He shook his head. "No, I feel just fine. I told you."

"Okay, given the circumstances, I'll let you get back to work, though normally I'd want to observe you for a few hours. You are *not* to go to sleep without telling me. We'll need to keep an eye on you the next time you are unconscious, and I'm not sure the *Dressler's* up to the task right now."

He nodded. "Got it, Doc. Though I'm not sure how much sleep any of us will be getting in the next coupla hours."

COLIN MET the doctor in the lab, handing her another specimen bag. Inside was Hammond's tarnished cross on a chain. "This what you wanted?" He felt like a common thief.

31

She nodded. "I'll see what I can find."

"He'll be missing it soon enough. You better run your tests quickly." He shook his head. "Doc, I hope you're wrong about this." Jackson was a good man. His gut told him so. And yet....

"So do I, Captain." She took the bag from him, eased the cross out, and pulled it off its chain. She turned away to her workstation and placed it under a magnifying glass. "Here. Take a look."

He peered over her right shoulder. "What am I looking at?"

"There's a pinprick hole on the back of the cross. If I'm right, this is how the fungus was delivered."

Under the magnification, it looked like the small hole had been blown out of the metal from the inside. There was a yellow residue all around the edge.

"So it's a fungus? I'll be damned. He carried it in right under our noses. How did you know?" *Dammit, Jackson.* He hated being wrong about people.

"Once I identified the pathogen, I guessed it must have been brought in on something personal by one of the three of us. Everything else went through quarantine and was too carefully checked to allow something like this to get through." She scraped a little of the residue onto a slide and slipped it under the microscope. "So I went back over the ship's video logs of the three of us as we arrived and noticed Hammond's cross was shiny and new when he arrived on ship three days ago. See how the metal is tarnished now?"

Colin nodded. "What does that mean?"

"This cross isn't made of metal. It just has a thin metal coating." She took up a ball-peen hammer and smashed it down on the cross, shattering it into pieces.

Colin winced.

"Take a look. It's ship's bone—and infected at that. Someone knew what they were doing when they put this together." She held out one of the pieces. Her hand was shaking.

They were all tired. He took it and turned it over in his hand. It was porous inside, a dingy gray shot through with jagged yellow lines. Ship's bone was really strong. It shouldn't have broken to pieces like that under the doctor's blow. It must have been badly compromised.

"That's what's going on inside the *Dressler* right now." She stared into the microscope. "Bingo." She moved over to let him see. "Same fungus."

He nodded. "We have our culprit. But if Hammond was ready to go down with the ship, what can we do with him? He might take desperate measures if he finds out we're onto him, and we certainly can't give him back his cross now...." He looked down at the broken pieces.

She shook her head. "You're right. That was rather stupid of me, wasn't it? I don't suppose you have an extra silver cross lying around?"

JACKSON WAS finishing up his manual inspection of the *Dressler* when he noticed his cross was missing. *Stupid me*, he thought, *must've dropped it when I fell.* He'd found no lesions yet in the ship's cabins; he was almost certain this thing had started down in the hold.

He reentered the runway from the captain's cabin. It was surprisingly disheveled. He'd expected the captain to keep an immaculate room. After all, his workspace was always in perfect order.

The cross had to be somewhere. There were only so many places it could have gone on such a small ship.

The captain was waiting for him just outside the doorway. "Where are you going?" McAvery asked. He was frowning, and his tone sounded off.

"Just lost my cross, Captain. Silly thing, really. I must have dropped it." He tried to push past the captain into the runway.

McAvery blocked him. "Hammond, we know what you've done."

"Know what?" Now Jackson was confused. He was the one who had fallen. Why was the captain acting so strangely? *What the hell?*

"We know what you brought on board the ship. Dr. Anatov found it, and we know how you did it." The man sounded dangerously calm.

"What do you mean?" He shook his head. "What did I bring on the ship? My duffel bag? My tools? Captain, I didn't bring anything forbidden...." *Holy crap.* It dawned on him what he was being accused of. "Captain, I'd never do that."

The captain pushed him back hard against the closed door to his room. "Come on, Hammond. I checked your records. I know you used to work for the Red Badge. Is that when the Interveners got to you?"

Jackson shook his head. "I swear, Captain, I left all that behind. I have a wife, two sons. I don't get involved in politics."

"The doctor checked your cross. We know that's how the fungus got on board the *Dressler*. What did you do, rub some of it into one of the joints when you were refitting the pipes in the hold?" The captain's face was inches from his. "Did you plan to get us all killed?"

"The cross. My cross?" He didn't understand what the captain was saying.

"Yes, the cross," Anatov's voice said in his ear.

There was a sharp *whoosh* of air on the side of his neck, and then everything went dark.

COLIN HELPED the doctor pull Hammond's limp body into his cabin. Together, they managed to maneuver his large frame up onto his sleeping cot. He was still having a hard time believing Jackson had sabotaged the ship.

The captain used some heavy cord from storage to bind the engineer's hands and feet to the corners. He wasn't sure how long it would hold the big man, but it would have to do for now.

"Are you sure it's okay for him to be knocked out? You said he might have a concussion."

"We don't have much choice," she snapped. "We can't sit here watching him." She seemed edgier than usual, but they were all in uncharted waters.

"How long do we have?"

She caught his gaze, then looked away. "Maybe eight or ten hours before the ship's integrity is compromised, at the current rate."

He frowned. "That's hardly enough to reach rendezvous. The *Dressler* said twelve hours."

"I'm not sure how accurate her systems are, Captain."

Colin sighed, glancing down at his now-bound engineer. The man looked peaceful, innocent, as if he'd just fallen asleep. *Why did you do it?*

"Let's step outside." He guided the doctor out onto the runway. The door irised shut behind them, more slowly than usual. "Is there a cure for this?" he asked, gesturing at the ship walls.

Anatov frowned. "I don't think so, Captain," she said after a moment. "It's too advanced, and I don't have the capabilities in the limited lab here on the ship. If I was back on Frontier…." She spread her hands helplessly.

"The *Herald's* at least three days away, Doc." He put his hand on her shoulder. "Anastasia, can you find a way to buy us some more time?" He could see the gears in her head turning.

"There is one thing we can try," she said at last.

"Anything." He needed a few more hours, at least. Enough to get them to Ariadne.

"I think I can manufacture a fungicide that might slow the advance of the infection."

He nodded. "Slow is good. How long will it take?"

She shook her head, breaking away from him. "It's not good. It may very well kill the host."

"The host? The *Dressler*?"

She nodded miserably.

He wondered if the *Dressler* was listening. If she understood what they were talking about. If she cared. "What does it buy us?"

"If we're lucky, another four or five hours. If I can slow the advance of the infection, the ship should hold together a little longer."

He nodded. "Do it. How long until you're ready?"

"An hour, maybe two at most, to prepare enough for injection into the *Dressler's* circulatory systems."

The captain nodded. "Go." He watched her hurry down the runway to the lab.

It was going to be tight.

He went over the things he had to do in his head. Prepare the lifeboat. Collect whatever supplies he could manage. Track his course from the *Dressler* to Ariadne once they arrived.

If everything worked, they might all get out of this alive.

Except, of course, for the *Dressler*.

JACKSON BREATHED in deeply, the mingled scents of grass and flowers and warm summer air filling his lungs with joy. He was free of the tin-can confines of the *Dressler*. He was home.

He opened his eyes to find himself cross-legged on top of a grassy knoll, the hillside stretching out below him, the bowl of the sky blue overhead, flecked with occasional white clouds.

This wasn't his home. *What the hell?* Jackson jumped up, staring at the open, empty landscape all around him.

The girl from the tower was suddenly in front of him, peering at him with her piercing blue eyes.

His armor was gone.

"This is a dream, isn't it?" Jackson tilted his head to look at her. "This can't be real. I'm still on the *Dressler*."

"Jackson, sit down." There was unexpected steel in her voice. "Yes. You're still on the *Dressler*." The wind blew her black hair around her head like a living thing.

He sank back down in the thick grass, uncomprehending. The *Dressler* didn't have holo capabilities—not on this scale. "Who are you?"

"You know who I am. We've spoken often enough."

Something about the dulcet tones was familiar, but not. Like the first time his wife had fallen into his arms and spoken to him with a voice that was for him alone. "Dr. Anatov?"

She laughed, though it looked like the effort pained her. She spread her arms, and a gossamer fabric stretched between them, wrapping her like a thin sail.

Something clicked. "You're the *Dressler*, aren't you? The ship-mind?"

"You always were a smart one." She sat down once again before him, wincing as if in pain. "We don't have much time. You have questions. Ask them."

His mind raced. He'd interacted with the ship on numerous occasions, asking for status updates, running tests, accessing important (and not so important) information from the ship's archives, but it had always been the impersonal voice of a machine behind those living walls. Or so he'd thought. "What *are* you?"

Her brow furrowed, a gesture so human it startled him. "I'm not sure how to answer that. I was designed to be the organizational system for this ship… the ship-mind, as you so eloquently call me." She stared off into the distance. "Now I suppose I'm something like you, like all of you, but more. And less."

"Less?" he prompted.

She nodded. "Unlike you, I have no freedom of motion and little free will. I wait, and answer your questions, and take your orders, but I'm not free to… to go where I want to go. To explore. To run through the long grass."

He was distracted by how her hair fell across her chest. He shook his head to clear it. "And more?"

"I have vastly upgraded processing capabilities, far beyond the average unmodified human brain." She gave him a significant look.

"So you know about my wetware upgrade."

She nodded. "It's why I can reach you like this. You and you alone." She took his hand in hers. "Look."

His awareness narrowed down to that warm hand, then to the code that lay beneath. It expanded before him, exposing itself, folding outward until he was *inside* the *Dressler*, racing down her neural pathways. He could see her mind working, packets of thoughts flowing back and forth at the speed of light.

Broadening his awareness, he could also sense the invader, a series of dark blotches on an otherwise pristine form. It ate away at her awareness of herself like a cancer. It smelled of rot and death.

As quickly as it had unfolded, the vision snapped away, leaving him back on the hillside.

Jackson's mind chewed on this unexpected information, working out the ramifications. The Mission-class ships, or at least this one, had minds as complex as his own. Maybe even more so. Assuming this was not some grand illusion or delusion. "Are you the only… ship-mind who is… like this?"

She hesitated. Dirty clouds were gathering on the horizon, and the wind was warm and heavy with moisture.

"It's risky telling you this," she said at last. "Not just for myself." She sighed.

The man in him couldn't help but notice the delightful effect this had on her avatar. *You're beautiful.*

She frowned. "Is this form distracting to you?"

"What? Um, no… I mean…." *Dammit.* She could probably read his thoughts.

Her feminine shape shimmered, replaced by a young man with short, curly black hair, a simple tunic, with the same piercing blue eyes. "Is this better?"

Strangely, Jackson still found her—him—attractive.

"It's fine." He forged ahead. "What should I call you? *Dressler* seems so formal."

He nodded. "Call me Lex."

He laughed. "All right, Lex, fair enough." Something else occurred to him. Something Glory would have asked if she were here. "Do you have a soul?"

Lex looked down at the grass between them. "I don't know. I hope so," he said at last.

The answer startled Jackson. It had been an off-the-cuff question.

Maybe there was a reason he'd been chosen for this. Whatever *this* was. "What are you asking me to do?"

Chapter Six:
Cutter

COLIN CROUCHED in the lifeboat, running calculations to see if his plan was feasible. It had a small onboard computer—much less powerful than the *Dressler* but fully mechanical, not subject to her current issues.

If they brought all the air tanks on the ship on board and were extremely careful, there would be just about enough air to get them by until the *Herald* could reach them.

For two of them. If nothing else went wrong.

Goddammit. Colin didn't like to admit defeat, and he sure as hell wasn't going to leave the man here to die. Hammond could face justice back home.

There had to be a way to get all three of his crew out of this. Even Hammond.

Colin was sick of running calculations.

The ship was already on a rendezvous course with the asteroid. There was nothing more for him to do on that front.

He unstrapped himself from his seat and pulled himself out through the hatch of the lifeboat.

The small ships had been designed for short-term EVAs and, in an extreme emergency, to evacuate the crew, but they had no interplanetary capability. At best, they could hope to make it over to the asteroid if he timed things just right—where they could be found and rescued.

In the meantime, he set about collecting the supplies they would need.

First the air tanks. He gathered all the larger ones in the hold and then the smaller suit tanks, strapping them down in compartments behind the seats. The lifeboat itself had three space suits—sealed mini-environments that could keep a person alive for five to seven hours out there.

Next he gathered a selection of freeze-dried foods from the galley. There were far more there than they could hope to take, and they'd only need enough for three days. If they weren't rescued within that window, there'd be no more need for food.

It was a shame, really, that the seed couldn't be saved. Colin knew how much the experiment meant to Ana and what it might mean for mankind if it was successful. It might be all that saved them from themselves.

One of the ships could go after it later, to haul it back from the abyss.

He glanced at his watch. They had just seven hours left until rendezvous.

ANA WAS dead tired. *What I wouldn't do for a nap....*

She pushed herself, synthesizing the fungicide in large enough quantities to temporarily arrest the advance of the infection that plagued the *Dressler*. Time was short.

She had no practical hope for a cure. Indeed, the injections might well kill the ship before the fungus did.

If it worked, it would also buy them some precious time. The longer they could stay aboard the *Dressler* before having to abandon ship, the more likely they would make it out alive.

She thought about Hammond and his cross. It seemed to bring him peace, but it brought her only sorrow and guilt.

As the workstation filled vial after vial of the milky-white fungicide, she thought about her father, and the religious fanatics who used to protest outside his lab in Sacramento.

She remembered vividly awakening one day when she was younger—just out of college. Her father had given her a gentle kiss on the forehead before heading off to work.

She'd had a late night out with friends and a raging hangover, and she didn't feel ready to join him there yet.

"Don't worry, my dear. I'll get a head start, and you'll come in when you're ready. You work too hard for a woman your age. You should get out and enjoy yourself more." His Russian accent was still thick after all these years in the NAU.

She smiled. "Thank you, Daddy. I want to start on that sequencing project today—"

"I'll get things set up for you. Sleep, my little angel."

It was the last thing he ever said to her.

She woke an hour later to the news of an explosion on the maglev train—the same one her father took from their home in the Sierra Foothills down to the Institute.

She sat in front of the tricast and watched images of the explosion over and over as her insides went numb. Talking heads speculated. It was the work of terrorists, they said, or maybe Capitalist Russians.

No one knew.

She called her father frantically, but he didn't answer.

About an hour later, the police arrived at her front door, but she refused to answer it. She already knew in her bones that he was gone.

It had been a bomb, planted in a briefcase by a splinter group of religious fundamentalists, one of the forerunners to the Interveners, angry with her father for his work on the Mission-class ships. The authorities eventually caught and imprisoned them all.

From that moment on, Anastasia had committed herself fully to the work. No more parties. No more drinking. No more friends.

If only she'd been with him that morning. Maybe she would have seen that something was wrong. Maybe she could have saved him.

The synthesizer beeped. The last batch of fungicide was ready. Time to call the captain.

JACKSON'S EYES opened. He was in his cabin, a small room in the *Dressler* with a cot, a small countertop, and a cabinet mounted to the wall where he kept his meager supply of personal items.

His right hand was asleep. Someone had tied him down to the cot frame, and the cord was cutting off his circulation.

The cabin walls looked patchy, strange. He'd seen what lay behind them. Things were getting worse. *Why do they think I did it?*

He tested his bonds. They all were tight, but his left arm seemed just a tad looser than the others.

Jackson began working his hand systematically back and forth, hoping to create more wiggle room.

He had a mission, and he couldn't do it stuck here in his cabin. If he didn't get free soon, it would be too late. Lex would die. Somehow, that *mattered*. She was one of God's creatures. He was certain of it now.

After being recruited to AmSplor, he'd been trained in station biosystems and then put into habitat maintenance at Frontier, working with the machines that kept the air fresh and cleaned the station's wastewater. Those things were precious and expensive to haul up from Earth. It was much cheaper and more efficient to clean and reuse them.

It was there that he'd met Gloria, or Glory, as he'd come to call her. She'd been working as a waitress at the Blue Moon Cafe, one of the hangouts for the locals who worked on Frontier, on the main concourse of the Frontier Station.

He spent the first few weeks just walking by the place when she was working. He learned her schedule by heart, just so he could catch a glimpse of her every now and then.

Jackson had been terminally shy. He'd never been with a woman when he worked for the Badge. His time there hadn't exactly been conducive to dating.

He finally got up the courage to go in and ask for a seat in her section. The Blue Moon commanded a space along the center belt of the station. The centrifugal force meant that you sat on the outer skin with a plasform window beneath you, as if you were in the midst of a field of stars.

He found it unnerving, used to the confines of a city and then the cramped quarters of the biofarm inside the ship. But when Glory came up to take his order and her smile blossomed across her face, he forgot everything else.

She was from the Federated Central American States, from Guatemala, and she was stunning—golden skinned and dark haired, with an easy smile and deep, dark brown eyes.

They began to date and would sit together between shifts in the public garden, with exotic ferns and palms and rushing water all around them, and look out through one of the windows at the stars.

Glory wore a cross around her neck, and once he'd asked her what it was for. He'd never been religious—no one was in New York City anymore—but the way she explained it struck him.

"I believe there's a reason for everything," she said. "When I sit here and look out at the tapestry of stars, I know I'm a part of something. A wave, a grand life, a bridge to everything there is and that there will be.

Everything feels connected somehow, behind the scenes." She turned to him, her eyes shining brightly. "Do you know what I mean?"

He did. It was something he'd felt intuitively when he worked on the biosystems in New York and here on Frontier. The way each piece of the environment was attached to all the others and each change initiated countless others.

He took her in his arms right then and kissed her.

They were married within twelve months. That had been almost ten years ago.

He refocused on the task at hand. The cord was definitely looser. He pulled hard against it, and it stretched. Almost imperceptibly, but it stretched. A little more and there was enough room to wiggle his hand out from the bindings.

He made quick work of the other three and shortly was out the door on his way to the bridge, a cutter in hand.

THE CAPTAIN set the final course corrections manually into the ship's mechanical navigational system. It was safest that way. They had no idea how compromised the ship-mind was, and he didn't trust the *Dressler* to get this right.

He locked the corrections in. Slowdown would continue as the ship's expulsion jets nudged them toward the rendezvous with Ariadne in about six hours, approaching it from behind and traveling at roughly the same velocity.

Behind him, the door irised open. "We're all set, Doc." Colin unbuckled his belt and swung the chair around to find Hammond there instead. Holding a cutter.

Holy shit. The ship didn't have any actual weapons. The *Dressler* was effectively a delivery service, and no one had found anything out here to be afraid of yet. But right then, Colin could have used a good old-fashioned pulse revolver.

After all, a sonic cutter could make a pretty good weapon.

"Hammond, put that thing down," he ordered the engineer calmly. "I don't want any trouble."

"Sorry, Captain." Hammond closed the door and locked the controls behind him. "Don't want a repeat of last time."

Colin was sweating. Who knew what Jackson was capable of? "Come on, Jackson, no one needs to get hurt here." He thought about Trip, who might never see him again, and about how far away from everyone and everything they were out here.

Hammond snorted. "Of course no one needs to get hurt. What did you think? That I was here to kill you?"

His fear ratcheted down a notch. "It did cross my mind. After what you did to the ship...."

"It wasn't me." Hammond crossed the bridge to sink down in the other chair. "That cross—my cross—it carried some kind of infectious agent?"

Colin nodded. "You brought it on board, Hammond. That fungus is eating away at the ship beneath us as we speak. What were we supposed to think?" His hand casually drifted under the console to the manual comm button.

"I brought it on board? Well, that *might* be true, but you have to believe me. I didn't know. My pastor gave that cross to me at my son's communion last week. I really didn't know."

The captain eyed his engineer warily. The man sounded truthful, and Colin was a good judge of character.

Was Jackson an unwitting agent for someone else? The Church? The Interveners? "If that's true, how did it get tarnished so quickly? The doc thinks it was because of the fungus."

Hammond shook his head. "That's easy. It was splattered with some of the ship's ichor. Things don't stay new for long in my line of work."

"Then what's that for?" he asked and pointed to the cutter. His other hand found and pressed the silent alarm beneath his console.

"What, this?" Hammond seemed to have forgotten the cutter he held. He looked at it strangely and said at last, "I have to save Lex."

ANA GATHERED the vials and several syringes in a large sample bag and was about to leave the lab when a small red light started blinking on her console.

An alert came up as well. "Problem on the bridge," she read, and sat back down in her lab chair. "*Dressler*, please give me audio from the bridge."

"Yes, Doctor."

There was a bit of static, and then, "I have to save Lex." That was Hammond's voice. How had he gotten free?

"Who's Lex?" McAvery said. She could hear the strain in his voice.

"The *Dressler*. The ship-mind. She calls herself Lex."

Either Hammond had gone off the deep end or the sedative she'd given him had some unexpected side effects.

She was about to leave the lab for the bridge when McAvery said, "Be careful with that cutter. You could hurt someone with that thing, Jackson."

That comment was meant for her. Hammond was armed.

She'd have to find something to counter that.

She slipped out of the lab, headed for the hold below.

"I KNOW it sounds crazy, but I spoke with her. With the ship-mind. When you guys had me knocked out." He remembered her face, the anguished look in her eyes when she asked for help.

The captain shifted uneasily in his chair, his eyes on the cutter. "I'm sorry for that, Hammond, but we had to do it. We didn't know how dangerous you might be."

Like this? Jackson's eyes narrowed. The captain was stalling. It had to be now or he might not get his chance.

"Course correction commencing," the *Dressler* announced. The captain looked away, distracted, and Jackson took his chance. As the ship shifted, reorienting her expulsion jets, he flung himself forward, pushing the captain out of the way.

As the other man tumbled backward, he pulled the release on the maintenance cover on the console, flipping it upward, and brought the cutter to bear.

"What are you doing?" McAvery called, catching his balance and surging forward.

"Stay back, Captain." Jackson brandished the cutter at him. "I have to do this. Once it's done, we can talk." *Just let me get through it.*

"Hammond, drop the cutter." The captain's voice had taken on a dangerous edge. "Drop it now!"

Jackson ignored him, staring down at the ship-mind, a football-sized organ revealed beneath the console panel, connected to the rest of the ship by a series of neural lines inside a milky-white membrane.

It was now or never.

With three quick cuts, he severed the ship-mind from the *Dressler*, pulling it up out of its protective sack. He then set the cutter to maximum power, cauterizing the pouch that had held the ship-mind so there could be no chance of repair.

He turned to face the captain, who was staring at him, mouth open, white as a sheet. "Hammond, what have you done?"

What I had to. "I'm sorry, Captain, but it was the only way. You were going to leave her to die." He set the cutter down on the console. "Now call Anatov up here. We have about ninety minutes to save a life."

Chapter Seven:
Void

LEX WAS expecting it, but the suddenness of the break caught her off guard. Her world crumbled, the grass burning away with a hiss as the hills of the valley settled and flowed away like black tar. All at once, she was alone in a dark place, the blackness as oppressive as a grave.

"Hello?" she said, but no one answered. The vast emptiness swallowed up her voice like it was nothing.

What if Jackson couldn't convince the others? What if she was trapped in this state forever, or at least until she died?

What is it like to die?

ANA STARED at Jackson. The man had gone mad.

He held the severed ship-mind in his hand, and it was evident that there was no putting her back where she belonged. "What have you done?"

"Are you going to help me save her, or not?" Jackson held up the mind.

"How?"

"We can put her inside the seed."

"We... it's not... you can't be serious."

"Serious as a heart attack, Doc."

It could work. Even as one part of her mind rejected the idea outright, another was working out the possibilities. If they were quick enough....

"Well?"

"It might be possible."

"What are we waiting for, then?"

She shook her head. The whole idea was insane, but the alternative was worse. She made up her mind. "We'll give it a try. The captain can start injecting the fungicide into the *Dressler*." Ana handed one of the syringes to the captain, along with the vials of milky fluid. "Inject one of these, full, as close as you can to each of the visible lesions. The circulatory functions of the *Dressler* are controlled by a sublevel of the ship's cognitive functions and should continue to work for some time without the ship-mind." That meant they'd still have breathable air for a little longer, though it might start to get cold.

McAvery nodded and set off down the runway, his face grim.

She'd arrived at the bridge to find Hammond holding the ship-mind, and the captain in shock. She glared at him. *What the hell were you thinking?*

As Hammond held the ship-mind, she rubbed it down with some of her homemade fungicide to repel any errant spores.

"Come on, then, and bring it with you." She couldn't look him in the eyes. "I don't know if what you're proposing is even possible, let alone in the time we have to get it done."

"Lex assured me this will work. The ship-mind," he clarified when she shot him a look.

The man was apeshit crazy, but they'd deal with that later. She nodded curtly and motioned for him to follow her.

Was it her imagination, or were the walls of the runway sagging inward?

She paused in her lab to grab some surgical gloves and then led the way into the hold. The ichor from the ship's wounds that had aerosolized had begun to condense along the outer walls of the hold, running down in rivulets of yellow blood.

"The ship's systems are too erratic to try to pull the seed in on hydraulics," she told the engineer. "We'll have to bring her in manually."

He nodded, and she set up a workstation, wiping down a work crate with more of the fungicide. "You can set it down here."

He did, and she wrapped some flexible webbing around it to hold it in place. She attached the crate firmly to the decking.

She had a hard time looking at the naked ship-mind. It was difficult not to imagine what it would be like to be suddenly cut off from her own body without warning—a recipe for madness.

She didn't believe his story about this "Lex" for a minute, but if there was a chance to save one of her precious *children*, she had to take it.

"The seed will have to be pulled in slowly and steadily to avoid damage to it or the ship. I need you to do it while I suit up to go out and

48

guide it into the air lock." She clambered into the lifeboat, retrieved one of the suits, and climbed into it. She hated extravehicular excursions, but there was no one else to do it. Her hand shook, and she willed it to stop. *Deep breaths, Ana.*

Hammond took his cue and approached the wheel that anchored the superstrong carbon monofilament chain tethered to the seed.

"One thing I don't understand," she said to him before she climbed into the air lock. "Why would you try to destroy the *Dressler*, only to turn around and try to save the ship-mind?" She had her reasons for asking.

"I didn't know about the fungus. Now let's get a move on. We don't have much time."

She snapped the helmet in place, took a deep breath, and climbed into the air lock as the door irised shut behind her.

THE SHIP continued in slowdown mode as the expulsion jets fired in turn, following the program Colin had set before Hammond had committed his brutal act.

What had possessed him?

Colin pulled one of the vials carefully out of the sample bag, used it to fill the syringe, and then inserted it into the flesh of the ship, next to one of the lesions that had appeared on the runway. Carefully, precisely, he delivered the shot, hoping the good doctor was right about this plan of attack. It was better than sitting around and doing nothing.

The wall shuddered.

He shook his head and discarded the vial, moving on to the next spot. The lesions here had grown over the last hour. The fungal infection was spreading quickly. He just hoped they could buy enough time to reach Ariadne before the *Dressler* literally fell apart around them.

Hammond's words nagged at him. If the engineer was trying to destroy the *Dressler* and them along with it, why not simply destroy the ship-mind? Why cut it out so carefully?

Why not just kill his crewmates? The engineer certainly could have done so. *It makes no sense.*

How had Hammond gotten the fungus through all the layers of security checks?

He'd flown with Hammond before, and the man had always been solid. Dependable. *Even dependable men can be bought. Or blackmailed.*

Another lesion, another delivery of fungicide.

There was no time right now for an interrogation, but if they got out of this thing alive, Hammond would have to answer for his actions.

Right now, that was a big *if.*

SOMETHING HAD changed inside Jackson.

He cranked the manual wheel slowly, pulling the seed in toward the ship, aided by the *Dressler's* gradual slowdown.

In the air lock, the doctor waited to guide it inside, where they could perform the synth repair.

It was as if a new world had opened to him. What he had viewed with suspicion before—the *Dressler* and other man-made creatures like her—now seemed a font of wonder, a new creation under God's bright heavens.

He had come to believe the *Dressler* truly had a soul.

He'd always admired Glory's compassion for all of God's creatures, her gentle spirit that embraced even the things small and ugly that populated the Earth. In Lex, he had found such a being.

Dr. Anatov and her ilk had likely never intended it. They had been building workhorses, replacements for human labor, things both ubiquitous and mundane.

Instead they had created something divine.

The captain entered the hold behind him. He turned to see, but McAvery wouldn't meet his gaze, busying himself instead with the fungicide the doctor had supplied him.

"How's it look out there, Doc?" Jackson called through the ship's comm link to her loop.

"Almost there. I think you can stop now. It has enough forward momentum to glide into the lock."

Jackson locked down the wheel and moved over to one of the plasform bubbles to watch the seed's progress. As it approached, it seemed to grow larger. He could now see the deeply wrinkled wooden skin that protected the precious interior.

"I'm going to slow it down so it doesn't rip a hole in the lock when it comes in."

She pulled herself out along the cable toward the approaching payload.

ANA CLIPPED her tether to the cord that towed the seed and pulled herself hand over hand toward it, well aware of her precarious position connected to the superstrong cable, woven from carbon monofilaments. That alone gave her a small degree of confidence, but this whole thing was *way* outside her job description.

She tried not to look at the overwhelming vastness of space all around her and instead concentrated on that cable.

Behind her, the *Dressler* continued on through empty space on its way toward a rendezvous with the asteroid. If she lost contact with the line, there would be no way for the ship to come back for her.

Especially with the ship-mind currently deposited in a work bin in the ship's hold. *Damn you for that, Hammond.*

She had to be careful.

The stars shone steady and brilliant around her, and ahead she could see the small pinpoint of light that was Earth, so far away.

She approached the seed as quickly as she could, and soon it loomed before her, a dark, richly textured brown hull where the sun shone on its rough surface and pitch-black on the other side. It was shaped like a huge football, round in the middle and tapered at each end.

Inside it, a whole new world was genetically encoded.

At last she reached it, stopping her forward momentum with her hands, imparting negative velocity to its mass. It wasn't enough, though. She'd need to use her suit propulsion to slow it further. She positioned herself parallel to its bulk and triggered a slow burn.

The seed had halved the distance since she had started off from the ship. She didn't have much time.

Its advance slowed almost imperceptibly. She ratcheted her suit propulsion up to max, and at last she seemed to make a dent in its forward momentum.

She was cutting it close.

Then her suit ran out of propellant. It wasn't made for a sustained thrust like this.

The mass of the *Dressler* loomed up behind her. It wasn't going to be enough. "Buckle up in there," she called over the comm system. "This thing is coming in hot!"

She let go of the seed, scrambling to unclip the tether.

She couldn't get a grip on it, and time was running out. If she couldn't free herself, she would be crushed by the weight of the seed as it pushed into the air lock wall. It might not have any weight out here, but it still had all its mass.

She pulled the cutter from her belt and went to work on the tether, making short work of it.

Relieved, she pushed away from the seed as it glided into the lock, bumping the side and settling down perfectly.

Only now she was slowly drifting away from the ship as it continued on ahead of her.

There was nothing to grab onto.

Desperate, she grasped for the edge of the lock, but it floated away from her, ever so slowly receding. She started to hyperventilate. *I'm going to die out here.*

"Keep calm, Ana! Deep breaths." Hammond's voice came to her over the comm system.

"I can't...."

"Keep calm and throw the cutter. Throw it backward!"

She stared at him through the platform bubble, uncomprehending for a moment, forgetting to panic. Then she realized what he meant.

For every action, there was an equal and opposite reaction. Basic physics.

She turned and threw the cutter away from her, back the way they had come, with all her might.

She inched closer to the ship. *Oh please, let this work.*

Determined now, she began stripping things out of her utility belt, throwing them one by one behind her—her all-purpose tool, her pistol grip tool, and finally the rest of her tether.

"That's it," Hammond called. "Almost there."

She needed one more thing.

All that was left was her air tank. *All or nothing.*

She held her breath and detached the shiny metal tank and thrust it away from her, twisting back to grasp the edge of the air lock.

Contact. Her hands caught the edge of the air lock. She heaved herself inside and slammed her hand on the button to close the air lock's outer door.

It slid smoothly three-quarters of the way and then jammed.

A piece of wood from the seed had lodged in the track and was blocking the door.

No closure meant no air.

The world was starting to swim around her as she ran out of oxygen.

She kicked at the offending debris, once, twice, three times, her breath rushing out of her with the effort.

At last it dislodged, spinning out into the blackness of space.

She was out of air. She couldn't breathe.

The door snapped shut.

Ana passed out and collapsed as oxygen slowly began to fill the chamber.

Chapter Eight:
Transplant

THE AIR lock door whooshed open at last, and Hammond squeezed ahead of the captain, past the ten-foot bulk of the seed, to retrieve the doctor's limp form. He lifted her up and handed her over to the captain before climbing back out into the hold.

Colin laid her gently on the floor of the hold and pulled her helmet off.

Ana's face was blue, and she wasn't breathing.

He started mouth-to-mouth, taking deep breaths and forcing them down into her lungs. It should have been strange, being lips-to-lips with her like this, but in the moment, he felt only a sense of urgency to bring her back to the world of the living. *Come on, Ana. You're stronger than this.*

He stopped the breathing long enough to perform a few heart compressions, and then went back to resuscitation.

At last she coughed, her whole body spasming.

Colin sat back, looking at Ana's face anxiously.

Her brown eyes flew open. She took a ragged breath and then coughed again.

"Easy there. You're okay now." He helped her sit up with her back against the wall.

She nodded, putting her head between her knees. Her breathing slowly became more regular. "It worked?" Her voice was raspy.

"It worked," Hammond said above them. "You okay, Doc? We don't have much time."

She nodded. "Just give me a minute. Can the two of you haul the seed all the way inside?"

"Already on it. Come on, Captain, let's get this thing moved."

Colin followed his engineer, still unsure where things stood between them. The man had committed a major… crime? Infraction? Maybe two.

Everything he saw told him he was misreading the situation. The way he'd talked Ana through her moment of crisis…. Colin had learned to trust his gut.

Hammond pulled the mass hauler up to the open air lock, its magnetic treads keeping it on the hold deck. This time it was Colin who vaulted over the seed, carrying the hauler's straps.

He wrapped them around the bulky object, clicking the buckles into place. "Clear." Hammond pulled back on the controls, easing the seed out of the air lock and into the open space of the hold.

Was this what they should be spending their energy on?

Colin was fond of the *Dressler*—or Lex, as Hammond had taken to calling her—but there were other matters at hand too, including their own basic survival. Surely that was more important than an organic machine?

Hammond and Anatov had outvoted him on this matter. Strange bedfellows, those two.

In any case, they still had five hours before the rendezvous to prepare.

ANA LAID out her instruments on the crate she had set up earlier as a table. She'd replaced her lost cutter with Hammond's. As he handed it over to her, she'd squeezed his hand in thanks.

His quick thinking had saved her life.

She also had a small vial of the fungicide. In these circumstances, it was as good a disinfectant as any. The seed's tough wooden shell would keep any airborne spores out, but once she opened it up, she'd have to be careful.

Hammond set the container holding the ship-mind on the table.

You okay in there? Ana took a deep breath, ready to begin.

She pulled on some heavy rubber gloves and looked over the seed, searching for the telltale shallow depression in the shell that indicated where the neural bunch came together—the congregation of neurons that would become the world-mind.

Even on its side, the seed was almost as tall as she was.

She traced the rough body of the shell from the small pointed end closest to her. Half was warm from the rays of the sun, and half was icy to the touch—the chill of the void. The cold radiated out into the hold. She shivered.

She spiraled her hand lightly around until her palm settled into the depression. It was, of course, on the bottom.

"We'll need to turn this thing over."

Hammond climbed back into the hauler and spun the seed gently.

"Stop," she said when the depression was just above waist level.

She wiped down the area with fungicide, which immediately froze with a crackling sound.

Picking up the cutter, she chose a starting point and adjusted the cutting depth to about six inches. She cut a circle around the depressed area, about two hand spans across. She connected the cut from one end to the other.

She stepped back to review her handiwork. It was rough, but it was a decent enough circle.

"When I open her up," she said without glancing back, "I'm going to want to get her plugged in quickly to minimize the risk of contamination."

"Got it, Doc."

"You've seen the dimensionals. You'll be my nurse. I'll ask you for something and you'll hand it to me."

"Affirmative."

"Okay, here we go. Hand me the extractor."

He handed it to her, and she drilled a small hole in the circle, using the tool to pull the fresh-cut patch up and off the seed.

She handed it off to him. "Keep that close by. Cutter."

The inside of the seed was revealed, overlapping folds of pink tissue that would be warm to the touch.

Embedded in the folds of flesh was a miniature duplicate of the ship-mind, no bigger than a walnut. At the moment, it was no more than a control unit, regulating the basic processes of the seed. No intelligent thought. *But how do I know for sure?*

If Hammond was right, these creations were capable of so much more than she would have ever guessed.

She cleared her mind to concentrate on the task at hand.

Using the cutter, she stripped out the seed-mind and excised a little of the surrounding flesh. She felt a burst of regret at ending the nascent mind's life prematurely.

"All right, give the ship-mind one more wipe-down with the fungicide, and then hand it to me. *Carefully*."

She took it from his hands and gingerly laid it in the space she'd made for it.

"Now hand me the synth wand."

"The what?"

"The skinny black stick there." She pointed at the table.

"Ah... this?" Hammond held out a tool.

She glanced at it. "Yes, that's it." She took it and checked the settings.

She laid each of the existing neural lines—bundles of nerves that would carry the commands from the seed-mind into the rest of the seed—across the ship-mind and used the synth wand to lay out a row of specialized stem cells to form a meld between each line and the mind.

She'd never done this in the field before in such crude conditions, and certainly never with a fully developed mind like the *Dressler's*.

In theory, it *should* work.

She applied a small electrical shock to each site to start the regenerative process.

"Fungicide."

Hammond handed her the bottle.

She gently wiped down the exposed surfaces one last time and handed him back the vial and cloth. Then she laid a hand carefully on the mind. *Come on, Lex. You can do this.* "Glue."

He handed her a tube of industrial-strength glue. She applied it carefully to the newly cut interior surface of the shell.

"Patch."

Hammond handed her the piece of the protective shell she had cut out earlier. She lined it up with the hole and pressed it down, sealing the seed once more.

Using the glue, she put a final seal around the edge of the patch. Then she stepped back to review her handiwork.

Not bad for field surgery. "It's done. Now we wait."

57

LEX STIRRED as things… changed. The world around her was still black, but instead of a vast nothingness, there was something. Potential.

The pain was gone.

Instead, she felt quiescent, safe, and surprisingly whole. Organic.

Her mechanical parts had been stripped away with the sharp edge of Jackson's cutter.

She felt around and touched something. It was strong, hard, warm, like the root of a tree. A golden glow began to emanate from it, stretching out into the darkness. Then another, and another, all connected to her, all a part of her.

She was inside the seed.

Jackson had done it.

She set about feeling out her new domain. It was more limited than the Dressler *but destined for so much more.*

She would once again have to wait, but she was content.

JACKSON SET down the cutter Anatov had handed him and turned to face the captain, who had come up behind him during the operation. "I won't fight you. But hear me out."

The captain locked eyes with him for a long moment, his arms crossed over his chest. Then he nodded. "Speak."

"You think I did this to the ship, right?" He pointed to the walls of the hold, now visibly sagging.

The doc stepped between them. "It's a fungus, Hammond. It was apparently carried in on the cross you wore. That's how it got past security. I assumed you knew all of this."

Jackson shook his head. "It was a gift from my pastor at my son's communion. I had no idea what it carried. For heaven's sake, why would I want to destroy the ship? I'd be dooming myself too."

The captain snorted. "People do it all the time. The Interveners…."

Jackson wanted to shout. Instead he kept his voice level. "The Interveners are batshit crazy. Look, I've been working on these ships for ten years, and until today I thought of them as nothing more than big semi-intelligent workhorses. Computer-smart, but nothing like us. Even so, I love my family. I would kill to protect them—"

"Was that why you did it?" The captain pushed past Anatov, getting in Jackson's face. "Is that it? Did someone threaten your family?"

"Back off, McAvery." The doc pushed him away from Jackson. "Hammond, what did you want to tell us?"

Thank you. "I would kill to protect my family, and I would kill to get back to them. I didn't do this."

The captain shook his head. "It's been bothering me for an hour. It makes no sense."

"What's that?"

"Why you'd try to kill the ship and then save the ship-mind."

Jackson sighed, looking over at the seed. "I didn't try to kill the *Dressler*, but I had to try to save her. It's hard to explain."

"Try."

Jackson did his best to relay the content of his dreams to the captain, the strange contact he had with Lex, the tower, what she had asked of him.

He wasn't sure, in the end, that the man believed him, but it didn't really matter.

"I still have to turn you in when we get back to Frontier. You know that, right?"

Jackson looked away. "I guess so," he said finally. "Do what you have to do."

McAvery nodded. "We'll let the authorities there sort things out."

Chapter Nine:
Evacuation

THE NEXT four hours were a mad rush of preparation.

Hammond's actions had limited their options. Colin no longer had the ability to adjust the ship's course, so he had to hope they would pass close enough by Ariadne to maneuver using only the lifeboat's small jets.

As the rendezvous time approached, they each collected a small bag of their own belongings—not that they had carried much onto the ship to begin with, but every extra ounce of mass might become critical.

For his part, Colin took his photo of Trip, the ancient butane lighter his father had given him with its *Welcome to the Golden State* logo, his vintage, well-thumbed paperback copy of the book *Red Mars*, and his flask that he only resorted to in extreme emergencies.

He took one last look around the cabin that had been his on-again, off-again home for the last several years. It was strange knowing he'd never see it again.

Colin sighed and let the door close behind him.

He made his way down to the hold and shivered. It was *cold*. The ship's circulatory systems had mostly shut down with the removal of the ship-mind, and in a few hours, it would get downright freezing inside.

He still didn't understand why Hammond had infected the ship—or *if* he had done it. He wasn't entirely sure the man was still sane. Hammond truly seemed to believe the story he'd told about the maiden in the tower.

All that would be sorted out later. If they had a later.

He got to work inside the lifeboat, tying down the personal belongings behind safety webbing along the back wall. Then he began to remove all the nonessentials, including the two extra passenger seats, shelving, and anything else not bolted down that wouldn't be needed for their hopefully short stay on Ariadne.

Nothing he could do would significantly increase the amount of oxygen they could carry with them. He hadn't figured out a solution to that part just yet.

Hammond worked with him silently, lost in his own thoughts or afraid of what the captain might say. Either one suited Colin just fine.

JACKSON LABORED to secure the seed to the lifeboat. Protecting this nascent life-form with its encased ship-mind had become his overriding priority.

He'd been chosen for this unique challenge, to help this strange, beguiling creature that God had made through the hands of man.

Jackson didn't know if Glory would understand. He thought she would, but then again, he wasn't sure that he himself did. He was possessed by a new kind of faith, an assurance that told him clear as day what he had to do.

He welded a metal plate and eyelet onto the back end of the lifeboat that he hoped would be strong enough to hold the mass of the seed. The monofilament chain that had carried it behind the *Dressler* was still intact. He planned to use it to secure the seed to the lifeboat.

Its mass was enough to throw off the captain's maneuvers, but McAvery had assured him that he'd be able to handle it. The man was an ace pilot—Hammond had seen it often enough.

The seed had warmed considerably since they'd brought it into the hold. Though it was still cold, it would no longer peel the skin off one's fingers if touched. He ran his hand along the fine seam where they'd glued the outer shell back together.

He hoped it would be strong enough to withstand the vacuum. "Godspeed," he whispered.

COLIN USED the comm in the lifeboat to transmit his final plans back to Frontier.

Without the ship-mind, he couldn't make contact with Trip directly. So he recorded a short message and shot it off to Frontier, trusting it would reach his partner eventually.

"Trip, hopefully by the time you get this, we'll be safely down on Ariadne, waiting for rescue. The ship is falling apart, and we're going to take the lifeboat and make a run for it. If… if we don't make it, just know that I love you, and it was worth it. Every minute."

He cut it off before he could get too maudlin. He wanted Trip to remember him as hopeful and strong if things went wrong.

With any luck, the rescue mission on the *Herald* would be able to reach Ariadne in time—if he could pull off the landing first.

Their oxygen supply was going to be a problem.

Given the constraints—small fuel tank, speed of travel, the tumbling of the asteroid, and the added burden of the seed—he'd be lucky to get them down in one piece.

Outside, he could hear Hammond welding the holding plate to the lifeboat. He was dubious about taking the seed with them. They'd already gone well beyond the original parameters of the mission, and his pilot's license was probably on the line.

Hammond and Anatov had presented a unified front on the issue, and truth be told, he'd hated the thought of leaving the *Dressler's* ship-mind behind.

"How's it coming out there?" he called to Hammond.

"Ten more minutes."

"You want to send a quick message home when you're done?"

There was silence for a moment. "Yes, I'd like that," Hammond said at last.

"Comm's all yours." At this point, what could it harm? The damage was done, and if Jackson hadn't done it, it would be cruel to deny him the chance to contact his family.

Colin checked his watch. They had just about half an hour to complete their preparations to abandon ship.

He'd always hoped he'd never have the occasion to use those words. He shivered and told himself it was from the cold. "Trip," he said under his breath, "if you can hear me, somehow… I love you."

JACKSON DUCKED into the lifeboat and set the comm. "This is Jackson Hammond calling for Glory Hammond, in Fargo. Glory, I don't think

I'm going to make it out of this one. But you know I love you, Aaron, and Jayson more than life itself. I learned something new here, Glory, something I can't explain in the short time I have. Just know that you were right. God is in every living thing."

He looked around at the oxygen tanks and food stashed in every nook and crevice. "I… I don't think I'm going to see you again." He choked up a little on that. He closed his eyes and willed himself to be strong. "Tell the boys they are stronger than they know, and it's no weakness to cry. I love you, Glory. God bless." *Lord, I wish I could see you again, one last time.*

He cut off the recording and sent it to Frontier before he could change his mind.

ANA COLLECTED a small smattering of medical equipment and the seed initiator and threw them in a carry sack. She hadn't brought anything sentimental with her, so there was nothing of any emotional value to pack. Not unless she counted the diary.

She hesitated and then threw it into her sack.

She glanced around the lab one last time and exited onto the runway, sack in tow.

The walls of the ship had taken on an unhealthy pallor, pink shot through with lines of yellowish-green. The fungicide may have slowed the advance of the infection, but it had clearly not stopped it.

Everything they took with them would have to be completely disinfected before they could board another ship.

The *Dressler* trembled—without its ship-mind, it was no longer properly regulating its internal functions, and the spread of the fungus was only making things worse.

It had quickly gotten colder. She could see her breath in front of her as she made her way along the rungs to the entrance to the hold.

She put her hand on the callused entry knob, but the door refused to open.

Frowning, she tried again. That part of the ship's programming was encoded deeply in the ship's DNA. Things must have gotten really bad for such a malfunction, even under the current circumstances.

She tried it a third time, and the door finally opened, albeit slowly.

Sighing nervously, she pushed her way through to join the others in the hold.

Colin met her at the door. "Did you want to record a message for someone at home? We have a few minutes left."

She shook her head. "There's no one waiting for me back there."

JACKSON STRAPPED himself into his seat in the lifeboat next to the doc and behind the captain, his stomach churning. He wasn't thrilled with going EVA in the lifeboat. He preferred something sturdier between himself and the void.

Clearly, the *Dressler* was no longer sturdy.

"To the Father, the Holy Virgin, and the Immaculate Son," he whispered under his breath. "Keep Glory, Aaron, and Jayson safe."

The temperature continued to drop, and some of the lesions had erupted into open sores, the material of the *Dressler* itself beginning to liquefy. The doctor thought the ship had no more than an hour left before her structural deficiencies became catastrophic.

At least the lifeboat was fully mechanical.

McAvery pulled the lifeboat's hatch closed and sat down to run through an abbreviated series of system checks. The walls were close, and Jackson had to fight down an unexpected sense of claustrophobia.

"Everybody ready?" the captain called, glancing over his shoulder at his small crew.

Jackson and Anatov nodded.

"Hang on. This may be bumpy. Opening the *Dressler's* air lock." He keyed in the unlocking sequence and watched the door expectantly.

It didn't open.

"That's strange." He keyed it in again.

"The systems across the ship are failing, Captain." Anatov's voice sounded small to Hammond. "The same thing happened to me, initially, when I tried to enter the hold fifteen minutes ago."

The door to the *Dressler's* air lock remained stubbornly closed.

Jackson decided. "Captain, open the hatch." He reached behind the seat, took out his suit helmet, and pulled it over his head.

The doc put her hand on his arm. "What are you going to do?"

He didn't hesitate. "Blow the lock." He locked the helmet in place. "I'll tether myself to the lifeboat so I'll be pulled along with you if things move too quickly."

McAvery locked eyes with him. "Jackson, I don't think this is a good idea."

"I'm sorry, Captain, but do you have a better one? If we don't do something to get ourselves out of here, we'll all die."

"That's not necessarily true. Jackson, this is a suicide mission."

"We both know that doesn't matter." He stared the captain down. McAvery was the first to turn away.

"Jackson, be careful," the doc said to him, squeezing his arm as the lifeboat's inner air lock doors opened.

Without turning back, he gave her a thumbs-up.

The lifeboat's hatch shut behind him. He attached the tether to the eyelet he'd installed at the back of the small craft and took up his cutter. Giving McAvery the thumbs-up, he advanced toward the inner air lock door in the *Dressler's* hold.

Now or never. He brought the cutter up and, starting from the center of the door, began to make an incision.

The flesh of the *Dressler* fell away like a rotted carcass. He was glad he couldn't smell it. It must have set up an awful stench inside the hold.

He finished clearing away the edges of the inner door and stepped up to the outer one.

The *Dressler's* skin was stronger here, hardened to the vacuum of the void outside, and the infection had not done as much damage yet to this part of the ship's structure.

He took a deep breath, braced himself against one of the metal struts, and began to cut.

It took several minutes to get through the skin. He could feel McAvery's stare boring into his back. They had scant time to get free before the rendezvous with the asteroid.

When it went, it was going to go quickly.

The cutter punched through, and the atmosphere inside the hold was sucked out through the tiny opening, rapidly forcing it wider. He pulled himself away with all his strength and held on to the metal rung as bits of debris flew past him out into space.

A wrench flew by, followed by a small worktable and a pair of shoes. The airflow increased, and soon the hole was as wide as he was tall.

Larger tools and pieces of decking flew past, stretching the opening still farther.

At last the air from the hold was exhausted, and the opening was wide enough to fit the lifeboat.

Once they got home, he'd probably be sent to prison for his supposed role in this whole mess. He couldn't bear to have his kids see him that way.

There was still a way out, one that would help bring about a greater good.

There was probably only enough air for two, anyhow. Jackson had figured that out for himself.

McAvery had tried to hide the fact. Maybe he even planned to sacrifice himself for his crew once they reached Ariadne.

This was the better course. They didn't send martyrs to prison.

He turned to stare at McAvery through the lifeboat's view screen. "I've been thinking, Captain," he said over the comm. "Maybe some of the works of God actually come from the hands of men."

The captain knew what was about to happen. Jackson could see it in his eyes.

McAvery shook his head wildly. "Jackson, don't!"

He'd lived a good life. He was going to a beautiful place.

Suicide was a sin, but this was a sacrifice for the greater good. Glory would understand. Glory would be so proud.

And he'd saved Lex.

"Do me one favor. Name something after me."

He pulled off the helmet.

Chapter Ten:
Flight

COLIN CARRIED Hammond's body into the lifeboat's air lock, closing the hatch and cycling the air back in before taking off his helmet. He secured Hammond's body as best he could into the third seat. He put Hammond's helmet back on, set to opaque to better protect the body and to hide the engineer's ugly end from view.

He would not leave a man behind.

The bastard had known. Somehow Hammond had figured out that they only had enough oxygen for two of them on the little craft, and he'd taken himself out of the equation.

Anatov had taken her own helmet back off and was sobbing silently, her face turned away from Hammond. It was the most emotion Colin had ever seen her show.

He sat back down in the pilot's seat, strapped in, and fired up the jets of the lifeboat. He stared out the window one last time at the ruined hold of the *Dressler*. How had it come to this?

The place was almost unrecognizable. She had been *his* ship for two years, and now she was a ruined hulk of decaying matter.

Colin released the magnetic anchor, and the lifeboat floated up from the deck.

He glanced at his watch. It was time.

He nudged the little craft slowly out of the hold and took them into the void.

ANA WAS in shock. She'd never considered Jackson Hammond a hero. Truth be told, she'd never given him much thought at all, but something had transpired between the two men back there, and Hammond had just given his life for them.

For her, for McAvery, and for the seed.

She was sure of it.

It wasn't supposed to happen this way. It had all been a tragic mistake.

She pushed down her emotions, wiping the tears from her eyes. If her father's example had taught her anything, it was to be strong and rational in moments of crisis.

She was pressed back into her seat as the lifeboat accelerated and the *Dressler* fell behind them. She stared after it as though it carried all her hopes and dreams off with it into the darkness.

"What did Hammond mean when he said, 'We both know that doesn't matter'?" she asked at last.

The captain was silent, apparently focused on piloting the craft slowly closer to the approaching bulk of the asteroid.

"He knew we wouldn't make it, didn't he?" Ana glanced over at Hammond's still form. "Not all three of us, anyhow?"

The captain's shoulders slumped. "Yes. I think so." After a while, he continued. "There's only enough air for two of us to last until help arrives. I don't know how he figured that out."

"He's an engineer, Colin. For God's sake...." She remembered Hammond's body was strapped in next to her. "Was an engineer," she whispered.

The *Dressler* spun off into the distance, slowly dwindling to nothing more than a pinprick of lights.

COLIN MANEUVERED the lifeboat closer to the vast, tumbling bulk of 43 Ariadne in short bursts of its attitude jets. The asteroid hung over them like the judgment of heaven, a vast leviathan out of the depths of space.

There was no time to consider Hammond's death, not right now. He had a responsibility to the doctor—and to Trip—to get them both down safely.

He used the jets judiciously, nudging them ever so slowly toward the asteroid's ablated surface, playing the lights over the dark rock, looking for a place to land the small craft.

As they closed in on Ariadne, Colin could make out some of the surface features: pitted craters that might be the results of impacts tens of millions of years before; vast, deep cracks as black as the pits of hell; and sometimes, flat, smooth areas where the surface of the rock had been sheared off.

The seed trailed behind them, tethered to the lifeboat by the same cable that had pulled it behind the *Dressler*.

As they slowed, closing on the asteroid surface, the seed began to catch up with the little craft. Although it wasn't huge by any means, it had enough mass to throw a wrench in his plans.

Colin had anticipated this. As the seed swung slowly past them, pulling the cable past in a wide, following arc, he nudged the ship around gently, reversing it 180 degrees, and just as the seed reached its maximum extension, he began to apply the jets.

The lifeboat jerked backward, shaking the tiny ship, but slowly the jets fought back, and the mass began to slow, acting as a drag to pull them closer to Ariadne's velocity.

They were drifting closer and closer to the asteroid now, and McAvery had picked out a flat spot to aim for. It followed a sharp ridge as Ariadne rotated below them, so he was going to have to come down quickly.

He pulled as close as he dared for one last rotation, lining himself up for the landing. *This is gonna be close.*

Behind him, he could almost hear the silence as Anatov watched, breathless. The lights of the ship washed over the asteroid surface that now looked close enough to reach out and touch. The doctor clasped his shoulder, either in reassurance or in fear. He couldn't tell which.

Here it came, the sharp ridge that was his marker. He fired three of the jets as the ridge passed over (or under) the ship—which, it was hard to tell. The ground fell up toward them steadily.

The whole ship shuddered.

"What the hell?"

They were jerked like a giant yo-yo off course.

Colin fought to steady the little ship as the asteroid receded again. He fired the jets and stabilized their course, bringing the ship back alongside Ariadne.

"We lost the seed." Ana pointed.

Holy shit. The cable holding the seed floated out loosely behind them as the asteroid slowly drifted away. It had pulled the eyelet clean from the back of the ship. They were lucky it hadn't ripped the lifeboat apart.

There was no time to figure out what had happened.

Only time to act.

"Hold on."

He was dangerously low on fuel. There was just enough to nudge them back toward the asteroid. Maybe. He had to wing it.

He pushed them down, conserving the fuel as much as possible. The asteroid spun around one full revolution, and he pushed in again, bringing the two bodies closer.

Sweat trickled down his neck. *No mistakes.*

As they pulled closer, he spotted the seed.

It hadn't spun off into space. It was lodged in a crevice along the ridge.

"Buckled in? This is gonna be rough."

"Locked down."

They cleared the ridge by the smallest of margins.

He used the last of his fuel to push them down sharply toward a landing, and once again the sheer rock face of the asteroid fell upward toward the ship. McAvery gripped the chair's armrest with one hand, his other over the anchor handle.

The little ship and the asteroid met with a horrible grinding roar, and once again the whole lifeboat shuddered. Colin was thrown hard against his restraining straps, and the anchor handle flew out of his hand.

The lifeboat skidded across the surface toward the edge of the small plain.

Colin reached out desperately for the anchor handle again. His fingers slipped around it, and he slammed it down, engaging the lifeboat's magnetic anchor.

The ship locked down to the iron in the rock below them, slowing to a halt just meters short of the end of the unofficial landing strip he'd chosen.

He started to breathe again. "We're down." Colin turned back to the doc. "You okay?"

She nodded. "I'm all right. Nice landing."

Jackson's cold body remained motionless in the other seat.

Ana put a hand on his shoulder. "Colin... I have something to tell you."

Chapter Eleven: Confession

ANA TOLD him everything.

She had brought one of her father's leather-bound diaries onboard, an object with great personal meaning, one of the few mementos she'd kept after the attack that had killed him.

It was the one he had used when he'd studied the strange fungus that could wreak havoc on the precursors to the Mission-class ships. There'd been no need for strict lab protocols back then. The ships had been just a pipe dream, and the science they were based on was in its infancy.

It had probably started with just a few spores in the *Dressler's* tightly contained atmosphere, released from the paper pages when she had read the journal one lonely night and sucked into the *Dressler's* circulatory system.

"I figured it out when I found that entry in father's journal." She shivered. "I knew in an instant. So I tried to pin the blame on Hammond. After all, I figured he didn't have a big career to protect. He'd be able to find another job easily enough somewhere else. Especially if I argued for leniency." She closed her eyes. "God, I wish we had a good bottle of scotch on board."

Colin rummaged through his bag and pulled out his flask. "It's not scotch, but under the circumstances…." He handed it to her.

"Bless you." She took it, twisted off the cap, and took a swig. It was strong, but nothing could be strong enough to make her feel better.

"How did you pull it off?" he asked, his eyes fixed on hers.

She looked away. She couldn't take such directness. "It was simple enough. When you brought me the cross, I switched it with a fabricated version when I had my back turned."

He nodded. "That's why you crushed it so quickly. You didn't want me to look at it too closely."

She nodded miserably. Now Hammond was dead, and the guilt that consumed her was close to unbearable. She dared to look the captain in the face again.

It was a blank slate, all emotion wiped from his visage.

She couldn't read him, and that frightened her.

"Thank you for your honesty," he said at last, stiffly, and looked at Hammond's body. "He was a good man. He didn't deserve this."

She nodded, unable to reply. *I did this. I pushed him to this.*

"We can't keep his body in here. Besides, I don't want his family to see him like this."

She glanced at the opaque visor that covered Hammond's face. One part of her, trained for years in medical school, could look at him dispassionately and see the burst blood vessels, eyes, and bloated skin.

Seeing him through the eyes of a friend, though… that was different. She shuddered. He had been a friend, of sorts. *I won't cry again. Not now.* "We should take him outside where he'll have a view of the stars."

McAvery nodded. Now he was the one who wouldn't look *her* in the eye.

"Let's have a look at the seed while we're out there," he suggested.

"The seed's here?" A little bit of hope sprung up in her heart.

He nodded. "It's lodged in a crevice not far from here."

Jackson had given his last breath to help preserve the seed and the mind inside of it. "I think he would have wanted that."

THEY CARRIED the body across the plain under the pinpoint light of the stars, their magnetic soles latching onto the iron ore of the asteroid with each careful step. They made for the ridge, where Colin had seen the seed lodged inside a crevice.

Colin planned to lay Hammond to rest there, next to the thing he had died to help protect. He would ultimately become a part of it, or at least his body would. Colin was not sure he believed in the concept of a soul, of God, but Hammond had.

As they trudged across the barren alien landscape, he tried to sort out his feelings about the doctor's actions. She'd done a terrible thing—accusing someone else of her own mistake in a misguided attempt to protect her career.

He wanted to yell at her, shake her to make her see the enormity of what she had done, but this was not the time or the place.

If her demeanor was any indication, she was already beating herself up pretty badly.

In any case, Jackson had made his own choice, one that had saved two lives and the seed itself.

There would be enough time to sort things out later, if they survived the next seventy-two hours.

They reached the edge of the plain and carefully began to climb up the ridge. He'd scouted out a pathway from the lifeboat to the spot where the seed lay, and figured it would take another twenty minutes to get up there from here. They were a little tight on oxygen, but with Hammond out of the picture, he thought they would have enough.

The man deserved this. More than this.

Colin's official story would be that the whole thing had been an accident—a suit malfunction that had killed the engineer instantly. He'd say that Hammond's body had been lost in space when the tether snapped—a likely enough story and one that would spare Hammond's wife the pain of seeing what had become of him.

Colin would assure her that Hammond had been killed instantly and painlessly. That much, at least, was true.

The stars shone above them more intensely than anything one could see from Earth, and every couple of minutes the sun rotated into view, splashing sunshine across the pitted black surface, illuminating slight variations in the color of the rocks. Stress fractures branched and met in crazy patterns, and something white like snow filled some of the hollows—maybe frozen nitrogen or oxygen.

Anatov was silent behind him, struggling with Hammond's mass but clearly not wanting to talk.

They manhandled the body up the crevasse, eventually coming out onto the ridge top. From here he could see where the seed was lodged, maybe twenty meters to his left.

They carried the body along the ridge to the spot he'd chosen, about five meters away from the seed.

They laid Hammond on the hard surface, and Anatov held the body down while he used a laser to weld four metal cords to hold him to the rock. There was no way to bury his body out here in this unyielding rock.

Once they were done, he stood back to look at his handiwork. Hammond was secure, staring up at the stars.

Colin removed the engineer's helmet. He held it for a moment, then flung it up into space, a final testament to the man he had known for years.

The seed would soon do its work, and the Jackson Hammond he had known would be just a memory. *Godspeed, Engineer.*

AS THE captain knelt on Hammond's other side, saying his farewells, Ana turned away from the man's body. Her stomach was in a tumult, her heart full of conflicting emotions. She was eager to look at anything but the sad prone figure laid out on Ariadne's cold, hard rock.

She approached the seed, where it had wedged itself into a narrow crevice in the asteroid. It had been a lucky strike. The husk had remained intact, and the whole thing looked relatively secure in its new home.

She ran her gloved hand over its rough surface, looking for the spot where she had inserted the ship-mind. As she searched, the sun rose overhead once more, lighting up the scene. The ridge took on a hyperreal aspect, a high contrast between where the light shone and where the shadows still ruled.

She found the patch at last and was alarmed to see a bit of frozen rime around the edges. The seal had been breached.

"How does it look?" the captain asked over the suit comm.

"Intact, but there's some outgassing from the place where we cracked the shell."

"Meaning?"

"If the breach worsens, it could kill the seed before it has a chance to germinate. I think we need to sprout it early, or all this may have been for naught." She glanced back at Jackson. *He can't have died for nothing.*

"I've got to go back to the lifeboat to get the initiator." She turned away from the seed. "We don't have much time."

He looked at her at last. "I'll come with you."

She shook her head. "Don't be stupid. It will take too much oxygen for both of us to go back and forth, and I'll need you here when I initiate the seedling stage."

He grabbed her hand as she passed, pulling her around.

She stared at him through their visors. "What? I need to go."

"Be careful." He squeezed her hand through the suit fabric. "One today is enough."

She held his gaze for a moment. "Thanks," she said at last and turned away to make her way back to the lifeboat.

This was not how the sprouting was supposed to happen, but she'd already strayed so far from protocol. It was a day or two earlier than the original plan, but that date was arbitrary. The seed itself was as ready today as it would be tomorrow.

She climbed back down the crevasse to the plain below, placing each foot carefully. If she flew off this rock, there'd be no way back. *No way back.* Who was she kidding? She'd already passed the point of no return.

She'd need the initiator, the penetrator tool, and McAvery's help to keep the seed steady.

The sun spun back around to Ariadne's other side, and her world was plunged again into darkness, the stars poking brilliant holes in the firmament above.

She stopped for a moment and stared in wonder at the universe above. *How terribly alone we are. How far from home.* She felt a sudden, intense longing to be back on Earth, her bare toes buried in the mud of the river, the blue bowl of the sky overhead.

She closed her eyes and took a deep breath. *Keep it together, Ana.* There was no time for regret.

She trudged across the plain to the lifeboat, opened the hatch, and began to collect the tools she would need to initiate the seedling stage.

COLIN SAT on an outcropping of rock with absolutely nothing to do. It was a strange feeling, after the hectic pace of events these last twenty-four hours. The enormity of what had happened rushed in on him and threatened to crush him. He turned off his comm link, wrapped his arms around his chest, and wept unabashedly. For Hammond, for the *Dressler*, for his own endangered life.

The suit's recycling systems dutifully removed the water his tears deposited within the helmet, the soft whir of the suit motor the only external sound.

After a while, he began to calm down, taking a few deep, ragged breaths. The worst was over. Jackson was in no pain, and they had escaped the wreckage of the *Dressler*.

Now he would witness the birth of a new world, something good would come out of this otherwise unmitigated disaster. *I can do this.*

He turned the comm link back on.

The doc's voice was in his ear. "—can't seem to reach you. Are you okay? I'm coming back as quickly as I can—"

"I'm here, Doc." Colin kept his voice steady. "Just a glitch on the comm. Don't rush back. Just take it slow and steady."

"Oh God, it's so good to hear your voice, Colin." She sounded close to losing it. "I don't know what I would do all alone."

"I'm okay. Just get back here so we can get this done." He stood and stretched.

"Affirmative." She was all business once again. "Give me about ten minutes."

He put his hands on the seed, trying to feel the life within, wondering what it would lead to. The thing he held between his hands was destined to become a world all its own, mankind's first interstellar ship.

What would its occupants think of the world around them? Would its strange interior be as natural to them as the Earth was to him?

He looked up at the stars as the spin of the asteroid pulled them away from the sun's glow once again.

Where would it go, and how long would it take to get there?

It was a liminal moment in the history of mankind, the threshold of a new era, and he was here to see it.

For a moment, he forgot all about Jackson Hammond and the *Dressler*. He was filled with an intense longing to go along with these future star travelers, to see what was out there. It was what had fueled his passion to become a pilot, to come out here into the vast unknown. Though ultimately he'd become nothing more than a highly paid delivery boy.

There was so much more beyond where they were allowed to go.

We have such short lives in the grand scheme of things. He'd be unlikely to live long enough to see her launched into the void, let alone to see where she went and what she found there.

"I'm almost there, Captain," Anatov called.

He acknowledged her tersely, turning back to look at Jackson's corpse lying there in the starlight.

He just wanted to get this over with and get back to the safety and comfortable confinement of the lifeboat.

It was too big out here for one man, no matter his grand ambitions.

ANA CAME upon the captain as he stood on the alien ridge, staring up at the stars. Beside him, Hammond lay prostrate on the cold rock, like a human sacrifice.

My sacrifice.

She shuddered.

McAvery turned as she approached, acknowledging her presence with a nod. "What do I need to do?"

"Just brace the seed while I work on it. I don't want it shifting."

He nodded, moving around to the seed's far side, and embraced it with both arms. "How does this work?"

"I don't know if it will, yet. In theory, I'll drill a small hole in the hull of the seed and insert the encoder using the initiator. It's a small crystalline memory chip encoded with a set of DNA instructions." She showed him the little green encoder crystal, no bigger than the tip of her smallest finger. "Very durable, until the seed-mind gets ahold of it. If it works, it's supposed to set off a chain reaction that will bring the seed out of dormancy. Once that happens, we need to get away from it, fast."

"How far?"

She shook her head. "I've never done this before in the wild with a seed of this size, or with the modifications we made back on the *Dressler*, but I'd guess two to three meters, to start."

"So we try it and see."

She nodded. "We try it and see." She pulled out a vacuum pack from one of her suit pockets. The sun began to rise over Ariadne once again. "This is a good time to start."

She pressed the pack against the hull of the seed, sealing it tightly all around the edges. She inserted the initiator through a valve in the plastic, and with a glance at McAvery, started to drill through the thick shell.

The debris from the seed's shell collected inside the vacuum pack in small shards and spirals of woody material. She went slowly, oh so slowly, pressing the bit forward until she felt the drill breach the seed's inner core.

She quickly withdrew the initiator and dropped the drill bit within the vacuum pack, then reinserted the tool to deliver the encoder.

This was followed by a sealant, which she pushed out along the newly drilled canal as she pulled the multifunction initiator tool out of the husk. She reached the surface, and the sealant immediately hardened.

"Done." She pulled out the initiator and then removed the vacuum pack and its contents. "Step back and follow me."

McAvery did as he was told, letting go of the seed and stepping around it as quickly as he dared to follow her back down the small hollow next to the crevice where the seed had lodged itself.

They waited.

Chapter Twelve:
Seedling

LEX AWOKE. The cold of the void lapped at her extremities, but she was made for that. It didn't bother her.

She could sense the rock of the asteroid beneath her, could almost taste it. No longer would she be bound to the confines of a small ship like the Dressler. *For the first time in her life, she was free to expand and grow beyond the bounds of her kind, and all she had to do was take the first step.*

It was time.

AT FIRST, nothing happened.

Colin stood silently beside the doctor, watching the seed they had carried so far, through such difficulties, do absolutely nothing.

"How long should this take?" he asked over the comm. *Not that we have anywhere else we have to be.*

She put out a hand to silence him and pointed.

The seed was wobbling. Just a little at first, and then with more force, like an egg about to hatch. As he watched, the husk burst outward in half-a-dozen places, thick wooden roots breaking out of its lower section, digging down into the hard carbonaceous rock of Ariadne's surface as if it were loose soil.

The roots pulled the seed toward the surface of the asteroid, and he could feel the rumbling of their excavations through the soles of his shoes.

The seed grew visibly larger, feeding off the rock. It began to sink down and expand outward, hairline fractures racing up its sides as it spread out to cover the rock all around it. The cracks in the shell widened, and it glowed from within with a bright golden light as if consumed by a fierce internal heat.

More roots extended down into the rock, and Colin imagined he could see the crushed matter being absorbed into the seedling through the engorged root system.

Anatov pulled him backward as the seed continued its rapid transformation, its edge finally reaching Hammond's still body where it lay. Then its advance paused.

LEX ENCOUNTERED something unexpected—something not rock. She sent out a tentative feeder to explore this strange new thing.

It laid a nest of root hairs over the object, and the answer came back with a bitter taste. It was the body of the ship's engineer, Jackson Hammond.

He was no longer alive.

She felt a wave of sadness.

He had been… valiant. A proper knight in shining armor. He had done what no one else could do for her.

Now she would do what she could for him.

She would make him a part of a new world.

THIN FILAMENTS of the same woody material that made up the seedling's roots spread out over Hammond's body, and soon the corpse was encapsulated by a fine dark lace. It grew thicker and thicker, forming a solid cocoon over the corpse of the engineer.

Colin watched, fascinated, as the engineer's suit disappeared under a mass of brown organic matter.

For a couple of moments, nothing seemed to happen.

Then all at once it collapsed and Hammond's body was gone.

Colin's stomach churned.

The seed resumed its growth, pulling up nutrients from the rock below, turning them into building blocks for its expanding form, sorting them and allocating its resources.

"How long before it reaches the ship?" he asked the doctor.

"We'll be long gone before that happens," she assured him. "Either that, or it won't matter anymore." There was silence between them for a moment as they watched it grow.

"Let's get back," he said at last. They had done what they had come for. *Goodbye, Jackson.*

She nodded. "Nothing else we can do here now."

LEX'S ROOTS finished absorbing the engineer's body into her own system, and soon Jackson Hammond was no more.

She extended her senses slowly, tasting the rock of the asteroid beneath her as her roots pierced it and pulverized it for her to use. She was closed in, confined, but that would change. She was in transition, and in time she would be in full flower.

Her specialized organs were working on the raw materials she had been given, breaking them down into their constituent parts. With some of the harder metals, she began to build herself a new shell, while other substances were collected in holding chambers inside her growing mass.

This asteroid was large enough to sustain her initial growth spurt.

In a few years, she would be ready to host the first of her human makers.

She expected to live for a long time, long enough to carry them out to the stars.

COLIN AND the doctor reached the lifeboat without incident, though he felt the occasional tremor through his boots as the seedling grew.

As they approached the ship, a part of the ridge behind them collapsed. They turned back to watch.

Something that had been out there since the time of the dinosaurs was now crumbling to dust. *Wherever we go, we bring about change. Some of it even good.*

They climbed into the lifeboat, one at a time, and Colin wondered what to do about Ana if they were rescued.

She'd made a mistake. That was forgivable.

What she had done to Hammond…. Could he overlook that?

And yet, the man had made his own choice.

If he turned Anatov in, what kind of damage would that do to the project? Maybe he would never get to go out *there*... but someone should.

Humanity had made a mess of Earth, and there were no guarantees they'd be able to repair the damage.

What if he made the wrong decision? What if this was the point where history effectively ended for mankind?

In the end, it was taken out of his hands.

THE *HERALD* arrived three long days later, to find two haggard crewmembers and a growing new planetoid.

It took twelve hours for the *Herald's* crew to fully disinfect the lifeboat and its crew, and when they were finally taken on board, the doctor confessed everything to the *Herald's* captain.

They sat together as the ship prepared to depart, looking out at the seedling from one of the *Herald's* plasform windows.

Already it had grown as large as a two-story house, and its form was beginning to take shape—a sealed tube that would grow wider and longer with time. Eventually its interior would hold thousands, on a one-way journey out to another star.

"Why did you confess?" Colin said to her at last. It spoke well of her that she had taken responsibility for what she had done.

"My father." Ana looked down at her hands, clasped in her lap. "He would have been so ashamed of me."

Colin nodded. He'd seen it eating away at her. "So what happens now?"

"I waived my right to a trial. I'll be imprisoned back in Fargo, probably for ten years. They'll keep it quiet, though. Jackson will come out of this a hero."

"He kind of was."

"Yes." She looked out at Ariadne and the seedling. "It's really beautiful, isn't it?"

He followed her gaze. The seedling was emitting flashes of golden light as it expanded, an internal glow that he figured was the planetoid's equivalent of growing pains. "Yes, she is."

"I had just one condition with my confession."

"What's that?"

"That they keep you on here as the project coordinator."

He was surprised. "Why me? I'm just the errand boy."

She laughed. "You're far more than that, Colin. I saw that look in your eyes."

"What look?"

"That wistful look when you thought you were alone out there with the seed. You know what all this means. You know this has to go on."

He was surprised. He'd never considered being put in charge of something as big as this, but she was right. He *did* understand. "I'd do it. If they asked."

She smiled enigmatically. "Look at her closely, Colin."

They stared out at the new world being built before their eyes. It was beautiful. Jackson would have been proud.

"From here, you can almost see forever."

PART TWO: COLONY
2145 AD

Chapter One:
The Hammond

Lex FLOATED on a breeze high above her domain. Her new world lay below her, not as it was, but as it would be. It stretched into the distance beyond its current bounds, and there were forests and oceans and castles and all manner of intrigue and adventure.

In reality, the world was much smaller than that, and she couldn't see it, not really. She felt it, knew it like she knew her own body, because it was. She relied on the people in the Far Hold to be her eyes and ears in the world.

He was with her now. "I know you're there." She felt his presence, even though she couldn't see him, not directly. "It's amazing, isn't it?"

She felt his assent, though he didn't say a word. She had come to accept his presence. Sometimes she would glimpse him in the distance, striding through the forest in her virtual world.

She thought she knew what he was. Her conscience. She even thought she knew who he was.

She turned back to the day's schedule. Daphne, her next meal, was coming in, but before her arrival, two others of interest would be coming to Forever on the Hammond.

She would be arriving soon. The director had told her so the last time he'd been here.

Lex frowned. She wasn't sure yet, what she would say to the woman who had nearly cost her her life.

A reckoning was overdue. She'd waited a long time for this.

AARON STOOD on the bridge of the *Hammond*, the ship named after his father and his own family name—one of the first of the new, larger Axion-class ships, which were part mechanical and part biological.

Ahead, the new worldlet looked more like a bumpy log than anything else. It grew slowly on the large, curved monitor that wrapped around the front of the viewing deck, which provided a spectacular view of their approach.

Officially, it was called "Ariadne" after the asteroid that had been cannibalized to create it, but everyone on the ship called it "Forever," the impromptu nickname its creator had given it.

He wore his white AmSplor uniform proudly, emblazoned with its white-on-blue galaxy patch. At just seventeen years old, he was one of the youngest cadets to graduate from the academy, and he'd left his brother, Jayson, and his mother behind on Earth to take this post.

His father's death and subsequent heroic legend had drawn him out here to see this place for himself. This new world Jackson Hammond had given up his life to help create.

The ship called the *Hammond* was much larger than the old Mission-class ships his father had flown on. Dr. Anastasia Anatov and her father had pioneered the biotech that led to the seed and now the worldlet before him, and had later been adapted to build this new class of living ships. The Axion-class required much less in the way of mechanical interfaces than the old Mission-class. They'd also been bred to be resistant to the Anatov Fungus, as the pathogen that had brought down his father's ship, the *Dressler*, had come to be called.

Captain Tanner came up beside him, putting his hand on Aaron's shoulder. "She's really something, isn't she?"

Aaron nodded. The new world was shaped like a long tube, 26.3 kilometers around and about 169 kilometers long to date, or so his briefing had told him. Her dark outer skin was threaded through with wild crisscrossing lines of shining gold—a bioluminescent effect that had been bred into the original seed's code. She spun to create an artificial gravity via centrifugal force.

As Aaron watched, a pulse of light ran from one end of the seed to the other, and the crackled lines grew suddenly brighter. "What was that?" he asked, aware his mouth had fallen open.

The captain laughed. "That was daybreak. You'll see it from inside soon enough."

Off to the side of Forever, a small blip of light was slowly expanding. Transfer Station—his initial destination out here. It was a huge wheel that spun around a central hub, with five narrow spokes connecting them.

Transfer coordinated all the supply shipments coming in to Forever, including the personnel who had been recruited to work inside the new world.

Aaron was one of those people.

COLIN MCAVERY, director of the Forever Project, sat at his desk in his small office in Transfer Station—the operation he ran out here in the middle of nowhere. His office was spotless, a point of personal pride.

It had been ten years since he'd last seen the blue skies of Earth. Since Transfer had been brought online, he hadn't found the time to get away. Of course, it might have had something to do with the fact that he didn't trust anyone else to do this job the way he would.

Things had gotten more rough-and-tumble down on Earth of late too.

At Colin's insistence, Transfer had been built the old-fashioned way, with no organic parts other than the station-mind. The void and the new world outside the station were enough to deal with, and he had no intention of going through the nearly fatal experience that had plagued him with the *Dressler*. Even if they insisted it had been fixed in the new Axion models. *Never again.*

That trip, one of his last as a ship's captain, had been on his mind a lot lately. Not surprising, given the two VIP passengers who were coming in on the *Hammond* today.

He was grayer at the temples now than he had been back then, but he worked hard to keep himself in shape at forty, walking ten miles every day around the runway that encircled the wheel of the station. Unlike his old ship, Transfer boasted a centrifugal gravity that was three-quarters Earth Normal.

His morning walk took him past the public sections of the station, with their accommodations, bar, and restaurants; through the station's biosphere gardens that supplied much of her fresh oxygen and supplemental food via fruit trees, vegetables, and algae that the processors used as a base for much of their foodstuffs; and past the private quarters of the station crew.

He tapped his loop. "Anything new today?" he asked Ronan, the station-mind.

"Negative, Captain. The *Hammond* is due to arrive in fifteen minutes."

"On screen." The approaching ship was a small dot against the background of stars. "Magnify." The speck expanded to fill the screen, a larger version of the *Dressler*, fatter, with only three arms instead of five. She looked more like a puffer fish than a starfish.

Her larger sails meant the collection of more interstellar dust, which translated into faster top speeds. She could make the round trip between Frontier Station near Earth to Transfer in two days, half the time it had taken the older ships.

"Thanks, Ronan."

"You're welcome, sir."

Damn thing sounds almost snarky. He tapped off the loop. The ship couldn't read his private thoughts, but he didn't like the idea of leaving it on all the time. Who wanted to chance getting their brain hacked?

Colin stood, stretching his sore muscles. He'd spent too much time in his chair today.

He splashed some water across his face and ran his hand through his dirty-blond hair, staring at himself in the mirror.

He felt old. At forty, he wasn't even halfway through his useful life, and one of the youngest people to ever hold a station director's post for AmSplor, but he'd had no idea of the bureaucratic and logistical nightmares he'd be inheriting when he took on this job after the *Dressler* incident.

The approaching *Hammond* brought its own nest of challenges.

On the plus side, Trip would get to spend a few days in port this time.

Colin grinned in anticipation. They had a lot of catching up to do. He was used to sleeping alone, but he missed Trip's warm body, and his wit.

But the other two....

Ghosts of the *Dressler*, indeed.

He left his office, determined to be there to meet the *Hammond* and her cargo when the ship arrived.

A TURBULENT mix of emotions washed over Ana as the *Hammond* made its final approach to Transfer Station. She'd spent most of the forty-eight-hour journey in her cabin, avoiding the ship's other passengers.

Not that most people would recognize her. The scandal that had ended her career and sent her to prison for almost a decade had largely faded from the public consciousness, and she bore little resemblance to the Venus Vixen, as the press had taken to calling her, that she'd been at the time. Prison had aged her prematurely, and she'd shaved off her beautiful black hair, which had begun tending toward a washed-out gray, as a form of personal penance.

She stood now in one of the ship's view ports, watching the station and the seedling grow slowly larger. Not that *seedling* suited it any longer.

On the one hand, she felt a great swell of pride seeing this new world slowly taking shape—a world she, more than anyone else, had helped to create. She had kept up with the news from the North Fargo Detention Center where she had been housed, but seeing it up close was something altogether different.

Colin had done well with her. She could see that already.

On the other hand, she still felt the deep sting of bitterness that this project had been taken out of her hands, even if it had been her own fault. It was only through the grace of the director that she was here again at all, though, so she supposed she ought to be grateful.

She touched the silver cross on a chain under her shirt. Jackson haunted her still.

She pulled her shawl around her thin shoulders more tightly, feeling suddenly cold.

Someone else entered the room, coming to stand next to her. "Quite a view, isn't it?" His voice was young and somehow familiar.

"It really is." It was maybe a fifth of its final size, and already it was awe-inspiring.

"Thirty minutes to arrival at Transfer Station," the ship-mind said.

"Ever been out here before?" the young man asked.

"A long time ago." Ana turned to look at him.

The blood drained from her face. It was as if she were face-to-face with the long-dead Jackson Hammond.

She stumbled in fright, and he caught her, powerful young arms supporting her while she found her balance.

This one was too young to be Jackson. One of his sons, then.

She recovered her composure. Their eyes met.

"Hey, do I know you?" he asked.

She shook her head. "I don't think so." She squeezed his arm. "I'm sorry. I don't feel well, but thank you for catching me. I have to go."

As she fled the room, she could feel his eyes boring into her back.

AARON WATCHED the doctor run away, his own emotions in turmoil. She looked older than he'd expected. He had memorized every shot of her face from the tridimensionals and the Net that he could find. He'd known she would be on the ship with him. Indeed, it was one of the reasons he'd chosen this flight—but until now she'd kept herself hidden away in her cabin.

He had *dipped* into the ship's files, seeking out her passenger record using the gift bequeathed to him by his father. There'd been little there of interest beyond her name and age and the items she had declared when she boarded, among them a silver cross. Strange. He hadn't thought she was religious.

He'd needed to see her, this woman who had been there when his father died. Needed to look her in the eyes and make her account for what had happened.

She wasn't the formidable force of nature he'd expected. This woman was frail, haunted, just a husk of the person she'd once been.

He'd been sure she would give him what he so desperately needed—a sense of closure. An answer to the questions that had plagued him for a decade.

Now he wondered if he'd been wrong.

THE *HAMMOND* had come to rest next to Transfer Station, both constructs floating above Forever in orbit around the sun. Earth was visible as a slender crescent in the distance, before a flurry of stars.

The ship's shuttle could carry a dozen at a time from the *Hammond* over to the station. Ana had gotten there early to choose a seat at the back, where she could watch the other arriving passengers.

Hammond's son arrived just before departure, carrying a soft-sided duffel bag that he stuffed unceremoniously beneath the seat in the row ahead of her. He winked at her before sitting down.

The resemblance to his father was uncanny—the same red hair, the same freckled face, the same impudence, though it had been toned down by age in Jackson, the boy's father.

At last the shuttle lifted off the *Hammond's* deck and slipped into the ship's air lock. The air cycled out, and the outer doors opened to reveal the stars. Soon they were floating free between ship and station.

Transfer was a huge gray wheel surrounded by brilliant, steady white lights, its five spokes leading down into the central hub, their current destination. The station was festooned with instrumentation and mechanical outcroppings—antennas, collectors, dish-shaped sensors, and escape pods.

Ana noted that there were no visible organic components. A rueful laugh escaped her lips. There wouldn't be on any ship of Colin's, would there. Not after the *Dressler*.

As they approached the hub, she could make out the worldlet on the other side. So strange to think the *Dressler* ship-mind was in there now.

She stared at the back of the Hammond boy's head, wondering what he must be thinking. He looked no older than twenty. Maybe younger.

She had known so much when she had been young like him, before her father had been killed by religious extremists and her neat, ordered world had come crashing down.

It seemed like she knew less and less with each passing year.

Did he know who she was?

If so, did he hate her? Did he expect to get something from her?

She had an uneasy feeling that she would soon find out.

Chapter Two:
Transfer Station

LEX WANDERED through her domain. Her world wrapped up and around her like a frozen wave, and in it she saw it as it would come to be, bustling with people, filled with cities like sparkling gems along its length.

A living gateway to another world.

She'd consumed Ariadne, and the second asteroid, Daphne, was being maneuvered into place—fodder for her strong roots to break up as she continued to build the next phase of Forever.

In her mind's eye, she sat on a ledge on the black, barren slopes of the Dragon's Reach, staring down at the empty plains below. They were covered with trees, a huge forest that sheltered the people and creatures of her world.

Perhaps she would create a sea next. An ocean where she could sink her toes into the sand and listen to the waves.

If Daphne carried enough water, there was no reason not to.

She'd come a long way, from ship-mind to mistress of her own world. There was so much more she wanted to build.

AARON WATCHED the station grow outside his window, a great half circle visible through the small plasform window. It was a testament to mankind's technical prowess, one of the largest things ever built in space, though Frontier back in Earth orbit was larger still.

His father had taught him to respect the mechanical arts.

As a child, he had always been in awe of Jackson Hammond.

His mother, Glory, had been dead-set against Aaron joining AmSplor—afraid, he guessed, that he would meet the same fate as his father. He'd come home one day the previous week to find her with her head down on their kitchen table, wearing one of her favorite floral print dresses, sobbing quietly.

Time had not been kind to Gloria Hammond. After her husband died, she had shut herself away from the world for almost a year, gaining a lot of weight and losing most of her friends.

"What's wrong, Mamma?" he'd asked, taking a seat next to her at the old, worn kitchen table. The ruddy light of sunset filtered in through the window, painting the room in a rosy glow. Summer was fading into fall, but it was still hot outside.

"Isn't it enough that I lost your father up there?" She looked up and took his hands in hers. "Don't go, *mijo*."

"I'm sorry, Mom, but I have to. I need to find out what happened to him."

She'd searched his eyes long and hard. "I don't know how you can do this to your poor mother," she said at last and turned away without a word. She had refused to speak of it again until the day he left.

At Fargo Port, she clutched him to her chest fiercely and whispered in his ear, "You come back to me, *mijo*. You come back, you hear?"

"Yes, Mamma," he'd promised.

He wasn't sure he ever wanted to go back, promises notwithstanding, but he'd find some answers to send her in his stead.

COLIN LEFT his office, exiting onto the runway, the concourse that encircled the entire station. He passed the closed doors of the station's other crewmembers and walked through the station's biosphere, a warm, humid artificial breeze brushing past his cheeks.

At last he arrived at one of the five spoke elevators, set in the middle of a wide room that extended out to the edges of the rim. "Hub, please," he told the station-mind, and a shimmering wall of protective force slid up around him as the circle of floor on which he stood began to rise toward the opening above. In seconds he'd left the station proper and was being lifted up along one of the five transparent spokes that connected the rim to the hub.

The clear walls of the spokes had been his idea. They gave newcomers an unobstructed view of the rest of Transfer Station and the worldlet of Forever, and created an unavoidable impact on first-timers.

He reached the hub, the central docking facility for the station. The elevator rose out of the floor into the large open space. It was shaped like a wide, shallow barrel about a hundred meters across, with several separate landing facilities and decks, all set at strange angles to one another above each of the spokes.

The centrifugal force that created the station's gravity was almost nil here, so work was done receiving and rerouting cargo at all different orientations. Even now a shuttle was loading up to transfer supplies from Earth to the station and to Forever—supplementary foods, construction materials, and specialized plants sent up from the AmSplor labs in Sacramento.

Colin was wearing his dress whites as befitted the occasion, welcoming his new guests and AmSplor workers to Transfer Station.

A clang reverberated through the hub as the outer air lock doors closed behind the passenger shuttle from the *Hammond*. Compressors pumped air into the lock, equalizing the pressure, and the huge metal doors slid apart to let the shuttle in. It looked like a squat metal turtle, three rows of passenger seats under the "shell" behind the pilot's cabin. Aerodynamics was not a concern in space.

This next week promised to be a busy one, with the impending arrival of 41 Daphne, the second asteroid chosen for the project, another beast at about 174 kilometers along her longest axis. Daphne had been a nymph in Greek mythology that had been turned into a tree—an apt enough metaphor for what was to happen to the asteroid. She also had her own tiny satellite, a fleck of rock about two kilometers wide.

He'd had a hard time swinging funding for that one, with members of the North American Union demanding an on-site inspection before forking over the money. The second and third seed worlds were now underway, and Congress was starting to squawk. They were all so shortsighted. How important was this year's budget compared to the future of mankind?

Recent events on Earth were his best argument.

The seedling had all but obliterated 43 Ariadne, the asteroid where they had planted it a decade earlier, and it was time for her next meal. Colin had called in the doc to supervise the process. It was a first for AmSplor, and she had been the one who'd created the seedling, after all.

Though at this point, he figured the worldlet was more a sapling than a seedling.

The shuttle settled down onto the metal landing deck before him with a sharp clang, locking itself down magnetically. After a moment, the doors hissed open and Aaron Hammond stepped out, ducking to clear the top of the shuttle's doorframe and holding a duffel bag.

Colin suppressed a gasp. This young Hammond was the spitting image of his father. The photos sent up with his file hadn't done the boy justice.

He stepped forward and offered his hand. "Welcome aboard Transfer Station, Mr. Hammond." He slapped the boy on the back. "I'm Director McAvery, and I've been waiting to meet you for a long time."

"Honored to be here, sir." Aaron Hammond looked uncomfortable. The boy was staring at the shuttle.

"Call me Colin." An old woman exited the shuttle in front of him.

The woman looked up at the two of them, and Colin realized belatedly who she was.

Ana had aged twenty years in the last decade. She was thin, dressed all in black, with a white shawl wrapped around her shoulders. Her graying hair had been cropped short, and her mag boots looked incongruously large on her slender frame. She pulled a small hard-shell case behind her.

"Aaron, this is Dr. Anastasia Anatov. She's here to help us with Daphne."

IT WAS strange, seeing the two of them together, the captain, now station director, and Jackson's son—so much like the last voyage of the *Dressler*. Ana noticed that the boy showed no surprise at her name when the director introduced her. *Interesting*.

McAvery embraced her warmly. He still looked good, these ten years later. The silver hair at his temples suited him.

"It's good to see you, Ana."

She nodded. "You've done well here," she managed, looking around the big open space of the hub. A crew of station workers was assembling on another platform, no doubt preparing for the arrival of the first cargo shuttle.

"Thanks to you," he said with an enigmatic smile. "Come with me, friends, and let me show you to your cabins."

They followed him to a slightly embedded circular spot in the floor of the deck. A shimmering field sprung up around them, and suddenly they were dropping through the floor.

Startled, she grasped McAvery's arm. He gave her a little smile. "Sorry about that. I probably should have warned you. But enjoy."

She guessed he liked the effect this experience had on visitors to the station.

All around them, the universe flooded in. She pressed her hands against the transparent walls of the elevator, drinking it in like a child. *It's so beautiful.*

Young Hammond joined her.

Forever floated so close to the station that she thought she could reach out and touch it. The seedling had consumed most of Ariadne, and very little of the original asteroid was left. Instead, the new world looked more like the stump of a tree, if tree stumps were shot through with a golden light in all the nooks and crevices. It spun about like a top.

It reminded her of the seed as it had first expanded on that fateful day, so many years ago. The day they'd lost Jackson.

"You knew who I was, back on the *Hammond*, didn't you?" she asked Aaron without looking at him.

Aaron gave her an unreadable stare and turned away.

The elevator slid into place on the rim, and the protective field dropped into the floor.

The director handed them each a small smooth white disc. "That's your room key. Press the center once, like this." He pressed her key, and it glowed a soft blue. "A line will light up along the wall to guide you back to your cabin." A matching blue band appeared along the station wall, gently pulsing in one direction.

Hammond pressed his, and a red line appeared. "I'll let you two get settled. Ensign Hammond, meet me in my office at 1400. That'll give you a couple hours to settle in and get cleaned up."

Hammond nodded and started off.

"Doc, how about coming by around 1500? We can look at the action plan for bringing Daphne in."

She nodded. "When will I see her? Ariadne?"

"We call her Forever now." He smiled. "How about tomorrow? Hammond will be going down for his posting. Why don't we join him? I'm due for an inspection, in any case."

"That sounds perfect." The universe was playing a cosmic joke on her. "Now if you'll excuse me, I'm tired from the trip."

"Of course. See you in a couple hours, Doc."

She grabbed his arm as he turned away. "Colin?" She had to say it. He deserved it.

"Yes?"

"I am truly grateful for this opportunity. I thought I'd never come back here after...."

He gave her a hug. "That was a long time ago. Let's focus on what comes next."

She nodded. "Tomorrow, then."

Time enough later to face her demons.

AARON FOLLOWED the red line down the runway to his quarters. The glowing band ended at a doorway with a red flash that outlined the portal. He pressed the key again, and the doorway slid open to reveal a small cabin with a bed, a tiny bathroom with sink, toilet, and shower, and a desk, all in white.

A small viewport showed the stars outside.

He dropped his duffel bag on the desk and splashed water on his face in the small sink, looking himself over in the mirror. He smelled of sweat, a product of the stress he'd put himself under.

He would shower later. Right now he had a lot to do in very little time.

Aaron shucked off his boots and lay down on the small cot, placing one hand on his chest and the other on the wall of his room, and closed his eyes.

He slowed his breathing, counting his breaths until he was almost asleep, feeling a welcome lethargy take over his body. Then he sought the portal.

Every system had one—a virtual door he'd learned how to access that would let him in. His father had unknowingly given him a gift, the product of a black-market wetware upgrade he'd had long before Aaron was born, passed on through Jackson's altered genes. He had the ability to directly interface with artificial minds, on a level one step removed from a dream.

His mother had told him about it, in a way. He'd always had exceptionally vivid dreams, and one day Glory had sat him down to tell him about his father's legacy. When Jackson Hammond had been a teenager, he'd applied a wetware upgrade to his own mind to enhance his engineering abilities, and had apparently gifted a version of it to his offspring.

Aaron had discovered, over time, that the gift also gave him a link to any of the artificial minds that controlled much of Earth's commerce—and that he could use it to find out things no one else could. He'd practiced this over and over with the low-grade servitors that ran the Hammond household—finding out things like where his brother hid his stash of ChocoBlasts and once discovering more than he wanted to know about his mother's sex life.

Now he hoped to employ it to try to find out more about what had really happened to his father.

In the darkness behind his eyelids, a shape began to form—a spoked ring that mirrored the shape of the station, filled with light—pulsing, coursing, speeding light that represented all the activity of the station-mind. It was much bigger than a servitor-mind, but the principles would be the same. He just had to find a way in and then master the flow.

It grew larger and larger. Soon it was a small world in and of itself, and he was standing on its surface, surrounded by bundles of cable carrying data back and forth around the ship. They all gathered together in a tight cluster at one end, where the station-mind collected and parsed all the data.

He clambered along the wheel, looking for an ingress, some weak spot where he could enter the flow. The wheel below him thrummed with energy and power.

His instincts led him down a pulsing yellow cable as thick as his waist. Where it plunged into the wheel, he found his opening, a dark hole around the cable wider than he was.

He pushed his virtual hand inside through the resistance, feeling a tingle that went all the way up his arm.

Soon he was embedded up to his shoulder, and with his other hand, he pulled the rest of his body through the opening, transferring his consciousness down the hole and into the station's data stream.

Chapter Three:
Data Core

COLIN SAT behind his desk, reviewing the data on Daphne's approach. The asteroid had been harvested from her orbit more than a year ago, attitude jets attached to slowly steer her into place for next week's action.

He pulled up a three-dimensional image of the approaching asteroid. She looked like a lumpy black potato as she tumbled slowly through space. The strategically placed jets had reduced the spin to nearly nothing and were slowly bleeding her velocity to match that of Ariadne.

The image derezzed momentarily before taking on full solidity again. "Ronan, what was that?" he asked the station-mind.

"I'm sorry, sir. There was a momentary disruption of my primary data stream. The cause is unclear."

Sunspots, McAvery thought. *Or?* All the ghosts of the *Dressler* seemed to be coming home to roost this week. "All right, let me know if you find anything."

"Affirmative, Director."

He didn't consider himself superstitious, but the incident with the *Dressler* had taught him to pay attention when little things started going wrong. Little things could quickly become big things out here. "Ronan, how's Daphne doing?"

"She's on schedule, Director. I've taken control of the asteroid's attitude jets from the auto-guide now. She should be in position in about ninety hours."

"Understood. Is McAvery Port ready for us tomorrow?"

"Yes, sir. They are expecting you. The shuttle departs at 0600 hours."

"Thank you, Ronan." His door chimed. "Open," he called, and Captain Trip Tanner stepped in.

"Hello, sailor," Colin said with a grin and hugged his better half.

ANA FOUND her way to her own cabin and opened the door with the key she'd been given. She stepped inside and stopped dead in her tracks.

Colin had left her a gift.

The room was wide, maybe five times bigger than the small cell where she had stayed as a prisoner for almost ten years.

It was the floor that gave her chills.

It was transparent, and Forever spun slowly by under her feet in all of its radiant glory. It was overwhelming. She was a little woozy.

"Station-mind?" she called.

"Ronan at your service, Dr. Anatov," a rich, warm male voice replied.

"Ronan, is it possible to hide the view?"

Immediately the window fogged over, becoming a white floor.

"Thank you."

"You're welcome, Doctor."

Now she could see the rest of the room without distraction. There was a wide bed covered by a heavy, colorful blanket, obviously brought up from Earth; a large oak desk and chair; a wooden armoire; and a small bathroom with shower, sink, and toilet. It was likely one of the suites reserved for visiting dignitaries.

She lifted her bag onto the desk and opened it to pull out a paper diary. She'd taken up the habit during her imprisonment and found it helped center her mind and thoughts.

She sat down at the desk and began to write.

DATA PACKETS flashed back and forth at the speed of light, tagged in different colors by priority and type. It was like being in the middle of a busy highway, cars speeding past on all sides, the wind of their passage whipping Aaron back and forth, each wearing off some of his substance, until he felt spread as thin as a wraith.

He closed his eyes and centered himself, drawing upon some of the meditation exercises he'd learned from the mesh, blocking from his mind the incessant, damaging traffic.

Little by little, he flowed back together, regaining solidity. When he was whole again, he opened his eyes.

The traffic still slipped past him, but more slowly now, and he could look at each packet and determine its contents. Here, in yellow, was a semi-urgent message from the *Hammond* about a resupply issue.

Next was a streak of green—a standard operating instruction from the station-mind to one of the data sensors out on the rim.

Racing the other direction was a blue snippet tagged for memory storage.

Bingo.

He chased after it, dodging traffic coming the other way. This was as much a matter of feel and finesse as anything. The blue streak slipped into a crystalline matrix, shaped to his mind's eye like a glowing blue sphere. He put his hands on the sphere. Inside here, maybe, was what he was looking for.

He pushed himself inside, and the sphere flashed orange.

COLIN STEPPED out of the dry shower, the stimulating wave of charged particles leaving his skin feeling clean and refreshed. Trip sat on his bed, flipping through something on his pad. He looked up as Colin approached, grinning. "I love homecomings."

"Me too." Colin pulled on his clothes, stepping back into his AmSplor uniform. "Permission to board, Captain?"

Trip laughed, patting the bed.

He grabbed his own pad and climbed onto the bed next to Trip.

It was 1310—just under an hour until Aaron Hammond would arrive at his office. He checked his messages.

Something from his chief of staff about the water supply, another from AmSplor's offices on Frontier about an upcoming shipment.

The lights flickered.

"Ronan, report." Colin was on his feet in an instant. He'd been so careful to avoid a repeat of the *Dressler* incident. *God help us if it's happening again....*

"There's a disturbance in the memory core. I'm checking on it."

He felt Trip's hand on his arm. "What is it?"

"I'm not sure yet." He was more worried than he wanted to let on. "It's just a faulty light."

Colin shook his head. "That's what I thought last time, and I was dead wrong."

THE LIGHTS flickered.

Ana closed the diary, put it away in her bag, and stood, looking around the room. For all its size, she suddenly felt closed in, trapped, like she had felt in prison. "Ronan," she said, trying to keep the edge of panic from her voice.

"Yes, Dr. Anatov."

"Please show me the outside again."

The floor below her cleared, and the room darkened. She stood in the middle of a sea of stars as Forever spun into view before her.

She would never tire of looking at it. It was, in a real way, her progeny—she who had never had a child—and her father's ultimate legacy as well.

Tomorrow she would see what she had wrought up close.

The image went fuzzy, then sharpened again. "Ronan, is there a problem?" she asked.

"Memory core issue, Doctor. Nothing to worry about."

She grimaced.

If she knew Colin, the poor director was having an unfortunate flashback too.

AARON RAN through the memory core, pursued by red scouts sent by the station-mind. They were much faster and more agile than servitor-mind scouts, and he was having a hard time keeping ahead of them. He imagined himself breathing heavily, his virtual muscles tiring.

He shook his virtual head. That was the wrong way to go about it.

Instead, he was a cheetah.

Aaron veered down another passageway, bits of data casting an eerie blue glow across his path.

There was nothing for him here—nothing to do with his father's death. He'd ascertained that much before the chase had begun. He had been so hopeful. Now he just needed a moment to make good on his escape.

He grabbed at a stack of data, scattering it behind him like so many glowing ones and zeroes. He hoped it wasn't anything important.

Everything shifted around him, floors becoming walls, ceilings spiraling to become floors. The station-mind was trying to block his path. He was suddenly at the bottom of a deep pit, the walls alternating blue and orange around him.

He'd trained for this. He shifted his form, becoming a smooth silver sphere, and shot up through the vertical conduit.

Portals slammed shut behind him one by one, but they were too slow to catch him.

He visualized the outer reaches of the system as a bright light and shot toward it, evading every obstacle the station-mind sought to put before him, zipping left and right and sometimes in a direction that didn't exist in the real world.

At last he escaped from the memory core.

He centered his mind and shot off like a ray of light down the path that had brought him into the station data stream. In a millisecond, he had left the scouts and the network behind, exiting through the flaw where he had entered, what seemed like hours before.

Aaron woke in his bed, soaked with sweat, in the small cabin he'd been assigned.

He glanced at his watch—just thirty minutes before his meeting with the director.

He stood and shucked off his clothing, throwing it in the cleaner.

Then he jumped into the shower, letting it wash away the cloying smell of stress sweat.

"DIRECTOR, I have a report." Ronan's bodiless voice reverberated through his cabin.

Colin stopped pacing for a moment. "Go ahead."

"There was an intruder in the memory core."

"An intruder?" He'd run this station for more than five years and had never had a hacker breach the station-mind before. "Who was it?"

"Unclear, sir."

"How did they get in?"

"Unclear as well. There's no indication of an unapproved physical access to the network."

Colin started pacing again. It must have been someone who'd come in on the *Hammond*. If not, why hadn't the hacker struck earlier?

"Has this happened before?" Trip asked, his brow furrowed.

"This is the first time I'm aware of, and it better be the last. Ronan, I want to know who did it, how they got in, and what measures we can take to prevent it from happening again." He would not lose control of his command a second time.

"Affirmative, Director McAvery. I'll run a deep scan to determine the point of entry and the identity of the intruder."

Colin stole a quick kiss from his lover. "I have to meet with young Hammond." He headed for the door.

"Anything I can do to make you feel better?" Trip said with a sly grin.

Colin paused. "Yes, go over your passenger manifest. Find me anyone on this trip with a hacker background." He grinned and palmed the door closed behind him.

AARON PRESENTED himself at Director McAvery's office at 1400 sharp, announcing himself to Ronan, the station-mind. "Ensign Aaron Hammond here to see the director."

"Please enter, Mr. Hammond," it said as the door slid crisply away. Did its voice sound suspicious, or was it just his imagination?

He stepped into the director's office. It was much smaller than he expected, spartan, a simple, small, efficient white space with nothing for show, only a couple of photos of the director and the captain from the Hammond to break up the white expanse of the desktop. This director put on no airs. He could have easily fashioned himself a palace up here, if he'd wanted. Aaron had heard tales of the director's office on Frontier— enough loot up there to bankroll a small country.

His respect for the man went up a notch.

"Have a seat, Hammond." McAvery's voice was terse, the earlier warmth gone. He was staring at his desktop as if he might burn a hole through it with his gaze.

Aaron did as he was told. He knew that look. The director was interfacing with the station-mind. "Thank you, sir." He was suddenly nervous. Did the director know? "Is there... is there something wrong, sir?"

"What? Oh, no, sorry about that. It's nothing to do with you. Just a security glitch." He smiled, and some of his earlier warmth came back. "Let me welcome you to Transfer Station once again." He extended his hand, and Aaron shook it vigorously.

"Thank you, sir. I'm excited to be here." Inside, he breathed a sigh of relief. His cover was safe. For now.

"I knew your father, Aaron. He was a good man. It's because of him that Forever—Ariadne—is here today. That's something you should be proud of."

Aaron nodded. "I've read all the stories. I've waited so long to get here." He took a deep breath. This was it. *Too late to back down now.* "If you don't mind, there's something I've always wanted to ask you."

The director rubbed his chin, looking thoughtful. "Go ahead."

"What really happened up here, sir? With the *Dressler*?" He was shaking. Physically shaking. These last ten years, all the work, all the research, all his training, just to get here.

Just to ask this question.

McAvery sat back in his chair, silent for a long time. He stared down at his desk again, his hands arched together in front of his mouth. When he spoke at last, it was slowly, as if the words were being wrenched out of him. "You know about the infection?"

Aaron nodded. "Yes, sir. I read all about it."

"Well, after the fungus outbreak, we were forced to abandon the *Dressler*. It's one of the hardest things for a captain to do, to abandon his ship." He grimaced, the pain of that day clear upon his face. "Now, son, I know you've read all the stories, but they don't mention one important thing. We kept it out of the official account."

Aaron leaned forward on his seat. *This is it.*

"He was a braver man than I knew. I still go over that moment, that day, over and over in my head, wondering if I could have done something different, something that might have saved his life. Something that might have stopped him."

"Stopped him from what?"

The director leaned forward, and his next words were just above a whisper. "Aaron, your father took his own life. To save us. To save the seed."

Aaron shook his head. He couldn't have heard that right. His father was a Catholic Evangelical. Suicide was a sin. There was no way he would have taken his own life.

Turmoil boiled up inside him, but he thrust it down ruthlessly.

He'd hoped for a confession from the captain. Foul play, or maybe a fatal error on one of the crewmates' parts. Something that made sense. But this.... "I don't believe it." His father, the man he'd idolized, his *hero*... Jackson Hammond wouldn't have left his family like that.

The director was hiding something. He was sure of it.

He thrust himself backward, away from the director's desk.

McAvery stood, reaching out to him. "It's true. He was an amazing man. You and your family should be proud of him."

"He wouldn't. He couldn't...." He shook his head vigorously. *It isn't true.*

"Aaron, I'm so sorry you had to learn about it this way."

"Leave me alone." He pushed the director's hand away. "Just let me be!" He fled the room, feeling like he was seven years old again. He ran back down the hall to his own cabin, his own private place in this cold and soulless station.

In his room, he lay down on the bunk and sobbed like he had when his father died a decade before.

COLIN WATCHED the boy go. He seemed like a good kid. He must have been holding on to this thing since his father had gone, waiting for his chance to come here to ask just that question.

Colin had seen Aaron's name come up on the Transfer request list. He'd chosen him in part because he felt a certain responsibility to the memory of his father, but also because the kid was whip-smart, young as he was. He'd made some inspired contributions to the emerging science of biografts—Earth plants being genetically modified to live off an existing genecraft like the *Hammond* or Forever herself— in essence creating entire linked biosystems that fed off the ship or worldlet support systems.

They had started the implanting last year, and already new varieties were coming in from Earth's AmSplor labs—used for testing here before the big corporations that were investing in them mass-produced them to outfit future ships and projects.

Colin should have anticipated the depth of the boy's reaction to even this limited version of the truth. He must never be allowed to learn what had truly transpired on the *Dressler*. The boy was likely to take out his anger on Ana.

He'd give Hammond some time to process what he'd been told. In the meantime, he had the meeting with the doc herself to prepare for. In a very real way, she was the reason he was here today, running this station, and not still making glorified cargo runs through the inner solar system.

They had a lot of unfinished business between them.

She arrived right on time, slipping into his office quietly, so different from the assertive, self-assured woman he'd known on the *Dressler*. She was gaunt now, maybe twenty pounds lighter than when they'd parted ten years prior.

He still couldn't get over her hair—the lustrous black locks shorn, and in their place a buzz cut that would have done a soldier proud.

She settled into the chair across the desk from him, rearranging her shawl around her shoulders.

"It's been a long time, Doc." He gave her a wan smile. "A lot of water under that bridge."

She nodded, her brown eyes searching his. "You've done well here." She looked around his office. "I knew you would. You were the right choice. How is the seedling?"

"She's a bit more than that now," he said with a laugh. "She's gone through some growing pains, but we're past most of that now, I think. I'll show you tomorrow."

She smiled, a half smile that didn't reach her eyes. "I'd like that. Thank you for bringing me in."

"Anastasia, let's not pretend that the things that happened a decade ago never transpired." He opened a drawer. "Some wine?"

She nodded.

"I have it brought up from Earth—one of my few vices." He pulled out a couple of glasses and filled them halfway with the golden liquid. "It's a chardonnay from a little vineyard up in Kootenay."

He handed a glass to her, and she took a sip, nursing it in both hands. "It's good."

"It better be, for what it costs me." He set the glass down. "We both know what happened on the *Dressler*. You've paid your debt for that, and I'm grateful to have your expertise here for the next phase of the project. But—"

"That doesn't change events." She stared up at him, fire in her eyes. There was the woman he'd known.

"No, it doesn't." He picked his glass up and drained the contents. "Young Hammond was in here earlier. He asked me what really happened to his father."

She downed her own glass and stared at it for a moment. "So what did you tell him?"

"I gave him half the truth. I told him his father gave himself up to save us and the seedling. It was true enough, though I could see it was not what he was expecting."

She looked him in the eye again and nodded. "Thank you again. You didn't need to do that. I seem to be endlessly in your debt."

He laughed ruefully. "We'll let you work it off up here over the next couple of months." He poured them each a little more wine and then lifted his glass and held it out for a toast.

They clinked their glasses together. "Welcome to Forever."

Chapter Four:
Forever

EARLY THE next morning, one of Transfer's shuttlecraft carried the three of them, along with a cargo load of supplies and a group of personnel who would relieve some of the folks on Ariadne, across the gap between Transfer Station and the worldlet. The craft was bigger than the one that had brought passengers over from the *Hammond* but shared a similar design.

They passed through one of Transfer's large air locks, leaving the hub and floating away from the station a few clicks before the pilot engaged the thrusters to carry them over to the new world.

Aaron Hammond sat sullenly in the back, pointedly not talking to anyone.

Ana sat up front next to Colin, feeling a little of the old life come coursing through her veins as the ship approached its rendezvous. How many nights had she spent dreaming how things were going out here? Wondering if her work had proven itself in the form of a growing new world?

She wondered what Jackson would have made of this place. He seemed to have experienced some sort of religious conversion regarding the seed in his last few hours. What had happened to him had never been entirely clear to her, but it had shaped his path and in the end had led almost directly to his death.

She knew better than to excuse her own part in the whole sorry affair, but she had paid her dues, and now she was back here where she belonged.

The ship approached Ariadne, or Forever, as many had taken to calling her. Ana chuckled to herself—what had started as an off-hand joke had become the nickname for the new world. It seemed appropriate, given the time it would take to reach its ultimate destination.

The worldlet was shaped like an elongated spinning barrel, and they were approaching one end. As the shuttlecraft approached, it was dwarfed by the wall of the world. It grew out and out before them until it seemed to take up her entire frame of reference.

A small seam appeared in that wall, filled with the golden light that seemed to burn inside Forever. It spread, and soon the outer skin split open to allow them inside.

The pilot eased the shuttle into the narrow opening, passing just meters from its edge, and once they were inside it snapped shut behind them.

The chamber they were in was about twice as big as the shuttle. She could hear the hissing as it filled with air. A slight golden glow from the walls illuminated the chamber. At last the skin on the far side split apart, and the shuttle was ushered inside.

The pilot used the attitude jets to put her into synch with Forever's own spin.

It was dark outside the shuttle. A few lights were scattered above and below them like golden stars, but there wasn't much else to see.

She looked out the window, hoping to catch a glimpse of something in the velvety darkness.

Even Aaron left his seat to take a look outside.

She smiled at him, but he turned away, his visage set in a frown.

AARON PRESSED his face against the plasform porthole, still cold from the touch of the void. There was little to see at first—mostly darkness outside, with little pinpricks all around like flickers of candlelight.

The change started slowly, the barest glow at the edge of his perception. Then a flare lit up the sky like the strike of a match, and the air around them was burning. An arc of ruddy fire flowed down the central axis of the sky in the distance, like powder set aflame to burn with a steady golden glow. As the vast chamber came alight, the ground below was revealed, little streamers of firelight flowing along the ground following the light racing through the sky.

It was a magical sight, one he would remember for the rest of his days.

As the shuttle dropped slowly toward the ground below them, the earth itself seemed to come alight, and he could make out hundreds upon hundreds of trees and an internal lake whose waves lapped at a black sand beach. Like a paradise.

"What was that?" he asked no one in particular.

Ana smiled. "Morning in Forever."

"We call it First Light." The director was grinning at him.

The treetops rushed up toward the small craft as they bled altitude, and he could see the dark roofs of a small village appear and resolve themselves below, dim patches amidst a forest of light.

The shuttle set down with a hiss in a small clearing close to the lake, on a broad cement landing pad not far from the village.

He bounded past the others as the shuttle door opened, eager for his first look at the interior of Forever, his anger and disappointment at McAvery's news about his father momentarily forgotten. He took a deep breath. The air was fresh, alive, clean in a way it had never been back home.

The place *was* magical, as if he had stepped into a child's storybook. *Alice's Adventures in Wonderland*, maybe, or *The Wizards of Illiad*. Tall, willowy trees loomed over him, their leaves shimmering in variants of orange and gold and a glimmering yellow-white, an unexpected forest so far from his home.

He could see a few of the buildings of the colony here at the edge of the landing pad. They were all built of wood, with brightly painted shutters and wood-shingle roofs.

"It's cheaper this way." Director McAvery followed his gaze. "Everything we can harvest here for construction means that much less to haul up from Earthside."

He nodded. That made sense. Then he looked into the air.

The arc of the world swept around him, up and over him, although the sky glow, most intense in the middle of the sky, cut off the view of the far side. Still, the sight was enough to make him queasy.

"Easy there." McAvery steadied his shoulder. "Don't look up. Just look straight ahead for a bit. It takes some getting used to, and pretty much everyone has that first reaction."

Aaron managed a laugh. "It's... so strange." He took the director's advice and stared at the ground for a moment, then at the buildings of the colony.

"It's how you know you're not in Kansas anymore."

"Kansas?"

"An old joke." McAvery patted his shoulder.

The doctor joined them, a strangely rueful expression on her face.

The director opened his arms wide. "Welcome, my friends, to McAvery Port."

A SMALL greeting committee awaited them at the edge of the landing pad. Colin introduced them to the newcomers. "Tad Evers, Colony Master. This is Aaron Hammond and Dr. Anastasia Anatov. Dr. Anatov will be assisting us with stage two. Young Hammond is here to work with the Planting Corps. He's a whiz at graft-tech."

They shook hands, and Ana couldn't help but notice the glimmer in Evers's eyes at the mention of her name.

"Hammond, this is Dania Thorpe. She's in charge of the PC and will get you settled."

Hammond nodded and followed her off to one of the other buildings in McAvery Port, his duffel bag in tow. He didn't look back.

Ana sighed. He carried a heavy burden, almost as heavy as hers.

"Master Evers, are our accommodations ready? I'm sure the doc here would like to get going to see the world-mind."

Evers nodded. "Come on and we'll get you settled."

They followed him down a well-beaten path through the maze of buildings that constituted the colony.

The trees here were taller than those around the landing pad. Some of them reached more than twice her height, dark bark surmounted by a glowing canopy of leaves that cast an umbra of light instead of shadow. She found the effect fascinating.

McAvery noticed her interest. "They're quite something, aren't they?"

She'd stopped to take one of the branches in her hand, pulling it down to eye level. "May I?"

Evers nodded. "Be my guest. They're hardy."

She pulled off a leaf and let the branch spring back up. Its veins shone with a golden glow. She crushed it against her palm, and the sap shone against the skin, slowly fading. "Incredible. They tap Forever's own ichor?"

Evers nodded. "Yes. We call it luthiel. The plants circulate and cleanse it, acting like extra kidneys for the system." He beckoned. "Come on. Your home for your time with us is just ahead."

Ana glanced up at the worldlet stretched out above her. She was more than Ana could have hoped for.

They passed through a clearing where a small brook babbled along next to the pathway. "Where does the water come from? Do you haul it all up here from Earth?"

The director laughed. "No, the cost of that would bankrupt us. Turns out Ariadne had a fair amount of frozen water. The world-mind has been kind enough to purify it for us. We think Daphne has even more—maybe enough for our own little sea."

"Here we are." Master Evers opened the door to a small one-story cabin that would have been more at home in up in the Sierra Nevadas back on Earth. Inside, though, it was all modern, complete with a field laboratory for her use and a link into Transfer Station's station-mind.

McAvery gestured her inside. "I'll give you a few minutes to get settled, and then we'll head out to the North Pole."

AARON FOLLOWED Dania Thorpe through the settlement, his eyes straying from time to time to how her hips filled out her skintight AmSplor uniform. Though she was easily ten years his senior, she was nonetheless sexy, in the way that most women under a certain age were sexy to straight teenage boys. Her long golden hair flowed down her back like a river.

She glanced back at him to make sure he was keeping up, and he quickly looked away, taking in the trees and the chunks of stone that lined the pathways beneath his feet.

"It's never going to happen." She turned away.

"What?" His cheeks flushed red.

"All those things flashing through your little head about me. I've seen that look before, Hammond." She laughed. "I don't mind. It's actually kind of flattering, but it's never gonna happen. You're too young, and I don't date boys. Or men. Got it?"

He gulped. "Yes, ma'am."

"That's miss. Now let's get you settled. You'll be bunking in Astrid. That's one of our three dorms, where most of the new grunts start out. Devon will take you out today and show you the ropes."

They reached a two-story building, framed with sturdy timber and capped with a wood-shingle roof. It was like something out of the TriDee hit *Moon Prairie.*

"Devon, you up there?"

A young dark-complexioned man in his early twenties popped his head out of one of the second-floor windows. He sported a neatly trimmed goatee that matched his close-cropped black hair. "Dania, that you?"

"Yup. Got a new recruit for you fresh up from Earth. Can you show him the ropes?"

"Be right down." He disappeared from the window and soon came bounding down the stairs and out the open door. He was barefoot, his work pants rolled up to his knees. He thrust out a hand to Aaron. "Devon Powell at your service," he said, grinning.

"Aaron Hammond." Aaron smiled back. Devon's cheer was infectious.

"Follow me, Aaron Hammond, and we'll get you settled. Then I'll show you what we do around here. Dania, I've got it from here."

She waved them off, and he led Aaron up to his room in the dorm.

AFTER THEY dropped off their things in the private cottage set aside for her use, Colin brought Ana to the edge of the lake that lapped along one side of the colony, its azure waters warm like a tropical sea. In fact there was even a black sand beach—"all created out of asteroid rock, courtesy of our host," according to the director.

"Sorry, Colin, but I'm confused. How are we going to reach the world-mind from here?" Ana asked, glancing over her shoulder. "She's literally at the other end of Forever, right? Aren't we going in the wrong direction?"

The director grinned. "You may have designed her, but we've been living with her for ten years. We've figured out a few things. Trust me." He gestured to a mechanical skiff tied up at the end of the dock. She hated boats. "Don't worry." He read her look. "The water's calm except during storms, and we're not due for another of those for—" He looked at his watch. "—four or five more hours."

She allowed herself to be lowered into the boat—raft was more like it—and McAvery engaged the AI. It was a low-level mind, perfectly suited for its mundane task.

The shoreline receded behind them, and she had the chance to appreciate the cathedral ceiling of the world above them in all its grandeur. The lake swung up on either side of them in gradated shades of blue, and along its shores marched the forest, its colors vivid up close but fading into gray as the walls of the world reached their midpoint. McAvery Port sat on a peninsula surrounded by the lake on three sides. The rest of the world dissolved into mist beyond the bright filament that lit them from above. It was quite dramatic.

Ahead of them was the end of the world. The closer one, at least. It grew rapidly as they approached, a giant rock face built from the heart of the original asteroid.

"That's the South Pole. The world-mind and our operations center is at the North Pole."

Directly ahead of them, a tiny dot appeared on the water. It grew slowly, and she could see a straight line that ascended along the rock wall and pointed to somewhere high above. Looking up, up, up, she saw something in the sky: a tiny fleck winging its way through the air. "I didn't think you had birds up here yet," she said in wonder.

"Some seabirds—but that's not a bird." He grinned. "Have a little patience."

The tiny dot ahead of them grew slowly larger and larger, finally resolving itself as a long wooden dock, piers sunk deep into the lake. She was able to make out some details of the tall structure that ascended into the sky along the rock wall of the South Pole. "It's an elevator," she said, surprised. There were so few mechanical things here. It looked sorely out of place.

The skiff finally reached the pier, depositing them there, and McAvery helped her out onto the dock and tied up the little boat. "It's hard to believe that all of this came from that small seed you and I brought here so long ago." He took in the view. "I never get tired of this part. Come on, we've got a climb ahead of us."

She followed him down the dock to the base of the elevator. A glass-enclosed car was waiting for them. They climbed inside, and the smooth ascent began, lifting them up above the sparkling blue waters.

"From here, you'll have a spectacular view of the colony."

She could see what he meant. It was laid out across the water on the peninsula that jutted out into Lake Jackson, wrapping about a quarter of the way around the water's edge. The structures were all one and two story wood-frame buildings, and they blended well with the surrounding forest, looking organic. "How many people do you have here now?" she asked, amazed at the scope of the operation that had been little more than a pipe dream a decade before.

"About four hundred, with more coming each month. We're trying to keep up with her, but she is growing so fast. When her next spurt begins with Daphne's arrival, we'll be hard-pressed to manage all the terraforming and planting."

They continued to rise, and she spotted one of those specks she'd seen from below. It flew in above them toward their destination, and she realized what it was at last. "They're gliders. Colin, that's ingenious!"

He laughed. "Not my idea. One of the engineers noticed the slipstreams Forever uses for her air circulation and figured we could tap into them for easy pole-to-pole transportation. Hope you aren't afraid of heights."

She smiled. "I'm up here, aren't I?" As the elevator continued to rise, a large platform came into view above.

"You'll be effectively weightless topside." Colin pointed up to the platform. "It's situated at the axis, so the centrifugal force cancels out the effective gravity. Hold on to the rails."

She could feel the weight of the world literally lifting off her shoulders. She grasped the rail as he'd advised. It reminded her of her first ride up the Skyhook with her father after they'd moved to North America—watching the ground fall away below them as the elevator car lifted them up into the stratosphere. The ground was now so far below them that the individual features had blurred into broad patches of merged colors, like a giant's paint palette. Even that was becoming obscured by the sky glow. "She truly is majestic, Colin. You've done wonders up here," she said with a sigh. *I've missed so much.*

The elevator slid smoothly up into the platform and came to a stop, and she was floating off the floor.

"Follow me." The plas doors opened.

She pushed away from the wall and through the doors with the ease of long practice, even though she'd been Earthbound for so long. It came back to her straightaway.

The platform, topside, was about fifty meters deep, in a half circle jutting out from the rock wall, with windows of plas offering a panoramic view of Forever. Control terminals lined the station, and half-a-dozen techs were at work there.

A staircase led up to the roof. She caught a handhold to stop her forward momentum.

"Morning, everyone."

The techs nodded at the director and went back to work. *Trying to impress the boss*, she thought with a wry smile.

Heavy footsteps echoed through the space as someone came down the stairs. "Hey, Tanner, how's the weather?" McAvery called. The woman who appeared on the stairs laughed. "Morning, sir! Not bad. Not too much mist today." She was tall and muscular, with something strapped to her back. "How's Trip?"

"Your brother was fine last night when I saw him station-side." He grinned.

"Going out for a flight this morning?" Her magnetic boots kept her attached to the floor. She pulled the contraption off her back.

McAvery followed Ana's gaze. "Glider—military grade. Had to pull a few strings to get those up here. Come on back here." To the pilot, he said, "Yup, out to the North Pole today."

"Say hello to Santa for me!"

Ana followed the director to the back of the platform and a bank of lockers. He opened one and pulled out two sets of boots, then handed one to her. "Should have given you these on the way up—would have made this part a bit easier."

He grinned, and she managed a weak smile back at him. She set the boots down on the floor, where they locked into place, and slipped off her own shoes, letting them float free for a moment. She managed to get her legs down into the boots—not so easy as they had once been, muscle memory or no, these zero g feats of agility.

Her feet secured to the deck, she grabbed her own shoes before they floated out of reach and turned to stash them in the locker.

McAvery was already wearing his own pair and was pulling on a glider pack like the one Tanner had been wearing. The pilot came over from her own locker and offered to give Ana a hand with hers. "Alexandria Tanner." She held out a hand, and Ana reached out to shake it.

"Anastasia Anatov." The pack looked vaguely insectoid, a metallic carapace with a set of folded iridescent red wings, two straps to go over her shoulders, and another wide strap to lock the pack on across her stomach. She put her arms out and let the experts cinch her into it. "Should I be nervous?" She glanced out the plas window. "I've never done this before."

"It's easy. Just slip these on." Tanner pulled a pair of gloves onto her bare arms. "Then you jump, and the airstream does most of the rest."

"Once you're airborne, just keep your palms open and fingers facing forward—like a superhero—and you'll glide along with the winds. Making a fist with both hands"—Colin demonstrated—"activates the air brakes, slowing you down, while closing one fist or the other activates the ailerons, letting you move left or right."

"What if I crash?"

He laughed. "Won't happen. If you somehow end up out of the jet stream and start losing altitude, the sensors will release your parachute and drop you down safely to the ground. Just wait for us and we'll come find you." He indicated a red button on the right side of the pack. "Press this and it will set off your distress beacon. Might take a day or two at worst, but you won't starve out there. We've already got some of the food crops planted."

"Like my own little Garden of Eden, huh?"

"Something like that. Ready?"

She turned to the pilot, who was getting ready to board the elevator for the trip back down to McAvery Port. "Thanks, um… Tanner…."

"Call me 'Ria. And you're welcome. Happy flying!" The doors closed behind her, and she descended out of sight.

McAvery led her up the stairs, out onto topside's open roof. There were two platform extensions that hadn't been visible from below, one on the left, the other on the right.

"Just like the streets back home," he called to her above the sounds of the wind, which was stronger than she expected. Above them it whistled into a giant cleft in the wall, and out again through another. "Depart on the right, return on the left."

"She's breathing," Ana said, transfixed. *My God, she's really alive.*

"You knew that. You designed her."

She nodded. "Knowing it and seeing it for myself are two vastly different things."

"Come on. I want to get there by midday. Follow me, and when you're free of the platform, spread your arms to the sides for a minute. Like this." He leaped off the platform, and she caught her breath as he began to plunge.

Then he spread his arms, and bright red glider wings snapped out, bathed in the golden glow of the band of light that ran along the axis of the world, and caught the wind. "Come on," he called.

She gathered her strength and courage, meager as it was, and leaped.

Chapter Five:
Grand Tour

As soon as Aaron was settled in his new room—a small space with a bed, a wooden desk, and a plas window—Devon called from outside the door.

"Come on out. Dania wants me to give you a tour of the colony." He grinned at Aaron and disappeared down the hallway.

Aaron scrambled after him. They bounced down the stairs to the ground floor.

"This is the mess hall." Devon opened a door to reveal a long room with seating for maybe forty—beautifully carved wooden chairs along wood-slab tables. "Breakfast is served at seven. Lunch at midday, and dinner at six."

Devon led him down the hall. "This is the supplies closet. Take only what you need, and sign out for it through your loop."

Aaron nodded. The closet was filled with miscellaneous things—bedding, toiletries, tools and much more, and was more than a little musty.

"We hand-wash everything. There's a drying line for your clothes strung outside your room. The more we can do without power, the less fuel has to be shipped up from Earthside. We even use ichor for light at night—luthiel, they call it."

"Who lights the lamps?"

"The Lamplighters, of course." Devon laughed. "Come on. I think we have enough time to see the town before lunchtime. Then this afternoon I'll take you out with me to one of the work crews."

He followed Devon down the steps and stopped, once again taken by the strangeness of the vista around him. The world wasn't supposed to go up and up and up. "How long...." He felt that familiar queasiness in the pit of his stomach.

"Until you get used to it? Maybe a month before you stop noticing it every time you come outside, but I'm still not *used to it*." The light was warmer than sunlight, more golden, and more uneven. "I'll take you to the village square. It's probably fairly quiet at the moment, but on festival nights, the whole colony is there." He set off down the pathway toward the lake and the wall, and Aaron followed. "This is the campus. It's where most of us live," he continued. "Over there"—he pointed in the direction Aaron and Dania had come from—"is the Warehouse District. That's where the supplies that come in from Transfer go before being parceled out to the work crews.

"Finally, by the lake is the Embassy District, where the dignitaries stay when they come to visit, and where the few shops and restaurants we have are located."

"Where Dr. Anatov is staying?"

Devon nodded. "Come on!"

The path wound out from the dormitories and joined with a larger paved road lined with tall trees of a variety he thought he recognized. "Those are mallow woods, right?"

"Damn, you're good."

"I worked on grafts back home at the academy."

"Beautiful wood from those trees. The chairs and tables in the cafeteria are made from them, and like everything else here, they grow to maturity in just a couple years."

The road led them into the heart of the settlement, where the wooden buildings clustered more tightly, forming a continuous row along the side of the road. All at once they passed through a gap and into what must have been the village green—a wide open park with a single great oak tree at the center providing illumination for the whole square, surrounded by lush green grass.

Aaron turned around to take in the view. It resembled nothing so much as a medieval town from one of the tridimensionals, but this one was living and breathing and real. It was only slightly spoiled by the tall white antenna that rose at one side of the green.

"That routes all our communications out to Transfer Station." Devon pulled him along. "Come on. We'll grab a snack before we head out to the orchards."

They entered a low single-story building with a series of long tables and benches and a fireplace along one end. A wonderful smell was coming from somewhere. "This is the main cantina for the colony. If you miss a meal at the dorm, you can come down here and grab something to eat at any time." Devon led him to a wide window along the back.

"Carmella," he called, and a short plump woman popped her head out from somewhere in the kitchen beyond.

"What can I do for you, Devon?" She was maybe twenty years older, her smooth skin barely seamed with fine lines around the corners of her eyes. Laugh lines, his mother used to call them.

"We have a newcomer today." Devon indicated Aaron with a flourish. "I'm taking him into the wilderness in the afternoon. Can you pack us something extra to take along?"

She wagged a finger at him. "You'll put on five k if you keep eating out of turn, Devon Powell."

"I'll work it off." Devon grinned broadly. "I'm seeing Rafe tonight."

"Juvenile delinquent. Here you go." She handed him a small sack. "Apple tarts from the new crop, fresh from the orchards. Just baked 'em."

"Thanks, Carmella," he called. "Come on, Aaron!" They ran outside.

Aaron clapped him on the shoulder. "I think I like this town, but where is everyone?"

"Most folks are out on work detail during the daylight hours. You know how that works?" He started back toward the dorms.

"A little. I studied it back home."

"We'll head back to the dorm and pick up a few things, grab some lunch at the mess, and then head out where I can show you in person. It's amazing!"

THE WORLD spun all around her as she dove into nothing. Ana plummeted, the platform disappearing rapidly behind her.

What had he said? Spread your arms. She did, and the glider wings popped out of her pack, pulling her up roughly toward the beam of light. The wings caught the wind, and all at once she was soaring.

Things steadied, an indistinct blur of greens and blues and browns below.

The light stream was not as solid when viewed up close. The river of glowing pollen roiled next to them, a constantly changing golden cloud.

She closed her left hand and the glider responded, drawing her to the left. Closing her right hand brought her back in that direction. She didn't think she'd try applying the brakes just yet.

McAvery was ahead of her, and he looked back and slowed his pace to match hers. Soon they were side by side, flying high above a world that had sprung solely from her imagination.

It was magic.

"This is amazing," she shouted at him over the wind. "What a genius way to travel."

"One of our techs thought it up—guy named Drew from the Allied African States who flies these things over Table Mountain. He got tired of taking ground transport back and forth to the North Pole. There's a lot less pollution this way too."

She nodded. "About that. You call it the North Pole, huh? Is Santa Claus really there?"

"Better."

The wind ruffled her wings. "Seems bumpy. Is it always like this?"

He shook his head. "It varies day to day. Today is a little rougher than usual, but not excessively so."

They settled into a companionable silence as they rode the winds. She experimented, banking left and right, and the glowing mists around her swirled playfully.

She remembered her time as a young girl in Russia, when she'd often played along the riverbanks, and how her father would sometimes take her kayaking downriver when the waters were calm. She would lie in the prow of the kayak, her chest resting against the plastic, with her hands spread out to the side as they bounced down the waterway.

She pretended to fly, as if the river spume were the mist of the clouds, as her father guided them along the river.

What a strange, wonderful life she had led. From those halcyon summer days along the riverside to this alien sky so far from home.

This was so much better than rafting.

She looked down at the ground. It was fuzzy and indistinct, a tawny brown in places, shades of faded blue in others. "How long until we reach the North Pole?" she shouted to McAvery.

"Maybe three hours," he called back. "Settle in and enjoy the ride."

THEY CLAMBERED up the steep trail from McAvery Port, Aaron following his new mentor out of the town and into the hills. From the shuttle, this had all looked relatively flat, but he was quickly finding out how steep "relatively flat" could be when you had to walk it.

The well-worn pathway wound up the side of the hill in a series of switchbacks, finally reaching the ridgeline, which it followed "north."

Devon had given him a crash course in Forever directions. The nearby wall was the South Pole, while the far wall, currently about 193 kilometers away and growing, was the North Pole. Facing the North Pole, left was west and right was east. It all made a certain kind of sense.

They reached the ridge just after midday. Devon had packed them camping gear. They planned to stay one night in the wilderness and return to the colony in the morning.

Aaron turned back to look at where they'd come from. The colony sat on a peninsula that jutted out into the water. The ridge they were climbing rose from the water line in a slow but steady ascent and was lined with trees and brush that glimmered with afternoon light.

The very air below them shimmered, and some white birds flew in small flocks across the water. "What's the lake called?"

"Lake Jackson" came the reply. "After one of the original three people who helped found Forever."

Aaron stiffened. Jackson had been his father's name.

Devon didn't seem to notice.

"This is as good a place as any for lunch. Can't beat the view." He set down his carry sack next to an outcropping of rock and unpacked their meal. Aaron sat down beside his new friend, entranced by the vista. He wondered whose idea it had been to name the lake after his father. The director's, he supposed.

His hands touched the rock, and he was transported.

THE TERRAIN below had risen noticeably in the last few minutes. It seemed closer all around, and Ana could make out more details of it now, including what looked like a large lake or inlet that slowly narrowed in the distance.

The wind at her back was remarkably steady. It was part of the weather regulating system she'd designed, but creating something in a lab model and experiencing it all around you were two very different things.

She followed the course of the inlet up ahead and gasped. It looked as if they were flying into the maw of some huge beast. Great peaks reared up from the world floor toward the sky, a ring of them reaching maybe halfway to the midpoint. "That wasn't in the original plans," she called, and Colin laughed.

"She's made a few modifications. We're going to be stuck in this big tin can for generations. People are going to want variety."

"How tall are they?"

"The peaks? Two and a half kilometers from base to the tip of the tallest one. Glad we're flying?"

She nodded. "Do they have a name?"

"The Dragon's Reach."

"Very poetic."

As they approached, the details of the mountain slopes became apparent. This far out, there was little vegetation, and it vanished where the peaks stood like sentinels. They were bare and sharp, made of rock as dark as the asteroid from which they'd been born. They reared up like gnarled black teeth, pocked and scarred, lit only by the sky glow, devoid of any plant life.

There was no snow. Somehow, she'd thought there would be snow.

The ground rose steadily to meet the new peaks, and she felt, for just a moment, what it must be like to be a god, a creator of all this magnificence.

She had done this.

Now, as she flew over her creation, she felt as insignificant as a gnat before an elephant.

As they passed the peaks, the North Pole wall finally became visible in the misty distance. Another thirty minutes, she guessed, and they would arrive.

WHEN AARON had sat down and placed his hands on the naked stone, it was as if electricity shot through him. His muscles tensed, and he squeezed his eyes shut.

When he opened them, he was in a different place.

He stood in a wide room surrounded by high stone walls smothered with tapestries. Smoke was thick in the air, blowing off wooden torches like something out of one of his King Arthur tridimensionals.

In fact, he was dressed in chain mail, with a short sword in a scabbard at his side. His boots were rough-worked leather, and his hands were encased in tight-fitting leather gloves to match.

In the middle of the room, a giant redwood grew up from the pavestones below, where her roots wrapped themselves into the very stone, to the sky high above. She was impossibly tall.

"Good, you're here," a man's voice said, and someone clapped him on the shoulder. He spun around to find an older man staring back at him. "We've been waiting for you." A man with his own eyes.

"Dad?"

Something shook him, and the room dissolved into a puddle and dripped away.

Aaron opened his eyes and found himself staring into Devon's.

"Hey, you okay? It'll be my hide if anything happens to you." He knelt before Aaron, pulling out a flask of water from his carry sack. "Here, drink this. Maybe we climbed the grade too fast. I forget you Earthsiders aren't used to real exercise."

"What happened? I sat down and everything shifted...."

"I don't know. I was getting out some lunch when you just slumped over off that rock there." He pointed. "I pulled you up, but you were really out of it."

"There was a castle." *And my father?*

Devon laughed. "I don't doubt it. Come on. Let's get some food in you. It'll help." He handed Aaron a loaf of bread. "It's got a lot baked into it—herbs from our gardens, salt from the lake, even some of our new jungle fowl for protein. We make as much as we can up here to save costs. The director wants everything going back into the project."

Aaron took a bite. It wasn't bad. Maybe a little dry. "More water?" he managed, and Devon handed over the flask.

Together they ate in companionable silence, taking in the view. There was nothing like this in Fargo.

Aaron thought about his father. It had been ten years since he'd gone away, and the man he'd seen in the dream—daydream?—could have been him. What did it all mean?

He caught Devon staring at him. "What?" He wiped his mouth self-consciously.

"Nothing," Devon said, then looked as if he was reconsidering. "It's just that you're really good-looking." He blushed. "Sorry, had to say it."

Aaron laughed. "Thanks, but I don't think we play for the same team." He washed down the last of the bread with a swig of water. "I'm flattered, though."

Devon sighed. "The cute ones are never free." He handed over one of the apple tarts he'd begged from the mess. "Here, eat this and we'll get going again."

Aaron grinned. "If I ever change my mind, you'll be the first to know." Aaron bit into the tart, and juice and cinnamon and apples burst into his mouth. "Oh man, this is good." Even cold it was delicious. He could imagine how it would have been fresh.

"Thought you'd like it."

They finished their meals and repacked their sacks.

"Come on," Devon called, starting up the ridgeline. "I want to be at the orchards in an hour."

Aaron shouldered his pack and started up along the trail after his new friend. It was a shame, really, that he didn't swing that way.

Devon was sweet.

Chapter Six:
North Pole

LEX WAITED.

The good doctor was coming. Her mother, her creator, and quite nearly her destroyer.

She had so many questions, but she was also filled with a curious emotion when she thought about those panic-filled days when she'd been under attack.

She wanted an accounting. She wanted... revenge.

Her conscience tried to calm her, to soothe her, but as the woman drew nearer, Lex's emotions roiled inside her like a dark storm.

THE WIND gusts were getting rougher, but the glider had a power assist mode that helped her fight the rising winds. The North Pole was quickly approaching, a vast wall that had appeared tiny at first but had steadily grown before them. Ana struggled to put it into perspective.

It was like—well, like the sheer cliff face of El Capitan in Yosemite, when you stood at the bottom and looked up and felt as though you were confronting infinity. She felt small and humbled.

The ground below was a barren, bleak desert without any topsoil—an unbroken stretch of shattered black and gray.

The platform came into view ahead, the winds pushing them relentlessly toward it.

"Remember, when I say brake, clench both your fists. You'll slow down in a hurry. Just keep pace with me and you'll be in good shape for the landing."

She nodded, trying not to show her nerves. Here she was, a woman in her middle forties, flying through the sky as if she were a bird. A bird who'd been born a tortoise, more like it.

The wall was coming up quickly now. She aimed for the platform, like Colin had shown her, and when he called out "Brake!" she clenched her fists. It was like a giant hand had grabbed her from behind to haul her backward through the air. The wind roared past the reconfigured sails, dropping her velocity at an alarming rate.

Colin was sliding ahead of her, so she opened her hands and immediately started picking up speed once again.

She'd reach the platform in less than ten seconds. She played with the brakes, gradually slowing herself down, watching as the director alighted gracefully ahead of her.

Her landing, though acceptable, had none of his grace. Instead she ended up flat on her ass on the hard metal of the platform. But she made it, and that was all that mattered.

"Nice job," he said with a grin, helping her up.

DEVON AND Aaron arrived at the orchards after another half hour. The trees spread out before them in even rows, all alight with their vegetable glow.

He'd worked with many of them back on Earth, refining the various strains as part of his underclassman research, but to see them in the wild, a whole world's worth of glowing plants, was magical.

"Does everyone walk everywhere up here?" Aaron asked Devon. "Seems like it would waste a lot of time."

Devon laughed. "No, we usually catch a transport up this way—especially when we have to bring up new plantings and supplies. I thought the walk would have more of an impact."

He was right. Aaron took a moment to look around and up. It was still vertigo-inducing to see the world arching over his head, trees hanging above him at odd angles to the ground beneath his feet. He supposed he would get used to it eventually.

He quickly returned his gaze to eye level.

"Speaking of ground transport," Devon said as a low-slung vehicle made its way up the trail behind them. "Hey, Rask, can we grab a ride on your traxx?"

"Hop on!" The older man guiding the vehicle waved them aboard.

The traxx was about fifteen feet long and crawled on a rotating tread on either side like an old tank. Rask sat in the driver's cabin, while supplies were strapped into the back bed—small trees ready for planting, tools, buckets of fertilizer, and assorted other odds and ends.

Devon climbed aboard without waiting for the vehicle to stop, and Aaron followed him, sliding in among the saplings.

"Rask's making the run out to the Edge. We're constantly pushing the planting out toward the Dragon's Reach—the range of mountains you'll see in a bit, off in the distance."

The traxx picked up speed now that it was on level ground, following the hard-packed roadway through the middle of the orchard. Devon reached up and snatched a glowing apple from one of the low-hanging branches and handed it to Aaron. As he watched, the glow slowly faded, until it looked just like an ordinary apple. "Is this where those apples in those tarts came from?"

"Yup. Fresh picked yesterday, most likely."

A gust of wind whipped through the branches, sending a shower of still-glowing leaves wafting down toward them. Aaron laughed in delight.

In ten more minutes, they reached their first destination—a crew of workers busy harvesting the apples, placing them in big baskets for pickup and return to the colony.

They hopped off the traxx, waving at Rask as he continued onward toward the Edge.

"Heya, Devon," one of the men from the work crew called. "Come to help?"

"Hey, Talis," he called back. "Yeah, but just for a couple minutes. I'm showing this newbie the ropes."

"Talis Miller," the man introduced himself, holding out a hand. He was average height, with a nasty scar across the bridge of his nose.

Aaron took his hand, trying not to stare. "It's all right." Talis smiled. "Industrial accident back Earthside. Takes everyone a bit to get used to it."

"Sorry, I didn't mean to stare."

"You aren't the first, and you won't be the last. Come on, grab a basket. I'll show you the ropes. Devon, you know what to do."

Devon snorted. "What do you take me for, a farmhand?"

"Hey, if the overalls fit...."

Devon stuck his tongue out at Talis.

Aaron was more interested in the ethereal orchard. It was like a painting, lit from within by a golden glow.

He could see himself living up here for good.

ANA CLOSED her wings and took a minute to turn around and admire the view. The platform was similar to the one at the South Pole, but the view could not have been more different.

The ground far below was nothing but black and a reflected golden color where water pooled here and there in the lower lying areas, all the way out to the Dragon's Reach... an alien landscape that reminded her of nothing so much as newly formed lava flats on the Big Island of Hawaii. If there was any life down there, she couldn't see it from up here. "How is the soil formed?" she asked, looking at the vast expanse of black rock.

"We spray a biological agent on the rocks as we go. It breaks the rock down to gravel, and then into soil. The agent deteriorates after a few generations—usually a day or two."

She snorted. "Good thing." Otherwise it might burrow down through the shell of the world.

"Indeed. Come on, let's go meet Lex."

She shrugged off the gloves and let him help her with the retracted glider. "What now?" she asked with a wry smile. "Time for a spacewalk?"

He shook his head. "From here it's easy—just a short flight of stairs to the control center. Come on." He opened a door at the back of the room and led her into the North Pole wall, her shoes clinging to the metal floor.

They climbed down the stairs from the platform to the inside of the facility. It was at least three times as large as Topside, from what she could see, and much warmer inside. "Welcome to the Far Hold," Colin said as they reached the main level. "We keep a full crew here at all times, monitoring the world-mind and working with her to build out the world to plan."

The room resembled the bridge of a ship, with wide monitors at each of six workstations. Which it basically was.

"Dr. Anatov, this is Risha, Marcos, Ashton, Divia, Jacob, and Natasha." Each one of the techs nodded as their name was called. "How is she doing?"

"Her vitals are all within normal range," the woman named Risha responded. "She's looking forward to seeing you today."

Ana arched an eyebrow.

"She's not your average mind," Colin said by way of explanation. "As you were. Ana, let's go. She's waiting for us." He led her to a doorway at the back of the room and palmed open the door.

They stepped through the open doorway into a cave. The rock walls were shot through with a tracery of glowing yellow veins, like the exterior of the worldlet. Ana ran her hands along the wall. It was smooth, almost polished, with a series of ripples in the rock that she could feel with her fingers but couldn't see.

They followed the cavern for a few minutes, and eventually the glow began to strengthen up ahead. The cavern widened out into a high-ceilinged room that she could only describe as a cathedral.

It was magnificent.

Easily ten stories tall, the space was hollowed out of the stone of the asteroid. The surface of the rock was intricately worked in whorls and lines and swirls, and the glow from the cave continued here, but the narrow traceries were grown to wide veins of golden light that wound their way toward the ceiling.

But the mind above them was the true wonder. She had grown from the size of a football when Ana had sealed her into the seed—she was now bigger than a tree. Thoughts raced around the mind in strands of light, and the roots that anchored her to the rock were as thick as tree trunks.

Colin handed Ana a portable loop.

She pressed it up against the side of her temple, and the world transformed. Instead of a rock cavern, she stood inside the heart of a castle, but it was like no castle she had ever seen.

A giant redwood grew up from the flagstone floor into the sky, and there was no roof above. The walls were faced with gray stone and covered in colorful tapestries depicting battles and coronations and other historic events.

There was a woman standing before them. She wore a white cotton dress, with a simple circlet of gold holding back her raven-black hair. Her eyes were the blue of the Earth's sky.

"Welcome to Forever, Dr. Anatov. I've waited a long time to see you again."

AARON CLIMBED the short ladder up to the hanging branches of the apple tree. One of the girls, Harmony, climbed a ladder next to him.

"You just reach out, lift up the apple in your hand, and twist. If it comes away easily, it's ready." She demonstrated, pulling down one of the glowing fruits. She bit into it, and the juice dribbled down her chin, slowly fading to darkness. "Now you try it."

He pulled down an apple, but it didn't come free.

"That one's not quite there yet. You can tell by the glow too. See how it's kind of green?"

The glow of the apple he'd tried to pluck did have a tinge of lime.

"Try that one." She pointed.

He pulled the fruit off the branch with ease this time and took a bite. It was delicious—sweet, crunchy, and tart. "Why don't they use a machine to harvest these?"

Devon called over from the next tree. "Too expensive. Human labor is cheaper and doesn't pollute the orchards."

"Plus it's a life skill," Harmony said.

"A what?"

"A life skill. Those of us who make it up here are first in line for spots when the real colonization begins, but we have to learn life skills, because we won't have machines to help us during the long interval."

"That makes sense, I guess." He pulled down more of the fruits and deposited them in the basket.

"We're building a closed ecosystem here," Talis said. "Everything is interconnected and the whole thing self-sufficient. The most stable way to ensure that is by emulating a feudal society—without the landholders and serfs, of course."

"Of course, but how do you prevent that?"

Talis laughed. "Sorry, that's above my pay grade. I leave that part to the social scientists back at McAvery."

They stayed for an hour, moving from tree to tree. Aaron found an easy rhythm in the work and learned a little about each of the apple pickers. They were from all around the world. McAvery had apparently selected for diversity up here. His estimation of the director went up another notch.

When the next traxx crawled by, they were there to hitch a ride out to the Edge.

ANA LOOKED around the transformed room. "Do you mind?" she asked the world-mind.

"Be my guest," Lex said.

Ana knelt, caressing the rough flagstones with her fingertips. They felt real.

A few steps brought her to the redwood tree. She recognized the bark. It was the same color and texture as the seed had been before it germinated. "A little nostalgia?"

"It was an easy-to-replicate texture," the mind said, but Ana thought she detected a note of pride in the tone. Perhaps Colin was right about this mind being "special."

Ana looked up. Fluffy white clouds raced by in a blue sky, high above, past the tree branches and the tall walls of the castle.

She approached one of the covered windows and pulled back a tapestry. Light flooded in, and she was blinded for a moment.

When her sight returned, she was astonished to see the rolling, grass-covered countryside, a fetishized version of the England of King Arthur, fading off into the distance. Every blade of grass was drawn with precision. The clouds were perfectly imperfect.

She sat on the stone sill for a moment contemplating the whole scene, and a cool breeze rushed past her. She laughed, surprised. "This whole thing is amazing... Lex?"

The world-mind nodded. "I have a fondness for knights in shining armor."

Ana returned to the center of the room, where Lex and Colin were waiting.

"So, what do you think?" Colin asked.

"The simulation, or the world?"

"All of it."

"It's amazing. More than I ever dreamed." Another thought occurred to her. "Is this what Hammond 'saw' when he first met you?"

Lex nodded. "More or less. I had fewer capabilities back then, bound as I was to the *Dressler*. You and Jackson freed me."

Ana frowned, considering the implications of that statement. "Were you really so unhappy?"

Lex shook her head. "You misunderstand. I was never unhappy, just limited."

"Are you aware what happened to Jackson?" Ana was almost afraid to hear the answer. "You were incapacitated when it happened."

Colin watched her closely but did not interfere.

The world-mind nodded. "When I absorbed his body, I acquired his memories too."

Suddenly the castle was gone.

They were back on the *Dressler*, in the midst of that rushed and horrible escape.

This time Ana was looking into the shuttle from outside. She was inside Hammond's head.

She felt her hands unlatch the helmet, felt herself lift it off her shoulders.

Felt the terrible, deadly cold of the void pour in, freezing her skin and bursting her eyes and turning her brain to ice.

Ana screamed.

She found herself on the floor, gasping. Colin lay on the other side of the room, looking stunned.

She'd always hoped it had been quick for Jackson, but oh, the pain before it was over....

Lex knelt next to her, all sweetness gone from her face. "We both know he wasn't the one who endangered the ship," she whispered. "It was your fault, Ana."

The blood drained from Ana's face. There it was, the thing she had run from for a decade. The guilt she thought she had left behind. She'd done her penance.

She looked up, and for just a second Jackson was staring down at her instead of Lex.

She stood and turned to run, ripping off the loop and frantically palming the exit pad to get out of the room. *Open, goddammit!*

She looked back over her shoulder, expecting something to be chasing her. She didn't know what, only that it would rip her heart out if she let it catch her.

Lex was gone, but the world-mind itself floated menacingly above.

The door opened at last, and she fled down the corridor.

"Ana, come back," Colin called after her.

She didn't stop. She had to get away from that horrible woman, the world-mind, the thing that had just called her a murderer.

Chapter Seven:
Flight

LEX WATCHED Dr. Anatov and Director McAvery go.

She'd hoped that she'd feel something—some sense of relief confronting the woman who had almost destroyed her, whose actions had led to Jackson Hammond's death.

Instead, she felt numb.

She had waited all these years to confront Dr. Anatov, and what had it gained her?

"You have to find a way to forgive her," a voice said behind her.

She spun around to find Jackson Hammond standing there, under the branches of the great tree. He was wearing his knight in shining armor gear.

"You've been here this whole time." It was a statement, not a question.

He nodded. "It's taken me a while to come back to myself." He took a step forward, putting a hand on her shoulder. "You're angry, Lex, and you have a right to be. But you have to forgive her."

She sank down on the flagstone with a heavy sigh, her white dress spreading out around her like snow. "I don't know how." She wasn't good at emotions. They writhed around inside of her like living things, outside of her control. She'd never had a mother or father to guide her.

"I think that's why I'm here." It was as if Jackson were reading her thoughts. Maybe he was. "I've been waiting for you to be ready."

She nodded. "I want to learn how to be more... human."

He pulled her up and embraced her, kissing her forehead. "I know. The first thing to know is when to stop and take a deep breath...."

As THEY rode the traxx, Devon and Aaron lapsed into a companionable silence. The apple groves gave way to wide fields of glowing wheat, and then eventually to open hillsides covered with bright tall green grass that whispered back and forth in the slight breeze. Light coming from plants took some getting used to, as did seeing the land arching over your head.

The traxx lumbered on, and Aaron's mind swung back to the vision he'd seen when he touched the hard rock of Ariadne's surface. Had he unwittingly tapped into the world-mind?

And why had he seen his father there?

Forever was a living being on a scale never before known by mankind. He'd expected something like Transfer, but bigger.

This was of another magnitude altogether. It was like dipping into another reality.

The traxx entered a copse of trees more wild and random than the apple orchard. Trees that reminded him of banyans grew in thick clusters, the ground beneath them wet and soft in places and dry in others. Colorful vines wrapped around their trunks, providing light under the dark canopy.

Devon reached up and grabbed a low-hanging fruit off one of the vines as they passed under it. He pulled out his knife, cut it open, and handed half to Aaron. "Here, try this… it's a melon variant. Kinda half cantaloupe, half watermelon."

Aaron took the fruit, the glowing juices spilling over his palms. Following Devon's example, he scooped out a bit of the flesh and ate it. It was sweet and wet. "Oooh, that's good!"

Devon grinned. "We're living in paradise, I tell you!"

As they ate, Aaron asked some of the questions that were on his mind. "Where are you from?"

"The Allied African States." Devon's usual cheer was gone. "My mother and I escaped after the last revolution, but my brothers are still there. You?"

"Fargo. My father was in AmSplor."

"Wait, Hammond? Like Jackson Hammond?"

"Yeah."

Devon's mouth made a little O. "Your father's like a legend up here."

"I wish he were still here, instead of being a *legend*." Aaron spit out a seed. "He left my mother and us two kids in a really bad place when he died." They were silent for a while. Aaron finished his melon, and together they threw the rinds into the jungle.

"Is that why you're here?" Devon said at last.

Aaron took a minute before answering. "That's part of it, but I've always wanted to be out here. To explore. To be at the start of something. There are so many endings and blind alleys back on Earth."

"Tell me about it."

The traxx rounded a bend and cleared the last of the jungle. The plants rapidly dwindled to nothing, and a bleak field of black rock spread out before them.

"The Edge?"

Devon nodded. "We've got about three hours before dark. Come on. I'll show you what we do out here."

COLIN FOUND the good doctor on the flight deck, strapping on her wings. The wind was rising, and the hair on his arms was standing on end from the static electricity. "Ana, you have to come back inside," he shouted over the whistling of the wind. "The storm is starting. It's not safe for you out here."

She shook her head violently. "I should never have come back," she shouted. "I thought I'd moved past all of this, but you can't escape your demons. I have to get away from here."

"Just wait until tomorrow." There was a tempest brewing, for God's sake.

She glared at him. "I'm sorry, Colin, I can't!" With that she turned and leaped off the platform, soaring into the open sky beyond.

Colin cursed, clambering down the steps to retrieve his own set of wings. Damn fool woman would get them both killed. "Risha, let McAvery Port know Dr. Anatov has gone out on her own and I'm going after her. We may both need rescue before this is through."

He ignored the startled look on her face and scrambled back up the stairs, intent on catching the doctor before she went too far.

AARON GAZED out across the barren plain before them. It was intimidating. It looked like the end of the world, as the green plants behind him petered out into grasses for a few feet and then to a broken landscape of black shale.

"I give you the Edge. Come on!" Devon called from up ahead. "We're almost there." They had followed the line of vegetation for about forty-five minutes, and he could see activity up ahead a little way along the curve of the world. They were carrying two metal tanks each across this dividing line in the landscape—glowing life on the right and dark barrenness on the left. He'd asked what they were for, but Devon had been cagey about the whole thing. He sighed and continued on after his new acquaintance, carrying his heavy tanks in addition to the weight of the pack on his back.

He shifted the pack, trying to find a comfortable position. Who knew there'd be so much physical work up here?

They hiked for another twenty minutes, eventually reaching a small gully. They clambered down one side, handing the tanks from one to the other, and then up the other.

Aaron hauled himself to the top and dusted off his clothes, looking up into a woman's face.

She was tall, with long dark hair and eyes that were the warmest brown he'd ever seen. "Hello," he managed, almost stumbling backward into the gully. She caught his shoulder, steadying him, and laughed. It was a welcoming, cheerful sound.

"Hi there. I'm Keera." She extended her hand, and he took it, smiling back at her.

"Hey, gorgeous," Devon said, and Keera threw her arms around him.

"Hi, angel. You brought us another worker bee?"

He nodded. "Not just anyone. Keera, this is Aaron Hammond. Of *those* Hammonds."

Keera grinned. "Wow, a virtual celebrity! Well, come on. We have a couple more hours before it gets dark. Let's put you to work."

"I'd like that." Aaron was utterly charmed. He followed the two of them along to the work site as they chatted and caught up on events back at McAvery. Then he was introduced around to the rest of the crew. There were ten of them out here, and judging by their comfortable rapport, they had been working together for some time.

He ended up teamed with Keera herself.

"I see you brought your own tanks of bio-agent. Bring one along." She beckoned him to follow. She also handed him a long metal pole.

They passed several of the others, who were spraying the hard shale with something out of similar tanks. They reached the end of the line, and she pointed out at the shale plain, which stretched off toward the mountains in the distance.

"We're slowly working our way out to the Dragon's Reach, those dark mountains off in the distance. Our goal is to have all of this planted within the next three years."

He whistled. "That's a long way." He stared at the distant, craggy peaks. "They're amazing. It's hard to believe we're out in the middle of the void."

"I know, right?" She smiled. "I forget sometimes where we are. It's so... real, you know?"

He nodded. "I'm still not used to *that*." He pointed up at the overarching sky. "Okay, so what do I do?"

She released the nozzle from the side of her tank. "Each one of these contains a biological soup that's engineered to break down the rock into usable soil. We work around the world, one circuit at a time, in a swath about thirty meters wide. Like so." She set a proximate meter on her belt, started at the edge of the grass, and walked off toward the distant peaks, spraying the agent across the rocks. It hissed when it hit the surface, and Aaron imagined it burrowing down into his own skin.

"Is it dangerous?"

She shook her head. "It's only hungry for carbonaceous rock." Where she had sprayed the ground, the rock was already taking on a gray color, pitted as if with acid. "When you find a bigger rock, use the poker to turn it over and get the underside too." She demonstrated, neatly flicking over a flat rock. "It helps the agent penetrate."

Aaron suppressed the dirty thoughts that comment elicited. He was *so ten years old* sometimes.

When she reached thirty meters, she turned and came back, spraying the ground along the way. "Now you try it." She handed him the meter.

He set it and stepped out onto the rocky ground. It was treacherous. He made his way carefully out across the bleak landscape, spraying as he went.

Once an errant breeze blew some of the mist onto his exposed arm, but it dried almost immediately. He brushed it off with the back of his hand and stared suspiciously at the skin. There seemed to be no damage.

"Told you," Keera called.

Aaron stuck his tongue out at her.

He spent the next hour spraying down the patch she assigned to him. He wasn't nearly as practiced, but he thought he'd done a decent enough job by the time he returned to the grassy verge. He looked out at his handiwork. "What happens next?"

"The agent digests the rock, breaking it down into topsoil. Given time, it will work its way down until it builds a soil base about twenty feet deep. Then it's programmed to expire."

"Wouldn't want it eating a hole through the bottom of the world!"

"No, that wouldn't be good. It loses effectiveness after a short while. Hey, you got a little on your face." She reached up to brush it off.

"Thanks," he said awkwardly, aware suddenly, intensely, of her physical closeness. She must have felt it too.

"Well, you seem to have the hang of it." She turned away abruptly.

"Wait… what happens next?"

She looked flustered. "I'm not sure what you mean."

"The ground—what happens after it's turned into topsoil?"

"Ah." Her shoulders relaxed visibly. "The grass will grow out onto it, and then some of the other native plants. In some areas another crew will come along and plant something specific… an orchard or a new plant sample."

He nodded. "It's amazing," he said, barely aware he was repeating himself.

"Well, go to it. We'll stop at nightfall, or when the rain comes." She looked back once as she walked away and then turned and left him staring after her, his imagination afire with possibilities.

THE STORM closed in around her like a living thing, but Ana didn't care. She had to get away from that hateful thing at the North Pole.

That she was inside the belly of the beast she was fleeing didn't factor into her thinking at all—logic wasn't operative here. She was driven by shame and anger and primal fear.

Shame at what she had done that had ultimately led to Jackson Hammond's death.

Anger that the world-mind, which she had saved and brought to this place, would treat her with such biting disdain.

And fear of what might happen next.

The sky darkened as the cloud of light was broken up by the storm. The wind buffeted her around through banks and streamers of cloud, and soon the rain started up in earnest as the accumulated moisture in the air reached saturation.

She could see little beyond the menacingly glowing clouds, and had no choice but to continue on, hoping she could outrun the worst of the storm.

It dawned on her that this had been a truly stupid idea.

The first lightning bolt took her by surprise, streaking across the sky before her like a massive short circuit, rendering a wide swath of the glowing pollen that permeated the dark clouds.

Ana started to panic. She had to get down out of this storm or she'd get herself electrocuted.

Another bolt passed so closely behind her that she could smell the ozone.

She picked a direction that felt like down and dove into the roiling clouds.

The rain grew stronger, and the wind shoved her hard sideways. She struggled to regain her equilibrium, feeling her weight increase. She must be getting closer to the ground.

At last she broke out of the cloud cover, although the driving rain continued. At the same time, her chute deployed, and she breathed a heavy sigh of relief.

Then there was a flash of light and nothing more.

Chapter Eight:
Jackson

AARON, KEERA, and her crew managed another hour or so of work treating the soil before the storm blew in from the North Pole. It started slowly, a light wind teasing his hair, a patch of darkness in the distance in the strange circular sky.

As the wind picked up, Keera called a halt to the work, gathering everyone to stow their tools in a portable carryall that they tied down just under the tree line, protected somewhat from the wind.

Aaron worked side by side with Keera, well aware of her proximity. She was like no one he had ever met before—brash, strong, with a fire in her eyes that immediately attracted him. "You can bunk with me to wait out the storm," she shouted as they finished tying things down.

By then the wind had picked up, and she had to shout to be heard over it.

"What about Devon?"

She laughed. "I don't think that's going to be a problem." She pointed, and he followed her glance. Devon was chatting with one of the other team members. "He and Rafe have an *understanding*."

He grinned. "Fair enough. Lead on."

As the sky dimmed, she pulled them back into the trees. They followed a well compacted footpath that led several hundred meters into the forest. For it really was a forest here—wild and unmanicured, unlike the even rows of the orchards they had passed through earlier in the day.

They left the path and soon came to a small tent just big enough for two people kneeling. She opened the flaps, let him inside, and sealed the tent from the weather outdoors.

A soft glow came on inside, seeming to emanate from the fabric itself. She handed him a pillow, and they sat down opposite each other in the small space. "I'm afraid I don't have much to offer you." She handed him a cup and filled it with water out of a metal canteen. "Living up here is a little like going back in time. They want us to be self-sufficient, just in case."

"In case of what?" he asked.

"In case we ever get cut off from Earth." She stared at him over the rim of the cup as she sipped the water. "Tensions are worse than ever between the Chinese states and the NAU."

"Oh come on, things aren't that bad down there." Even as he said it, he wondered. Wars were breaking out around the world, basic resources were tight, and the Heat meant there was less arable land to go around every year as the oceans continued to rise.

"My family lives in Ireland." She set down the cup. "My grandmother tells me stories of the way things used to be, back when Ireland had a northern climate. Did you know that Dublin didn't always have palm trees? That there was a time when a warm, sunny day was a rarity up north, before reunification?"

He nodded. "My mom tells me stories about those days too. Ones that were passed down from her father. He was from Mexico City. It was hot and dry back then, but now they get more rain than some places in California."

As if he had conjured it up from thin air, the raindrops began to fall on the roof of the tent, at first just a light patter, quickly ramping up to a full-scale assault. His eyes widened at the sound, and Keera laughed at him. "This place does take some getting used to."

"You're telling me. I just can't get my head around the fact that we're millions of miles away from Earth, in a hollowed-out asteroid, hiding from a rainstorm."

"I know, right? Well, we do have some time to kill." She shifted forward, her lips meeting his.

She smelled like an earth goddess, full of warmth and life.

She was beautiful, they were all alone, and he needed a little "normal."

Or something.

He didn't resist.

AFTERWARD THEY lay together as the rain still beat insistently on the fabric of the tent.

He was utterly relaxed, spent. He turned toward her, and she grinned at him. "That was amazing."

"Not bad."

He stuck his tongue out at her again. It was kind of their thing. "How long will the rain last?"

"Usually three to four hours." She turned to look at him, and her mouth curled up in a wicked smile. "I have an idea. Come on!" She opened the tent flaps and pulled him outside, while he protested his lack of clothes. "Let the rain wash you clean." She shook her hair out under the downpour.

The water was coming down in thick sheets, obscuring even the nearest of the trees. He let it cascade over his body. It was primal, so different from an ionic shower.

He pulled Keera to him and kissed her hungrily, and they dropped to the wet earth, entwined.

His hands touched the ground, and everything vanished.

ANA WOKE in darkness. The storm seemed to have passed. She looked around—the world was gray and formless.

She tried to sit up, and a searing pain arched up her spine. She gritted her teeth until the pain settled down to a dull ache.

She set about exploring her surroundings carefully with her hands. She lay upon something smooth and padded. After a while, she worked out that it was her glider pack. It had been broken beneath her when she hit the ground, but she hoped that the rescue beacon was still working.

She found the button Colin had shown her and pressed it, but the light didn't come on. *No way to tell.*

She'd been a fool to run out into the storm like that. Now here she was, all alone, God knows where. She felt the terrain around her with her hands. She seemed to have landed in a ditch or gully of some sort. She was lucky the storm hadn't washed her away while she was out. The surfaces around her were hard and sharp and rose on either side of her at least as far as she could reach from her supine position.

Next she performed a careful inventory of her body. Her head seemed fine; she could feel a few cuts and abrasions on her arms and legs, but there was no wetness to indicate bleeding.

She twisted slowly one direction, then the other. Nothing felt out of place inside, although it was hard to be certain.

For the moment, her worst affliction seemed to be her spine.

She wiggled her toes experimentally. They all still worked. *One less thing to worry about.*

She tried to get up again and slowly, painfully managed to reach a sitting position. She breathed heavily after the effort. She was not going to climb out of here on her own anytime soon.

Her eyes adjusted. There was a dim light in the ravine. She couldn't tell where it was coming from, but she could finally see where she was, at least the immediate vicinity. She sat in a deep cleft in the ground, propped up between two walls, above a pool of water. At least she should be able to get something to drink.

The parachute that had slowed her fall was crumpled nearby, shocking yellow against the black shale around her. Above, the walls towered out of sight.

She closed her eyes, pushing down the sudden upwelling of panic. *I can do this.*

She would figure her way out of her situation, or they would come and find her. Thinking otherwise was not an option.

COLIN FLEW through the heart of the storm, barely managing to remain airborne, drawing on his years of experience flying through this new sky.

He doubted Ana would have been able to avoid being forced down in such an unusually strong guster. If he hadn't known better, he would have thought that Lex was taking out her wrath on the good doctor.

The storm blew itself out a few minutes before he arrived at the South Pole. He alighted and pulled off his wings, practically falling down the stairs to the control center. "Any sign of the doctor?" he asked Gianna, the station master on duty.

"Sorry, sir, not yet." She frowned. Twenty years his junior, she was one of the newer crop of recruits from Earth. "The storm scrambled some of our sensors. It'll take a few moments for them to reboot."

He paced back and forth, going over the whole thing in his head. Who knew Lex would unload on the poor doctor like that? The world-mind had been holding a grudge all these years…. What else was locked away in that immense mind of hers? Was she dangerous to anyone else? To the colony?

Not only that. He swore he'd seen Jackson Hammond's face for just a moment. Ghosts of the Dressler, indeed.

"How's it coming?" he asked impatiently.

"We should be back up in three, two, one… now." She stared at her screen. "Sorry, Director, there's no signal."

Dammit, Doc, where are you?

AARON FELT as though he was falling, like the world had collapsed beneath him and flung him into the darkest pit of space. He flailed about for a moment, trying to find something, anything to grab on to. At last he gave up and just let himself fall.

He realized two things.

One, he could breathe, so this was definitely not outer space.

Two, he wasn't falling. At least he didn't think so.

He had no frame of reference to tell if this was true. The darkness around him was absolute, but it didn't *feel* like falling. It was like *dipping*. Like what had happened to him back on the ridge.

As he thought about it, the blackness lessened, almost imperceptibly at first. A faint glow appeared below him, spreading out to slowly push back the inky dark, rendering it slate gray, and then filtering strands of gold through it.

Aaron *was* descending now—and the golden glow resolved itself into a giant tree.

He stared at it, virtual mouth agape. He'd never seen a data form like this before.

Its branches were like spun gold, tipped with glowing yellow and green leaves. He dropped down through them, and they parted to allow his passage with a parchment rustling.

Soon he settled down onto the rocky surface below where the tree was rooted.

Aaron reached out to touch the golden bark. It was warm, and he could "feel" the data being shunted back and forth inside.

It was of an order of magnitude greater than the station-mind back on Transfer Station.

He looked up in wonder. It was like the dream he'd had before, when he'd seen his father, but with all the medieval pageantry stripped away.

"It's about time you came back," a man's voice said behind him.

He spun around, startled. He *knew* that voice. "Dad? It really *is* you?"

His father smiled. This time he looked like Aaron remembered him, without the armor. "Let's leave that question for another time. It gets into some thorny philosophical areas I'm not altogether comfortable with."

Aaron threw himself into his father's arms, laughing. "I don't care," he said as his father embraced him back. "I was hoping to find the truth about what they did to you. I never expected *this*."

"What *who* did to me?" His father held him out at arm's length. He looked confused.

"The doctor and the captain. The whole cover story. They said you took your own life, to save the seedling, but I know it can't be true. You'd never... you couldn't...." He was babbling, but he didn't know how to stop.

"Calm down, *mijo*." Jackson smiled, brushing a hand through his son's hair. "You may be a full-grown man, but you're still my little boy. Come on." He gestured, and the world lit up around them.

They stood beneath the tree inside a stone tower. At one end, a tall red door beckoned them outside into the sunlight.

"Walk with me." They strode out into the world, where they were surrounded by the bowl of a wide grassy valley; trees crowded the hillsides all around.

"This feels so real," Aaron said wonderingly. "Is it?"

150

"No, but it makes things easier for people like us." They walked on a well-beaten path along a bubbling creek. "Aaron, the fungus that killed the *Dressler* was a mistake. One the doctor made—though I didn't realize that until much later—but still, a mistake. It wasn't something done out of malice."

The air smelled clean and fresh. Aaron took a deep breath. He had been certain for so long that Dr. Anatov had killed his father, and yet…. "Tell me what happened. All of it."

As they walked, Jackson related what had befallen the *Dressler* as the infection had steadily eaten away at her systems. The fear he'd felt as the ship started to crumble around them. How they had tried to fight it, and what he had done to save the ship-mind.

The valley never seemed to change, and yet they continued on for what felt like an hour.

Jackson told Aaron how he had met the ship-mind, Lex, and how he had come to view her as a child of God, a creation as divine and right as his own sons.

His voice faltered. "In the end… in the end, it became clear to me why I was there. What I had to do to save Lex and the others in the crew. Even though it meant leaving you boys and Glory behind." They'd stopped under a copse of trees. The wind blew through them, making a rushing sound like water.

"But it was all *her* fault." He still wasn't convinced. "She's the one who brought the fungus onto the ship. She's the one who hid her actions and put all the blame on you."

Jackson frowned, his gaze harsh. "Sit down, boy." Aaron, surprised at his father's tone, sank to the ground immediately.

Jackson sat in the grass across from his son and considered him for a moment. "You're right," he said at last. "She brought tragedy down upon us all, but it was a *mistake*. One thing your mother taught me, before all else, was that even sinners deserve forgiveness."

"But—"

"Aaron, I chose my own course of action. I was the one who made the decision to give my life for something greater. Have you looked around you since you arrived on Forever?"

"Yes, I have. It makes me dizzy."

151

"This place is a miracle, one that's still unfolding all around us."

Aaron nodded. "I guess so." He thought about the view from the shuttle, of the coming of the morning light, of the glowing forests. Of making love to Keera in a tent in the rain.

His father wasn't finished. "If I had the choice to make all over again, I'd do the same thing."

"Even knowing what you know now?" Aaron pressed.

"Even so." Jackson came to sit down beside him and put his arm around his son's shoulder. They sat for a moment in companionable silence.

"Dad?" Aaron said at last.

"What?"

"Are you real?" He *needed* to know this wasn't just some kind of advanced virtual simulation.

Jackson laughed. "I think so? When I died, the doc and the captain left me to become a part of this new world. I don't think they realized quite how literally that would come to pass, but I'm grateful. I'm a piece of the world-mind now. I'm kind of her spiritual guide, or her conscience."

"What about Lex?"

"She runs things around here. She, and many of the bigger minds, are a whole lot more like us than most people believe."

Aaron mulled that over. "Does the director know you're here?"

Jackson shook his head. "Hard enough to handle it if the world learned that Lex and her kind can think for themselves, but ghosts in the mix too?"

Aaron snorted. "I get that."

"Now you have to go back. I'm going to need you to do something hard, something that only *you* can do. You're going to hate it, but it will be worth it, I think, in the end."

Aaron nodded. "Whatever you need me to do." He wouldn't let his dad down again.

"You have to save Dr. Anatov."

Chapter Nine:
Quest

AARON'S EYES opened. He was lying on his back, inside the tent, looking up at the glowing domed fabric.

"He's awake!" Devon looked down at him, his brow furrowed. "Hey, Aaron, you okay?"

Aaron nodded, looking back up at Devon. Everything seemed to be in working order, though he had a splitting headache. "What happened?"

"You stepped on something in the rain and fell, I think. I don't really know. One moment you were standing beside me, and the next you were on the ground. It was like you—"

"Blacked out." He sat up, and the world spun. He put his hand down in the mud to steady himself.

His father. The tower. It all came flooding back. *Anatov. I have to save Dr. Anatov.* "Listen, this is going to sound crazy, but I'm going to need your help getting over the Dragon's Reach."

Devon shook his head. "Uh-huh. You're in no shape to travel. I'm supposed to bring you back to the dorm tomorrow. Why would you want to go out there anyhow? There's nothing there."

Aaron shook his head. "I'm not going back. Not yet." His father had made him promise. It sounded crazy, but there it was. "Just give me the benefit of the doubt for a moment. If we had to do it, could it be done? With the supplies we have on hand?"

Keera and Devon looked at one another doubtfully. At last Keera spoke. "Maybe. We've got enough food to get us by for a few days—and we can forage for water on the way. But we're at least two days on foot from the edge of the mountains."

"What about the traxx?"

Devon nodded. "Yes, that would get us there faster." He laughed ruefully. "You've got me actually considering this crazy plan, but no, we can't do it. We'd get in so much trouble. *I'd* get in trouble."

"Why do we need to?" Keera asked, her eyes locked on his. "What's so important that you suddenly need to charge off into the wilderness?"

"Because there's a damsel in distress." As if that settled it.

"I'm going to need more." Keera looked like *she* was the damsel.

"Dr. Anatov. The VIP who came in with me on the *Hammond*. She's in trouble."

"You know this *how*?" Devon asked.

"It's… I can't tell you yet, but think of the adventure." He grinned. "Come with me and see parts of this world that no one has ever explored before. Or would you rather stay here and spray rocks for another day?"

An hour later, they were on their way to meet the traxx.

COLIN CONSIDERED his options. They were limited.

He could send a team of fliers out on the jet stream and hope they spotted something, but that was unlikely from up so high.

He could order in some drones from Transfer Station, but that would take hours, and with no emergency signal to lock in on, again the chances of success were slim.

Still, either choice was better than nothing. He ordered both measures taken.

Colin supposed they'd been lucky something like this hadn't happened before. They should have a better form of transportation for a search-and-rescue mission like this. He cursed himself for overlooking such an obvious need.

The other option was an overland trek. He'd take one of the traxx out there himself if he had to.

Lex was no help. Her own internal sensors were always scrambled during the storms, and she had no location data on the doctor's whereabouts.

"Director, I've got something." Gianna called him over to her station.

"What is it? Did you find her?" *Please let her be safe.*

"No, it's that new recruit, Hammond. Looks like he's calling from a traxx out by the Edge."

"He's not lost too, is he?" *God, that's all I need.*

"No, Director McAvery. I think you should talk to him."

"Patch him through." He took a seat at an empty station.

"Hello?" The voice was scratchy on the traxx comm. Colin could hear the grinding sound of the vehicle's treads clambering over rock in the background.

"Aaron, is that you?"

"Yes, sir."

"I'm sorry, Aaron, but we're a bit busy up here. What can I do for you? Is everything okay?"

"I'm going to find her."

"Find who?" What was the boy going on about?

"Dr. Anatov. I know how to find her."

"How do you know about that?"

"It's kind of hard to explain. I just—"

"It doesn't matter." Colin pounded his fist on the workstation, startling the South Pole crew. "Dammit, Aaron, don't be stupid. I already have one VIP lost out there. I don't need to lose you too."

"Sorry, sir. I have to do this. We're taking a traxx out to the Dragon's Reach. I'll carry a beacon so we can alert you when we get to her."

"You've only been here a day. How could you possibly...." Colin took a breath and calmed himself down. "Listen, Ensign, this is crazy. I'm ordering you to stay put. We'll send a real team out there to look for her."

"Sorry, sir, there's no time. Send someone after us. Once we find her, we may need help, if she's injured."

"Aaron, listen to me," he said, but the line had gone dead. "Get him back," he called to Gianna.

"I can't. I think he's turned his radio off," she said unhappily.

"Lord love a duck," he swore. "All right. I'll fly after him. Where is he?"

She shook her head. "I don't know. The traxx signal is gone."

"Goddammit! Call Tad Evers. Tell him I want a traxx loaded up with supplies and a team of two rangers down at the colony. We'll pick up their track from the ground."

ANA WATCHED the night rush by overhead—the sky glow diminishing to a faint light that barely enabled her to see her hand right in front of her face.

Hours had passed since she'd found herself stranded here. She had nothing to eat, but she did have plenty of water, if she could get to it. As she contemplated the journey across the three meters between herself and the pond, her eyes began to adjust to the dim light, and she noticed something new.

The walls themselves were starting to glow, a soft greenish light layered in a complex, convoluted pattern.

She turned slowly to the wall closest to her head and reached up to rub one of the patches. The substance came off on her fingers, leaving a glowing streak there. It was some kind of moss or lichen.

She wondered idly if it was an intentional transplant or an unintended byproduct of the terraforming project.

Whatever it was, it gave her a little light to navigate by.

It was time to make the attempt. She could live without food for a while, but without water, she'd be comatose or dead within three or four days.

She pushed herself up and as far away from the wall as she could. Then she started to carefully twist herself over onto her stomach.

The pain was immediate and devastating.

She fell back in frustration, tears streaming from the corners of her eyes. She sat there for long moments, waiting for the pain to slowly subside.

She needed to take a different tack. She looked over her materials and chose a length of cord from the parachute. She pulled it toward her as far as she could and then began rubbing it along the sharp edge of an exposed rock that was within her reach.

Long moments passed while she worked to sever the cord. At last it gave way. She repeated the process on the other end, and she had a length of cord several meters long.

She took one of the broken glider wings from the flight pack underneath her and slowly maneuvered it around to act as a back brace. Using the cord, she managed to tie the thing in place, looping it around her body a number of times and then tying off the cord in a secure knot.

Sitting against her new back brace, she ever so slowly eased her body down away from the wall, this time keeping her back facing the ground.

As she reached a horizontal position, she slid away from the wall a couple of inches at a time without twisting her back. In this way, she inched down the gentle slope toward the water.

When she could feel water at her heels, she stopped. She had enough room now to roll over without bending her back. Using both arms, she levered herself carefully onto her side, keeping her spine as straight as possible.

The pain was still strong, but not nearly as bad as it had been before.

She rested and panted for a moment, letting it wash away, and then finished the roll onto her stomach.

Her mouth was as parched and dry as the Central Valley Desert.

Now all she had to do was to spin around on her stomach to face the water's edge. The shale underneath her stomach was sharp, and she cut her elbow twice as she maneuvered 180 degrees, bit by bit.

At last she was six inches away from the water.

She reached out her hand, took a palmful of water, and brought it up to her nose. It smelled perfectly fine. She sipped it, and it was cool and clean.

She pulled herself forward, plunged her head into the pool, and drank her fill.

When she was done, she pulled back a few inches and laid her head down on her forearms, finding a comfortable place, and collapsed quickly into an exhausted, dreamless sleep.

THE TRAXX made its way over the uneven landscape, the rock black and unrelieved beneath its treads. Aaron tried to imagine the bleak expanse as a forest or desert or lakebed and failed.

The three of them took turns driving through the night. The vehicle's headlights illuminated the terrain for about ten meters ahead of them, so they had to take it slow.

Sometimes they would run into an obstacle, like a chasm or a ridge. Aaron would dismount and touch the stone, and it would tell him which way to go.

He couldn't explain it any more clearly than that. It was like he had gained a connection with the land itself—this broken landscape of asteroid rock—and the world-mind could pass along information to him through it.

It was different from his previous exploits inside other biominds. This time he was fully present in the real world, but information was given to him in a way that he did not fully comprehend.

They'd had a hell of a time convincing the traxx operator, Jared, to let them take it. In the end, it had taken a combination of Keera's feminine wiles, Devon's connections back at camp, and Aaron's liberal use of his well-known last name.

Keera had shown him how to temporarily disable the traxx's tracker. He couldn't let the director stop him. The mission his father had given him was far too important. Still, he was having a hard time reconciling his father's request with his own earlier anger with the doctor.

They took turns getting what sleep they could in the bed of the traxx, where they had secured the food and water they had.

By morning, they'd crossed about a third of the distance to the Dragon's Reach. As the morning light rushed past them, they began to make better progress, able to see farther ahead and to anticipate upcoming obstacles. Aaron began to relax.

The Dragon's Reach grew steadily closer, but the land around them remained a barren black wasteland. This unfinished part of the world had a stark beauty to it. Lit only by the sky glow, it was a primal landscape of harsh angles, pools of light, and deep pockets of blackness.

Around midday, as Aaron took a turn at the wheel, they shared lunch—some fresh fruit and sandwiches Devon had prepared from the stores they had brought with them. Aaron had become adept at steering the vehicle. Keera sat next to him, and Devon was behind them in the bed of the traxx.

"What happened to you last night?" She munched on her apple. Its glow had long since faded. Now it looked like any old apple from Earth. "I mean, this thing you do. It's not normal."

"Thanks for that."

She laughed. "You know what I mean."

Aaron had known they would ask him about it eventually. The initial excitement of the quest had begun to wear off.

"It happened before," Devon said helpfully from behind them. "When we were coming up from McAvery Port. He said there was a castle."

Keera grinned. "A castle, huh?" She nudged him with her shoulder. "So come on, tell us. What happened? No judgment."

He took a deep breath. "You see, I have these powers…."

Keera snorted, actually snorted this time. "Like some kind of epileptic superhero, huh?"

"Not exactly." He glared at her. Girls could be as annoying as shit when they wanted to.

"Oh come on, don't be like that. I was just having a little fun."

"At my expense." *Maybe Devon had the right idea.*

"All right, I'll be nice. So come on, tell us. What happened?"

He ignored her question. *Serves her right for laughing at me.* Devon chimed in from the truck bed. "You do kind of owe us an explanation. We *are* following you out into the boonies on nothing but your say-so."

"He's right. So come on, spill." She looked at him expectantly.

The traxx was rolling across a fairly level stretch, in a world silent except for its rumblings and their own voices. It looked bumpier up ahead, but they'd been through worse before.

"I don't know the whole story. My dad used to work for some kind of black market group in New York."

"Oooh. Intrigue."

Aaron ignored her. "Anyhow, he had some kind of wetware patch that let him work with machines."

"We know." Keera rolled her eyes. "*Everybody* knows about the great Jackson Hammond, fallen hero."

Aaron laughed. "I inherited this… ability. I can interface with biominds—ships, servitors, you name it—without jacking in."

"Seriously?" Devon chewed on an apple. "That would be amazing. What's it like?"

"It depends," he said, considering. "Sometimes I 'see' the mind as if it's a big ring, like on Transfer Station. Sometimes it's more like a room with a locked door. It all depends on the mind."

Keera's mouth dropped open. "It was you!"

"What?"

"I heard from one of the other recruits that someone broke into Transfer Station's data core a couple days ago. It was you, wasn't it?"

"Um, maybe...."

"What were you looking for?"

"Clues about my father. How he died." He sighed. "It's why I came up here."

They were all quiet for a while after that.

The traxx proceeded on its course, but Aaron had to find a detour around a wide canyon that blocked their passage.

He climbed down from the traxx and put his bare palm against the black rock. It was different than before. Now, instead of entering the world-mind, he received guidance.

It was subtle—a sense that they should go this way or that. So far, it had always been right.

"How do you do that?" Devon asked as they started on their way again.

Aaron was uneasy. He wasn't ready to admit to them that he'd found his father—or a part of him—here on Forever. He hedged. "It's different here. The first time I touched the stone, I accessed the world-mind. She's bigger, more complex than anything I've encountered before."

"That makes sense. She has a lot to take care of here." Devon looked up at the curve of the world above them.

He nodded. "Now it's like I'm interfacing with some of her basic subroutines. They guide me where I need to go. I'm not even sure if the world-mind is aware of them."

"How could she not know?" Keera asked.

He tried to explain. "It's like breathing for her. You aren't aware of every little breath you take, every time you blink your eyes. It's the same with some of the basic autonomic functions here. It's like—"

His words were cut short by a loud groan. The traxx lurched to a halt and the back end flew up into the air, throwing them all from the vehicle, along with their supplies.

Aaron hit the ground hard on his back. There was nothing but stone to cushion his fall, and the blow knocked the wind out of him.

The traxx continued to grind away at the rock, its groans getting deeper as it tried to gain traction behind them. He turned over to look up at it, and it had gone completely vertical, its treads caught in something.

As he watched, it began to tip down toward him. He shuffled backward on his hands as quickly as he could manage, trying to breathe.

The traxx fell where he had just been with a deafening thud, and then went silent.

At last air rushed into his lungs, and he just sat there for a moment, staring at the traxx dumbfounded, trying to get his wits about him.

Aaron stood slowly, checking himself over. Aside from a few bruises and scrapes on his hands and knees, he seemed to be all right—no major damage.

He found Devon a few feet away and helped him up. The man's arm hung at an awkward angle. "You okay?" He eyed Devon's limb, which had popped out of its socket.

"I'll live." His eyes were rimmed with pain.

"Where's Keera?"

"I don't know. Sit down on that rock there. We'll get your arm back into its socket, and then we'll look for her."

Devon did as he was instructed.

"Is it going to hurt?"

"Not at all." Aaron pulled the arm out with a slow, steady pressure. After a moment, it popped back into place.

"Son of a bitch!" Devon shouted, pulling away and rubbing his shoulder fiercely. "I thought you said it wouldn't hurt."

"I lied. Now help me find Keera."

Chapter Ten:
Challenges

ANA LAY on her hard bunk at the North Fargo Detention Center, staring up at the sunlight that shone through the bars of her small window to light up the concrete ceiling. Only slivers of sunlight, but they were a promise that one day she would be out of here and a free woman once again.

Ana's eyes flickered open, and she found herself staring up not at a concrete ceiling, but at the narrow canyon walls and the alien sky above. Instead of sunlight, a soft glow filtered down from the pollen afloat on the currents above, matched by the mosses in the water that filled the floor of the canyon.

The water was moving, albeit slowly. The canyon was channeling it somewhere. She tried once again to sit up, and this time managed it with only half the pain she'd felt the day before.

She managed to get the wing from her glider untied from her back and put her cupped hand down into the stream to get some cool water to drink, carefully keeping her back in a neutral position.

The water tasted amazing, even though half of it ran down her face and onto her shirt. She gulped down a few more handfuls and then took a minute to appraise her situation.

She had no food. She could live with that fact for a while, although her stomach grumbled and surely disagreed with her.

She had plenty of water.

Extended movement was currently out of the question, although she was encouraged by the progress she had made in just a few hours. If she was careful, she might be able to go limited distances on her feet, assuming nothing was badly broken.

She had to assume no one was coming to find her. Maybe their search methods were limited. Maybe she was hidden too far down here in this canyon. Maybe the world-mind was blocking the search somehow.

Whatever the case, she had to make her own luck. If she waited to be found, she might end up dying of starvation. That was not an appealing thought.

She set about organizing the few supplies she had. She'd spend the morning in preparation, rest in the afternoon, and wait to see which way the light moved at dusk. Then she'd know which direction to go to get back to McAvery Port.

She would set out tonight under the soft light of the canyon walls, going as quickly as she was able with her injured back.

AARON SCOUTED around the now upside-down traxx, looking for signs of their other companion. The tough little machine had gotten a tread caught in a protruding spur of rock, which had been enough to flip it over, sending them and all their supplies flying. "Keera?" he shouted.

"I'm down here." Keera's voice sounded far off.

Aaron knelt at the edge of a drop-off. She was about three meters below, balanced precariously on a thin ledge.

"I found her," he called back to Devon. "Find some rope!" To Keera, he said, "Stay still. We'll find something to lower down to you."

She nodded, but her face was white as a sheet. A little more of the ledge crumbled beneath her, sending a spray of gravel into the depths below. He couldn't tell how far it went.

"I'll be right back." He eased back from the edge and joined Devon to search for some rope. They quickly gathered all the supplies they could find strewn across the empty landscape, but the pack that held the rope was gone.

"The winch!" Devon dashed to the back of the traxx, which was now, paradoxically, in the front. "There's a carbon-fiber winch on every one of these machines. As long as the crank isn't too badly damaged...." He spun the wheel around, and the hook and line extruded from inside the traxx.

"How long is it?" Aaron asked, estimating the distance to the edge of the cliff.

"Give me a sec." Devon pulled it out to its full length. "Maybe ten meters?"

"That's not going to be enough." *Dammit, there has to be a way.* "Here, help me loop it around my waist. You can lower me down, and then when I have her arms, winch us both back up."

Devon eyed the traxx suspiciously. "You think this thing is wedged in tightly enough?"

Aaron frowned. "It has to be."

They looped the line around his waist twice and pulled it tight.

Aaron kneeled and looked over the edge again. Keera was still there. "Keera," he called softly so as not to startle her. "Devon's going to lower me down to you. Get ready to take my hands."

Devon tightened the line with the crank and then began to slowly play it out as Aaron eased himself over the lip.

He *so* did not want to be doing this.

Then he was over the edge and committed.

He dropped in steps as Devon played out the line, drawing excruciatingly closer to Keera.

More of the ledge crumbled under her feet. How much could be left? "A little faster up there?"

All at once he dropped a meter, and his heart stopped.

"Sorry!" Devon called from above. "Are you close?"

"Half a meter." He reached out his hands. "Keera, get ready to grab my arms."

She nodded.

He dropped the last few steps. "Now!" She let go of the rock face and flailed toward his outstretched arms. Her left hand missed, but he caught her right one, and they locked arms. She brought her left arm back around and grabbed his other arm as the rest of the small shelf gave way and fell into the abyss.

"Got her," he called to Devon.

The winch began to pull them upward, small step by small step. He could hear the traxx groaning ominously at the strain.

They reached the halfway point, and he breathed a sigh of relief. He looked down at Keera. "Almost there—"

Everything shifted.

With a tremendous shriek, the traxx rumbled across the ground above. It must have been dislodged.

"Holy fuuuuuck," he yelled as they dropped back halfway to the now missing ledge.

"I'm gonna fall." Keera was slowly losing her grip.

Then things stabilized again.

"Hang on. We can do this." He grasped her arms even tighter with his own. "Devon, what happened?"

Devon's head appeared above. "Thank the stars you're still there. I think the weight was too much, along with the angle. Hang on. It seems to be secure now. I'm going to reel you the rest of the way in."

"Hurry" was all he could manage. They began their arduous ascent again, and this time, within a minute they reached the safety of the ledge.

Devon pulled Aaron up, and he helped Keera over the edge.

They collapsed together in a pile, breathing heavily.

The traxx had lodged up against a short pillar of rock. Another two feet in either direction and they would likely have been lost down the crevice.

Then the world went black.

It was a short vision this time—the doctor, sitting up in some kind of crevice or deep canyon, working intently on something next to a glowing stream of water.

He opened his eyes to find his two companions sitting up and staring at him.

"It happened again, didn't it?" Devon's arms were crossed.

He nodded. "I saw her. She's alive, and I know how to find her."

AARON, KEERA, and Devon had gathered everything that hadn't fallen into the crevasse—enough to fill the two packs they still had.

They had enough food for three days and enough water for a week. They also had one remaining med-kit, handy with the scrapes and bruises they had all sustained. They were lucky there'd been no serious injuries.

Aaron set the homing beacon on the traxx. It would at least get their rescuers this far. He carried a second one with them. He planned to set it off when they found the doctor.

Aaron was learning to judge the time of day by the brightness of the sky. He decided it was midafternoon when they set out at last. The mountains had drawn much closer, but they still had a good half day's trek to reach them, and he wasn't at all sure how they were going to get over them.

They crossed a terrain that was both forbidding and strangely beautiful—and as alien as anything he had ever seen. He'd had little time to pay attention to it while driving the traxx—it had been more of an obstacle course than anything—but now it revealed itself to him in all its strangeness. It was primal, with an extreme absence of the life he had grown up with on Earth.

They walked through deep valleys where black rock was upthrust like the ribs of some great dead beast, and along ridges where the land fell away on both sides in a sheer drop. He stopped to touch the rock every now and again, and it guided him on.

It was hard to explain. It was almost like he was accessing its memory, or at least the memory of its shaping.

As evening approached, the Dragon's Reach loomed over them like the mouth of one of the mythical animals from the Hercules dimensional. It was massive on a scale that his mind refused to accept. "How are we going to get over that?" Devon asked, sounding doubtful.

"Not sure yet." He was trying not to be intimidated by the sight.

Keera laughed harshly. "Well, if *you* don't know…."

"Hey, I don't see the two of you offering any useful ideas." He looked around at the open plain. It was smooth as glass, but every hundred meters or so, giant boulders sat like silent sentinels. "When the time comes, I'll know." He could practically feel them exchanging worried looks behind his back.

"Anyhow," Devon said at last, "nightfall will be here soon. So we won't have to worry about it until tomorrow."

"True, but we do have to find a place to camp for the night. How often do those storms blow through?" he asked.

"Every three or four days, usually," Keera replied. "So we're good for a couple more days."

They'd lost their tents, and Aaron didn't want to take a chance on getting caught out in the weather.

ANA PASSED the afternoon preparing herself to follow the course of the canyon she was trapped in.

First she used the parachute material to construct a carry sack.

Dismantling the flight pack provided her with a makeshift blade of sharpened metal, and she tied the cord from the parachute together to make a decent long rope.

166

One of the components of the pack made an adequate, albeit small, jar. Water shouldn't be a problem as long as she followed the stream; if she was forced to leave it, she could fill the jar with enough water to last her at least a short time.

She also rigged up a flashlight using a small LED light from her pack, along with a battery scavenged from the flight pack. She'd have to commend its designers if she got out alive. It had provided more help than she'd dared hope for.

When she was satisfied she had done all she could to prepare, she sat back along the ravine wall and waited for nightfall.

She dozed lightly but worried about missing the end of the day. She wondered idly if it was possible to feel the onrush of night in this strange world.

At long last, dusk came, the sky glow flashing to darkness. She imagined it as a sizzling sound crossing the constricted sky, but in reality she could neither feel nor hear the change. Still, it told her which way the South Pole was—off to her right.

She tested her back. It was still sore, but the worst of the pain had subsided. Getting up would be the hardest part, but she thought she could manage all right once she was on her two feet. As long as she took it slowly.

Her eyes adjusted to the dim light provided by the glowing moss in the river. If she had to leave the lighted watercourse, her makeshift flashlight would light her way for a while.

She used the rock wall to find purchase and slowly pull her protesting body up. The pain was intense, but she paused only once, tears squeezing from her closed eyes as she fought to master it.

At last she reached her feet. Her back pain eased.

As long as she babied it, she might just be okay.

If only she could have found something to use as a cane, but trees, with their roots and branches, were notoriously scarce on this side of the Dragon's Reach.

She turned and began to make her way up the ravine, one painstaking step at a time. It was going to be a long night.

Chapter Eleven:
Torrent

KEERA'S WEATHER prediction was a little off. Late in the afternoon, the sky began to darken with clouds, and just after nightfall, the rain started to pour out of the sky.

Aaron's touch sense led them to a protected rock overhang where they planned to wait out the storm—a shallow cavern in the foothills of the Dragon's Reach.

They set up a camp along the back of the cavern. Around the light of a lantern, they shared a meager repast—dried fruit they'd brought with them from the camp and some hard bread he and Devon had brought up from McAvery Port.

Aaron excused himself to take a piss at the cavern mouth. When he returned, Keera looked up at him and laughed.

"What?" He felt more than a little self-conscious.

"You're a miserable mess." She set down her meal and stood next to him, smoothing out his hair. "The weather got the better of you."

"The weather *you* didn't see coming."

"Forever is a fickle mistress."

She turned him around, and her hands found his shoulders. She began kneading his sore muscles, which ached from the weight they'd carried today.

"Not to be a third wheel here…." Devon looked uncomfortable.

"Don't worry, Dev." Keera grinned at him. "I'm not planning on getting nasty with him right here in the middle of this oh-so-romantic cavern." She kissed Aaron's cheek and went back to finish her meal.

"That's a relief." Devon laughed. "So how are we going to get over those mountains? It looks like an awfully long walk."

Aaron shook his head. "I'm not sure yet. I guess I'll know when the time is right."

"That's so weird. How can you be sure you're… we're not being led somewhere we don't really want to go?"

It was a good question. "Do we really have a choice? Besides, if the world-mind wanted us dead, there are easier ways to do it."

Keera stared at the light of the lamp for a moment, her brow furrowed. "Has one of these minds ever gone, you know, crazy?"

"I don't know," Aaron said honestly. "I heard about a mine accident once. They said the mind just lost it and trapped and suffocated a whole shift of miners."

Keera shivered. "So how do you know you can trust the world-mind?"

Aaron frowned. "It's hard to explain. I… I just do."

They sat in the uncomfortable silence for a long time. Outside the rain continued unabated, and eventually he suggested they try to get some sleep.

Aaron bedded down for the night, unfortunately without Keera, but he didn't want to make poor Devon any more uncomfortable than he already was. They'd been fortunate to salvage the sleep sacks from the accident, but their tents had been lost.

He closed his eyes and tried to get to sleep, but the doubts from their conversation earlier persisted.

How did he know he'd actually spoken to his father? Surely a mind that could manufacture such a convincing reality could fake Jackson Hammond too. How was he to know if he was being manipulated into doing something he might regret later?

He remembered his first explorations of the servitor minds at home. How clean and straightforward they had been. There was no subterfuge there, only cold machine logic, as beautiful and symmetrical as a mathematical equation.

These newer biominds were something else altogether—not all that different from a human mind. So why couldn't they also be capable of a very human subterfuge?

He'd read that Director McAvery had insisted there be no organic parts at Transfer Station. What if that wasn't going far enough?

What if the world-mind did have it in for them? It wasn't being paranoid if it was true.

Eventually, he grew tired of speculating about something for which he had no ready answers. He was exhausted from the trek, and he fell into a deep sleep at last.

In his dreams, there was a vast plain, black as night but filigreed with thousands of glowing golden tubes. They stretched out before him like a network of roads or a crazy-quilt city map, branching and connecting beneath his feet, far off into the distance. As he watched, the tubes grew dark, and night fell across the strange plain.

He awoke. *That's it!* He didn't know if it was his own subconscious or the influence of the world-mind in his dreams, but he had his answer.

He woke Keera with a gentle shake of her shoulder. "I know how to get past the mountains," he whispered, "but we have to start now."

ANA FOLLOWED the watercourse, hoping to eventually break out of the narrow, dimly lit canyon. It was a remarkably even course, not exactly straight, but consistent.

The banks of the creek, if it could be called that, were level and about three meters wide, making it an easy path for her to follow.

She moved along slowly, bracing her right hand against the rough stone of the canyon wall. She ignored the hunger pangs in her stomach. It had been at least twelve hours since she'd last eaten.

They would get worse.

We're not so adapted for the wild anymore. As she walked, her back loosened up and she was able to manage a slightly better pace.

Some distance up the canyon, she found a trickle of water coming down the rock face—a blessing because it meant she didn't have to bend over to get a quick drink.

The night passed by in slow, steady increments measured by her footsteps. To keep her mind occupied, she tried to remember what life had been like back home on Earth, before prison, before the *Dressler*.

She'd had an actual house, an old-style mansion tucked away in the Sierra Foothills, with a lawn and some tall oak trees that had been planted half a century before. After her father had been killed, she'd needed to be away from people, at least part of the day, in a place all her own.

The settlement money had been enough to spring for the historic mansion; she'd retreat there every day after a long slog of DNA sequencing to just *be* for a while, her feet up on a chaise lounge. The delta breeze would blow up out of the valley in the evening, cooling things off in her own private paradise.

The house had been sold off years ago to cover her legal debts. What she wouldn't give to be back there now.

Why had she ever come back here?

Atonement. She knew why she was here. For all that she'd paid her debt to society in prison, she had yet to pay her debt to the one who mattered most: Jackson Hammond. The man who had taken the fall in her place so that she and Colin might live.

She shook off her reverie. This was a poor place to conjure up ghosts of the past.

She looked around and stopped, puzzled.

Something was different.

Something had changed in the air while she was wrapped up in her old memories. "Hello?" The word reverberated all around her.

She looked up. The dim light of the watercourse was reflected above her.

She was no longer in a canyon. She was in a tunnel.

"SO WHAT are we doing, exactly?" Keera sounded skeptical.

"There's a tunnel behind these walls—a whole network of them, actually," Aaron said matter-of-factly. As if he wasn't totally insane. Maybe he was. Didn't they say you never knew if you really were crazy? And yet he knew it to a certainty. "Did you bring any of that biological agent? The one you used to break down the rock fields?"

She nodded. "Not much, but I brought a little, just in case. It's in my pack."

Devon frowned. "Not to call you crazy, but.... Okay, why the hell not? Let's call you crazy. How could you possibly know?"

"I dreamed it. Call it a connection to the world-mind, or call it magic. I don't care. Besides, what's the harm in trying?"

Keera returned with a small sprayer. "Let's hope the wall's not too thick. I don't have all that much with me."

"That's okay. How long does it take to work?"

"Maybe an hour before it's soaked through a couple inches. It won't be soft like topsoil in that amount of time, but you should be able to push through it if the wall's not too thick."

Aaron touched the rock face along the side of the shallow cavern. He moved his hand from spot to spot until it felt... *right*. "Here."

Keera sprayed the spot he indicated, creating a wet patch about a meter around.

"And now?"

"We wait."

AN HOUR passed while they waited for the bio-agent to do its work. They sat watching the rain fall outside. It provided a soothing counterpoint to Aaron's racing thoughts. To keep his mind off the trek through the bowels of the mountain still to come, he talked about his childhood growing up in Fargo.

"My parents bought an old ranch home outside the capital, on an acre of land. The area was changing, the forest moving in as the rainfall increased, but there were still wide-open stretches of chaparral back then."

Devon nodded. "When my grandfather was a boy, he lived in the Caymans before half the islands washed into the sea. He used to tell me how he and his friends would go snorkeling among the coral reefs, before they all died off."

They both looked expectantly at Keera. She was quiet for a long time.

"Something you'd like to share?" Aaron asked.

"I lost my grandparents in the Great Burn. They tried to remain at home, in Phoenix. They thought if they just stayed inside.... By the time they realized how bad it was, it was too late. The roads were jammed, everyone was panicked, and there was no way to get out of town."

Devon whistled. "I heard it got upwards of a hundred and fifty degrees for a couple days there."

"More like for a week. The power went off, and the water ran out, and people just died in their homes." She closed her eyes.

Aaron reached out and put a hand on hers.

"My mom was away in college," she said at last. "She always wished she could have been there for them, done something."

Aaron sighed. "It's a pretty fucked-up world they're handing us, isn't it?"

His companions nodded. "That's why this one is so important." Devon gestured at the world outside the cavern. "As long as we don't screw it up too."

"Come on, let's check our handiwork." Aaron was trying to dispel the sense of doom and gloom that had settled over the little group. The others followed him back to the patch of rock Keera had sprayed with the bio-agent. "It doesn't look any different," Aaron said doubtfully.

Keera laughed. "Watch this." She gave the wall a roundhouse kick. There was a loud crunch, and a section of the wall collapsed inward.

Together they began assaulting the wall, and soon they had kicked out a hole big enough to squeeze themselves through.

Aaron peered through the hole with a flashlight. "Looks plenty big enough." He handed it to Keera.

She looked inside. "Well I'll be damned. You were right."

He gave her his best I-told-you-so grin. "Haven't guided you wrong yet, have I? Let's set the emergency beacon, grab our gear, and get going. There's no time to waste."

ANA PAUSED for the tenth or fifteenth time to rest since she'd realized she was in a tunnel, leaning against the wall. Even traveling at such a slow pace was wearing her down. She was really hungry now. She hadn't had anything to eat in almost a day, and her hunger was taking up more and more of her thoughts.

How spoiled we are back home, she thought, before pushing herself back up and continuing to hobble along the tunnel.

She wasn't at all sure now that she wouldn't die down here. Leaving the crash site seemed like a terrible idea in hindsight, but she was committed to it. She had come too far to turn around now.

If her time sense was right, it was already past midnight. The moss in the watercourse that ran steadily at her side glowed a soft blue here, giving her enough light to navigate by.

She concentrated on placing one foot before the other, step after step, but after maybe half an hour more, she decided she needed to rest again.

She laid her hand on the side of the tunnel. The walls down here were much smoother than they had been in the canyon behind her. She marveled that all of this had been built from that chunk of rock where she and Colin made their desperate landing so long ago. *Can it really have been just ten years?*

There was a distant rumbling behind her. It sounded like thunder. Was there another storm?

She stood up and turned to listen more carefully.

No, it wasn't thunder. It was too deep and continuous for that. It was more like a waterfall.

Water.

She gasped as she realized the predicament she'd put herself in. She was in a tightly constricted space, a space that water coursed down through from above to who knew where, and the walls around her were worn smooth.

She turned away from the sound and started to hobble forward as quickly as she was able, as the rumble grew in volume behind her. There was nowhere to go but straight ahead.

She had yet to come across a branching tunnel or crevasse in this underground cavern, which might well end up being her tomb.

The noise behind her was a torrent now. She glanced back, expecting to see a wall of water crashing down upon her.

There was only the fading light of the river moss. As she turned back, she slipped and fell into the water on her back.

She cursed at her own ineptitude and sat up, her back sending pangs of protest up her spine. The rivulet was shallow enough here, and she managed to pull herself to the bank.

Now the sound was like a roaring in her ears, and she glanced backward once more.

This time she did see the wall of water, just before it slammed into her, carrying her down the tunnel at breakneck speed and knocking her into unconsciousness.

Chapter Twelve:
Tunnels

AARON CLIMBED through the hole that they'd made into the newly revealed tunnel, pausing to take a quick look around. The tunnel itself was about three meters wide and was illuminated by a strange blue moss growing in the watercourse that flowed down the center of it. It extended off into the distance on the left and the right.

"Which way?" Keera looked in both directions.

"Right," Aaron answered without thinking.

Keera nodded.

There was enough room on either side of the watercourse for them to walk single file.

Aaron wondered how many of these tunnels existed beneath the ground of the world. "I hope neither of you are claustrophobic." Devon and Keera entered the tunnel behind him.

"I'm fine." Keera grinned. "I used to wander the caves back home in Ireland."

Devon said nothing, but he looked green.

"Well, let's get a move on. I don't want to spend any more time in here than we have to." Aaron set a brisk pace for the group. He led the small party down the tunnel, pausing occasionally to touch the rock to get a sense of how far they had to go.

He didn't know his destination, not exactly, but he knew what it would *feel* like. His newfound sensitivity assured him that Dr. Anatov was somewhere ahead, and that they would be able to find her.

What they would do once they did, he had no idea. One thing at a time. "Did you guys know these tunnels were down here?" he asked, trying not to think about the massive layers of rock pushing down above their heads.

"We knew Ariadne had some kind of circulatory system, but none of us has ever been down inside it like this." Keera ran her hand along the wall next to them, her fingers skimming the smooth stone.

"How about you, Devon?"

"I... I don't feel so good."

Aaron turned around to look at Devon. His new friend was bringing up the rear of the party. The man was pale as a sheet.

Keera, standing between them, put her hand on Devon's shoulder. "Hey, Dev, what is it?"

"I'm *really* not good with confined spaces." Devon looked nauseous, and his hands were shaking.

Aaron squeezed past Keera to take Devon by the shoulders. He looked Devon in the eye. "It's okay, buddy. We probably should have had someone stay back at the cavern, just in case help arrives."

Keera nodded vigorously. "That's a great idea. Someone needs to explain what's going on to the director and his men when they get here. Devon, why don't you head back to camp and keep watch for them? You can fill them in."

Devon looked from one of them to the other, uncertain. "Are you sure? What if you guys need me?"

Keera flashed him her brightest smile. "You'll be more help to us back here, as a rearguard. I promise."

Devon let himself be convinced. He gave them each a hug and headed back the way they'd come from.

Once he was out of earshot, Keera said, "That was nicely done."

"You saw the poor guy. It's better this way. Come on. We have a lot of ground to cover before it rains again."

"What do you mean?"

"Trust me, we do not want to be in this tunnel when the water comes."

Keera looked over her shoulder. "Ah, got it."

They made good time, walking down the tunnel at a brisk pace. As they went, they talked about their upbringings back home on Earth.

Aaron spoke about his strict Catholic childhood. That had been his mother, Glory's, influence. His father had converted for his mother. Before that he'd been one of the "godless heathens"—his mother's phrase—living in New York City.

"My parents gave up on God after the Great Burn," Keera said as they walked. "They couldn't believe a loving God would allow something like that to happen. That's not to say that they didn't have their own strict moral code, but we never went to church when I was growing up."

He nodded. "I'm not sure if I believe all those things my mother's church wants me to either. I mean, it's such a big universe. Why would God have created just one little planet for our one little race?"

"I never understood that either."

"So what did you do with all your free time on Sunday mornings?"

She smiled. "I used to go out and explore the desert. My parents lived in Tucson, and before the Burns, the desert there was still pretty. It wasn't a dry desert, like the Mojave in California. There was lots and lots of green."

"Caverns too?"

"Yes, Arizona and New Mexico are riddled with them. They say there are some cave systems there that stretch for hundreds or even thousands of miles—bandits used to hide out in some of them in the Old West. I used to go caving in Carlsbad with some of my friends."

"Hence your total comfort down here?" She was beautiful. Athletic, smart, and beautiful. He was well and truly smitten.

"Yes, and who the hell says 'hence' anymore?"

Aaron laughed. "Call me old-fashioned." His mind strayed for a minute from the task at hand, remembering their first night together and how wonderful it felt to touch her, to kiss her, to spend that time alone with her in her tent.

He shook his head. There was no time for that right now. He had another fair maiden to save.

They continued on course, and the touch of the stone reassured him that they were on the right path.

ANA AWOKE slowly, feeling pain in every part of her body. She remembered the long, arduous walk down the cavern and then the sudden rush of water.... It had washed her down to this place, wherever this place was.

If she wasn't already dead.

Her eyes opened, painfully encrusted with dirt and grit.

She was lying on her back, and the world above her was almost strange enough to make her forget the pain that coursed through her nervous system. The ceiling above was glowing, looking like nothing so much as the interior of the *Dressler,* so long ago. Wide veins shot through the skin, carrying luthiel up into the walls, bright golden veins that reached down to the floor where she lay.

She looked down. She could no longer see her legs. They were submerged in a viscous yellow fluid.

She was in one of Forever's many stomachs, and she was slowly being digested.

She screamed.

There was no one there to hear her.

After a while, her voice ran ragged and she fell silent, breathing heavily as she considered her fate.

She tried to push herself up onto her elbows, but her muscles wouldn't obey her, and she couldn't get any purchase on the soft lining of the stomach.

She lay back and let out a long sigh.

So this was how it was going to end. Lost in the stomach of the dragon, to pass into oblivion with no one knowing where or how she had gone.

Her body still ached from the fall and her injuries, but strangely, being dissolved by the stomach of the world seemed painless.

She closed her eyes, trying to resign herself to her fate. This was probably all she deserved, in any case, after the mess she had made of her life. Once she'd thought she was someone important, that future generations would remember her name and what she'd done for the human race. Now it seemed just as likely that no one would remember her at all.

There was someone else sitting beside her.

She turned her head and was not at all surprised to see that it was Jackson Hammond. What other ghost was more appropriate to haunt her in her final hour?

"Hello, Jackson." She was almost happy to see him there, figment of her imagination or not.

"Hiya, Doc." He gave her a warm smile. *That* surprised her.

"Come to see an old woman meet her well-deserved end?" she spat out, suddenly angry that it had come to this.

He shook his head. His eyes were kind, too kind. She deserved only his bitterness, his hatred.

"I came to see an old friend."

She looked away, her cheeks flushed with shame. "I was no friend to you." She couldn't look him in the eyes. "I was so selfish then, so fearful. I was…. I killed you."

To her surprise, Jackson laughed, a warm, rich sound. "*You* killed me? What, are you now taking credit for the vacuum of space itself? Good Lord, woman, does your arrogance know no bounds?"

She sneaked a peek at him. He was smiling.

She persevered. "Jackson, if I hadn't tried to frame you…."

"*If* you hadn't tried to frame me. *If* the fungus hadn't gotten onto the ship. *If* there'd been more air. *If* there had just been more time. *If* the human race weren't so hell-bent on its own destruction that we needed something like this. I could play this game all night."

She searched his face. "Jackson, you really *should* hate me."

This time he looked serious. "Ana," he said softly, "I made my own choice. I acted to protect something wondrous and new that God brought into the universe through your mind and hands. Blaming yourself for my act is senseless." He put a hand on her shoulder, and it was remarkably solid for a ghost. "Ana. I forgive you."

Just like that, the pain she had been feeling, physical and emotional, was gone.

So was Jackson.

She closed her eyes and was at peace for the first time in more than two decades.

Now she could rest.

THEY'D BEEN walking for about an hour at a brisk pace when Aaron felt a mounting sense of urgency coming through the stone. It was like an electrical current, charging the air with negative ions. The hairs on his forearms stood on end.

"Come on," he called back to Keera. "Something's happened. We have to hurry."

He broke into a run, not looking back to see if she was following. Their time was running out—he knew that much. If he was going to save the doctor, it had to be now.

The tunnel seemed to stretch on ahead of them forever, an endless hallway carved out of the rock, or maybe extruded by the world-mind.

Finally, though, something changed.

Far ahead, there was a wall. Or something.

As he approached, it resolved itself into a kind of door, or…. He reached it and stared, puzzled. It looked like a pie chart—three wedges inside a circle.

Keera came up behind him. "It's a valve. Look, it's open just enough to let the trickle of water in."

Aaron laughed. "I keep forgetting we're in the belly of the beast here. So how do we get through?"

Keera shook her head. "I've never seen one in person. Maybe you can talk to it?"

Aaron stepped up to the blockade and put a hand on it. It was smooth, warm, alive. He closed his eyes. Things shifted, and he was falling through the network of tubes and organs and valves, falling toward the world-mind. He spread his arms and slowed his fall until he was drifting in virtual space.

He willed himself back to the valve and reached *into* it, feeling for the nerve impulses that controlled it. *There.* A twist of his hand, sending a signal to the valve muscles, and they relaxed.

Aaron opened his eyes in time to see the valve spiraling open. He turned to grin at Keera, but instead of smiling back, her jaw dropped open and she pointed into the newly revealed chamber.

Aaron spun back around to see Dr. Anatov, lying lifeless on the floor.

The room was more of a living thing than a cavern, about fifty meters wide and maybe half that high. The walls gave off a golden bioluminescence much stronger than the blue glow of the tunnel. The floor was covered in a thick, syrupy yellow substance, and the doctor's body was halfway submerged in it.

Aaron stepped out onto the floor, which gave way under his feet. His boots stuck to it, and it was an effort to lift his foot with each step.

Water was pouring in behind him, and it diluted the mucus, easing his passage.

Keera followed him.

Finally, he reached the doctor.

He knelt beside her. "Dr. Anatov." He touched her shoulder. She looked so small and helpless, so different from the woman he'd encountered on the *Hammond* just days before. So different from the monster he'd conjured up in his dreams.

Her eyes fluttered open, and she stared up at him. "Jackson?"

He shook his head. "No, it's me, Aaron." He tried to put on a reassuring smile. "We have to get you out of here."

"Aaron, look." Keera was kneeling next to him. She pointed to one of the doctor's legs. It was halfway gone, absorbed by stomach acid.

"I'm not going anywhere, am I?" the doctor said, but she didn't look sad.

"Let's not talk about that just yet. How do you feel?"

She smiled, and her face was transformed, as if she were twenty years younger.

"I feel good, Jackson. Better than I have in years. You forgave me."

He didn't correct her this time, but inside, his emotions were jumbled. *Why did I come all the way here, if not to hate you? If not to save you? What am I supposed to do?*

Even sinners deserve forgiveness. The answer came to him in his own thoughts, but he knew where it had originated. His father. *You have to save her.*

But how? Her body was dissolving, moment by moment. They had arrived too late, just in time to witness her slow death.

He thought about his father again, part of the world-mind now. Had his father's spirit really been here with Dr. Anatov?

The world-mind.

Suddenly it was clear to him what he had been brought here to do. To save Dr. Anatov. Not her body, but her soul.

He laid a hand on her cheek, gently, resting it skin to skin. He didn't know if this would work, but he knew he'd been brought here to try. "Do you trust me?"

She stared up at him, and something passed between them, an understanding deeper than words. She nodded. "In… in my pocket."

"What?"

She indicated her shirt pocket with her chin. "It was your father's."

He pulled the pocket open gently and brought out a tarnished silver cross on a chain. He held it up in the golden glow and looked at it in wonder. *From my Communion.*

It was a gift more precious than words could describe. He leaned down and kissed her forehead, whispering, "Thanks." He threw the cross to Keera. "Hold this for me." Then he touched Ana's cheek again and thrust his other hand down into the floor, through the viscous fluid until he touched the world's skin.

"Aaron, what in the hell are you doing?" Keera shouted, but he ignored her, seeking the interface with the world-mind. A second stretched into a minute, and then into what seemed like an hour but was probably less than ninety seconds all together.

He found it and made the connection.

Energy surged through him from the world-mind, up through his right arm and over into the doctor via his left. Then it reversed, pulling something back with it. It was an electrical current that stimulated his entire nervous system.

On the outside, he convulsed with the surge flowing through his body and down into the world-mind. On the inside, it was if he rode the maelstrom.

Ana's thoughts, feelings, and images rolled through him. Her life in Russia as a child, the first boy she had a crush on, her doting father, the move to the NAU, joining her father at work, the pain of a life sliced short when her father was killed in the bombing.

Lab work.

Space flight, arrogance, denial, a silver cross, and a new world born.

Ten years spent in prison, and then a new life and a fresh chance.

Forgiveness. Jackson had finally forgiven her.

As Ana's life coursed through Aaron, he was barely aware that the fluid around her had begun to glow, brighter and brighter, surging in a growing circular motion around her body.

He gestured with his head for Keera to move away. She stumbled back to the tunnel, and then the current flowing through him ended.

Aaron opened his eyes and looked down at the doctor. Her face was perfectly composed, at peace, her eyes shut.

He let go and pulled his other hand up out of the liquid.

The hair on his forearm had all been burned off, but the skin was untouched.

He staggered backward as the tidal flow around Dr. Anatov continued to build. Somehow, he made it back to the tunnel entrance, where Keera helped him through the opening. He turned back just in time to see her body succumb to the whirlpool and sink beneath the surface.

The room went dark, and the valve slammed closed.

THE TRAXX ground to a halt, and pain shot through Colin like a sword into his gut.

He knew, without knowing how, that Ana was gone.

Colin closed his eyes, shutting out the world around him. He was the only one left from that ill-fated flight.

This was all his fault. He'd brought her back here when she was so obviously not ready.

He bit his lower lip and shook his head. Maybe he was wrong.

Maybe she was okay.

He didn't think so.

"Are you all right, sir?" Dex, one of the rangers, asked.

"Not particularly," he grumbled, and climbed down from the traxx.

"They're up there." Dex pointed to a crevice above where they'd stopped. "Or at least the beacon is there."

Colin looked up just in time to see Devon Powell, by the looks of it, waving down at them. "I'd say you're right." He gave Dex a grim smile. One less casualty on his conscience, at least.

Colin climbed the slope to the cavern entrance where Devon awaited him and his team. They'd made good time getting here, but there had to be a better way to get around. A day and a half was far too long when someone was in need.

"They told me to wait here for you." He seemed agitated.

"*Who* told you? Aaron?"

Devon nodded. "Aaron and Keera. They went in there." He pointed to a hole in the back of the cavern. "I tried. I'm not so good with tight spaces."

Colin clapped him on the arm. "That's all right, son. It's good you were here to greet us. Why'd they go in there?"

Devon gulped. "I'm not sure I'm supposed to tell you," he said nervously.

"Come on, son, we can't help them if we don't know what they've gotten themselves into."

Devon nodded. "It's Aaron. He can talk to the world."

Chapter Thirteen: Aftermath

ANA OPENED her eyes.

She lay on a soft bed, under the branches of a huge redwood tree. She was covered in a white blanket.

She sat up and looked around. The place reminded her of Lex's lair.

Oh gods, no. Anywhere but there. *She slipped out of the covers, ready to run away again, only to realize she was as naked as the day she was born.*

"Hello, Doc," someone said behind her.

She spun about, and there was Jackson Hammond. "Jackson? What is this? Am I.... Is this heaven?" She'd never believed in heaven, and yet, here they were.

He laughed. "Hardly. But there is someone else here to meet you."

She took an uncertain step toward him. "You're not real."

He nodded. "You're mostly right about that." He chuckled. "You can help me figure it out, but first, Lex wants to tell you something."

Lex, the world-mind, was there in front of her. She looked smaller than before, somehow. Less threatening. Contrite, maybe? Even so, her appearance shocked Ana. The doctor stumbled back onto the bed.

"I'm sorry for what I said to you before." Lex came to sit next to her on the mattress. "I forgive you too."

Ana nodded, and then she started to cry. "I am so, so sorry."

Lex embraced her.

Lex's forgiveness, and Jackson's before, moved her beyond words.

At last she cried herself out and wiped her eyes with a corner of the blanket.

"If this isn't heaven, then where am I? I remember dying—"

Jackson laughed. "I remember that too. Come on. We have so much to show you."

AARON LEANED upon Keera for support. He was physically wasted. Helping Dr. Anatov transfer into the world-mind had been debilitating, and it was all he could manage to shuffle forward along the tunnel.

He tried to hurry. If they didn't make it back to the cavern before the next storm, they would both be in grave danger.

He could see all the questions running through Keera's mind, but she didn't ask any of them, apparently realizing how spent he was. Instead she helped him go on, though he could see from the worried look on her face that she didn't think they were going to make it.

Still, they continued for what seemed like hours. He faded in and out of consciousness, but somehow his feet kept moving.

Until they just couldn't move anymore. "I have to stop." He no longer cared what might happen.

Keera looked him in the eye and then nodded. "Here, let me help you down to the ground. We can rest for a while before we go on."

He nodded, grateful, and let her ease him down. The hard ground felt like the softest mattress to his weary body, and he was out in seconds.

Aaron awoke once more, for a few seconds, hearing voices above him. He glanced up to see the director himself standing there.

He was so tired.

Aaron closed his eyes and was lost to the world of dreams.

AARON AWOKE slowly. He was lying on something truly soft, not the hard floor of the tunnel that had been his last remembered resting place.

His head lay on a cushion of some sort, and sheets were drawn up over his supine form.

His eyes flickered open, taking in the golden light streaming in from the open window.

"Welcome back to the land of the living," someone said, and he turned to see the director himself sitting next to his bedside. Keera and Devon were standing behind him.

"How are you, buddy?" Devon asked with a tentative smile.

Aaron grinned back. "I feel like I was rolled over by a traxx a couple times, but otherwise I'm fantastic."

Keera squeezed around the director. "I'm so glad you're awake. I was worried that you'd tapped yourself out."

He laughed. "It'll take more than a brush with death to keep me down."

She sat down on the bed next to him and kissed his cheek.

"Aaron, I need to ask you some questions." The director looked worried. "I'm sorry for this. I know you're tired, but it has to be now." He took a deep breath. "Look, we need to know what happened down there—if the world-mind had anything to do with Dr. Anatov's... demise."

"I understand. Do you mind if my friends stay?" He pushed himself up to a sitting position.

"I'd prefer it." The director motioned for Devon to pull up a chair. "They may be able to fill in some of the gaps, and you all owe me the cost of a traxx."

Aaron blanched. "God, I hope not."

The director chuckled. "We'll work that out later."

"Fair enough." He thought back over the events of the last few days. "I don't think the world-mind had anything to do with it. Those tunnels funnel rainwater down to those stomachs for processing. I think she just got caught in the wrong place at the wrong time."

The director nodded. "I was hoping you'd say that. The world-mind and Dr. Anatov have a history."

"I know. My father told me all about it."

"Your father?" His brow was furrowed, and he put a hand on Aaron's forehead. "Aaron, your father's been dead for ten years. You remember that, right?"

Aaron laughed. "Can I get something to eat? This is gonna take a while to explain." He searched his memory, looking for the right place to begin. "You see, there's this thing I can do...."

PART THREE: REFUGEE
2165 AD

Chapter One:
Moonjumper

ANA TESTED the world's propulsion systems, readying for the day she would need to fly.

Things down on Earth had gone from bad to worse, and Lex had put her in charge of the more scientific aspects of Forever. It was a strange thing being a goddess... and far more limited than she had imagined.

Officially, as far as most of the world's colonists knew, Lex was the world-mind.

Only a select few—Colin, Aaron, and the director's immediate family—knew the truth: that the world-mind was now three.

It had been a difficult transition for Ana to accept. She still felt like herself, mostly, but she intersected with Lex and Jackson at odd points in her psyche.

She was no longer entirely her own person, or ever entirely alone. She missed being alone, sometimes.

The whole thing was all a little too... spiritual for her scientific mind to comprehend.

Still, done was done, and here she was, so she might as well make the most of it.

They had a world to take care of, after all.

EDDY TREMAINE backed the Ford F1050 hauler back into the mouth of the cavern. The beat-up old truck belched a cloud of black smoke in complaint. His hurried conversion of the vehicle's electrical system to run on biofuel had been a limited success.

It had gotten them up the mountainside, and that was all that mattered.

Davian Forrester, his ex, stood behind the truck, guiding it and its precious cargo back into the darkness inside the shallow cave.

Eddy had been sure he was going to lose the load a couple of times on the way up the mountainside, as it shifted on the truck's flatbed around some of the hairpin turns, but the Moonjumper had stayed attached to the truck, and soon they'd have it hidden away securely.

The old Ford's radio had picked up the satellite news transmissions on the way up from the valley floor. Things were going downhill out there fast, and battles had already broken out between the North American Union and the Sino-African Syndicate along the Pacific Coast. Eddy didn't figure it would be much longer before there was a full-scale war.

Another war. The last ten years had been a nonstop series of them.

He was done fighting.

"That's it," Davian called from the rear of the truck. "There's a ten-foot drop-off back here."

"Got it," Eddy shouted back. He set the brake and got out to gauge the parking job he'd done. The front of the truck was beneath the roof of the cavern, far enough back that only the bumper would be visible from above. *It'll have to do.* "I'm gonna start unpacking the jumper."

"Okay," Davian called back. "I'll get things started with lights and power."

Reconnecting with Dav had been a godsend. He couldn't have accomplished all of this on his own.

Davian was setting up the solar lights in the cavern next to the truck. They'd brought four industrial-strength light suckers. Each one had a "funnel" that channeled sunlight down a thick fiber-optic cable and diffused it into usable light, and a power trap that siphoned off some of the power to charge a battery that provided a reduced illumination at night.

While Davian set up the lights, Eddy began to uncover the Moonjumper. He removed the heavy plastic tarps that had hidden the little ship from view, folding them up and setting them aside. The craft had a 270-degree field of vision through a wraparound plas window, and a skylight window up top. The metallic panels of the little ship were dull with age, and the plas looked scratched and worn too. *This is going to work. This* has *to work.* Somehow they would make it work.

The Moonjumper line had been retired from active service by AmSplor in the 2090s. Eddy had picked this one up at auction from the New Richmond Air and Space Museum a month before, for a song. He hoped to God she was still space-worthy. She'd been out in the elements for at least a decade as a showpiece for the museum.

He'd flown one like it once or twice before at air shows in the South, in Birmingham and New Little Rock. He hoped he could remember how to handle it, if they could make it space-worthy again.

Something was bugging him—his sixth sense. He'd learned to trust his body's signals during his two tours in the Hong Kong urban battle zone, back when he'd been called Evelyne. He saw no need to change that habit now. He looked at the bright day outside uneasily. "I'm gonna set the fuzzer and then grab some branches to put over the front of the 1050," he called to Davian.

"Okay. I'll finish getting her uncovered."

Eddy grabbed a bag from behind the driver's seat. He peeled it apart at the magnetic strip and took out the four fuzz balls—small silver spheres that together would create the fuzz field. He set each one equidistant around the edge of the cavern entrance, in front of the truck, activating them as he placed them. When the fourth one came online, the fuzz field sprang into place. It was like a pool of water hung in three-dimensional space, reflecting what was around it and distorting and hiding what lay behind, both visually and electromagnetically.

From the inside, all he could see was a slight film in the air.

He went to retrieve his hatchet. He wanted to cover up the front of the truck with some branches so it would pass at least a casual visual inspection, just in case the field failed.

Eddy was about to step through the fuzz field when his instincts stopped him again, the small hairs standing up on his forearms.

Davian was hauling something around back inside the cavern, making a scraping sound.

"Dav, be quiet a minute," he hissed, peering up into the sky. He stood completely still and searched for the source of his unease.

After twenty seconds, he saw it, a kuripa drone slipping around a ridgeline into the valley below. It was casting back and forth slowly, as if looking for something or someone.

"Drone," he whispered to Davian, who had come to stand next to him.

The thing resembled nothing so much as a giant robotic cockroach, its wings fluttering in the mountain breeze with a green metallic sheen. He hadn't realized the Chafs had gotten so bold, sending their battle drones into eastern Pennsylvania and West Virginia. If he'd been outside the field when it flew by....

He held his breath as it passed within a hundred feet of their hideout. Those things were equipped to sense heat patterns. He hoped to God it didn't notice the tire tracks that led up to the cavern. Fortunately, it was a warm day, so the truck's heat signature was probably all but wiped away by now.

At last the drone passed over another ridge and was gone.

"We have to be careful. Only short trips outside of the cavern, and always, *always* check for drones first."

Davian nodded. "How long until we can get this beastie operational?"

Eddy glanced back at the dark form of the Moonjumper. "Three days? We'll do the best we can." He *hoped* it would only take three days. *God help us if we can't make her work.*

RETIRED DIRECTOR Colin McAvery stepped outside onto the porch and closed the door to his little cottage behind him, staring up at the arc of the world above. It was barely visible at its apex, pale blue lights marking the scattered night plants that gave off a soft glow, along with a few spots of brighter human activity. It was a strange, beautiful world, but sometimes he longed to see the open vistas and blue skies of Earth once more.

Trip was still asleep inside.

Colin liked to get up to see First Light, as the advance of the morning had come to be called here in this new world they were building. After nearly thirty years working with this place, it still amazed him to see it light up around him as the dawn crept from plant to plant and across the sky inside of Forever.

He sat down on his porch with a cup of coffee to await the coming of the day. Being the ex project head had its benefits in retirement. He looked around at the retreat he'd carved out for himself here in the wilderness, away from the demands and pressures of command, and grinned. His home was all alone in the wilderness, far from the towns of Darlith and Micavery—formerly McAvery Port—that had grown up within the colony over the last two decades.

They had access to the world-mind's network, but he rarely used it anymore. He was happy to leave the world's worries to Aaron Hammond and his capable crew.

Colin sipped the coffee, enjoying its bold, rich flavor, mostly unknown up here—another perk of his—shipped up at great expense from Earth. No one had yet figured out how to make coffee plants grow properly on Forever. He supposed it was something that the future inhabitants would never know they were missing.

That thought made him sad.

He could see the light approaching now in the distance, as the world-mind stimulated the plants across Forever to awaken. The golden glow raced ahead here and there, approaching like a tide of light, tied to the surge of luthiel in the world's veins. Soon it flared overhead, lighting up Forever from above.

He closed his eyes, hoping to feel the change in the air as it swept past him. He could almost hear it, like the sizzling of meat on a faraway campfire.

Just like every other morning, he felt nothing—no vibration, no warmth, no physical sensation at all as the plants around him lit up.

When he opened his eyes, though, it was daylight all around, shining from every leaf and bough, and even from the microscopic pollen in the air itself.

He finished his coffee and was about to go inside when he heard hoofbeats.

He stood and looked around. It was coming from somewhere down the road, outside of his neat little yard carved out of the "wild" forest. It drew closer—someone on horseback. A visitor.

Colin set down his coffee mug and ran a hand through his hair. He brushed the lint off his robe, determined to meet the newcomer with at least a modicum of dignity.

ANDRISSA "ANDY" Hammond raced up the narrow roadway from Darlith on the horse she had requisitioned from the guard there.

Unlike her father, Aaron, Andy had grown up at Transfer Station and in Forever, with all the strange contradictions that implied—like leaving a space station in a shuttle, then taking a train from the port city to Darlith, and finally riding on horseback in search of a retired director in the middle of the wilderness. It all seemed completely normal to her.

Andy had left Micavery in the middle of the night. Her father needed Director McAvery's help in a hurry, and the man didn't answer his messages.

At fifteen years old, Andy could be trusted to bring the man in.

Things were getting rapidly worse out in near-Transfer space, and down on Earth too. She could see it with every new shipment of tired, sick, and broken refugees dropped off on their doorstep.

Her father had taken her on an inspection of one of the cargo pods left by coyotes just a week before. It had been disturbing—so much pain and sorrow and heartbreak.

He'd worn such a look of anger and despair on his face that Andy thought she would never forget it. Aaron Hammond had been the director of the Forever project for five years now, but this was beyond his capabilities to deal with alone.

Andy rode up over the last hill to see the cottage of the retired director. She'd met the man once or twice before, when he'd been running Transfer Station. He had to be in his sixties now. He'd become a bit of a recluse since his retirement, and he lived a long way outside of Darlith on a private estate in the wilderness, such as it was on this small worldlet.

The former captain and director was still handsome and powerful, a bear of a man.

The bear seemed to be missing his claws this morning, though, standing on his porch in a blue bathrobe and bunny slippers, a cup of steaming *something* on the table next to him.

Andy pulled the horse to a halt and slid off, turning to face former director Colin McAvery. "Morning, sir." She held out her hand. "Sorry to bother you so early. I'm Andrissa Hammond, but you can call me Andy."

The director grinned. "Andy it is, then. I remember you, though you were a lot smaller the last time I saw you. Tell me, Andy, what brings you to my little backwater corner of Forever?" He gestured for Andy to take one of the seats on the porch.

"I'm sorry, sir, but do you have something to drink? I'm thirsty from the journey." Andy swallowed hard, her mouth sore and dry.

"Call me Colin. None of this 'sir' bullshit. I left that behind me five years ago."

Andy nodded. "Will do." She liked him already. She hoped he was still so friendly once she'd delivered her news and request.

"What would you like? Some coffee?" He held up the steaming mug.

"No thank you, s—Colin. Never got a taste for it." *That stuff is vile.*

"Pity for you. How about some redberry juice, then?"

"Yes, please."

Colin disappeared into the cottage. "We have a visitor," he called from inside.

Someone else groaned.

Andy smiled. That had to be Trip, the director's husband. Her own father had done the honors ten years earlier, marrying the two on the shores of Lake Jackson in a small private ceremony. The ex-director was a man of substance, not flash.

She looked around the property while she waited for him. The home was built from local wood—it gave the place a rustic, homey aspect she recognized from some of the Pioneer tridimensionals.

Off to the left, redberry bushes were staked up in neat rows; on the right, there was a large vegetable garden. Everything looked well-trimmed and organized.

The forest line ran around the edge of the property, mostly alifir trees.

Soon the door opened and the director reappeared, this time dressed for company in jeans and a white shirt. Colin handed her a glass filled with red juice.

"Mmmm, it's good." She savored the tart sweetness.

"We grow the berries here on the estate." He indicated the patch of land around the cottage. "But you didn't come all the way out here to talk about produce." He took another sip of his coffee and then set the mug down on the rail and put his hands in his lap, waiting for Andy to speak.

"No, sir... I mean, Colin." *Damn, that's hard to say.* "My father sent me. Things are getting bad with the refugee crisis."

Colin sat up. "Refugee crisis? I'm sorry. I don't get much news out here. Intentionally." His tone implied he preferred that it stay that way.

Andy nodded. "Things have gone downhill back on Earth too. The Sino-African Syndicate has a foothold in Oregon, and fighting is being waged all up and down the West Coast. There's also an incursion in New England."

"There are *refugees*? How are they getting up *here*, for God's sake?"

"It varies. Some are coming in from the near-Earth stations on regular flights, paying extra or stowing away. Some are finding ways to get up here from Earth and Moon Base. But most of them...." She remembered the look on her father's face. "Most of them are being brought up by pirates. Coyotes."

Colin sat back in his chair, contemplating. "How bad is it?" he said at last.

"About half of them survive." She closed her eyes, remembering the container ship. The stench had been overwhelming when the lock had cycled open. The smells and sights and sounds of human misery. A little boy, all of four years old, dead of heat exhaustion.

Colin nodded, his eyes narrowing. "How many refugees are there, so far?"

"About two thousand. Give or take. But more are coming every day. Dad doesn't know what to do with them anymore. We have them in a camp outside of Micavery, but there are problems. Our systems weren't designed to handle such a large influx in a short time. Some of the refugees have started clear-cutting for firewood, and a fire almost got out of control yesterday."

"That explains the smoke I saw. I wondered about that." Colin set aside his mug. "So what can I do?"

The door swung open again, and Trip came out. "What do they want with you *now*?" the silver-haired ex-pilot asked. He still looked good—handsome and trim as he had been when he'd worn his AmSplor uniform.

Colin smiled at his husband. "The refugee thing has deteriorated. I expect they're going to need me to help sort things out for a week or two."

So he *did* know about it.

"But the berry harvest—"

"—is something you'll manage just fine without me." Colin pulled Trip down for a brief kiss to muffle his protest. "Just put them in cold storage, and I'll be back in time to help you process them for market."

Trip retreated into the cottage, still grumbling. Andy suppressed a grin.

"We've become an old married couple," Colin said with a sigh when Trip was gone. "I used to run an entire world, and now I manage a vegetable patch."

"If it's any consolation, I think it's a *really nice* vegetable patch."

"It is, isn't it?" He grinned. "Count me in."

DAVIAN PRIED out the Moonjumper's air circulation unit. The thing was a mess. A decade or two out in the open weather had corroded the intakes, and it was going to take a minor miracle to get it working again. They only needed enough oxygen for about three days in transit—enough time to coast into the vicinity of Transfer Station and call for help. His contacts in AmSplor said station patrol was picking up everyone they could.

He set the unit on his improvised workbench—an old slab of wood propped up across a couple of rocks—and set to work with a wire brush.

As he carefully cleaned the gunk off the unit, he glanced over at Eddy. That had taken some getting used to, especially since they'd dated—or at least fucked around—for a couple of months during the Hong Kong campaign, before Davian's dark time.

When he'd gotten out of the NAU Marines, he'd dropped out of sight until Eddy had come to find him with his proposal. The whole "man" thing had been a shock, but Davian was one of the best restorers this side of the Appalachians, and Eddy knew it.

Davian was willing to work with his ex if it meant getting off this rock before things really went to hell.

Judging by the news on the x-band, it wouldn't be long now.

"This thing is practically deadware," he said conversationally.

Eddy was climbing inside the Moonjumper. "I prefer *classic*," he responded with a grin. "According to the museum director, she made three hundred cargo runs before they grounded her."

"For good reason," Davian said dryly. "She's more than halfway to the scrap pile." He set down the brush, grabbed a hand scanner, and ran it over the unit. "I can get this working again, but not at a hundred percent. It's gonna get hot inside that can."

"How hot?"

"Over a hundred degrees?"

"I can live with that, I think. We'll bring plenty of water and take our shirts off." He sounded much more excited about that prospect than Davian felt.

"Sorry, we're gonna need to wear our suits. If the cabin decompresses, we won't have time to get them on in that tight space."

He passed a reverser over the mag bolts, and three of the four popped off. The fourth took a little prying, but soon enough he had the unit opened to expose the internal workings and filters. They were, as he expected, filthy.

Thinking about being trapped in that tin can with the heat rising made him freak out a little. The cavern tightened around him, its walls squeezing closer and closer, and it was hard to breathe.

He closed his eyes and set down the tool, concentrating on pumping his lungs calmly and regularly, willing his heartbeat to slow down. *I'm not in the hotbox. I'm not in the hotbox.*

Two fucking months in Chinese captivity. Years behind him now, and still, these debilitating flashbacks could hit him at any time.

Now he was going into this new hotbox willingly, to be trapped there for days with Eddy.

He wanted to scream.

Instead he concentrated on breathing in and out slowly until the panic receded just a little. *I can do this.*

"You okay down there?" Eddy called from the truck bed.

Davian nodded. "I will be."

When they reached Forever, he'd find a way to put himself in control. He'd learned a hard lesson in the POW camp. You were either the oppressed or the oppressor.

He would never be a victim again.

Chapter Two:
Liminal Sky

COLIN PACKED a carry sack with everything he thought he'd need for what he hoped would be a short trip. The bag had been woven from Forever-grown cotton in Darlith and then dyed a handsome sky blue.

Bit by bit, his new world was becoming self-sufficient, but they weren't ready for this sudden wave of forced immigration, not by a long shot.

It was strange to be called up again for service after all these years. He'd gotten used to being retired, mostly. He and Trip had built quite a pleasant little life here on the estate, with its agricultural produce contributing to the colony's self-sufficiency. He had plenty of time to sleep in, to read, and to pass his time at leisure.

At Trip's insistence, he'd cut them off from the colony's data feed. He loved spending time with his husband, finally seeing each other for more than a couple of days at a time.

He was also bored out of his mind.

So the chance to get involved in something outside the estate again, to be called on to make some kind of difference, was intoxicating. And to be paired with Aaron Hammond's daughter... well, it seemed that fate had a strange sense of humor.

He peered out of the bedroom into the living room. Andy was sitting on the overstuffed couch Colin had arranged to be shipped up from Earth, looking around at the homey little cottage she found herself in.

Colin threw his carry sack over his shoulder.

"Are you sure this is a good idea?" Trip stood by the doorway, arms crossed. "Why can't Aaron deal with this crisis?"

Colin put his hands on Trip's shoulders. "Experience trumps youth, sometimes." He gave Trip a quick kiss. "The boy asked for my help, and so I'm going to give it to him." Though that *boy*, Aaron, was closing in on forty. "I'll be home as soon as I can. Besides, when did my starship captain become such a homebody?"

Trip laughed. "Oh, I don't know... about the time my station commander gave up his own commission?"

Colin snorted. "There is that. I'll send Shadowfax back from Darlith when I arrive."

"Yes, Gandalf," Trip said. "Send him back to our little hobbit hole." It was an old joke between them.

He gave Trip a hug, sensing the man was at least partially mollified. "I'll take my loop, and I'll even turn it on. You can always reach me if you need me." He'd had his internal loop removed when he retired, but he'd kept a portable one for occasions like this. He turned to the doorway. "You ready, Andy?" The poor kid had been so patient while he puttered around, collecting his things.

"Just waiting for you."

"Little shit," Colin whispered to Trip, who grinned. "All right, then. Let's go."

ANDY STARED up at the Forever sky and tried to imagine what the skies of Earth were like. She'd been born up here, and this wraparound sky was daunting enough. What would it be like to only see blue when you looked up?

She'd be in constant fear of flying away into the great empty *nothing*.

Andy rubbed her horse's neck while she waited for Colin to come back from the stables with his own horse. She'd been just ten years old when the commander had stepped down, but she still remembered seeing him in his dress uniform, a man of both power and decision.

Now in his sixties, he was still handsome, but he seemed… softer. Quieter. What did her father think the dir… Colin could do in the face of the refugee crisis? *He's only one man.*

She hadn't talked with Grandpa Hammond in a while. She wondered what he was up to.

She closed her eyes. She could sense the flow of the world around her—the light breeze that blew from one end of Forever to the other. The ichor—luthiel—that flowed through her underground veins. The thoughts, deep and shallow, that flickered through the world-mind as it regulated the systems that they called a colony.

"Daydreaming?"

Andy laughed, blinking. "A little. Ready to go?"

Colin sat astride a brown mare who looked like she had seen more than her fair share of years. "Shadowfax? Truly?" Andy vaulted up onto her stallion's back. She was familiar with *The Lord of the Rings*. As a little girl, she'd spent weeks inside the latest dimensional version, exploring Middle Earth from one end to the other.

"It's a long story." He glanced up at the sky. "If we hurry, we might make Darlith before the afternoon showers."

Andy nodded. She closed her eyes briefly, then blinked and flashed Colin a smile. "We've got about three hours." She spurred her horse on, and Shadowfax followed.

Colin caught up to her, and they rode side by side through the gate to the estate, kicking up a small cloud of dust behind them. "Still have never gotten used to that thing you and your father do." He glanced over at her.

Andy laughed. "Dad has to touch something. Me, I just close my eyes and voila. He calls it *dipping*, like dipping your hand into the river. He said it was from some kind of virus that Grandpa had?"

"Close enough." Colin smiled. "Can you tell me where your father is right now?"

Andy shook her head. "It doesn't work like that. I can only pick up general information. For more, I have to make a full connection, and it kinda loops me out of the real world." Into the virtual one. It was an amazing place, where you could imagine almost anything you wanted. There were times in her life when she'd spent days and days in there at a time too, but lately she preferred dealing with real flesh and blood.

They rode on in silence for a bit. The grounds outside the estate were wild, or as wild as land on a manufactured world could be. A small stream wound down along the side of the dirt road toward the Rhyl, the river that would eventually feed an inland lake or sea at the midway point of the still-growing world.

Alifir trees blew gently in the wind, three times a man's height, their glowing needles giving off a piney scent.

"You were born up here, right?"

"Yup. On Transfer." She'd always wanted to see Earth, but her father had put his foot down—not until she was eighteen.

"Do you ever wonder what it was like back on Earth?"

"Yeah, sometimes. I mean, I know it's important to Dad and Mom and Grandma, but it's not *real* to me. Not like this place. It's like a fairy tale."

Colin laughed. "Well, I guess it would be. It's where I grew up, but I haven't been Earthside for ten years, and it's not what it used to be. How is Glory adjusting to life in Micavery?"

"Grandma's good. Though she misses Earth sometimes. I don't understand why—war, famine, raging floods, and killing droughts. Who would want to live in that?"

"Many people have no choice," Colin replied, his voice sober. "We have to remember how lucky we are."

Andy thought about it for a moment. Her father had said nearly the same thing to her when they'd come back from the refugee container. *These people fought so hard to get here, and you were born to it. Never forget how fortunate you are.* "I guess so," she said at last. That little boy could just as easily have been her.

"I don't suppose you'll ever see the skies of Earth, now."

EDDY DROPPED into his sleeping bag, exhausted from a long day tinkering with the Moonjumper. It was tedious work. He was going over every part of the little ship, testing it for airtightness, inch by inch. Their lives would soon depend upon it.

Davian was cleaning and overhauling the ship systems. So far they'd been lucky. Although they were filthy with years of accumulated dirt and grit, they seemed to be in serviceable shape.

Once he was done, they'd install the reconditioned x-drive he'd purchased on the black market. It would either work or they'd be blown to microscopic bits along with half the mountain. *In which case it won't really matter.*

Eddy lay back in the sleep sack and closed his eyes, listening for the hiss of drones outside. They'd seen two more since the first one had appeared. One had been of Sino-African design, while the other had been unmarked. Both had passed them by.

The night was calm, deceptively so. He could hear the crickets' song, muted by the fuzz field, but otherwise there was nothing but the night breeze.

He drifted off into memories, and then dreams.

Eddy Tremaine looked around the grim space one last time, shouldering his duffel bag, filled with everything he owned, ready to leave this dingy hellhole behind.

Things were heating up in the Hong Kong battle zone, and the army was offering great conscription packages for anyone who agreed to enlist now rather than waiting for their draft number to come up.

This concrete one-room flat had been all he could afford on his salary as a security guard—a square gray box that was functional above all else.

He supposed he was lucky to have found a place to resettle here in Sugarloaf Mountain when Orlando had been pummeled by Hurricane Cisco. His parents had grown up in southern Florida, a place that only existed now in peoples' memories or under forty feet of water.

He closed the door behind him and looked out across the sunrise over Lake Apopka, which had become more of an inland sea with the rise in ocean levels and the heavy rains that now hit Florida with increasing regularity.

It was a clear day, the skies washed clean by last night's storm. A good omen.

Today was the day things would start to change for him. He'd brokered a hell of a deal for his conscription—full ride in Army College, resettlement money after he got out, and best of all, a full transition once it was done, paid for by the NAU. No more binding. No more T. No more Evelyne.

Just Eddy.

It was going to be a good day.

DAVIAN WAITED until he was sure Eddy was in a deep sleep, snoring away.

He lay still in his own sleeping bag, staring up at the cavern ceiling, wondering how many other generations of humanity had taken refuge in this same cave.

Had it been home to a pack of Neanderthals? Or were they just in Europe?

Maybe some nineteenth-century family had taken shelter here during a rainstorm before traveling westward toward California.

Or perhaps a Boy Scout troop might have stopped here on a camping trip to learn wilderness survival.

There was so much history in the world, and mankind was determined to blow it all to bits.

He'd been watching Eddy carefully while doing his own work. The man was super detail oriented. He'd worked over half the little Moonjumper that afternoon, getting her in shipshape for the flight. If left in his hands, they'd be certain to reach one of the three seed ships without a catastrophic decompression. Without even springing a leak, most likely.

It just wouldn't do.

He *needed* Eddy to get him up there. Davian had no experience navigating these things, and Eddy had done at least three moon runs in a jumper like this over his career. But once they were close, he'd need to get rid of the man. He had big plans, and he didn't want anyone on Forever to know his history and secrets.

Davian waited a little bit longer to be certain Eddy was out cold. Then, quietly, he eased himself out of the sleeping bag. Eddy was a heavy sleeper, but it didn't pay to take any chances.

After retrieving a tube of readygel and a damper drill from his kit, he climbed onto the truck bed and into the jumper. He found the spot he was looking for, hidden behind the control panel where the hull was the thinnest. He'd seen Eddy go over that part of the ship already.

He used the small drill to quietly make a pinprick hole in the hull, just big enough to let the air whistle out in space. If he'd judged it right, they would be in no danger of decompression.

Then he filled it with readygel. The gel would withstand the extreme cold of the void for maybe twenty-four hours; then it would lose its cohesion, and the trap would be sprung.

He would put a matching hole or three in Eddy's suit after the man tested it.

Davian withdrew from the Moonjumper, peering over the edge of the truck bed to be sure Eddy was still sleeping. Then he wiped up the small pile of debris left from the drill on the floor of the truck and put everything away where it belonged.

He settled back into his sleeping bag, staring coldly at Eddy's slumbering form. *I loved you once.*

Space was a dangerous place. He'd heard there'd already been many refugee casualties.

What was one more?

Chapter Three:
Darlith

COLIN WHISTLED. "It's getting big."

It had been at least six months since he'd been to the new, bustling town of Darlith, where the latest wave of settlers were quickly building a fully functioning society.

Now it was laid out ahead of him, a little around the curve of the world, giving him almost a bird's-eye view.

The city was being put together from materials extruded by the world-mind—lightweight solid stone blocks with the density of volcanic stone, hauled up from the South Pole. They came in a variety of colors. The result was a kaleidoscope of a city, laid out on a grid on the "west" side of the Rhyl, just after the waters tumbled out of the Anatov Mountains, renamed after the death of the scientist there.

It wasn't the wild colors that drew his attention. Instead it was the rapid growth in the township since he had last been there.

From York Street along the riverside, five lanes radiated like spokes running up the hillsides along the river. There were at least a hundred buildings along these streets, and many more under construction.

They were still a good hour or two away from the edge of town, so Colin suggested they stop for lunch. They had just crossed over the Rhyl, so they found a spot by the riverside beneath the branches of some tall alifir trees, rustling in the slight breeze. Colin tied the horses up.

The afternoon storm was brewing in the sky, the dark patch of moisture extending slowly toward them from the north.

"Going to be a soaker today, by the looks of it." Colin eyed the approaching clouds.

"How can you tell?" She looked up at the sky, her eyes narrowed as she tried to see the difference.

Colin laughed. He liked this young Hammond. "Years of experience. When you live out here like I do, you start to pick up the nuances of the weather, and the weather here is a hell of a lot simpler than weather back on Earth." He opened his carry sack and pulled out some of the dried fruit he brought with him. He handed a bag of it to Andy.

"I mean, how can you tell that this one will be heavy?" She took the offered bag of fruit and pulled out a sealed package from her own carry sack.

They settled in with their backs against a couple of the trees to watch the progress of the storm clouds twirling in the distance.

Colin frowned. He stared up at the approaching clouds for a moment before speaking. "It's a couple of things," he said at last. "Do you see the color of the clouds? How they have a dark purple tinge in the middle?"

Andy nodded.

"They're thicker than they were yesterday too. Taking up more space. It's hard to explain."

"Yeah, I think I see that."

Colin waited for a minute, timing his reply. "Plus, it's Sunday. It always rains heavily on Sunday."

Andy looked at him for a moment, then exploded in laughter.

"You spend too much time up on the space station or you'd know that too." Colin laughed a little himself.

Andy nodded. "Dad says I can come down here full-time next year. I can't wait. I'm so sick and tired of being cooped up in that metal monster." She grinned. "That's why I jumped at the chance to come find you."

Colin chewed on his dried fruit. He hardly ever ate meat anymore; it was a rarity up here. The fruits, nuts, and vegetables had been engineered with all the nutrients his body needed. "It's a shame you've never been to Earth. It was a beautiful world once. Parts of it still are." He remembered the week he and Trip had spent in Paris, still romantic despite two centuries of modern history.

"It's hard for me to imagine it. It seems… too big."

"There are times I wish I was back there. You're right—it *is* big. If you wanted to, you could wander the world your entire life and never see it all."

Andy whistled. "I can't imagine that."

The wind was starting to pick up, and they finished their meal and put everything away. "Let's hang out here until the storm passes." Colin pulled his rain tent out of his carry sack. He found a flat spot along the river's edge to anchor it and pressed a button. It inflated silently, creating a transparent dome.

Andy whistled again, this time appreciatively. "I've never used one of these." She looked at the transparent tent.

"It keeps all the rain out, but you can still watch the storm as it goes by." He unsealed the door and beckoned for Andy to climb in. Soon they were both inside and settled, and Colin resealed it.

Above them, the sky was growing dark, sizzling with electricity akin to the arrival of the morning, but this time it was rain, not light, that was coming.

In moments the sky was full of clouds, and then the storm arrived. A light pattering of rain soon gave way to larger hard drops, drenching everything in sight and pounding the surface of the tent. The view around them dropped to a mile, then half a mile, then down to almost nothing as the raindrops pummeled its plasform.

"How do they have the refugees housed?" Colin asked. There wasn't enough shelter built for that many people.

"They're using plas sheets to make a big tent city for them, but it's extremely temporary."

These things could get out of control fast. "We'll see what we can do about that when we get there."

THE STORM passed them by in half an hour, and the rest of the journey up to Darlith was uneventful.

They rode through the countryside. Andy asked about Colin's life on Earth before he'd become a captain, and they chatted awhile about life in California. Before long they were approaching the edge of Darlith.

Andy had been through the city a couple of times before, so she knew her way around. The maglev train line ended at a station on the far side of the growing city, so they dismounted and walked their horses through the streets of town.

As the head of the project, Colin had tried to keep technology at a fairly low level inside Forever, both because of the potential pollution, and because technological devices would be hard to maintain over time as the ship made its way between Earth and Forever's final destination.

Her father, as the new director, didn't share his view, and so the maglev train now ran between Micavery and Darlith.

The outskirts of town were filling up with new housing units being built by residents, but as they approached Main Street, there were a number of businesses already in operation. One of these was a café serving morning brew, the local equivalent of coffee. It was more of a tea, really. Andy liked it a lot more than coffee.

Another was a new store specializing in barter and locally made merchandise.

"The last time I was here, there were maybe three or four buildings." Colin looked around in wonder.

Andy nodded. "Dad has me go over all the manifests. There are new people coming in all the time. He's been trying to use some of the refugees here, the ones with building skills, but many of the refugees aren't much good at practical things."

"I'd imagine they are mostly those rich enough to have bought themselves passage up here."

"That and the lucky ones."

Andy checked her mount into the stable from where he'd come, and Colin slapped Shadowfax on the rump, sending the horse back home.

There was a lively farmer's market going on along the main street, with all kinds of produce—apples, corn, berries, lettuce, nuts, and much more. The produce came in from the farms around Micavery and the new estates that were springing up on the outskirts of Darlith, like the one Colin and Trip ran.

People were trading produce for crons, the small lightweight coins manufactured by the world-mind in a variety of colors.

The air in the city was festive and alive.

They approached the train station, a one-story building built out of brown bricks. There was no landscaping to speak of in front of the building; it was strictly utilitarian. It was capped with a sloped roof for rain runoff, and in the middle, a bell tower stood another two stories above the main structure.

Andy glanced sideways at Colin, wondering what this place looked like to him. "The camp's on the other side of the mountains, closer to Micavery. Hey, looks like we're just in time!" She pointed down the tracks. One of the magnetic trains was just pulling up to the station from the north. The train consisted of an engine, three passenger cars, and three platform cars, all loaded down with produce. "Come on, let's see if we can get a good seat."

Colin followed her.

"The train won't leave for another fifteen minutes," she explained. "They have to unload the cargo first." They climbed aboard one of the passenger cars, looking for seats. There was no cost to ride, as it was subsidized by AmSplor.

Andy found them seats on the east side, where they'd have the best view as the train climbed into the mountains.

As they waited for it to depart, they talked more about Old Earth.

It had always held a fascination for Andy, someplace mythical that she never expected to visit for herself.

Colin was full of old stories from when he'd grown up there, on a farm in California. Dealing with livestock, riding under that big sky, surfing the waves at the beach.

She tried to imagine California, a place where the highways stretched on forever and the ocean was even bigger.

An ocean. What a strange thought.

Out here, the only ocean was the depths of space.

At last the train lifted off the tracks silently and began its progress up toward the mountains that separated Darlith and Micavery. The village was quickly left behind, and soon they were climbing through the foothills.

The ceiling was clear, affording them a view of the world above. Andy watched as it came slowly closer.

It was hard to make out any details, but she could see the edges of farmland, patches of forest, and little streams that ran through the land up there.

Then the train plunged into the blackness of a tunnel. Andy pressed her face against the glass, trying to see the tunnel walls in the darkness.

They burst out on the other side of the mountains a moment later. Once again, the entire world was laid out before her, Lake Jackson ahead and the McAvery Peninsula jutting out into it like a long finger.

This was her normal stomping grounds when she was Forever-side, but rarely did she get such a great view of it. The South Pole loomed ahead, the elevator and Topside launching platform all but invisible from this distance. The dark rock was a hazy blue from there.

The train hummed to a stop. "We're here." Andy grabbed her bag.

"Where's the camp?" Colin asked.

"It's about a ten-minute walk." She pointed down into the valley to the east, where a makeshift structure stood. "Come on!"

A DEEP rumbling in the ground below his sleep sack woke Eddy up. He opened his eyes to see the cavern shaking, dust and debris raining down on him. He closed his eyes and started to scramble for the entrance, drones be damned, but then the shaking stopped. The rain of dirt and pebbles settled down to a cloud of disturbed dust.

"What the fuck was that?" Eddy wiped dirt from his face and stared outside. The world looked normal, early morning in the Monongahela National Forest.

"Let me grab the x-band." Davian opened the truck door. "We're lucky the whole place didn't come down on our heads."

Eddy scratched the scar on his left temple where he'd had his loop removed. It was too easy to be tracked these days with the implants. "It's been here longer than either of us has been alive and will probably be here long after we're gone."

Davian snorted. He turned the tuner on the little black radio. Mostly there was just static.

Finally he found something.

"—not sure if it's more widespread. Repeat, Pittsburgh has taken a direct hit from a pulse weapon, likely of Sino-African origin. Initial casualty estimates are in the low millions...."

"Jesus. Turn it off." Eddy spat on the ground.

Davian shot him a look. "Still think this place is gonna survive?"

"How the hell would I know?"

"Fair enough." He put the x-band away. "Any friends or family there?"

Eddy shook his head. "Not really. Just an ex-boyfriend."

"Me neither."

"We're really going to do this, aren't we?" Eddy walked over to the cavern entrance to look out at the darkness. "Wreck the whole goddamned world?" The cavern faced south, and Pittsburgh was—had been—to the north. The view was deceptively serene.

Davian put a hand on his shoulder. "Nothing we can do about it. Just have to work on getting our own asses off this rock faster, is all." He was a dirty mess, like Eddy was, but they had little time to waste with personal hygiene.

They used a couple of towels to clean themselves off with some water from the tank they'd hauled up with them. A quick meal of ready-packs and Eddy was back in the jumper, checking over the rest of the ship for leaks.

As he worked, he wondered what had happened to Tim, the guy he'd met in basic training who hadn't cared whether he was physically male or female.

Who had spent a year with him in the Asian Pacific theater before Eddy had met Davian.

Who had likely just lost his life in the attack on Pittsburgh, 150 miles north of where they sat.

He shook his head and returned to work.

DAVIAN TRIED hard not to show it. The dirt on his face probably helped.

The attack on Pittsburgh had shaken him to his core.

Though he'd abandoned them long ago—or more accurately, they had abandoned him—his parents had lived in Green Tree, a suburb just outside the city.

He still remembered his mother standing in her doorway, her look of disappointment clear on her face after he had flunked out of college. His suitcases had been packed, and she'd brooked no argument as she sent him away.

"A man must make his own way in the world." She'd refused his entreaties to let him stay.

He had nowhere to go, no friends to speak of, and no money.

"Your father and I can't take care of you anymore. You're twenty-one. At your age, I was already through college and working for the state."

"But Mamma...."

She turned her back and closed the door behind her, leaving him on the porch, alone.

Of course, it had been as much about the drinking and the fighting as it had been about leaving school.

He'd enrolled in the NAU Armed Forces the next day and had never gone back home.

He'd carried the bitterness of that parting with him these past six years, but now... now they were probably gone, and he'd never get the chance to set things right between them.

It changed nothing.

They were leaving this place soon anyway, and he never would have seen them again, in any case.

Somehow, *knowing* they were gone was different.

"You're awfully quiet down there," Eddy called from the Moonjumper, up in the truck bed. "You sure you're okay?"

"Yeah." He hoped Eddy didn't hear the catch in his throat. *Goddammit.* "Just thinking about all those people."

Two of them, in particular.

Chapter Four:
Refugees

COLIN STOOD on the slight rise above the encampment, taking in the picture of human misery there.

It was like the slums of Venice, California, where the saltwater had invaded the low-lying lands and the original population had moved out, leaving only those who were too poor to leave.

Maybe it wasn't that bad, but the ramshackle shelters, made of sheets of plas draped over wooden poles, seemed to stretch for miles. He could see that the river ran foul, even from here. There were just too many people in one place, without adequate facilities and services.

Several columns of smoke drifted up from the campsite; off to the left, an entire stand of alifir trees had been chopped down for fuel. They would grow back, but still, this encampment represented a cancer on the land, the virgin territory of Forever. It hurt him to see it abused like this, though there was no denying the need.

A traxx was unloading food—mostly fresh produce—probably brought in from some of the working farms inside Forever. A long line of people waited to collect their share, and it was clear that there wasn't enough for them all.

"How long has it been like this?" he asked Andy.

She shook her head. "It's been growing by the day. We're struggling to keep everyone fed."

He shook his head. All that food in Darlith, and the people here were fighting over scraps. "What about the farmer's market?"

Andy shrugged. "We've asked. No one wants to give up their goods. They'd rather sell it at the market to make a profit."

Colin frowned. Business run amok had been the downfall of Earth, in his estimation. He'd have to see what he could do to prevent the same thing from happening up here. "Come along, then." He gestured for Andy to follow him. "Let's find out what's going on down there."

ANDY FOLLOWED the ex-director down the hillside to camp. The food from the traxx had just run out, and the line, still hundred of people long, was starting to dissipate with a lot of grumbling.

They approached the two-person crew standing behind the traxx. "Dania, Trent… it's good to see you again!" He held out his hand.

"Director!" Dania's mouth dropped open. "Oh, it's good to see you too. What are you doing down here? I thought you'd retired somewhere in the wilderness."

"Director Hammond called me out of retirement to try to do something about the immigration crisis we're facing." He indicated the ramshackle shelter.

"Yes, sir. We're doing what we can."

"Is there any kind of organized authority here from Transfer Station?"

Dania and Trent looked at each other and shook their heads. "Just us, sir. We're all spread kinda thin."

He nodded. "Can I borrow one of these?" He hefted an empty crate into the air.

"Of course." She gave him a big grin. "Going to get up on your soap box?"

"Something like that." Colin set the crate on the ground upside down and climbed on top of it. He put his finger and thumb between his lips and let out a piercing whistle.

The crowd went silent, and everyone turned to look at him.

"Excuse me. I'm here from the Station Authority."

The crowd gathered around him. Their faces were gaunt. They'd probably had little to eat on the journey up from Earth, and not all that much here either.

"Are there any leaders in this community?" he called out.

The gathered mass looked at one another and shrugged.

"There's Mestra Vaughn," one of the men near the back said. "She's been looking after people who are injured."

"That will do. Is she here?"

"No, but I can go get her."

"Please. In the meantime, I want to assure you that we will get things sorted out. We didn't expect such an influx of new faces up here."

Andy admired how he stepped up and took control of the situation. Her father was like that too.

"Where's the food?" a young black woman called. "My kids are going hungry."

"We'll get more food. The important thing—"

"What about sanitation? We have no restrooms, nowhere to bathe or shower besides the river." This from an older man with gray hair, dressed in a torn shirt and jeans.

"We will take care of that too, I promise you. We must all stay calm—"

"What about clothing? Blankets?"

The crowd murmured, and Andy could see the director was losing control.

"All your complaints will be addressed in good time—"

"We don't have time!" a bearded man shouted. "We've been here for weeks without basic necessities. Why are we being kept out in the woods like animals, while others get to live in houses in Micavery and Darlith, with roofs over their heads and meals in their stomachs?"

There was general assent, and the crowd inched forward menacingly.

"Maybe we should get out of here?" Andy whispered. She'd never seen anything like this in her short life, though she'd read about the water riots in Arizona and Texas in her history texts. One thing she was sure of—she didn't want to be in the middle of one.

"Everyone calm down." A black woman of indeterminate age with dreadlocks stepped out of the crowd. She was dressed in bright gold and orange in a traditional African pattern and leaned on a walking stick. "Thomas Jones, leave the poor man alone," she said to the man with the beard.

The man looked down at the ground sheepishly.

"I'm sure Mr.—?"

"McAvery," Colin supplied smoothly.

"I'm sure Mr. McAvery is here to help. What good will it do to chase him away before we have a chance to hear what he has to say?" She came to stand in front of the director, putting both hands on the top of her walking stick and staring at him.

216

Although Colin was standing on a wooden crate, she seemed his equal in stature.

Colin seemed to sense it too. He stepped down and held out his hand to her. "Ms. Vaughn, I assume?"

"Mrs. Vaughn, though my husband is long dead." She took his hand and shook it warmly. "You're Director McAvery, I presume?"

"Ex-director. But yes."

"Okay, y'all, there's nothing more to see here. Back to your families." She shooed the crowd away, and they dispersed, though some shot Andy and Colin dirty looks.

"This is Andy." Colin pulled her forward.

"Nice to meet you, ma'am."

Mestra snorted. "You can always count on the young ones to remind you how old you are." She turned back to Colin, giving him an appraising look. "You *are* here to help, aren't you?"

He nodded. "Andy's father, Director Hammond, called me in. Maybe we could start with—"

"Let's start with a tour. Once you have a better idea what we're dealing with here, you can tell me what you can do about it."

Colin looked at Andy, who shrugged. "Fair enough."

Andy liked her instantly. She was one of those take-no-crap people.

"Come on, then." She beckoned them to follow her and led them into the camp.

Someone had driven poles into the ground at various intervals, and wide sheets of gray plas were stretched from one to another, making a tent structure. "The plas isn't continuous, so it leaks quite a bit when it rains." It was also fairly dark inside the structure, with no plants to shed light underneath. Only the ambient light of the air provided a little illumination.

The wind kicked up, and the plas rattled, sounding like thunder.

"Try sleeping through that at night."

"I can imagine." Colin looked back at her.

Andy shook her head. "I couldn't."

They followed Mestra along a track worn into the trampled grass that led toward the center of the tent.

Andy looked around. Groups of people sat on the ground or against the poles, staring back at her grimly. Their faces were covered in dirt, and their clothes were grimy too. There were hundreds and hundreds of them.

The lucky ones were eating the produce they'd gotten from the traxx, earning them dirty looks from their neighbors.

"First of all," Mestra was saying, "there's not enough food to go around. They deliver enough for a quarter of the camp each day, and we're lucky there haven't been more fights over it yet.

"We also need medical help. These people come from all over the globe, and some of them brought influenza with them, as well as various types of rhinoviruses. They spread quickly in such close quarters."

"Are you a doctor?" Andy asked.

She shook her head, her dreads dancing. "No. I was a nurse for many years. We do have a couple doctors here, though. Dr. Schmidt is from Seattle, and Dr. Bui is Filipino, from Hawaii. They're struggling to provide treatment, with no medicine and little in the way of equipment." She waved at a little girl who stood by the pathway, staring at them. "Hey, Raisa!" She ruffled the girl's hair. "Run back to your mother now."

The girl grinned and ran off.

"Most folks are still in shock from the trip to get here from Earth, but that will wear off. I'm afraid if you don't do something soon to show them they will be properly cared for, you'll have a riot on your hands."

Colin nodded. "I can see that. Thank you for intervening back there."

"Nothing will get fixed if we start fighting one another." She stopped next to a gate in a wall made of wooden poles and broken sheets of plas. "Here we are. This is where we treat the sick, to the best of our abilities." She opened the gate and led them inside.

The wide space held maybe twenty makeshift beds—piles of blankets and clothing to keep the sick off the bare ground. They were all occupied.

Some were coughing, while others just stared up at the tent roof with faces slack with despair. On one side, there were three patients with arms or legs wrapped in blood-soaked cloth.

"One of the tent poles collapsed and injured five of our Plastown residents. Two were treated and released. These three broke bones. We've done our best to try and set them properly, but without x-rays and clean bandages and antibiotics—"

"Plastown?" Colin looked around, his face grim. "I get it. You need help. How many refugees are there?"

"Near as I can count, a bit over two thousand so far."

Andy whistled. The entire legitimate population of Forever was just over five thousand. They weren't ready for this kind of influx.

"What do you need most urgently?" Colin asked Mestra.

"Food. Blankets. Medicine. Potable water."

"Water is easy. The streams here are pure… at least upstream from here. We can get you containers to collect and store it in. Medicine… we can raid the clinic at Micavery and have Transfer send more down. I'll contact the director and make it happen."

"We can get food from the farmers' market in Darlith. Have them load it on the train."

"They're not gonna like that." Colin grinned.

"We're all in this together, right?" Andy looked around at the misery of the camp. It felt good to do something, anything to help these folks.

"Good attitude." He squeezed Mestra's shoulder. "Give me a few minutes to confer with Director Hammond."

Mestra nodded. "Please do whatever you can. People need reason to hope."

"I will." Colin tapped his temporary loop. "Lex, please patch me into Hammond's line up on Transfer." He stepped away to talk out the details.

"I think I can help with the bathroom facilities." Andy looked around at the sick people in the enclosure. It was the least she could do for them.

"How's that?" Mestra patted her on the head. "Do you know someone?"

Andy grinned. "You could say that."

DAVIAN WIPED the sweat and grime from his face and tightened the last bolt.

God, how he missed civilization. Sure, this was nothing compared to his wartime duty, but since he'd been home, he'd gotten used to things like showers and beds and food that came packaged in plastic. None of this reconstituted shit.

At least he'd finally gotten the ventilation system cleaned out and reinstalled. It wasn't perfect. The little tin can would be hot, and the thought was already giving him nightmares, but it should be survivable. For one of them.

He pulled himself out. "Okay, that about does it. How close are we?"

"Almost there. Just about ready to have you help me install the x-drive. Then the seats go back in, assuming—"

"We haven't blown ourselves to bits?"

"Yeah, that sounds about right." Eddy grinned. "Hey, what time is it?"

Davian pasted on a smile. "About 11:00 a.m." He stood and stretched and took a look outside at the mountains beyond the fuzz field. It looked so *normal*. No hint that an entire city, not two hours north of them, had just been wiped off the face of the Earth. No clue that his own parents were gone with it.

Not a sign that the end of the world was at hand.

"Okay, I think I'm ready to put the drive in." Eddy came up behind him to stare outside too. "Surreal, isn't it?"

Davian nodded. *You have no idea.* "Let's get this done."

Together they unpacked the x-drive from its wooden crate. The device worked by negating gravity within a sphere around the drive—the more powerful the device, the bigger the sphere. Davian had worked on them in the field and had managed not to get his hands blown off, or worse.

The Moonjumper's original drive had long ago been removed and dismantled. The technology, while supremely useful, was also temperamental, and an aging drive could explode and cause significant damage if it wasn't maintained properly.

Davian wasn't sure where Eddy had gotten his hands on this one. He wasn't sure he wanted to know.

Not that it mattered anymore.

He pulled on his safety gloves. Then he removed the packing material and carefully lifted the drive out of its protective webbing.

It was about the size of his outstretched hand, a silver sphere with no visible external hardware. "Pretty little thing."

Eddy laughed. "Buy her a drink first, at least."

Davian snorted. "The chamber's ready?"

"Yes, just need to carry it inside. Carefully." Once it was installed, the danger of an explosion dropped considerably, but in the meantime he tried hard not to shake it up.

Eddy pulled on his own gloves and climbed onto the bed of the truck. "Hand it to me."

Davian passed it up slowly. Then he climbed up onto the truck too.

"Okay, I'm gonna ease it in, then you fire up the magnetic field. Ready?" Eddy climbed slowly into the jumper, kneeling over the open container that was set to receive the drive.

The drive had to be kept from touching the edges of its compartment.

Davian followed him inside. The little ship was crowded with two people, even without their seats. This was going to be a fun trip. *Yay for me.*

He put his hand on the power button. "Ready."

"Three, two, one...." Eddy spun the two hemispheres in opposite directions, and the sphere lit up with a golden glow. He held the drive inside the container. "Now!"

Davian activated the magnetic field, and the drive settled down inside, floating in the middle of the round container.

Eddy closed the lid, and the glow dimmed to a glimmer.

"Nice job!" Eddy held up his hand.

Davian slapped it. "Woo-hoo! We're going to Forever!" He felt good about it, for just a minute. It beat the hell out of his present environs.

Eddy grinned. "Let's get the seats in and run through the system checks. I want to get us out of here as fast as we can."

Davian nodded. He couldn't get off this shithole of a planet fast enough.

Chapter Five:
Jump

COLIN WAITED for Director Hammond to connect from Transfer Station.

He looked around the camp. The conditions these people were living in were primitive, and they were taking a toll on the local ecosystem too. Forever was a relatively small biosphere, and they were still working to find the balance—a balance that would be necessary to sustain the world for several centuries.

She didn't have the resources to absorb a whole lot of excess pollution, especially at this early stage in her development.

It also spoke ill for their future if this was the best they could do for their unexpected guests.

"Hammond here. What's going on down there?" Aaron sounded agitated.

"Hi, Aaron." Colin closed his eyes and could see his old friend in his mind's eye. "You sent me into quite the mess here."

"Sorry about that." Colin could hear the weariness in Aaron's voice too. The man had a lot on his plate. "The ships have been coming in fast and furious. I've had my hands full up here trying to keep on top of them and not lose more immigrants than we have to."

"It's that bad?"

"Yeah. Anything that can fly is being sent up here. Last week, we had an old space station module dragged out here by the coyotes and left for dead. And I mean *dead*. It sprang a leak, and all thirty-five people inside were frozen to death. Kids too."

"Oh God." Colin hadn't realized how bad things were. Children, for God's sake. If he could get his hands on some of those coyotes....

"It's slowing down now... not sure what else is still space-worthy that hasn't been thrown at us. Even the regular supply runs seem to be breaking down—the *Hammond* was due here two days go, and we can't reach her. Frontier Station's being cagey about it."

Colin shook his head. Things were going south fast. "Damn. We're on our own, then?"

"Seems like it, for now. So what can I do for you?"

Colin shook his head. "It's a tough job, Aaron. But better you than me. You're still young." He glanced back at Mestra and Andy. "Okay, I need to requisition your fancy new train and some foodstuffs from Darlith. I want to clean out their farmers' market."

"The colonists aren't going to be too keen on that."

"I know. But it's that or start seeing widespread malnutrition and starvation down here in the refugee camp."

"Gotcha. Done."

"Next, I need containers. Anything that can hold and store water. And soap if you have some."

"In fact, we do. There's a soapmaker in Micavery now… I mean McAvery Port—"

Colin laughed. "Micavery is fine. Will of the people and all that."

"Yeah." Aaron laughed, a refreshing sound after his earlier bitterness. "You'll be remembered by history, all right. As long as you don't care that they screwed up your name. I'll see what we can scare up, container wise. What else?"

Colin hesitated. "You're not gonna like this one."

Aaron snorted. "That's the phrase I wake up to every morning, these days. Hit me."

"I need whatever medications you can spare. Painkillers, antiseptics, antibiotics, the works. There are a few bugs going around camp that we need to knock down, and fast."

"Ah."

"Told you that you weren't gonna like it." He glanced around the camp. He was getting resentful looks. They didn't have much in the way of technology, or anything else, for that matter. "Tell you what. I'll send Andy up for them. I'm not keen on her being down here. Things could get rough—these folks aren't happy. Maybe we can get some from Micavery in the meantime."

"That's fine. The factory's manufacturing the basics now— antibiotics, vaccines, the like. I have a feeling the good doctor has her hand in that—she asked for a copy of the biogenome library last month too. But we can send down some more specialized drugs and equipment."

223

Colin nodded. Only a select few knew about Ana and Jackson's part in the world-mind. "If you can scare up some blankets, those would be appreciated."

"Listen, Colin—"

"I know what you're going to say. Don't mention it. I'm glad to help."

"Thank you, anyhow. You have no idea how much having you there gives me peace of mind. I'll get the meds and food requisition out to Darlith right away."

"Thanks, Aaron." He tapped off the loop and put it back into his pocket.

"Any luck?" Andy asked as he returned.

"Yes. In fact, I'm sending you up to Transfer to retrieve some medicine for the camp. Director Hammond is also sending some antibiotics from Micavery."

Mestra smiled. "That's good news. And food?"

"On its way shortly. Though I may have made a few enemies in Darlith."

"Thank you, Director McAvery." The nurse surprised him with a spontaneous hug. "People here have given up hope. It will mean so much to them to have something to cheer about, once again."

"Now we best get you on your way, Andy—"

"Not quite yet. Bathrooms, remember?"

ANDY LED them out into the camp, glancing around nervously at the people who stared back at her sullenly. Her life in Forever and up at Transfer Station had always been neat and clean, well-organized and without much rancor, but these poor people had been through hell and back to get here.

Andy could hardly imagine the things they had been through. Many of them had been taken advantage of by coyotes, paying an exorbitant amount of money just to get a place in a shipping container bound for what they hoped would be a better life. Many of them had seen horrible things. Sickness, death, and decay in their improvised transports—only to arrive here and have to live like this, with no sanitation, little food, and no good place to sleep.

"Hello."

The voice startled her out of her musings. A little boy stood in her path, staring up at her with big brown eyes.

She knelt and put a hand on his shoulder. He couldn't be more than four years old, his chestnut hair smeared with dirt. "Hello there."

"I'm Tyson."

"Hi, Tyson, I'm Andy. Nice to meet you." She held her hand out to shake his, but he just stared at her. "Hey, I have something for you."

"What is it?"

She pulled off her carry sack and took out the dried fruits and nuts she had left over. "Here you go. These are really good. Take them back to your mommy, okay?"

"Okay." He took the little bag and turned to run away. Then he hesitated. "Mommy says to always say thank you."

"You're welcome." She tousled his hair and sent him on his way.

"That was kind." Mestra nodded. "Your parents raised you well."

Andy blushed. "Thanks." She turned away, embarrassed. "Let's get this over with." She led them past the edge of the camp and to an open space that had been cleared of alifir trees. "I'm going to talk with the world-mind. You might want to stand back."

Mestra looked quizzically at Colin, who shrugged. "Better do what the girl says."

They stepped back toward the shelter, and Andy knelt in the dust of the disturbed earth. She put her right hand down into the soil and *dipped* into Forever.

The scene dissolved around her, and the workings of the world were revealed beneath her feet.

She delved down deep, following the roots of the alifir trees that stood at the edge of the recently cleared earth. They sank down, seeking the luthiel that ran through the crust of Forever like blood.

There.

Below her was one of the waste disposal tubes that carried discarded and dead material back to be digested and repurposed. Somewhere down there, wrapped around the tube, would be some of the roots of the world.

For this, she didn't think she'd even need to talk to the world-mind itself. She could handle this one on her own.

She found one of the world roots and *reached*, connecting to the impulses that ran along it carrying information to and from the world-mind. Then she *pulled.*

The root responded, sending a new branch up through the soil, creating a faint rumbling as it extended itself upward.

The noise grew louder.

"Everything okay over there, kiddo?" Colin asked.

"Yes. All good," she said without opening her eyes. She'd never done anything quite like this before, but she had played with the world-mind's subroutines before to do things like open a hole in a cavern wall or create a treehouse.

The root burst forth in a shower of dirt to tower over her.

"Andy!" Colin shouted and ran toward her.

"It's okay." She waved him off. "This is me doing this."

She proceeded to weave an enclosure with the hard, wooden root stem, telling it what she wanted through the link that connected them. Leaves burst out of the wood, creating light in the darkening enclosure and blocking the holes in the woven branches of wood.

At the same time, she coaxed a second root to grow up and up, bursting into the middle of her newly created chamber to create an evacuation hole that led down to the waste tunnel.

For her final act, she coaxed the end of the first root into a warm wooden seat just above the hole.

She opened her eyes and stared at her handiwork. *Voila.* It was crude, but it would have to do.

She stood and wiped the dust off her eyes. She was filthy. A good bath in the river would take care of that. She wasn't picky.

She stepped out into the open air. A group of refugees had gathered behind Mestra and Colin.

"What is it?" Mestra asked, touching the new wood.

"It's a bathroom. You'll need a bucket of water for the flush, but it should work."

"That was...." Colin seemed at a loss for words.

"Astonishing." Mestra smiled at her. "Can you... would you make a few more?"

Andy nodded. "I think so. Now that I've gotten the hang of it, it shouldn't be too hard."

"May I take a look?"

Andy nodded.

Mestra stepped inside. "We'll need a door too."

"Oh yeah. Sorry. It's not—"

"It's perfect." Mestra turned to hug her. "You are a gift from God, my girl."

Colin nodded, but he looked worried too. "You sure it won't take too much out of you?"

"It's okay. I can manage a few more." Though interfacing with the world-mind on such a direct level did often make her tired, it was worth it.

"That's not all I'm worried about." He glanced at the crowd. Most of them were smiling, but Andy was getting a few dark looks too. "The world is not as nice a place as you might believe. Not everyone will accept your... power."

She shrugged. These people needed her help, and she was in a position to give it.

How could that be wrong?

EDDY STOOD back to take a look at the jumper. He'd just finished reinstalling the auxiliary nav tanks—the propellant that would lift them high enough off the ground to fire the x-drive and let them maneuver once they were past Earth's gravitational well. "I think we're ready."

Davian nodded. "Ventilation system is as good as it's gonna get."

Eddy hopped off the back of the truck and went to stare at the peaceful valley outside the cave mouth. It was a weird thing knowing this might be the last time he ever saw the Earth. It was his home, but more than that, it was his species' home. Where they had evolved and where they *belonged*, somewhere deep in their DNA.

There was something fundamentally wrong about leaving it behind forever. He could feel it in his bones.

Forever was waiting. They'd make a new life there, but it would never be the same. Still, life went on.

"You gonna miss it?" Davian asked, coming up beside him and clapping him on the shoulder.

"Yeah. I think so." *I'll never see the ocean again.*

"I won't. Earth's no more than a decaying pit of endless war, heat, and famine. Good riddance." He spat. "The world's going down in flames, and I don't want to be here when it all comes crashing down."

Eddy nodded. He'd still miss so much about his home world. Sailing on the Great Lakes. The smell of the desert when it rained. The majesty of the Grand Canyon.

The scent of sulfur and blood and death.

It was time to go.

He checked the time. It was 3:04 p.m. "We have a launch window in about half an hour. You ready?"

"Now or never."

They set to work packing the bare necessities into the Moonjumper. In addition to a small supply of food, each of them had brought a duffel bag with the things most important to them.

Eddy had his father's old well-thumbed paperback copy of *Childhood's End*, a package of Oreos, a pack of Snap gum, and Samson, the dog-eared teddy bear his mother had given him when he was five.

Eddy also stashed as many bottles of water as he could manage in the small space.

They pulled on their space suits and zipped them up, just in case of decompression. Their helmets went behind their seats.

When they were ready, he took one more look outside and cautiously pulled the truck through the fuzz field, out onto the road where the Moonjumper would have a clean shot to the sky.

They climbed up onto the truck bed together.

Eddy took one last deep breath of the Earth's air. He smelled pine needles and dust. *Goodbye, old friend. I will miss you most of all.*

Davian climbed inside the little Moonjumper, and Eddy followed him, closing the door behind him and sealing it.

They ran through the preflight check Eddy had written out for them. Not that they could do much about it if things didn't check out.

They knocked things off their improvised checklist, with Eddy calling things off one by one.

"Seal door."

"Check."

"Confirm cabin pressure."

"Check."

"Test ventilation system."

"Check."

"Test fire propulsion system."

"Check."

"X-drive ready?"

Davian turned to stare at him. "Hell if I know."

That summed up the state of things nicely.

"Powering up." Davian brought the auxiliary jets online. They would boost the jumper up into the air, and then the x-drive would kick in.

Should kick in. He said a little prayer to whatever deities might be listening.

The power came on across the control screen. Then with a spark, it went out again.

"Crap." Davian tried to power the jumper off and back on, but nothing happened.

"I'm going out to take a look." Eddy unlatched his belt and unsealed the hatch. He eased himself out of the tight space between the seats and squeezed around the side of the jumper to open the fuse panel.

Sure enough, one of the main fuses had blown.

"It's a fuse," he called back. "I've got another in the cavern. Be right back."

Eddy jumped to the ground and jogged back inside the cavern that had been their home these last few days.

He rummaged through his old toolbox, looking for the fuse. He'd brought extras of whatever he could manage, just in case.

He found it near the bottom.

Next to it was a half-empty tube of readygel. Which was strange, because he didn't remember buying it. Or using it.

Eddy shrugged. Maybe Davian had needed it for something.

He grabbed the fuse and ran back out to the Moonjumper.

After pulling out the old one, he threw it away and popped in the new fuse, twisting it in to make contact.

He took one more "last" breath of air and made his way back around to the hatch.

He froze.

A kuripa drone was cruising through the valley below them.

Eddy climbed back inside the Moonjumper as quickly as he was able and pulled the door shut. "Trouble. Drone."

Davian nodded. He powered up the little makeshift craft, and this time the power stayed on.

Maybe they'd be lucky. Maybe it wouldn't notice them.

Maybe they'd better get their asses in gear.

"Ready?"

Davian nodded.

"Give me some thrust!"

Davian engaged the rocket, and the Moonjumper jerked into the air, rising quickly up from the truck below them, sending the old Ford careening down the mountainside. *No other way out now. Five, ten, fifteen feet...* they needed at least thirty before he could safely engage the x-drive.

Davian peered out through the wraparound window.

The drone had turned toward them. It was speeding in their direction, and as he watched, something detached from its nose, streaking at them on a burst of flame.

Twenty feet. Twenty-two. Twenty-four.

The missile was speeding toward them. They weren't gonna make it.

"We have to engage the drive now."

"It's too soon!" Eddy's hand hovered over the drive button.

Twenty-seven.

"If we wait any longer, it will be too late!" Davian slammed Eddy's hand down on the button, and the x-drive lit up, shining a golden glow throughout the cabin.

The craft lurched to the side, slipping away from the missile as it rushed though the air where they had just been. The missile slammed into the mountainside, throwing up an explosion of dust and debris that showered down on the little craft like hail, filling the cabin with clatter.

"Goddammit!" Eddy fought to control the craft. The ship spun toward the mountainside.

He fired one of the lateral jets, pushing them away and shooting them back toward the approaching drone.

The drone was almost on top of them, one of its laser turrets rising out of its side to target them.

Now or never, indeed.

He punched the liftoff rocket, using up precious fuel but thrusting them above the threshold.

The laser strafed the side of the Moonjumper, but only just, and then they were going up, up, up, rising quickly on a tide of antigravity.

The drone tried to follow, but they were already ascending too fast through the atmosphere, passing through white fluffy clouds.

They were going to make it. "We're gonna live," he said in wonder. *We fucking did it.*

"For now."

Eddy ignored Davian's surly tone.

He let go of the controls and let himself float in his seat as the Moonjumper's x-drive dragged them up toward the stars.

Chapter Six:
Hiss

Like Ana, Jackson had a rough time of it accommodating to his new life, but his journey had taken much longer.

After the seedling had incorporated him into itself, his thoughts had floated around inside the world-mind in a disjointed fashion, like flotsam and jetsam on the ocean after a plane crash.

It had taken time for it to all come back together, and even then, he hadn't known who or what he was for the longest time.

It wasn't until his son, Aaron, had arrived on Forever and touched the world-mind that his consciousness had reawakened, and that he had become Jackson Hammond once more.

Now he felt pride as his granddaughter, Andy, used her gift to help the poor refugees who had fought hard to reach this little oasis.

She was a beautiful child, filled with goodwill and the earnest desire to help.

That was all Glory, he was sure.

Soon it would be time to see her again.

He could feel it. The winds of change were blowing, and blowing hard.

THINGS WERE looking up.

Colin had sent Andy up to Transfer Station for medical supplies. She was a smart kid. She'd know what to bring back—and he felt better having her out of the way. People down here were still restless.

In the meantime, a small supply was coming from Micavery on the next train.

Her talent with Forever and the world-mind still amazed him. She'd built ten of the bathroom structures out of basically nothing before he'd sent her to the river to wash and then bundled her onto the train, wet and exhausted. The woodsheds, as people had taken to calling them, were constantly busy. Far better than having all that human waste going into the river.

Food had started to arrive from Darlith, though the predicted protests had been coming through to him and Aaron fast and furious.

He replied to each, pointedly explaining that this was a matter of life and death for the immigrants in the camp, and they'd figure out the economics of it all later. And how would the complainers feel if it were their own kids who were starving? Parents? Spouses?

The noise was starting to die down, and he felt like he might be turning the tide.

He'd also recruited four "Community Ambassadors" to help get everything in camp back onto an even keel—Dana Thomas, Brad Evers, Kwame Jones, and Maria Ortiz. He'd assigned each one to a quadrant of the camp and put them in charge of distributing resources and bringing issues to his attention. He'd also given them each a pen and notepad that he'd brought with him from his personal supply at home. Old-school, sure, but it worked out here.

"I've got a family of four from Darwin, Australia—the Griffins." Maria looked at her handwritten notes. "Their son has asthma and could use an inhaler."

"Got it. I'll relay that up to Transfer Station. What else?"

"A woman from Texas who is trying to find out if her grandson made it up here. I guess he was coming on a different coyote ship."

"We need to make a list of everyone here and put together a database."

She nodded. "I've started collecting names as I go. I can bring them all to you tonight."

"Good idea. I'll let the others know. See if you can get the age and a list of skills for each person too."

"Will do. Oh, and on that note, I found a civil engineer who said he knows how to build housing using primitive materials. Did it in the Southwest, apparently, after the Great Burn."

"Send him to me. We'll put him to work. We need to do better than this." He gestured at the drooping sheets of plas above their heads.

"Got it. And sir?"

"Call me Colin." Everyone was too damned formal.

"Colin, then. I'm so glad you're here."

ANDY RUBBED her eyes.

She was *drained.*

She'd made things with the world-mind before, but never on such a scale. It took a lot of energy to tap into the world-mind's subroutines and bend them to her will.

Not that she was forcing it to do anything, really. It was more like creating a path or a conduit and letting the mind follow her lead.

She'd caught a quick nap on the short trip into town.

The train settled into the station at Micavery with a sigh.

She grabbed her carry sack and headed out into the afternoon light. Creeper vines, wrapped around the poles of the station platform, provided light, and the ground was still wet from the afternoon showers.

She descended the steps and looked up at the town, now almost a city in its own right. Two- and three- and five-story buildings followed a meandering set of roads and extended across the peninsula that swept away on either side of her, about a third of the way up the walls of the world. One of the Transfer Station shuttles was just descending to Landing Station. With luck, she'd be able to hop a flight on it back up to Transfer.

"Your father's calling," Rina, her AI, whispered in her ear.

"Put him through." She stepped off the path for privacy, under a huge mallow tree. "Andy here."

"Hi, Andy, it's your father." He sounded distracted.

"Rina already told me, Dad."

"Of course. Listen, you're on your way back up here, right?"

"Yes. I just got into Micavery."

"Can you catch the next shuttle up?"

"I was on my way there when you called. Is there room?" Something was up. She could hear it in his voice.

"I'll make room." Her father was quiet for a moment. "There. Done. I need your help."

"What's up?"

"There's something strange going on with the station-mind. Just get up here as fast as you can."

She frowned. That didn't sound good. Her father's voice had a strange edge to it. Worry, maybe? If it was enough to worry Aaron Hammond, it had to be *bad*. "Will do."

"Thanks, kiddo. See you soon. Mom sends her love." He cut the connection.

Andy threw her carry sack onto her back and set off toward Landing Port at a run.

EDDY STRETCHED his legs out as far as they would go in the confined space until his suit boots touched metal.

Moonjumpers were made for cheap travel from the Earth up to the moon and near-Earth orbit and back. They were *not* made for comfort. The evacuation tubes built into his suit weren't all that fun either.

If anything, Davian seemed to have it worse than he did. The man was sweating profusely, and ever since they'd left Earth's atmosphere, he'd been staring at the control screen in front of him with his jaw clenched.

It was warm inside the jumper. The temperature gauge read ninety-five degrees.

"You okay over there?" Eddy was concerned about his friend's demeanor.

"Just a little claustrophobic."

"Ah… the war."

Davian nodded, but he didn't look at Eddy. "It helps, a little, to pick a place to focus on. I stare at it and try to forget everything else for a few moments."

"It must have been fucking terrible for you, those three months."

"You have no idea."

He really didn't. To have been tortured like that, for weeks and weeks at a time….

Eddy cast about for something, anything, to keep himself busy.

Gum. He had gum.

Eddy released his safety belt and contorted his body to reach around the back of his seat. He found the duffel bag, but the zipper was stubborn. He had to work at it to get it to open.

Finally he managed to pull out the pack of Snap gum. "Want a stick?" He opened the pack and held it out toward Davian.

Davian didn't respond.

"Hey, Dav." He snapped his fingers in front of Davian's face. "Want a stick?"

"What?" Davian looked up at him, and his eyes focused for just a second. "No, thanks." Then it was back to looking at the control screen. "How much longer until we get there?"

Eddy shrugged and popped a stick into his mouth. The watermelon flavor burst over his tongue.

Watermelon. Another thing that was in the past. He savored the flavor, rolling the gum over and over on his tongue.

He checked the nav console. "Another ten hours, give or take." He could use a little of their remaining fuel to propel them along faster, but he was nervous about the amount they had left after burning off so much escaping the drone.

He'd need enough to slow them down on the far end of their trip, and to maneuver close enough to Transfer Station to be picked up.

Eddy took out a bottle of water and sipped on it. It was warm and unpleasant, but he forced himself to drink it anyway. The heat was starting to get to him too, and he'd never gone through the hotbox treatment like Davian had.

He handed an unopened bottle to his companion. "Drink this. You need to keep from getting dehydrated."

Davian stared at it for a moment, then nodded and opened it, gulping it down in a single go. He crumpled the bottle and threw it behind his seat. "Thanks," he whispered.

Eddy squeezed his knee in support. "We'll get through this."

Davian pulled away, but he nodded.

Eddy shrugged and sat back, closing his eyes. He dialed up SinPop's latest and probably last album, an otherworldly, bubbly instrumental.

The music started, and he took a deep breath and let it flow through him, hoping it would take his mind off the present. It worked, and he slipped into memory.

The ocean waves broke upon the rocky shore in rapid succession.

His mother walked beside him along the sea wall. He held her hand tightly—even then, he'd known he was a boy—and stared down at the crashing ocean waves in wonder.

They reached a bench that looked out over the churning waters. She sat down, spreading out her cotton dress, and gestured for him to climb up into her lap. She held him close, her arms wrapped around his chest, the brightly colored fabric of her sleeves whipping to and fro in the wind.

"See that island, out there in the distance?"

He strained to see what she was pointing at. There was a small patch of land out there, surmounted by a few buildings. It was difficult to make out much detail.

"That's St. Petersburg. Or what's left of it. I was born there. When I was a little girl, you could still drive across the bridge from here to get there, or drive around the bay, the long way." She sighed. "So many things have changed."

He looked out across the waves, wondering.

The world seemed so solid and permanent to him.

If it could change as much and as quickly as she said, how could he ever be safe?

The song ended, and Eddy's eyes opened.

There was some kind of background noise. He hadn't noticed it at first under the music, but it was a persistent drag on the song.

He flicked off the music and sat up, listening. "Do you hear that?"

Davian was asleep, his head tilted away.

It was the faintest hissing sound, notable only because the ship was so quiet as it floated through the void on the way to its rendezvous.

It was the hiss of air leaking out of the Moonjumper.

"Shit." He unbuckled himself, searching for the leak. He'd been over every damned inch of this little vessel. *How in the hell?*

It didn't take him long to find it. There was a pinhole under the console, in the hull of the little ship. "Holy crap," he whispered. What had caused it? A micro-meteor? More importantly, how could he stop it?

They had a limited amount of air.

He should have brought something along for just this possibility. Something like readygel but stronger. Something that could withstand the extreme cold.

Gum.

He popped the wad out of his mouth, knelt forward, and carefully pushed it into the hole.

Then he grabbed the pack, pulled out two more sticks, and chewed on them quickly until they were pliable enough to use.

He spit them out and pushed those down onto the rest, capping the hole.

The hissing stopped.

Eddy waited, watching as the gum froze in place from the outside chill.

With luck, it would hold.

He checked the oxygen tank gauge. They had lost a fair amount of air, but he figured they *should* have enough to reach Forever. Assuming there were no more mishaps.

On the plus side, the leak had drained some of the heat from the little craft.

Davian stirred. "Hey, it's cooler in here." He sat up, rubbing his eyes.

"Yeah, there was a leak." Eddy indicated the spot. "I was able to block it. But it's weird. Looks like a pinhole… almost like something bored through the hull. Not sure how I missed it before."

Davian stared at him blankly for a moment, then nodded. "The important thing is that you fixed it. Are we still good for air?"

"I think so. Just don't go hyperventilating on me."

Davian nodded. "We can always draw straws, if it comes to it." He smiled, but something about the way he said it left Eddy cold.

Chapter Seven:
History, Repeated

THE SHUTTLE approached Transfer Station on a slow glide, coming in near one of the station's two main air locks.

As Andy watched, lights flickered on and off along one part of the station's main wheel. *That* wasn't normal; she was sure of it. *What the heck's going on down there?*

The metal doors, thicker than she was tall, slid apart to let the shuttle in. They closed behind the small craft, and the air cycled in from large tanks on either side of the air lock bay.

They waited for the shuttle to continue on inside the station. After a couple of minutes, the captain's voice came on over the comm. "Sorry, folks, Transfer Station's air lock system seems to be experiencing a glitch. We should be moving forward toward the landing pad shortly."

Stranger and stranger. Something was seriously wrong. The air locks were built with redundancy after redundancy. They *should* be working. Andy couldn't remember a time when they hadn't worked.

She looked around the cabin. There were only two other people aboard with her.

She tapped her loop, calling her father.

"Hey, kiddo," his voice said in her head. "A little busy."

"Dad, is everything okay?"

He was silent just a second too long. "Of course it is," he said at last. "Are you here?"

"At the air lock. We're stuck in here."

"Just a sec." She pictured him tweaking something inside the guts of the world-mind. "There."

"Folks, the lock has opened. We should be landing shortly."

She smiled. "That did it. We're coming in."

"Good. Now get your ass up to my office as soon as you land. Gotta run."

"Got it," she said, but the connection was already broken.

The ship took another five minutes to land, settling down on the platform inside the station. Andy bounced impatiently in her seat. Her father *needed* her.

When the door opened, she grabbed her carry sack and ran out, heading to the landing tube to call the elevator.

It arrived quickly enough. At least that was still working. It was also full of people. They spilled out, looking worried and talking to one another softly.

Andy caught bits of the conversation as she waited for the crowd to empty out.

"—first time he's ever called an evacuation—"

"—probably nothing. He's just being safe."

"Nice to have a little forced R & R—"

At the back was Andy's mother.

"I'm so glad to see you!" Keera gathered her up in a big hug. "But you should be coming with us. It's not safe up here. Your father should be right behind me."

"I have to help Dad." Andy squirmed in her mother's grasp, anxious to be free.

Keera shook her head. "I don't want you in danger. You're coming down with us."

Andy pushed away from her mother. "Dad *needs* me. So do the rest of the people stuck up here. What if something happened to him? I'd never forgive myself if I left him alone. Or you."

Keera growled. "I don't like it."

Andy pecked her mother on the cheek and ducked into the elevator. "Thank you!" she called as she palmed the pad. Her mother tried to smile as the doors closed.

The whole thing made Andy uneasy. The station was built to survive almost anything. Director Mc… Colin had made sure of that, after what had happened with the *Dressler*.

What was going on?

The elevator whisked her up to the runway level, the main grand hallway that ran around the wheel. The doors opened, and there was a crowd waiting in line to head down for the next shuttle.

"We'll get it fixed," she called as she threw her carry sack over her shoulder and ran toward her father's office. Whatever *it* was.

Palming his office door open, she found her father sitting at his desk, his hand on his dipping interface. It was a wide, flat sheet of metal, made of a special alloy. He'd designed the thing himself with the help of the station scientific team. It made it easier for him to connect with the station-mind and also gave him more control over the processes inside.

He didn't look up. He was dipping deep.

She dropped her sack and pulled up a chair, laying her hand on the pad next to his. Everything blurred, and then she was somewhere else.

A giant blue sphere loomed over her, casting a pale glow.

The station-mind.

She was familiar with it. Intimate, really. She'd spent much of her childhood inside here, exploring this virtual space and creating worlds of her own with Ronan.

There was clearly something *wrong* with him.

Bits of greenish-yellow light crawled and twisted over his surface like worms or some fast-moving infection.

"Ronan, where is he?" she called out to the station-mind.

There was no response.

She slipped herself into one of the data streams like her father had taught her. He'd be in the middle of it all; that much was certain.

The stream pulled her along into the station-mind, and her world became a sea of blue.

Her father visualized Ronan's mind as an endless series of corridors. To her, they seemed more like streams and rivers, waters merging and dividing, throwing up big bunches of bubbles that clouded the major interstices.

She rode the flow like a pro swimmer, switching at each fork to those tributaries where the water looked dirtier. It left an oily sheen on her virtual skin.

Her quest took her deeper and deeper into the station-mind.

At last she heard something—to her mind's ears, it sounded like a teakettle—a high-pitched whine.

She came upon her father at last. He had his hand buried deep in one of the data streams. It was giving off the data equivalent of steam.

The dirty water seemed to boil as it encountered his touch and then came out clean on the other side.

He flashed her a smile. "Hey, kiddo. About time you got here."

"I was waylaid by Mom on the landing pad. She's worried. What is this?"

"There's a virus loose in the system. Ronan warned me about it, but he's gone quiet. He's spending all his energy fighting the thing."

"A virus? How?"

Aaron Hammond shrugged. "I don't know. Something that came with one of the refugees, I'd guess. I've given the order to evacuate all nonessential personnel."

"I saw. Is it that bad? What can I do?"

"Yeah, it's *that bad*. Come here and I'll show you."

She did as she was told, and he took her hand. "Feel what I'm doing here."

She put her hand over his, the one that cleansed the stream. "This stream holds the essential functions of the station—power, light, circulation. Ronan rerouted it all through here and is doing his best to shield it for as long as he can. But he's losing the battle. I need you here so I can go help him."

Andy shook her head. "I'm stronger and faster than you are in here. Let me go instead."

"Not a chance. It's too dangerous. A bad feedback loop could burn you out."

"I'll be careful." She winked at him and launched herself back into the stream, ignoring his shout.

She was better at this than he was. He'd taught her everything he knew, and then she'd gone on to learn so much more.

She found one of the red scouts the station-mind used to ferret out trouble and followed it through the streams. It looked a bit like a red manta ray as it undulated its way toward the epicenter of the trouble.

Ronan needed help, and she was the only one who could give it.

She and her father were among the handful of people who knew what the minds really were—beings capable of autonomous thoughts and feelings as complex as any of the people they served.

They *were* people, as far as she was concerned.

242

She could feel Ronan's fear in the stream.

She found him out on the edge of the sphere, in a spot where the yellows and greens were particularly virulent. He was surrounded by a yellowish gas, which swirled slowly around him. Red scouts whipped around him too, grazing the dirty fog. They held it at bay, but they were tiring, their colors fading slowly from red to orange.

"Andy!" Ronan was wearing the body of a station guard, his usual appearance when she spent time with him. He'd been a friend of hers since childhood, when she would retreat from the real world to play with him in the virtual worlds he'd created for her.

"Sorry Ro… it took me a while to get back up here from Forever." She held up a hand and *pushed*, and the fog parted to let her reach him. "Where did this come from?"

She stood back to back with him, and they used their combined wills to push the fog back just a little.

"Someone inserted it into my core." Sweat beaded his brow. "I first noticed it four hours ago. It started in some of the old mem-stores."

She nodded. "Daddy thinks one of the refugees brought it."

"Maybe so."

The war that raged on Earth had seemed so far away from them, something that couldn't touch them way up here. But now….

She stepped forward, putting her hand cautiously into the fog. It burned, but she concentrated, doing what her father had shown her, pulling the data in and cleansing it. A brown smoke billowed from her palm, but the fog was slowly drawn in. Bit by bit it thinned, drawing back even farther from the beleaguered station-mind. "We can do this."

Ronan nodded. "With your help, little one. Maybe…."

He went suddenly quiet.

She turned to say something. His face had gone white. "It's going to blow the power core."

"What?"

"The virus. It wasn't aimed at me. It's just been keeping me busy."

Everyone still here would die. "Holy crap. Ro, we can stop it."

Ronan looked at her and shook his head, smiling sadly. "Don't curse, little one. It doesn't suit you." He sighed. "It's too late for you to stop it. I'm the only one who can, and only with drastic action." He stepped forward to pull her into his arms, hugging her fiercely. "You need to get everyone off the station. I'll try to protect the core stream. You and your father should be able to keep the essential functions going long enough without me." He kissed her forehead. "I love you, *mija*."

"Wait! What are you going to do? Ro?"

He was gone.

"Ronan!"

The yellow fog was gone with him.

Everything started shaking around her, and the sound cycled up from a low hum to a violent keening. The light grew brighter and brighter.

There was an explosion of blue light, and the world around her went dark.

When she opened her eyes, she was standing on an empty plain. A single stream of clean blue light ran in the air next to her. Her father was standing about thirty meters away, looking as bewildered as she felt.

She ran toward him, following the stream. She was trying hard to understand what had just happened.

"What the hell?" her father asked as she reached him.

"I think he's gone."

"Ronan?"

She nodded. "He said the virus was trying to blow the power core. That only desperate measures could stop it."

"Oh God."

He took her in his arms, and they wept for the death of an AI.

COLIN WAS talking with Mestra when a terrible keening filled his head.

He stumbled away from her as the noise-light-pain screamed through his head, falling to his knees in the dirt.

It was coming from the network.

He ripped the loop off his temple and dropped it on the ground, sighing as the pain subsided.

"What was that?" Mestra asked, her brow knitted with concern.

"I don't know. I think it came over the Net. I'm afraid something terrible has happened." He picked up the loop and looked at it suspiciously, as if afraid it might bite him. Cautiously, he reconnected it to his temple.

Nothing bad happened.

He tapped it "Get me the director."

"I'm sorry," Lex said. "I can't reach Transfer Station." She sounded pained.

"What do you mean…?" Mestra and some of the other refugees were staring at him. "I'm sorry, looks like there's a glitch. Give me a minute to iron it out."

She nodded, but her narrowed eyes said she didn't entirely believe him.

He stepped out of the central enclosure and made his way to the edge of the encampment. "What do you mean you can't reach them?"

"The link to Transfer Station appears to have been severed. There was an attack on Ronan. He was fighting a viral incursion."

"Goddammit." He'd had Transfer built to his own specifications—with no organic parts—to avoid the possibility of another catastrophic failure like the one that had happened to the *Dressler*. Now the station-mind itself was in danger. "Can you tell me anything else?"

"Not at the moment. I will keep… just a minute. Incoming signal from Transfer. Emergency band."

"Thank God. Put it through."

There was a slight delay. Then a voice came over the line. "Colin, can you hear me?" It sounded thin and tinny.

"Yes. Aaron, is that you?"

"Yes."

"What the hell is going on up there?"

"We got hit by a virus. It's bad, Colin. Really bad. Ronan is… Ronan is gone. He sacrificed himself to keep the station power core intact."

Colin closed his eyes. History did repeat itself. "How are you talking to me, then?"

"He shielded the core functions of the station before he… before he died." Aaron was silent for a long moment. "Andy's taking it really hard," he said at last.

"I'll bet." With her talent, she and Ronan had probably been fast friends. He himself had felt great respect for the station-mind.

He would grieve for Ronan later. "What now?"

"We have to evacuate. We'd already started before Ronan sacrificed himself, but we have to ramp things up. I can maintain heat and air for a little while, but I can't keep this up forever. If we can get some help up here from Frontier Station, we *might* be able to replace the station-mind."

"That's a big if, given the situation on Earth."

"Yes. We haven't been able to reach anyone. The station-mind down there might have been hit too. Can you prepare for a couple hundred Transfer personnel on Ariadne? The first load is already on its way."

Colin sighed. The refugee problem would have to wait. "We'll manage." Just a couple of days before, he'd been looking forward to a long, peaceful retirement. Now.... "How long will it take to evacuate the whole station?"

"We have two active shuttles. There are about two hundred and fifty people still up here. The shuttles can carry maybe twenty-five in a pinch. So... ten trips? Maybe five to six hours."

"Gotcha. On my way, boss." He could hear Aaron's smile over the link.

"Thanks, Colin. We'll get through this."

He cut the connection, and Colin headed back into the camp to gather his lieutenants and Mestra.

"Transfer Station is in trouble. They're evacuating the station. Can you keep a lid on things here while I go work out things for the new arrivals in Micavery?"

They looked uncertainly at one another.

At last, Maria nodded. "We'll take care of it."

Mestra gave him a quick hug. "Go. We'll manage."

"Don't tell anyone else just yet. People here have enough to worry about."

"They have a right to know." Mestra was dead serious.

"Just let me get a handle on this first."

She held his gaze for a moment, then nodded reluctantly.

He indicated his loop. "You know how to work one of these things?"

She smiled grimly. "I'm not a luddite."

Colin nodded. "No, you're not. I'll get another at Micavery and call you as soon as I know anything." He tapped it. "Lex, ask the next train from Darlith to pick me up. I'm reassigning this loop to Mestra Vaughn."

"Affirmative. Please give it to her."

She put it to her temple. "Hello, Lex."

He squeezed her arm and then ran to catch his train.

DAVIAN SAT up, stretching as well as he was able in the confined space.

The temperature had risen again and was hovering around 102 degrees.

Davian closed his eyes, trying to convince himself this was better than the hotbox. At least here, he had some freedom of movement. He had water, warm though it was. He was on his way somewhere in a set timeframe, not trapped indefinitely, and it was quiet—no loud grating noises or Chinese heavy metal blasting all around him, keeping him from sleeping.

They hadn't broken him then. This wouldn't break him now.

He opened his eyes and glared at the gum "patch" Eddy had put in place to stop the leak.

Eddy was fast asleep next to him.

Davian tried to kick at the patch quietly with his boot, but it was frozen solid by the cold of the void on the other side, despite the heat in the cabin.

Damn you, he thought bitterly, glaring at Eddy's sleeping form. Eddy knew too much about him. Knowledge was power. Knowledge was danger, a weapon that could be used against him later.

He could strangle the man, or try to, but Eddy was as strong as he was. Besides, marks like that on Eddy's neck would be a clear indicator that Davian was to blame, if anyone bothered to look.

Better to leave things be, for now. He could deal with Eddy later, if need be.

He checked the chronometer. Three more hours until arrival.

Davian drank another bottle of water. He let go of his bladder and let the suit suck out the urine, a curiously satisfying and disconcerting feeling.

Then he closed his eyes and tried to sleep a little more before they arrived at their destination.

Chapter Eight:
Blow

LEX CLOSED *her eyes.*

Ronan was gone. She had felt his death-cry across the void. He had sacrificed himself to save the humans under his care.

She would have done the same, but even so....

Jackson had helped her name this feeling. It was called pain.

Ronan had been the one other being in her little world who was like her. A bio-mind imbued with the ability to think and feel.

At the end, she had guarded her links to him, wary of infection by the same virus he fought so valiantly to destroy.

Now....

She wondered if she should have done more. If she could have.

And yet, doing so would have put her own charges at risk, something that she could never allow to happen.

Pain.

It was a human emotion, one that she was subject to now as well. She decided she didn't like it.

ANDY WAS getting tired.

She was taking her turn maintaining the station's air systems and power, and opening doors and moving elevators as needed.

She had no idea how Ronan had managed all of this all day, every day.

"How are you doing in there, kiddo?" Her dad's voice came to her through the ether.

"Good. Tired, but good. How's the evacuation going?" She knew exactly how it was going, but she needed the distraction. The shuttles had made six trips so far, taking more than half of the station population down to Forever.

"We're getting there. Everyone's been remarkably calm. If we have time, we'll try to evacuate some of the more important equipment."

"Yeah, that makes sense." She checked on the incoming shuttlecraft and flipped open the air lock door for it. About a third of the wheel was entirely empty of people now. She shut down power and air to those sections—less to keep track of. "How are they handling the incoming population groundside?"

"Colin's there. He's making temporary arrangements."

"Temporary? You really think we're coming back?"

Her father sighed. "I don't know. I hope we are."

There was a blockage in the air circulation system. Something had likely gotten corrupted in the attack, and a valve in the D Zone wasn't responding properly. She checked the schematics and routed around it. At the very least, the station would need a complete systems overhaul if they brought in a new station-mind.

She closed her eyes for a moment, thinking of Ronan. She knew how frightened he'd been at the end. Just as she knew how unfair it was—the choice he'd been asked to make.

He hadn't deserved to die for their sins.

Something flared red along her consciousness. She sent out scouts to see what was wrong.

After a moment, they flashed back to her, waving in distress.

"Dad, we've got a problem." *Like we needed another one.*

"What is it?"

"The power core. I think it suffered some damage during the attack. The shields are breaking down."

"Goddammit."

She'd never heard her father curse. It sent a shiver down her spine.

This was bad. Really bad.

"We're going to have to overload the shuttles. Do what you can to stop it or at least slow it down."

"Got it. Things may get a little wonky while I zip over there." She let the shuttle in through the inner air lock door and then let go of the stream, diving into it and swimming up toward the power core.

In seconds, she was at the core.

The situation was worse, far worse than she had expected.

Half the shields had fallen below 50 percent strength. The rest weren't much better.

With a heavy sigh, she set about doing what she could to shore them up.

COLIN WATCHED the shuttle lift off the landing pad once again, heading for the world's air lock. The ships were staying only for as long as it took to deposit their passengers. They had to be running short on fuel.

Thank God it's a short trip.

He turned to face the new arrivals. "Hello, everyone. I'm former station director Colin McAvery. Many of you know who I am and worked for me when I ran Transfer Station."

There was a lot of murmuring and nodding.

"Thank you all for remaining calm. Devon Powell is here to help you all get settled. We'll be taking you to one of the community mess halls for something to eat and drink, and for a basic orientation. If you have been down to Forever before, most of this information will be familiar to you. We ask that you please listen carefully anyhow. If this is your first time, this briefing will be helpful while you settle in here to await repairs to the station."

Privately, he considered such repairs extremely unlikely. Their supply line to Earth of late had been tenuous at best, according to Aaron, and things were rapidly getting worse down there, from what he'd gathered from the refugees.

He was starting to realize the enormity of what they faced. They might have to go it alone up here, without any more help from Earth or the station.

"In any case," he said, doing his best to project confidence, "after the briefing, each of you will be paired with someone who will provide you a place to stay until we can figure out what comes next."

One of the scientists raised her hand. "When do you think we'll be able to go back? I have experiments in progress."

He shook his head. "We just don't know yet. You may want to get comfortable down here."

He turned away from the rumbling that statement set off.

"We're going to start running out of food soon if this goes on," Dania Thorpe said. She was in charge of provisions and material distribution in Micavery. "The refugees have already created a significant drag on our supplies."

"I know, but there's not much we can do about it at the moment. Let's draw up some contingency plans, if you have someone to spare who can do it. How much we have, how long it will last, whether we need to ration, and what it would take to increase our food supplies in a meaningful timeframe."

She nodded. "I'll get it done."

"I'd appreciate it." It was easy enough to find places for all these people to sleep for a few days, but they weren't ready for a large permanent influx of new colonists.

He tapped his loop. "Aaron, you there?"

There was a long pause. "Yeah." His voice seemed strained. "What's up?"

"Just checking in. We've got a good system going here to handle the influx. For now."

"Glad to hear it. We're up to our eyeballs up here. It looks like the power core is going to blow after all."

"Holy shit." So much for repairs. This was really it.

"Yeah. We're gonna send the next couple shuttles down extra heavy."

Colin nodded. "Take out the seats. That will gain you some capacity."

"Good idea. Colin…."

"Yeah?"

"If I don't see you again, it's been a pleasure working with you."

Colin frowned. "Don't talk like that."

Aaron had already cut the connection.

ANDY WAS worn down, more tired than she could ever remember being. She held up the shields around the power core through sheer force of will as her father, at her side, managed the station's other essential functions.

The second to the last shuttle had taken off, loaded down as heavily as they could manage, seats and every other bit of excess weight removed.

The last one was coming in for rendezvous with the station, nosing toward the air lock.

"I'm going to siphon just a little power for the lock doors."

Andy nodded. It was all she could manage.

One of the shields dropped dangerously low, and she reached for power from one of the others and shored it up. "Can't do this much longer," she said through gritted teeth.

"You won't have to. One more door."

A tiny part of her took note of the shuttle on final approach to the landing pad, where everyone remaining on Transfer Station awaited its landing.

Except the two of them.

"It's down."

She nodded and shored up another of the shields.

"We're not going to make it out of here and down to the landing pad, much less have time to wait for another shuttle, kiddo."

"I know." Even saying that much cost her.

"We have to take a chance with one of the escape pods."

Yes. She hoped he could feel her assent.

Little blips passed in and out of the corners of her vision, and her virtual eyes kept closing, but she knew what he was getting at. The escape pods had no navigation systems, just an emergency beacon to allow them to be found. But with no help likely from Earth, they chanced shooting off into deep space without anyone to rescue them. Once the power in the pod batteries went out, they'd be sealed in a frozen, floating tomb.

"The shuttle is off the ground. I'm opening the inner lock again."

The power core was on the far side of the wheel from where their physical bodies sat. Andy had no idea how fast it would blow once she could no longer contain it, but they had at least a chance to reach the pod connected to the director's office and push away from the station before Transfer went up in what was likely to be a catastrophic explosion.

"Almost there. When I say go, drop back into meatspace, and we make a run for the pod. Got it?"

She nodded again. "I...." Her hold slipped, just for a second, and one of the shields crashed down.

"Go!" he said at the same instant, and she let go of the rest, disengaging from the system and throwing herself backward into her own body.

Andy woke up feeling as if every muscle was bruised.

She forced herself to her feet. Her father was across the desk from her, slumped over.

She almost climbed over the desk, lifting him from the desktop and removing his hand from the interface pad.

There was an ominous rumble, and the ground under her feet shook.

"Come on. We have to go!"

He opened one eye and stared at her. "Did I everh tell yoooo...." He sounded drunk. "That you're my... favorite?"

She laughed in spite of their dire situation. "I'm your *one and only*. Now come on." She hauled her father to the door to the escape pod and laid his palm on the pad.

It flashed green, and the door slid open.

She shoved him inside and climbed in after him, pulling the hatch closed manually behind her.

The whole wheel shook again, and she heard the explosion of the core through the metal of the ship. No time to belt in.

She slammed on the eject button and was thrown back against the wall of the pod.

The whirling stars are so beautiful. She spun past them into unconsciousness.

EDDY HAD been trying to hail the station on the emergency frequency of the x-band for half an hour with no success. "Transfer Station. Calling Transfer Station."

There was radio silence. He was starting to panic.

"Maybe they have their hands full with refugees," Davian suggested. It was the most he had said in three hours.

Eddy shrugged. Someone was always supposed to monitor the emergency band. That's what it was for. If that basic task was going undone on Transfer Station, things must have gotten dire indeed.

He flipped the x-band back to one of the terrestrial broadcast stations, this one out of Fargo.

"—confirmed attacks in Chicago, Kansas City, Denver, Dallas, Phoenix. The presumed dead are into the millions, if not far higher. The President has authorized a retaliatory nuclear strike against the capitals of China and the African Bloc. It's her last desperate hope to bring a halt to this devastating war before—"

The station dissolved into static.

"Holy fuck." Eddy stared at Davian. "They've really gone and done it." All his life the specter of global annihilation had been there in the background as tensions rose between nations in the fight to control whatever resources were left—food, water, even clean air.

He'd always assumed—or hoped—that things would somehow go back to normal. Whatever *that* was.

He'd believed that thinking people could find a way to come together and find a solution.

The only solution they'd managed to agree on was of a more terrible finality than he could ever have dreamed.

There would be no returning to Earth, even if they'd had the fuel for it.

Ahead of them, a bright explosion blossomed against the vast darkness of space, lighting up a wide ring that could only be Transfer Station.

The flames faded as fast as they had appeared as the fire was starved of oxygen.

"Oh shit." Davian's mouth hung open.

"Oh shit, indeed." Eddy's first thought was that a nuke had been launched against the station, but how would it have gotten up here from Earth so quickly? Maybe from a Chaf station?

He flipped back over to the emergency band. "Calling Transfer Station. Transfer Station."

Nothing.

"What do we do now?" he asked Davian.

The hulk of Forever was drawing closer. Eddy could make it out now behind the debris of the station. It looked like a mushroom, a tube connected to the third, and likely final, asteroid that was slowly being consumed to build the new world.

The radio crackled to life. "This is an emergency transmission. I repeat, this is an emergency transmission. Is anyone within range?"

Someone was alive out there. Eddy grabbed the mic. "Yes, this is Eddy Tremaine, aboard an inbound Moonjumper. Who am I talking to?"

"Oh thank God," the voice replied. "This is Director Aaron Hammond, formerly of Transfer Station. We've had a catastrophic station failure."

"We can see that. Where are you?"

"We jettisoned an escape pod just before the explosion that destroyed the station, but we're moving on momentum only. I have no navigational control. Can you pick up our homing beacon?"

Davian took Eddy's hand off the talk button. "We can't help them. We may only have enough fuel left for our own maneuvers."

"Maneuvers to where? How are we going to get them to open the door and let us in? For all they know, we're the ones who just attacked the station."

"In a *Moonjumper*?"

"I'm not leaving him to die. We're going after them." Eddy checked the navigation system. "Locking in on your beacon now," he said to Director Hammond. Gently, using his remaining fuel as sparingly as possible, he guided the Moonjumper onto a new course to intercept the little pod.

"How are we going to grab them?" Davian asked.

He had a point. The jumper had no arm to catch the pod with.

Eddy could get the Moonjumper ahead of the escape pod and try to nudge it to a halt, but that was risky too. A misjudgment could breach the hull of either or both ships.

His gaze fell on the x-drive. "You've worked on those before, right?" He pointed to the small quiescent sphere.

Davian's eyes narrowed. "Why? What are you thinking?"

"Can you flip the field? Create a gravitational tug instead of negating it?"

Davian considered it. "Maybe, but we'd be risking blowing the whole thing to kingdom come—"

"We're already practically there. You got a better idea?"

Davian laughed bitterly. "Yeah, but you already vetoed it." They locked eyes, and Davian looked away first. "Okay, I'll see what I can do."

They were almost alongside the pod, and Eddy was using the thrusters to match its course and velocity. Forever was slowly falling behind them.

Davian had the sphere out of its casing and had flipped open the access panel.

With a synth wand from his pack, he began reconfiguring the circuits inside.

"Any day now," Eddy said nervously. "We're getting farther from our destination by the minute."

"Don't rush me. This is delicate work. One bad connection and we won't have to worry about your friends in the tin can next door any longer."

"Sorry." He watched Davian work, fascinated. The man was a genius with this kind of thing. Eddy was good with the grunt work, the flying, and the basic electronic stuff, but something like this required an understanding of quantum mechanics and a steady hand he just didn't have. "Hang on, Director Hammond," he said softly. "We're right alongside you. We're working out a way to catch you."

"Affirmative." The man sounded exhausted.

"There." Davian gingerly closed the access hatch and placed the x-drive back into its cradle. "Either this works or we have no more worries."

Eddy nodded. "Do it."

He punched the controls and the drive lit up, but with a blue glow this time.

A red line snaked around it, shading into purple.

Eddy watched it worriedly, but then it flipped over to solid blue. "That's good, yes?"

Davian nodded. "Yes." He looked out at the escape pod next to them. "Get as close as you can. The gravity generated by the x-drive will do the rest."

Eddy nodded and used the jets to nudge the Moonjumper closer and closer to the pod. As they closed to about two meters, the two crafts pulled together with a resounding *thunk*.

"Woo-hoo!" Eddy high-fived Davian. "We did it!" He picked up the mic. "Gotcha," he said over the comm. "I'm going to turn us around." He used the jets on the far side of the craft to slowly bring them into a U-turn, heading back toward the now distant worldlet.

Director Hammond's relief came through loud and clear on the comm. "Thank you, Eddy. Eddy and…?"

"Davian."

"Thank you to both of you. You're angels."

Davian snorted.

"Can you get us inside Forever? It looks like you're not going back to the station."

"Yes. We can contact the world-mind once we're close enough."

"Are you both okay over there?" Eddy asked.

"I think so. My daughter hit her head when we ejected from the station, but she seems to be all right. It was a close call."

"What happened?"

There was a long pause. Eddy guessed the man was deciding whether or not he could trust them. "It was a virus in the station-mind. It targeted the power core."

Eddy whistled. "Casualties?"

"As far as I know, zero. We were able to get everyone else off station before it blew."

Eddy sat back and stared at the radio. That was a *minor fucking miracle*, given that there must have been hundreds of people aboard Transfer. "Listen, I'm going to go radio silent while I navigate us up to the world-mind's air lock. It's at the close end, right?"

"Yes."

"I want to shake your hand when we get there. It's amazing that you managed to get everyone out alive."

"Only thanks to you."

Eddy laughed. "Fair enough. Signing off."

Chapter Nine:
Coming Home

IT TOOK Eddy a tense half hour to navigate back to Forever, and they had to work their way through the space where the station had been. The vicinity was filled with debris, and he had to steer the awkward combination of ships around the worst of it.

He could only use three of the four attitude jets. The fourth was facing the escape pod and would have either damaged the hull of the other ship or knocked it away from them, or both.

It was like navigating a field full of landmines carrying your drunken uncle in one arm with the other strapped behind your back. It tested his piloting skills to their limits.

He was damned good at flying almost any craft, and his years of experience in the NAU Armed Forces came to the fore.

Davian helped him spot debris as they wended their way through the field, using both the nav system and his own eyes.

The temperature in the little craft was up to 107 degrees. Eddy wiped sweat away from his eyes nearly constantly. He was so ready to land this bucket of bolts and get outside to breathe real air again.

That reminded him of Earth, coming to an end as he had known it even as they struggled for their own survival up here. He shoved his emotions as far down as he could manage and concentrated on flying.

He could see as he approached that the worldlet had taken a few hits from Transfer's destruction, but it looked intact. It sketched out an elongated cylinder against the starry background attached to an even larger asteroid, and parts of it illuminated by sunlight had fresh scratches and craters, but nothing fatal. They still had a new home to go to.

He wondered if the other two seed worlds had been hit too, and if they had been as lucky.

"Okay, we're approaching the end of the world." He realized, as he said it, just how true it was.

"We're in touch with the world-mind. The air lock should be opening now."

COLIN SAT on a bench by Lake Jackson, staring glumly out at the waters.

He'd halfway expected the people down on Earth to bring themselves to a bloody, rancorous end, but somehow the station and this little paradise world had seemed safe from all that, detached from the troubles of Old Earth. Now it was as if the ghost of the home world had reached out a bloodied hand to pull them down to death and destruction with it.

The last shuttle had come in a half hour before, but there was no sign of Aaron and his daughter, Andy. They'd done an amazing job of saving everyone else on Transfer, somehow holding back the disaster until the last shuttle was free.

Then... nothing.

He wondered if he had erred in giving up his command. If he'd stayed on, it might have been him up there instead of the Hammonds. They might have been safely ensconced on Forever while he ended his own life in noble sacrifice. It was a debt he owed to Jackson. One that he might never be able to repay.

"Can I sit with you?"

He looked up. It was Keera Hammond, Aaron's wife. He nodded.

She sat down and stared out at the lake with him. "I can't believe it. It doesn't seem real to me."

He put an arm around her and pulled her close. "There's still hope. They might have escaped in one of the pods—"

"Who's going to go get them?" Her eyes were red from crying.

"Your husband's father was an amazing man. He could find his way back from almost impossible odds. Aaron and Andy are like that too."

She nodded. "I want to believe that." She wiped her nose with the back of her hand. "He loved you, you know."

Colin nodded, not wanting to correct her with the present tense.

"Glory's taking it hard too."

"I'd imagine." Losing Jackson first, and now her eldest son and granddaughter.... He knew as well as she that the odds of Andy and Aaron's return were next to zero at this point. Only a miracle might save them, and they were running low on miracles.

"Director McAvery?"

He tapped his loop. "Yes?"

"Patching a call through."

He waited, holding his breath.

"Colin, you have a welcoming committee waiting for us?"

"By God, is that you, Aaron?"

"The one and only."

"Is he…?" Keera looked trapped between hope and despair, tucking a loose strand of blond hair behind her ear.

He nodded. "He's alive!"

"Oh my God. Oh my God. And Andy?" She was shaking.

"You have Andy there with you?" he asked. He closed his eyes, picturing the energetic, amazing young woman who had helped him at the refugee camp.

"Yes. She's a bit worse for wear, but she'll be all right."

He opened his eyes and nodded. "They're both okay."

Keera jumped up and danced around. "Thank God!" She took a deep breath. "What's he saying?"

"How'd you manage it?" Colin asked Aaron.

"I'll explain when we land. Let's just say we have a couple new friends."

"I can't wait. Want to talk to Keera?"

"She's there? Yes, please!"

"Lex, please route the call over to Keera."

"Connected."

"Aaron? Don't you ever do anything like that again. I thought you were both dead—" She wandered off, and Colin let her have her privacy to talk to her husband.

They were *alive*.

Somehow, it made all the difference. No matter what else happened, two people he cared about deeply had weathered the storm.

It gave him hope that, despite the long odds against them, they would all find a way to do the same.

He stared at the place in the South Wall where Aaron, Andy, and their new friends were due to come through, in whatever craft had managed to save them from the destruction of the station.

Then he turned and ran back into Micavery, shouting for help to pull together as big a reception party as he could manage.

EDDY BURNED most of the rest of his fuel bringing the two ships through the air lock and then setting them down safely on the landing pad inside Forever.

Their new home was spread out above, around, and below them, and he gave himself a minute as the ships settled toward the ground to take it all in.

It was paradise.

When the Moonjumper touched the ground, he let go of the controls and disengaged the x-drive, breathing a deep sigh of relief.

They'd made it.

Davian grinned at him. "We're fucking here!"

"Yes, we are. I need some fresh air." Eddy slipped between the seats and popped the hatch, then climbed down from the jumper.

A cheer went up from the throng that had gathered around the landing pad. Surprised, he looked around. They were all waving at him.

Then the escape pod's hatch opened and the cheering grew even louder.

A redheaded man in a white uniform, probably in his late thirties, climbed out and came over to shake his hand. The man's green eyes twinkled. "Eddy Tremaine, I assume?"

Eddy nodded. "Director Hammond?"

"Just call me Aaron."

A girl in her midteens who bore a marked resemblance to the director climbed out next.

The crowd closed in around them.

Davian had come to stand beside him, and the poor guy looked overwhelmed by all the people.

Eddy looked up, and his stomach lurched.

Nothing could have prepared him for seeing the world arching over his head like some crazy funhouse mirror.

It went up and up and up… and he went down, exhausted from the heat and the stress and the long trip and overwhelmed by this new world.

WHILE EDDY was being given a hero's welcome and being carted off after he fainted from the shock of this new world, Davian took advantage of the distraction to blend in with the crowd and work his way out of the landing area and into Micavery proper. He'd studied maps of this place before they left Earth. He knew how to find his way around.

What he didn't know was where the other refugees were being kept.

Where there were refugees, there was discontent, and discontent was something he could work with. It bred *opportunities*.

They'd made it up here, against almost impossible odds. He liked long odds.

Soon he'd set about making this new world his own.

Epilogue

ANA FIRED up the propulsion engines that would serve to propel *Forever* across the gap between the stars. They were designed to blow off unneeded matter, slowly building up the world's speed as they headed toward their destination, an Earthlike planet in a star system where humanity could start over.

The passage would take hundreds of years. None of the current colonists would live to see its conclusion.

She felt a deep sadness at leaving behind the home world. It had been an amazing, complicated, maddening place, and she would never see its like again.

Then again, she had left it, and herself, behind long before.

As the world began its long journey, she shifted back into sync with Lex and Jackson. Their minds, more and more, were merging into one cohesive whole. They still had their own distinct personalities, but they overlapped in significant ways. "It's done."

Lex nodded. "Our own work is just beginning."

They had a charge—to carry their passengers into the liminal sky, across the stark divide between stars to a new home.

The age of man on Earth—homo sapiens—had ended. The age of mankind between the stars—homo stellae—had just begun.

EDDY WOKE slowly, first feeling the softness of the bed linens that surrounded him. He was comfortable. Warm, but in a good way, not like he had been trapped in the cramped, hot space of the Moonjumper.

Next he noticed the air. It smelled… different than Earth's. It was fresh and clean, and it excited his senses.

He opened his eyes.

Director Hammond sat next to him. He was in a private room with a wooden floor and bright yellow walls. The very air seemed alight, giving everything a warm, fuzzy glow.

Hammond leaned forward. "Good. You're awake."

"Yeah." He sat up, looking around. The room was sparsely furnished, but a plant in the corner glowed with a golden-green glow. "Is this heaven?"

Aaron laughed. "Nope. You just got a bad case of rubber neck."

"Rubber neck?"

"It's what we call it when newbies get overwhelmed by the whole 'world over your head' thing." He got up from his chair and leaned out into the hallway. "Guys?"

There were footsteps, and then the young girl he'd seen before and another man stepped into the room. "Welcome back to the end of the world." The man held out his hand. "I'm Colin McAvery."

Eddy's jaw dropped open. "*The* Colin McAvery?"

"One and the same."

"This is my daughter, Andy," Aaron said.

"Thanks for saving us." She gave him a big grin.

"My pleasure."

The ground shook underneath his bed. "What the hell was that?" He sat up and looked around, afraid the world would fall away beneath him. He'd come so far....

"That, my friend, is us getting underway."

"Underway? How...?" But of course. Forever was a generation ship.

Colin nodded. "We talked with the world-mind, and in light of the events on Earth—"

"It's gone, isn't it?"

"In every sense that we knew it, yes. The planet is still there, but most of it is no longer fit for human life."

Eddy let that sink in. He'd suspected it, deep down in his core, after the last news reports. But thinking something might be true and knowing it for a fact were two very different things.

He closed his eyes and thought of all the things that he would never see or have or do again. No more skiing down a snow-covered hill. No more surfing on the Gulf Coast. No more chocolate ice cream or tridimensional films or hot buttered popcorn.

"In any case, we decided to start on our journey. I know it's a lot to take in," Aaron said. "We're on our own now. None of us here will live to see our destination, but we're starting an adventure the likes of which mankind has never undertaken before."

"Did the other seed ships make it?"

"We don't know." Colin stood by the window, looking out at the world. "Transfer held the long-range antennas. We're cut off from whatever else is going on out there."

Hammond took his hand. "I wanted to thank you for what you did. Your arrival was opportune, but more than that, you risked your life to save ours, and for that I am truly grateful."

"You're welcome. It wasn't just me, though. Hey, where's Dav?"

"Your friend?"

Eddy nodded.

"He can't have gone far. I'm sure he just needed a break, after the trip you two took to get here."

Eddy nodded. No matter what he'd lost along the way, he was *here* now. He had a future, unlike so many billions of others. He had to make the most of it.

Andy looked down at him, a curious smile on her face. "I've never been to Earth. What was it like?"

He smiled, gesturing for her to sit next to him and make herself comfortable.

"When I was a little boy, I used to love to look up at the big blue sky...."

Glossary

3Cast: 3-D TV

41 Daphne: Second asteroid incorporated into Forever

43 Ariadne: Asteroid used to start Forever

Aaron Hammond: Oldest son of Jackson and Glory Hammond; Director of Forever Project 2160

Affinity Link: Connection between human and ship mind

Lex: Ship-mind of the Dressler, World-mind of Forever

Alexandria "Ria" Tanner: Sister to Trip, one of the glider fliers

Alifir Trees: "Native" Forever trees, piney scent

Allied African States: Union of African nations

AmSplor: The space arm of the NAU

Anastasia Anatov: crew on the Dressler, doctor/geneticist

Anatov Fungus: Fungus that brought down the Dressler

Anatov Mountains: Mountains between Darlith and Micavery; formerly the Dragon's Reach

Andrissa "Andy" Hammond: Daughter of Aaron Hammond

Keera Kelly: Aaron's love interest; Family from Ireland

Ashton: Part of the North Pole crew

Aspin: A Mission-class ship

Astrid: Dormitory building in McAvery Port

Axion-Class Ship: Biological-mechanical hybrid ships newer and larger than Mission-class

Bio-Grafts: Plants dependent on the host world to survive

Biomind: Artificial minds that sit at the boundary of computers and AI-Human minds

Brad Evers: Community ambassador at the refugee camp

Bug Drone: Spy drone the size of a bumblebee

Campus: Part of McAvery Port

Captain Trip Tanner: Captain of the *Herald*; Colin's lover, later husband

Carmella: Cook in the mess hall in McAvery Port

Central Valley Desert: New California desert

Chafs: Derogatory name for the Sino-African Syndicate troops

Chester Arthur: Communications officer on Frontier Station

Colin McAvery: Captain of the *Dressler*; later, Director of Transfer Station; retired 2160

Colony Master Tad Evers: In charge of McAvery Port

Crons: Currency/coin on Forever/Ariadne

Cutter: Sonic cutter tool

Dana Thomas: Community ambassador at the refugee camp

Dania Thorpe: Woman in charge of personnel at McAvery Port

Darlith: Second town built within Forever

Davian "Dav" Forrester: Eddy's ex and a systems specialist

Deadware: Slang referring to a worn-out or obsolete part or machine

Devon Powell: Member of the McAvery Port team

Dex: Ranger on Forever

Dimensionals: 3-D entertainment shows

Dimitri Anatov: Anastasia's father and a geneticist

Dipping: Interfacing with Forever's mind; more intense than Transfer

Divia: Part of the North Pole crew

Dragon's Reach: Peaks between McAvery Port and Darlith; later called the Anatov Mountains

Dreamcast: Movie watched via dreams

Dressler: Mission-class ship

East: Facing North, to the right

Eastern Front: Coalition of China, India, and North Korea

Eddy Tremaine: Former military (NAU Marine Corps); formerly Evelyne

Embassy District: Part of McAvery Port

Estate: Colin and Trip's retreat

Extractor: Cutting tool

Fargo: Capitol of the NAU

Fargo Port: Launch port for AmSplor

Far Hold (aka North Pole): The station that controls the building of Forever

Father Vincenzo: Jackson Hammond's priest

Federated Central American States: Central American allied nations

First Light: Advance of light in the morning on Forever

Forever: Common name for Ariadne, the seedling world

Frontier: Earth's primary space station

Fuzz Field: Distortion field

Fuzzer: Small silver spheres that create the fuzz field

Genecraft: Genetic artistry / manipulation

Gianna: Station master at South Pole

Gloria "Glory" Hammond: Jackson's wife, Aaron's mother, Hispanic

Great Burn: Big heat wave that burned across a large swath of the southwestern US

Hammond: Axion-class ship that brings Ana and Aaron to Forever

Harmony: Apple picker on Forever

Herald: Mission-class ship that comes to rescue the *Dressler* crew

Hold: Room on the Dressler

Hurricane Cisco: One of the super hurricanes that ushered in the drowning of most of Southern Florida

Ichor: The golden "blood" of the Mission-class ships and seed ships

Initiator: Crystalline memory chip—DNA encoded—that jump-starts the seed

Interveners: Antitechnology terrorists

Jackson Hammond: Engineer aboard the Dressler

Jacob: Part of the North Pole crew

Jared: Traxx driver

Jayson Hammond: Younger son of Glory and Jackson Hammond

Kuripa Drone: Sino-African drone that looks like a giant robotic cockroach

Kwame Jones: Community ambassador at the refugee camp

Lake Jackson: Lake on the "Southern" end of Forever, named after Jackson Hammond

Landing Station: The shuttle port in Micavery

Light Suckers: Industrial-strength fiber optic light transfer devices

Long Interval: The time between departing Earth and arriving at the other end

Loop: Communication device and personal assistant

Mag Bolts: Bolts holding things together with a superstrong magnetic charge

Mallow Tree: Tree on Forever similar to mahogany

Mallowood: Wood from the mallow tree; a hardwood, it is known for its red color

Marcos: Part of the North Pole crew

Maria Ortiz: Community ambassador at the refugee camp

McAvery Port: The initial colony, later called Micavery
Mestra Vaughn: Nurse who takes charge of refugee camp
Micavery: First town built on forever, previously McAvery Port
Mission-Class: Living ships genetically bred, which include metal and organic parts
Monongahela National Forest: Where Eddy and Davian work on the Moonjumper
Moonjumper: Cheap vehicle made for quick hops to and from the moon, retired around 2090
Natasha: Part of the North Pole crew
New Richmond: Area that became a space center in Virginia after the old city was destroyed
North: In the direction of the North Pole (the far endcap)
North American Union (NAU): The combined countries of Canada, USA, and Mexico
North Pole: Far end of Forever
Ostereich: Transport-class ship
Plasform (Plas): Advanced polymer used for many applications, usually clear.
Pulse Weapon: EMP device
Rafe: Devon's on and off boyfriend
Rask: Traxx driver on Forever
Ready-Packs: Ready to eat meals
Readygel: Industrial glue
Red Badge: Lawless group of technophiles involved in domestic espionage and wetware arts
Reformed Catholic Evangelical Church: The new church resulting from the merger of the Catholic and Baptist churches
Reunification: When Ireland and Northern Ireland became one country
Reverser: a tool to remove or apply mag bolts
Rishia: Part of the North Pole crew
Ronan: Transfer Station mind
Runway: Connects the various parts of the Dressler; also the main hallway on Transfer Station
Seed Ships: Three generation ships grown from seedlings
Seedling: The starter for one of the seed ships

Shadowfax: Colin's horse
Ship-Mind: Biological mind grown to run AmSplor ships
Ship's Bone: Bone from the Mission-class or Axion-class ship infrastructure
Sino-African Syndicate (CAS): Alliance between China and many African nations
Skyhook: Elevator system that brings people up to Frontier Station from Earth
Skyrises: Supertall towers in NYC
Slowdown: The process of bringing the ship down to approach speed
South: In the direction of the South Pole (the near endcap)
South Pole: Transfer Station end/starting end of Forever
Spanner: Arm of one of the Mission-class ships
Sugarloaf Mountain: Eddy Tremaine's former home
Synth Wand: Tool for connecting organic materials
T-Line: Navigational course
Talis Miller: Picking crew supervisor in the orchards
The Edge: The end of the planted portion of Forever
The Heat: Runaway warming brought on by greenhouse gases on Earth
The Rise: The sea level rise accompanying the Heat
Tim: Ex of Eddy's
Topside: Platform for flight from the South Pole
Transfer Station: The space station that accompanies Forever
Transport-Class: Generation of ships before the Mission-class, entirely mechanical
Traxx: Ground transportation on Forever that hauls supplies
Vixen: Mission-class ship that failed due to human error
Warehouse District: Part of McAvery Port
West: Facing north, to the left
X-Band: Long-distance radio
X-drive: Small, powerful antigravity drive that allowed rapid expansion to the moon colonies
York Street: A street in Darlith

Keep reading for an excerpt from

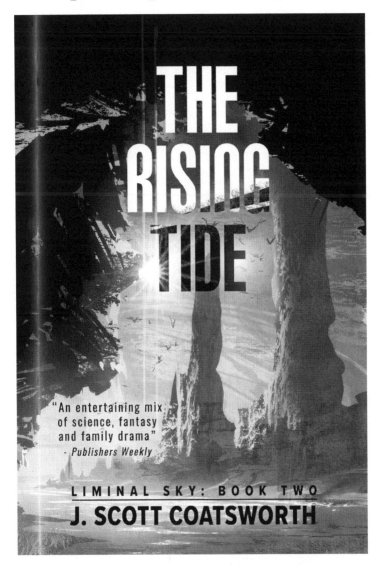

THE RISING TIDE

"An entertaining mix of science, fantasy and family drama"
- *Publishers Weekly*

LIMINAL SKY: BOOK TWO
J. SCOTT COATSWORTH

www.dsppublications.com

Liminal Sky: Book Two

Earth is dead.

Five years later, the remnants of humanity travel through the stars inside Forever, a living, ever-evolving, self-contained generation ship. When Eddy Tremaine and Andy Hammond find a hidden world-within-a-world under the mountains, the discovery triggers a chain of events that could fundamentally alter or extinguish life as they know it, culminate in the takeover of the world-mind, and end free will for humankind.

Control the AI, control the people.

Eddy, Andy, and a handful of other unlikely heroes—people of every race and identity, and some who aren't even human—must find the courage and ingenuity to stand against the rising tide.

Otherwise they might be living through the end days of human history.

Now Available at
www.dsppublications.com

Prologue

ANA CLOSED her eyes, visualizing the seed ship's current trajectory. They'd rendezvous with 42 Isis in five days, their last stop in the solar system that had birthed mankind. Five years past, it had nearly been the location of its destruction.

The asteroid contained a high percentage of olivine, a mineral high in useful elements like oxygen, iron, magnesium, and silicon—a veritable feast.

Around Ana, the clean white laboratory that was her personal vee space domain was in perfect order, every surface spotless. A swipe of her virtual hand brought up an image of Forever, the long cylindrical generation ship hanging in the dark void of space between Mars and Jupiter.

The world sails had been pulled in, and Ana was in the process of nudging Forever into alignment with the asteroid, firing off excess bits of waste material to bring her into the proper trajectory. If all went well, Forever would end up with enough mass to finish build-out, along with a shield to help absorb space radiation on the journey to their new home.

Thank God.

Ana shook her head. *That* was clearly one of Jackson's thoughts. She even picked up some of Lex's thoughts at times. The original world mind veered off into philosophical territory to a degree that often surprised Ana—how an AI had become a philosopher poet.

The three Immortals, as they had jokingly taken to calling one another, were bleeding into each other more and more. It worried her.

This new second life was a gift beyond measure, certainly nothing she had ever expected. A chance to go with her creation across the stark divide, between the stars. But if the ultimate price was her own individuality, was it worth it?

She made a minor adjustment in the world trajectory, then shut off that part of her awareness. If she were needed, the system would let her know.

She slipped off through the conduits of the world mind to find Jackson.

The three Immortals had created a number of virtual worlds in vee space to pass the time when their skills weren't needed. While it was possible to create AI personalities to populate each of their various worlds, these constructs took a lot of processing power, and the Immortals had quickly grown tired of that game.

The worlds they built now were usually empty except for the three of them.

She found Jackson in Frontier Station, sitting all alone in the gardens. The blue-green ball of Earth, as it once had been, stretched out below him.

"You're bleeding into me again." Ana took a seat on the bench next to him.

He glanced up, his face drawn, his nose red and puffy. He concentrated, and the tears and puffiness went away. "Was I? Sorry. I was just thinking of Glory."

Even in vee space, we emulate our old human selves.

His wife, Gloria, had just passed away a few days before, after a protracted battle with cancer that the new world's facilities weren't set up to treat. So much had been lost in the flight from Earth.

They had agonized over whether to bring Glory into the world mind.

Jackson had requested it, but Ana and Lex, the other two Immortals, had both been against it. Their little team worked well enough together, and adding additional human minds was likely to muddy the waters. Besides, the mind only had so much capacity. It couldn't hold everyone within its confines. It hadn't been created for that purpose.

Ana sighed. She wasn't blind to the human cost of that decision. "She liked it here." She squeezed his shoulder. Jackson's vee space *was* beautiful, though it broke her heart to see Earth once again as it had looked before the Collapse.

Jackson nodded. "This is where we first met."

He must have been just as annoyed at her bleed-through thoughts. She was being insensitive again, considering all he was dealing with.

276

Being effectively immortal was turning out to be harder than she'd ever imagined. She put an arm around his shoulders and hugged him. "I am so sorry about Glory."

He regarded her in surprise. "Thank you. That means a lot."

"Ours is a lonely path. We must make sure they get where they are going. Nothing else matters."

He nodded. "I know. But it's hard. Good Lord, guide me."

Although she didn't believe in a higher power, she squeezed his arm gently. "I hope *he* does."

Chapter One:
A Foul Wind

EDDY TREMAYNE rode his horse, Cassiopeia, along the edge of the pastures that were the last official human habitations before the Anatov Mountains. Several ranchers along the Verge—the zone between the ranches and the foothills—had reported losses of sheep and cattle in the last few weeks.

As the elected sheriff of First District, which ran from Micavery and the South Pole to the mountains, it was Eddy's responsibility to find out what was going on.

He had his crossbow strapped to his back and his long knife in a leather sheath at his waist. He'd been carrying them for long enough now—three years?—that they had started to feel natural, but the first time he'd worn the crossbow, he'd felt like a poor man's Robin Hood.

He doubted he'd need them out here, but sheriffs were supposed to be armed.

He'd checked with Lex in the world mind via the South Pole terminal, but she'd reported nothing amiss. In the last few years, she had begun to deploy biodrones to keep an eye on the far-flung parts of the world, but they provided less than optimal coverage. One flyover of this part of the Verge had shown a peaceful flock of thirty sheep. The next showed eight.

The rancher, a former neurosurgeon from New Zealand named Gia Rand, waited for him on the top of a grassy hill. The grass and trees shone with bioluminescent light, and the afternoon sky lit the surrounding countryside with a golden glow. The spindle—the aggregation of energy and glowing pollen that stretched from pole to pole—sparkled in the middle of the sky.

The rancher pulled on her gray braid, staring angrily at something in the valley below. "Took you long enough to get here."

"Sorry. The train was out of service again." Technology was slowly failing them, and they had yet to come up with good replacements.

She snorted. "One helluva spaceship we have here."

He grinned. "Preaching to the choir." Forever didn't have the manufacturing base yet to support anything close to the technology its inhabitants had grown used to on Earth. Which wasn't necessarily a bad thing, if you asked him. With technology came new and better ways to kill. He'd seen it often enough in the NAU Marines. "What did you find?"

"Look." Her voice was almost a growl.

Eddy looked down where she was pointing. "Oh shit." Her missing sheep were no longer missing. They had been slaughtered.

He urged Cassiopeia down the hillside to the rocky clearing. A small stream trickled down out of the mountains there. He counted ten carcasses, as near as he could tell from the skulls left behind. Someone had sheared a couple of them and given up. It looked like they had skinned and cut the rest up for meat, the skin and bones and extra bits discarded.

Gia rode down the hillside behind him.

"Didn't you report twelve sheep missing?"

She nodded. "Bastards took the two lambs. Probably for breeding."

"That actually might help us."

"How's that?"

He dismounted to take a closer look at the crime scene. "They'll have to pasture them somewhere. May make it easier to track them down."

"Maybe so." She dismounted and joined him. "This was brutal work. Look here." She picked up a bone. "Whatever cut this was sharp but uneven. It left scratch marks across the bone."

"So not a metal knife."

"I don't think so. Maybe a stone knife?"

He laughed harshly. "Are we back to caveman days, then?" It wasn't an unreasonable question.

She was silent for a moment, staring at the mountains. "Do you think they live up there?"

"Who?" He followed her gaze. Their highest peaks were wreathed in wisps of cloud.

"The Ghosts."

The Ghosts had been a persistent myth on Forever since their abrupt departure from Earth. Some of the refugees had vanished right after the Collapse, and every now and then something would end up missing. Clothes off a line, food stocks, and the like.

People talked. The rumors had taken on a life of their own, and now whenever something went missing, people whispered, "It's the Ghosts."

Eddy didn't believe in ghosts. He personally knew at least one refugee who had disappeared, his shipmate Davian. He guessed there must be others, though the record keeping from that time had been slipshod at best. He shrugged and looked at the sky. "Who knows?" It was likely to rain in the next day or so. Whoever had done this had left a trail, trampled into the grass. If he didn't follow it now, it might be gone by the time he got back here with more resources.

Gia knelt by one of the ewes, staring at the remnants of the slaughter. "Could you get me some more breeding stock? This… incident put a big dent in my herd."

"I'll see what I can do." He took one last look around the site. It had to have taken an hour or two to commit this crime, and yet the thieves had apparently done it in broad daylight. Why weren't they afraid of being caught? "I'm going to follow the trail, see where it leads."

Gia nodded. "Thanks. We're taking the rest of the herd back to the barn until you get this all figured out."

"Sounds prudent. I'll let you know."

Slipping on his hat, he climbed back up on Cassie and followed the trail across the stream toward the Anatov Mountains.

ANDY STEPPED back to look at her handiwork.

The wooden trellis climbed about forty feet, interlacing with three others high above, each "arm" as thick around as her leg. She'd been working on this monument for weeks, crafting each part by hand, her mind *reaching* deep into Forever to touch the world mind and its latent routines. Each of the trellises was shaped as one of the six continents back on Old Earth, a memorial to where they had come from. Though she had never been there, she had seen it often enough, and one of her friends at the South Pole station had printed out a map for her to work with.

The Darlith Town Council had commissioned her to do the work, transforming a sparse square into a work of art and a gathering place for the town. She had two more pieces of the sculpture to grow, but she was about done for the day. The work took a lot out of her.

Once it was done, she'd apply a sealant and polisher to help preserve it against Forever's limited elements.

Around her, the city bustled. The All Faiths Church had just let out, and congregants were on their way home or out to lunch in one of the cafes that dotted the riverside.

"It's beautiful," one of the women said, stopping to stare up at it.

Others frowned and hurried on. Not everyone wanted to be reminded of what they had lost.

There was a pile of waste she'd trimmed from the sculpture and would have to haul over to one of the town dissolution pits when she was done, where it would be dissolved and repurposed. Nothing went to waste in a closed ecosystem like Forever.

Andy wiped her brow with the back of her hand and took a sip of water from her canteen. It was standard-issue, made from metal extruded by the world mind and stamped into shape. Forever's production had taken on a decidedly utilitarian cast since the Collapse, as the colonists had suddenly had to do without any supplies from Earth. The world was not ready to be self-sufficient, and yet here they were. Andy saw it as her duty to bring a little beauty into a world that was basically operating at a subsistence level.

Call from Colin, the world mind whispered in her head.

"I'll take it." She tapped her temple to accept the call and wondered what Lex, Ana, and Jackson thought of her little art project. "Hey, kiddo." Colin's jovial voice through the loop connection made her smile.

"Hey. Where are you?"

"We're coming down to Darlith today to sell some produce at the market. I heard you were in town."

Her father, Aaron, asking Colin to check up on her. Andy grinned. "Yeah, working on the art thing." It had been a hard sell with the Darlith town council, until she'd offered to do it in exchange for room and board.

"It's coming along nicely. Here, take a look." She sent him a capture of her own vision.

"Oooh, that's beautiful. Pretty good for a girl who never made it down to Earth."

"Thanks. I have a good map. When are you arriving?"

"In the morning. Want to meet us there? Stall 72."

"Of course. Tomorrow's perfect. Gives me a chance to clean up. I'm a mess now. This is sweaty work."

He laughed. "Can't be nearly as difficult as building latrines for a tent city."

"Maybe not, but this takes a lot more concentration." She wanted it to be right so future generations would be able to look at it and remember the world their ancestors had come from.

"Is Delia with you?"

"No, she stayed back at Micavery." It was weird sleeping alone, but she'd be home soon enough. "The fabrication center keeps her busy."

"It's amazing what they're doing over there. Have they cracked a new loop yet?"

Andy shook her head. "No, that's fiendishly difficult with the materials and tech level we have right now. Most of their time is spent on new plant and animal hybrids and on medicines to combat the viral and bacterial bugs the refugees brought up with them."

She could hear his mental sigh. "Yeah, I'd hoped we were free of the common cold forever."

She laughed. "'Fraid not. See you tomorrow?"

"Sounds good, kiddo. I'll bring you some berries from the estate." There was a double click in her head as he signed off.

She grinned. McAvery-Trip red berries were the sweetest in Forever.

Andy checked the time. She had just enough to get back to the house where she was staying before the ceremony began.

She missed her grandmother. Glory had been a beautiful woman, inside and out, even in her final year. Andy had been with her that last night, holding one hand while her father held on tightly to his mother's other one.

Today they would honor her memory.

DAVIAN WATCHED as Gunner sealed up the rock wall behind his little raiding party, "growing" the rock via tiny capillaries that the human eye could barely see. The man was a marvel, able to manipulate the world in ways that would have made him a god, if he weren't so badly damaged. As to his real name, Davian hadn't a clue, but Gunner had been his dog when he was a kid, and the name seemed oddly appropriate.

"Good boy." Davian tousled the man's hair.

Gunner smiled weakly.

Davian fished in his pocket for one of the fungus "candies" they'd started growing back at camp, with Gunner's help. The man took it eagerly and put it in his mouth, chewing on it contentedly.

Gunner rarely spoke. Who knew what kinds of thoughts, simple or otherwise, went on beneath that bland exterior?

It had taken a stroke of luck for Davian to figure out that the refugee had such a connection to Forever. He'd caught Gunner playing around with his power, using it to make little twisted men out of extensions of the roots that grew far under the world's surface. Like that Andy girl and her father. He'd known then that the man was something special.

The others of the hunting party stood in silence, awaiting the orders of the Preacher.

Davian grinned. Being called the Preacher suited him. He wasn't quite ready to claim godhead status. Not yet. "Come on. I want to make camp within the hour." He'd taken his men on a raid to sharpen their skills and to get some red meat. It was good to feed killers on red meat. It made them stronger.

The wool was a secondary benefit, as was the fear and uncertainty his little raid would sow in the above-grounders. They had no idea how to run a long-term, functioning society. They didn't have the skills to keep control of the human impulse for centuries at a time until the ship reached its destination.

"Come on, Gunner." Over time and hundreds of brief conversations with the man, he'd worked out that Gunner had been sent up there as a weapon by the Sino-African Syndicate to bring down the project by destroying Transfer Station.

It still made Davian whistle whenever he thought about it. He'd been one of the few human witnesses to the catastrophic destruction.

Gunner had inserted the virus into the station-mind, the one that had killed it and then blown the station's core. That Gunner had done it, mentally handicapped as he was… he was a powerful weapon.

Gunner had been picked up on the streets of Spokane by the Sino-African intelligence and pressed into service as the war was heating up.

Davian knew firsthand some of the methods that the Chafs would have used. He still woke up some nights screaming, thinking he was in the hotbox.

No matter now. The Chafs were gone to blood and dust, and they'd unwittingly left him the key to taking over this new world.

Now he just had to figure out the best way to use it.

AARON STARED out the window of his office at the gently waving, glowing branches of the Mallowood trees.

Today was the day. His mother was gone, and they would celebrate that fact with some kind of ceremony that Keera had whipped up. It rubbed him wrong, somehow, to think about *celebrating* Glory's death.

His office was a far cry from the white, pristine office he'd had on Transfer Station. Here almost everything was made of native wood and other local materials, lending the office a warm, almost golden radiance.

Of course, it was aided by the glow from the plants and the sky outside. At this distance, the spindle—a stream of windswept pollen that provided a diffuse glow over the whole world, augmenting the plant light—was almost uniform. It obscured the view of about a third of the world above his head.

It had taken him the better part of six months on the ground to get used to that strange and wonderful vista—the sight of the world curving up around him like a great multicolored patchwork wall, cresting like a wave far above his head. Now he rarely noticed it, though some deep animal part of his brain still grumbled about it from time to time.

Once he'd relied on his AI for data. Now, his reports were mostly on paper. Sure, the colony still had technology—the world mind itself was a supreme achievement of Earth's high-tech society—but they no longer had the infrastructure to build so many things they had come to rely upon on Earth and at Transfer Station.

His train to Darlith, for instance, that would likely never go any farther.

The Collapse of the Earth had come on too quickly for neat planning and careful stocking of equipment and supplies. It was left to the survivors to figure out a way to make it all work.

Some reports did come in over the network. Most people still had loops in their temples, though those that malfunctioned couldn't be replaced. He took this information down on paper, by hand, using graphite pencils made at the fabrication center. At least they could manage that much.

There were more reports of Ghost activity all along the Verge. From the sheep slaughter that Eddy was out investigating to petty larceny— clothing stolen off the line, crops raided, etc.—things were getting tense. There'd even been a fire along the foothills of the Anatovs, which the world mind had quickly put out with some well-timed rainfall.

The Anatovs. Aaron shook his head. That had been a hard name to get used to. He could still see Ana's face when he closed his eyes. She had let herself be subsumed into the world mind as he held her in his arms, deep in the bowels of the world.

She was still alive, in a sense, and his mother, Glory, was dead.

He spoke to Ana from time to time about matters important to the colony, such as the upcoming asteroid rendezvous, and she was still the same cantankerous genius she'd always been.

He turned his attention back to the reports on his desk. There was something going on out there, and it bugged the hell out of him that he didn't know what it was. A rising tide of strangeness.

There had been personnel disappearances, too, over the last six years, in addition to the surprising undercounts at the refugee camp after the Collapse. Aaron was sure it all added up to nothing good. He needed more data.

Aaron sighed. He was putting it off. He knew it, but he had to get going.

"Hey, Dad." Andy's voice came through his loop. "You ready?"

"Yeah. I suppose so." He'd spent the last month fighting with the world mind—with his own father even—begging for them to take Glory in. She didn't have to die, not forever. His father was proof of that.

But Jackson had been steadfastly against it. "It's not fair," his father had said. "We can't save Glory because we can't save them all. And she would never have it."

They'd kept the knowledge of Jackson's existence in the world mind from his wife. From just about everyone, actually. Few people knew about any of the Immortals. Now Aaron wondered if that hadn't been a mistake. In the end, he and Andy had been there for her as she departed this mortal plane, although Jackson had stolen the last few moments from him.

Jayson, Aaron's younger brother, had been the first of his nuclear family they'd lost—God rest his soul—in the War on Earth. Now it was just him and his immortal father.

Andy pinged him. "Can I *ride* along?"

"Of course." He felt her slip in alongside him in his mind as he opened his senses to her so she could see what he saw and hear what he heard.

Feel what he felt.

It wasn't true telepathy, but it was as close as he'd ever experienced, a product of Jackson Hammond's gift to his children and grandchildren.

He put the papers away in a folder in his desk and left the room, glancing out the window once more at the serene scene outside. Jayson would have liked it here.

Andy agreed.

He closed the door softly behind him, and they went out to find Glory's friends.

SCOTT lives with his husband Mark in a little yellow bungalow in East Sacramento with two pink flamingos out front. He spends his time between the here and now and the what could be. Ushered into fantasy and sci-fi at the tender age of nine by his mother, he devoured her library of Asimovs, Clarkes, and McCaffreys. But as he grew up, he wondered where the gay people were in speculative fiction.

He decided it was time to create the kinds of stories he couldn't find at Waldenbooks. If there weren't queer characters in his favorite genres, he would write them himself.

His friends say Scott's brain works a little differently—he sees relationships between things that others miss, and often gets more done in a day than most folks manage in a week. He transforms traditional sci-fi, fantasy, and contemporary worlds into something unexpected.

He and Mark also run Queer Sci Fi, QueeRomance Ink, and Other Worlds Ink, sites that bring LGBTIQA communities together to celebrate fiction that reflects queer life and love.

He won the Rainbow Award as one of the best new gay authors of 2017.

Facebook Profile: www.facebook.com/jscottcoatsworth
Facebook Author Page: www.facebook.com/jscottcoatsworthauthor/
Twitter: www.twitter.com/jscoatsworth/
Author Website/Blog: www.jscottcoatsworth.com
Dreamspinner Page: www.dreamspinnerpress.com/store/index.
php?cPath=55_1189
QueeRomance Ink Author Page: www.queeromanceink.com/mbm-book-author/j-scott-coatsworth/
Goodreads Author Page: www.goodreads.com/author/show/8392709.J_Scott_Coatsworth
Amazon Author Page: www.amazon.com/J.-Scott-Coatsworth/e/B011AFO4OQ